D1324100

Meg Sanders and Annie Ashworth have written twelve successful non-fiction books together. Both have families and live in Stratford-upon-Avon. *The Gap Year for Grown Ups* is their fifth novel. Their first four novels, the bestselling *Goodbye, Jimmy Choo*, *Warnings of Gales*, *The Xmas Factor* and *Busy Woman Seeks Wife* are also available in Orion paperback.

By Annie Sanders

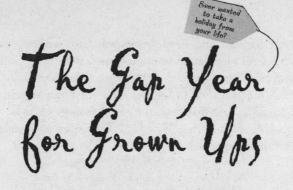

Ever wanted to take a holiday from your life?

The Gap Year for Grown Ups

Annie Sanders

An Orion paperback

First published in Great Britain in 2008
by Orion
This paperback edition published in 2009
by Orion Books Ltd,
Orion House, 5 Upper Saint Martin's Lane
London, WC2H 9EA

An Hachette UK company

A CIP catalogue record for this book is
available from the British Library.

Typeset by Deltatype Ltd, Birkenhead, Merseyside

Printed in Great Britain by Clays Ltd, St Ives plc

The Orion Publishing Group's policy is to use papers that are natural,
renewable and recyclable products and made from wood grown in sustainable
forests. The logging and manufacturing processes are expected to
conform to the environmental regulations of the country of origin.

www.orionbooks.co.uk

To the men in our lives

What did your last slave die of?

'A successful marriage requires falling in love many times,
always with the same person'

Mignon McLaughlin (Author and Journalist, 1913–1983)

'For two people in a marriage to live together day after day is
unquestionably the one miracle the Vatican has overlooked'

Bill Cosby (Actor and Comedian)

Chapter 1

'Come on, Mum,' Claire urged, leaning forward over the kitchen table. 'Put us out of our misery.'

Working on the principle that it's always best to confront an uncomfortable situation – like root canal work or a smear test – with a brave face, Sarah tentatively pulled at the wrapping paper. Resplendent with Thomas the Tank Engine, she recognised it as the leftovers from the roll she'd bought for a godchild's birthday. David had obviously forgotten to buy any and had plundered her resources.

'Nice paper,' Sarah said pointedly and he looked sheepish.

'Sorry, love, but it's what's inside that counts, isn't it?' He looked concerned, and she laughed.

'Is that your excuse for wrapping last year's offering in the *Sunday Times* Property Section?'

'Okay, okay not that again.'

Sarah tore off the paper, keen to get the agony over with. The parcel felt soft and squashy so she already had a strong suspicion what it might be and, sure enough, when she pulled the paper away, a fleecy sweatshirt lay on the kitchen table, like evidence in a court case, the beady black eyes of an embroidered squirrel staring balefully up at them.

Claire leaned back in her chair and sighed. 'Oh, Dad.'

'What's wrong with it?' David jumped in. 'It'll be so practical for gardening, and I got it big and roomy cos I know you hate tight things.'

'Couldn't you at least have got her something a bit more

feminine? Even the ubiquitous lacy knickers would have been an attempt at least—'

'Claire—' Sarah began.

'Happy birthday, Mum,' Tom interrupted, walking into the kitchen and yawning, pyjama bottoms hanging off narrow hips. He planted a kiss on his mother's head. 'Sorry I wasn't up to serenade you earlier. I didn't get in till late. What the hell's that?'

'It's from Dad. A fleece for gardening.' Sarah smiled up at her lanky son, his fair hair swept off his face and, as ever, in need of a wash.

'Well, it's certainly the colour of shit,' he laughed. He flicked on the kettle, then dropped a small package onto the table, a box from her favourite shop tied with a pink ribbon. He hadn't gone into town to meet friends until five yesterday afternoon so it must have been purchased pretty smartish. David had gone quiet and was busying himself with some papers on the side. Sarah felt a wave of guilt.

'It's lovely, darling. Thank you. It will be very useful.' She got up from her seat, quashing a vague feeling of disappointment and avoiding her daughter's disapproving eyes. At eighteen, and scrupulously polite with everyone else, Claire still hadn't quite learned the necessity of discretion over honesty when it came to family.

'I'll just take it upstairs and change.' Sarah put her coffee cup into the dishwasher, automatically adding David's that had been left on the side. 'What time's the table?'

'One o'clock. We'll pick your dad up on the way.' Characteristically he rubbed his hands together nervously. 'I booked The Old Bell. We all like it there.'

'Oh God, Dad. We did when we were ten. Isn't there anywhere else?'

'Claire, that's enough!' Sarah said sharply, shooting her daughter an admonishing look. She picked up her parcels off the table. 'I'll take your presents with me to open there or we're going to be late. And, Tom, remember to make the acquaintance of the shampoo when you get in the shower.'

Sarah made her way upstairs to the landing, shutting the airing-cupboard door with her foot as best she could as she passed. The catch, broken for years, kept jumping open on its own. She must ask David to fix it again. In her bedroom, she avoided looking at herself in the mirror and, picking up David's jeans from the floor and laying them on the chair, she opened the wardrobe and tucked the green fleece with the squirrel motif inside next to a chunky oatmeal cardigan ... a chunky oatmeal cardigan that had been wrapped last year in newspaper and was as yet unworn. It looked down at her censoriously and she shoved it further back onto the shelf, hiding it behind another jumper.

'Bye, love. Have a good day.' David deposited a quick kiss somewhere in the vicinity of Sarah's head as he bent to pick up his briefcase. He was already humming as he let himself out of the door – some song the twins had been listening to on the car radio on the way back to university the night before, after the birthday celebration. Sarah had been asleep by the time he'd got back and he hadn't wanted to wake her, so they hadn't had the usual birthday bonk. Shame, because, with the twins now safely out of the way, it wouldn't have had to be one of those muf-fled, whispered affairs. You'd have thought ... well, David had thought they could have started being a bit more spontaneous now they were alone in the house but it hadn't happened that way. Still, early days.

David leaned over to put his briefcase in the passenger footwell and winced as he felt the waistband of his trousers dig in. Surely he wasn't putting on weight? He'd always been the fittest of their friends, able to tease Phil about his beer belly without any jibes coming his way. God! He'd already cut out Sunday-morning fry-ups – admittedly, at Sarah's urging – what next? He slid into the driver's seat and prodded his stomach. Maybe not a six-pack, but not yet a party seven. Sarah must have washed his trousers too hot again.

David put his brain in neutral on the drive to work and yawned as he pulled into the car park. How many times had he driven that same route? Once the question occurred to him he couldn't resist a quick mental calculation. Well, guesstimate really. At least five thousand. He shook his head and smiled. It was amazing, really, how the years went by. Could it really be twenty years since he'd started work here? He turned off the engine, dropped his mobile into his briefcase and clicked it shut. He took his jacket off the back seat, shrugged it on, shut the door and headed towards the office, locking the car with the keyfob.

Now that was something that had changed over the years. Being able to lock your car remotely. Definite progress! He hadn't been able to do that in those days. They'd had a Fiesta then. Light blue. And Sarah had ridden her bike to school. He smiled to himself, remembering how she'd looked with her violin on her back, her cheeks all pink and her hair sticking out in all directions. Her hair never stuck out any more – the bike was long gone, and they had a car each: hers a little black Renault; his a company saloon. Just before he entered the building, he glanced at it over his shoulder in quiet satisfaction.

Sarah picked up the cards from the window sill in the kitchen. She only ever left birthday cards there for a few days – they tended to fall over and were a pain to clean around. One had arrived only this morning from one of her oldest friends, Nathalie in France – late as always and saying something stupid but in French. Sarah dropped it into the bin next to one with an unseasonal picture of daffodils from David, and a lovely montage of fairy cakes from Claire, who always managed to pick beautiful cards, and had given her a silk covered notebook of no particular use

4

but pretty all the same. There hadn't been a card from Tom, but the necklace, however hastily it might have been bought, had been a sweet plastic heart and she'd put it on at lunch on Sunday at The Old Bell as soon as she'd opened it.

Sarah sighed and looked out at the garden, bleak and denuded now from the November winds. Though it had been lovely having the children home for her birthday, she had hated them going back to university; really hadn't got used to them being there in the first place. Having had them noisily home from school every night of their lives, their absence was an echoing void.

Sarah propped up the card from her father on the recipe-book stand, not able to bring herself to throw it away, turned off the kitchen light and let herself out into the dank chill of the morning.

'C, F, A,' she sighed two and half hours and five lessons later. Was it actually illegal to do this much damage to a Mozart piece? 'Gregory, just how much practice have you done this week?' The dark-haired boy hung his head in shame.

'Bit,' he mumbled, scuffing the floor with his shoe.

'Too busy playing on the computer? You'll need to do a bit more, you know, if you want to get grade one.' He nodded again. Pulling out his practice book from his music case, Sarah felt a surprisingly strong wave of What Do I Care? wash over her. She'd lost count of the times she'd heard these exam pieces annihilated by children. *I'm concerned Gregory isn't progressing when he has such promise*, read the handwritten note at the bottom of last week's page. *Surely he is ready to move on to grade 3 by now?* It was signed with a flourish of initials, clearly in haste. Sarah had met Gregory's mother at a parents' evening. A brisk, immaculately turned-out woman who Gregory had once said 'sold ladies things'. Sarah assumed he meant clothes, not sanitary products or, God forbid, sex-aids, though with her dominatrix heels and short black skirt, she could well do. You never could tell with private-school parents. Sarah smiled, and replied in her careful hand with her score-marking pencil: *One step at a time. A little more practice would be a start.*

She watched as Gregory stuffed his books into the bag, not to see the light of day again until next week, then shuffled out of the room with a mumbled goodbye. Sarah glanced at the clock. There wouldn't even be time for a cup of coffee before the Christmas concert rehearsal started. She picked up the scores and headed for the school hall, and another year of smug Mary, mischievous innkeeper and a bunch of disgruntled sheep who hadn't got the main parts. She smiled to herself. She must be getting old.

The sound his key made sliding into the lock always filled David with a kind of low-key happiness. It was like the full stop at the end of the working day and the start of his real life. Coming in and finding Sarah pottering around was comforting after a day of dealing with Barry's bullshit. No smell of cooking yet. Maybe he'd suggest a take-away. That'd be nice for her after a busy day. A jalfrezi and keema naan would hit the spot nicely.

He put down his briefcase, just loud enough so she'd hear it and appear from wherever she was – upstairs, maybe, making the bed. He shrugged off his jacket and slung it on the back of a chair. It could probably do with dry-cleaning. He'd mention it to Sarah later. He prised off his work shoes, pushing the heel of each one down with the opposite foot, then flicked them in turn towards the chair. Not bad! One on the seat, one underneath. 'Yesssss!' He punched the air. 'He shoots! He scores!'

An exasperated sigh from behind him took him by surprise. 'Oh hello, love. Good day?'

Sarah looked at him for a long moment, then rather pointedly at his shoes. 'Yes, fine.'

Uh-oh. 'You all right?' he asked a little defensively. Well, just enough to suggest she was being a bit of a killjoy but not enough to start a row. He pushed the errant shoe onto the floor next to its mate and turned to face her. 'Fancy a cuppa?' He waited for her to offer.

She softened a little. 'Yes, that'd be great. Thanks.' He could have sworn her smile was triumphant.

Chapter 2

Christmas came and went as ever for Sarah, hurried on by the usual absurd orgy of supermarket shopping. She had bumped into friends and acquaintances and they had all sighed theatrically at the pressure of it all, before continuing to throw too much food into trolleys as if they were in for a siege. Despite promising herself she wouldn't be sucked in this year, Sarah inevitably was, dragging out the decorations from the attic as David made heavy weather of positioning the tree in the lounge window, a job which, like barbecues, he considered his alone.

Her mother-in-law, Heather, elegant in pink cashmere, threw her usual Christmas Eve drinks party with its exquisite canapés to which they dragged a reluctant Claire and Tom, still exhausted from too many late nights with friends since coming back from university. It wasn't until they were sitting on the sofa after Christmas lunch, stuffed with an excess of food and good wine, watching Kevin Costner playing a hero in the afternoon film, that Sarah had noticed the expression of total despair on her father's face.

They'd all avoided the glaring gap at the table left by her mother's death in September, though David had raised a toast to her at lunch. Sarah had gone over and silently taken her father's hand, which he'd squeezed gratefully and said nothing, isolated in his grief. This had been another milestone, and Sarah realised how much she'd missed buying her mother a present, and receiving one from her – always something unusual and carefully thought through.

'Shall we open our presents now?' David had asked brightly,

and they'd lumbered slowly from their prone positions to hand out the pile of parcels under the tree. She watched with pleasure as everyone opened theirs. She knew she'd got it right with the twins – they were so easy to buy for – and David was thrilled, as she knew he would be, with the electric lawn edger.

'You've dropped enough hints,' she snorted, as he pored excitedly over the instruction manual.

For Sarah, the haul was the usual kitchen implements, soaps and paperbacks. She'd left David's offering till last, and had to summon up all her enthusiasm for the ubiquitous cookery book by a TV chef. Her heart sank. Surely he knew how much she loathed those programmes, incensed by how vapid they were. She slipped the book to one side, hoping he wouldn't notice that she'd opened it at all.

The present from her friend Trish – another book – sat in a pile by her bed until well after the New Year, which dawned grey and dank accompanied by a hangover from a very late New Year's Eve party with friends. *This was marvellous for me*, Trish had scrawled inside. *Be forty and fabulous.*

Sarah read the title again: *Meeting Yourself. Knowing Yourself. Loving Yourself*; an American publication, no doubt. She flicked through the pages full of shortlists for feeling marvellous about yourself, snorting at the hyperbole, and put it back in the pile.

She dusted and hovered around it for another three weeks before picking it up again idly one afternoon as she changed out of work clothes. 'Take a long look at yourself and who you are. Begin with an analysis of your naked body as a starting place to finding your inner beauty and contentment. By reaching a point of total self-acceptance and love for yourself, you empower yourself to make those changes in your life that will reveal a core happiness. Here's what you need to do …' All bilge, she thought, about to close the book again then, what the hell? Trish had some off-the-wall ideas, but the house was empty, and it beat doing the ironing. Was it worth a go?

She drew the curtains, feeling faintly furtive, even a little sordid, blocking out the milky afternoon light, then slowly unbuttoned her blouse. It slid down over her shoulders, making her shiver. She dropped it at her feet, kicked off her shoes and, hooking her thumbs into the waistband of her trousers, pushed them down slowly. She wobbled a little as she stepped out of them and briefly opened her eyes, shutting them again quickly. Taking a deep breath, she reached behind her back, undid the catch of her bra, a little ashamed of its grey dowdiness as it slipped to the floor, her breasts falling heavily as they were released.

She paused as she slid her thumbs into the sides of her knickers then, suddenly impatient, she pushed them down. She'd done it. Slowly, she turned round and opened her eyes.

There in front of her was her reflection in the bedroom mirror, and she forced her gaze downwards over her naked body. 'Oh dear God!' she gasped, her worst fears confirmed. 'It's all going south.'

Picking up the book, she hurled it across the room. *Meeting Yourself. Knowing Yourself. Loving Yourself* hit the wall with a dull thud and a flutter of loose pages.

They could stuff their cod psychology. Self-acceptance? It might have worked for Trish but it wasn't working for her.

Chapter 3

'Morning, David.' Doreen looked up from reception and beamed at him. 'How's things today?' Good old Doreen. She'd been there even longer than he had, as reliable as the annual pay review. Of course, her weight had yo-yoed – didn't it always with women? – but he knew enough to make the right noises.

'Fine, fine. Clive in yet?'

Sealing a large white envelope and dropping it into the post tray, she said, 'Brown as a berry, lucky bugger. And you don't get that colour in Dorset!' She knew all about Dorset, of course. She'd never holidayed anywhere else. And in the same hotel year after year because it could cater for her husband's wheelchair, yet she revealed not a trace of bitterness.

David headed for the stairs. By the time he reached the top he was a little out of breath. Tut tut, he admonished himself. You used to be able to do those two at a time, old man.

'David, a word in your shell-like.' Barry Fox appeared from somewhere, today wearing the pink-stripe version of his perennial white-collared shirts. The short, bumptious line-manager had never subscribed to the 'dress down' code. It was all of a piece with his one-upmanship, as if it somehow meant he was more focused than the rest of the team. Reluctantly, David turned to face him.

'Yes, Barry? And what can I do for you?'

'The ODS training on Monday. Can you make sure Malcolm is up to speed? I want to drive this content management initiative as hard as we can and he needs to know the ropes. Good man.' Without waiting for a response, he slapped David's back and headed off, calling heartily across the office.

Tosser. David placed his briefcase on the desk, logged on, and went to prepare his first coffee of the day, before settling contentedly into his tidy workstation, ready to see what the day would bring. But first, the list. He fished out his A4 pad from the top draw and ruled the usual three columns: work, home, mates. Tackling 'home' first he wrote: *Wedding anniversary – present? Ideas? Dinner? Ask lads.*

He rubbed his temples. Oh God, another present. This was torture. How can you know a woman so well, have spent so many years with her, yet not know what to get her? What would Sarah really like? What would make her eyes light up? Make her throw her arms round his neck? Perhaps he shouldn't have gone for the clichéd lingerie after all.

He sighed, took a swig of coffee, hot enough to burn his tongue. Just the way he liked it. This was just too difficult. He turned, almost with relief, to the list for Barry's meeting and the schedule for the Fat Dads, the ageing five-a-side team he'd played football with for the last fifteen years. This he could manage.

Chapter 4

February and Sarah was awake, as always, before the alarm went off. Something, she had no idea what, had been waking her every day recently at 6.18 precisely. She'd briefly toyed with the idea of setting the alarm for 6.15 so she'd be awake to hear what it was that was waking her up, but even she could see that was absurd.

Lying in the darkness, listening to David's gentle, untroubled breathing, she ran through what the day had in store. Oh rapture. Three hours of teaching, followed by string orchestra at lunchtime – fiddling with music stands and tuning half-size violins for children who couldn't play in tune if their lives depended on it. She made a mental note to collect David's bloody jacket from the cleaner's. She yawned and shifted in the bed, turning her back on his motionless body and waiting for the radio to leap into life, for James Naughtie to give her the headlines and for the day to officially begin.

The weather was biting hard and, wrapped warmly, she headed for her car. If she'd known how long it would take her to scrape the ice off the windscreen with the edge of a CD box, she would have got going earlier. She'd had no idea the frost would be so tenacious. It hung on the leaves and branches of the hedges like icing, and she reversed cautiously out of the drive into the road, already aware she would be late. In fact, by the time she was unravelling her scarf in the staff room, the bell was going for first lesson and she had time only to grab a cup of stewed coffee from the pot and head for the music room.

'Off to the hairdresser, Jean,' Sarah said, waving at the school secretary a week later as the three-fifteen bell filled the corridor and children began to pour noisily out of classrooms, pushing past Sarah as they went. Jean Kemp, tucked away in her eyrie in reception, looked up over the head of the small child to whom she was returning a mobile phone, her overlong hair curiously pasted to her head as if with glue.

'Having a trim?' she enquired.

Sarah put her hand up self-consciously to her own sensible bob. 'Actually, I fancy a bit of a change.'

'But your hair always looks lovely,' Jean gushed. 'Don't change things just for the sake of it. You'll only regret it.' And she turned back to another child demanding her attention. Sarah smiled to herself. She'd always liked Jean on a superficial level, but it had never gone deeper than that, Sarah being a bit unsure she had anything in common with a woman who consciously chose to wear her hair that way. Indeed, Jean's compliment was confirmation that Sarah needed a haircut and fast.

The frost had thawed under the harsh sunshine, but already it was beginning to get cold again by the time Sarah found a parking space in town and went into the steamy salon. Condensation ran down the windows and the strong smell of 'product' hit her as she opened the door. Stylists in black – such an impractical colour with all that hair around – were busy clipping away, standing behind their gown-wrapped clients, and juniors rushed around with brooms, sweeping up the showers of hair.

Sarah felt a frisson of anticipation. Burying the Kalashnikov attack to her confidence raised by her recent encounter with her naked body in the mirror, and convinced now that no amount of power walking or running upstairs could hold back the ravages of time, she knew her hair was something she *could* change. With just a snip here and there she could, she would, look totally fresh and different. She paused as she was ushered towards the basins, looking at her reflection in a mirror beside her in the glass. Maybe something a little more feminine? Younger perhaps? Claire would have been able to advise, but her daughter was too wrapped up in university to be able to help. Yes, she'd talk to Andre about a complete change. He'd know what would suit her. He'd been cutting her hair for long enough.

Shampooed, conditioned and head-massaged, she was escorted back to the hot seat as Andre glided over and squeezed her shoulders warmly, looking at her now in the long mirror. 'Hel-*lo*! Lovely to see you, darling. Now what are we doing today?'

'Well, I was thinking something a bit younger. A bit more contemporary. What do you think?' She looked at his face uncertainly in the mirror.

He unwrapped the towel from her head and started to run a comb through her wet hair, his head thoughtfully to one side. Sarah tried to avoid her own eyes in the mirror, knowing this was when she looked her ugliest. Andre stopped and screwed his face up. 'Well, we're a bit limited with the length. It's neither one thing or the other. There's nowhere we can go except really urchin. And that might be … Perhaps you're a little bit … Tell you what, why don't I just put in a bit of graduation round the back here. Sharpen it up. Maybe we could go a bit Helen Mirren. What do you think?'

Sarah could feel a sense of deflation. She looked in the mirror, realising that she'd never really looked at him eye to eye, just at his reflection looking back at hers. Had he ever really looked at her properly? She watched as he touched her hair – such an intimate gesture, yet he had an air of vague boredom, at the same time glancing around the salon at the juniors gossiping in the corner.

He wasn't listening. He wasn't even trying to be imaginative. Did she have to spell it out to him that she needed help here? That age wasn't very kind to women? Could he at least try to do something to make her feel different? And Helen Mirren? Was that how he saw her? Just some housewife who craved to look like Helen bloody Mirren?

Defeated, Sarah sighed. 'Oh, just do the usual.' And she buried her nose in an old copy of *Heat*.

The house smelled of cooking. He sniffed. Fish pie, maybe? Sarah's campaign to keep him healthy was all very well – as long as it was topped with plenty of mash. He threw his jacket on the back of a chair and kicked off his shoes, casting about for his loafers, which, as always, Sarah had tucked neatly under the chair. He tutted – why did she do that? – and hooked them out with his foot. He called out her name and peeped into the kitchen.

Hairdresser. Must remember she's been to the hairdresser.

She wasn't downstairs. 'I'm home, love! Back from the trenches!' He smiled to himself as he called the familiar greeting. 'Hellooo! Are you in the loo?'

The bedroom door creaked open – he really must have a go at those hinges – and Sarah emerged, a pile of dirty washing in her arms. 'Hiya,' she called down. 'Did you want this sweatshirt washing?'

He squinted up at her. 'Yeah, I'll need it for footie.'

'Okay, but next time can you put it in the laundry basket? I'm not telepathic, you know.'

Ouch. David did a quick mental scan. Had there been anything on today that might have put her out of sorts? The hair. Mention the hair.

'Your hair looks nice, love. Really ... smooth.'

She seemed to thaw a bit and came down the stairs. 'Good day?'

That was more like it. He leaned forward and gave her a kiss. Her hair smelled unfamiliarly of coconuts. David recounted events, as he always did. She knew all the personalities involved, and understood the politics without him having to explain. She'd see instantly why it was so irritating that Barry had palmed off all the arrangements for the meeting onto David when he knew he'd been opposed to the whole bloody initiative in the first place. He followed her into the kitchen, still talking.

Sarah busied herself with the supper, her head bowed as she concentrated, pointedly moving him out of the way of the cutlery drawer or the sink as she worked and he talked. Then she suddenly turned round, cutting him off mid-flow.

'Rachel called about going through Mum's things.'

He took a slow breath. 'I'm sorry, love. That's going to be hard.'

He watched as her eyes filled with tears, hoping it would be no more than that, but already she was blinking them away. She hadn't really blubbed at all since her mother's sudden death, but Sarah never had been one for big scenes. Thank goodness.

'Look' – he scanned his mental diary – 'shall I take a day off and come and help you?'

She smiled weakly. 'What, so you can miss that meeting? No, don't worry. I'll be fine. Then Rachel will only drive one of us mad. You know how she gets.'

'Mmm. Stand by your beds!'

He took a surreptitious peep at the supper, warming on the oven shelf. Not pie at all. Just a slab of pink fish – salmon? – with some bits of green stuff on top and a few carrots. There was a bowl of mixed salad. No potatoes in sight. He sighed. It was too late to put any on to cook. Maybe there was some pudding. Dejectedly he forced down the contents of the over-flowing bin, getting the morning's scraped cereal on his hands, before tying it and tugging it out. Why did she always let it get so full?

'Never mind, love.' He opened the back door on his way to the bins. 'It's bound to be hard, but you've got to get rid of her things sooner rather than later, and everything will get back to normal, you'll see.'

'Yes.' Sarah turned away to get the cutlery from the drawer and muttered quietly, 'That's exactly what I'm afraid of.'

David stared for a moment then shrugged. He must have misheard her.

Chapter 5

'Can you meet me at Dad's at eleven?' Her sister Rachel's tone on the phone when she'd called suggested that Sarah could only comply. 'We'll need Marigolds and a roll of bin liners. I'll bring those.' It had been Sarah's sister who'd finally galvanised everyone into moving their father Wilf into a small flat in town. 'The Firs is way too big for him now – well, it was too big for both of them,' she had declared some weeks before Christmas and, even though Sarah knew she was right, the five-bedroomed family house being totally impractical for an elderly widower, moving him would simply confirm that nothing would ever be the same again.

Her dad had been as phlegmatic as ever. 'Shame to give up the old place after forty years, but without your mother it rattles horribly. I dare say it'll make some young family a lovely home.' He'd paused and looked out of the window at the winter lawn and shrugged. 'Unless of course it's snapped up by a developer and they bulldoze the whole place and put up some ghastly executive homes cheek by jowl with each other. They seem to do that everywhere these days.'

Sarah pulled up in front of the house just after eleven, parking in the same place she had since she'd owned her first car at seventeen. It wasn't a pretty house – far from it. Grey render and dark windows, a forbidding porch, and in the dank winter morning had an air of sadness about it; but there had already been an offer in on the house from a gentleman who'd viewed it with alarming speed. Perhaps her father's prediction was right.

'Hello, love, your hair looks pretty.' Her father had obviously heard the car and had come out to meet her. He kissed her on the forehead. Funny how you can see people all the time and suddenly you will notice changes that have crept up on you. Sarah hadn't noticed how gaunt he had become.

'Oh, I just had a trim the other day. My attempts at reinvention were thwarted. Are you eating properly, Dad?'

He shrugged as she followed his back to the dimly lit kitchen, his familiar tall lean frame in corduroy trousers and the deep red sweater she had given him for Christmas. 'Oh, I bundle along, you know. And you girls are marvellous with the suppers you drop by. Your cottage pie is almost as good as your mother's.'

'I learned at the hand of the maestro,' Sarah said with a smile, flicking on the kettle and opening the fridge for milk. Inside was a wasteland: half a piece of cheese, a tub of margarine (something her mother would never have given fridge-room to), a half-used jar of pasta sauce and a lemon, the essential for his evening G&T. God, how sad. Sarah turned back to the kettle and blinked hard.

'I'll be better once I'm in town with the shops nearby. You'll see.' He patted her gently on the arm. Sarah smiled weakly, but the thought of the wonderful contents of their family home being shoehorned into the tiny geriatric's flat over-looking the river – the remainder being bought by some shady house clearance company – was almost too much to bear.

'Come and live with us!' she burst out. She hadn't even discussed this with David, knowing it was totally impractical. They lived even further from the centre of town than The Firs and they were both out all day. He'd be lonely. Perhaps she could give up work and ...

'You are a love, and your sister has already offered,' he said with a twinkle, and the two of them chuckled, complicit in the living hell that arrangement would be for him. 'She'd have me whipped into shape good and proper,' he whispered. 'Bless you both, my lovely girls, but I shall be fine in my little shoebox. I shall feed the ducks and talk to strangers and toddle along to Probus meetings.' He paused. 'I might even take up some awful habit like poker or darts.' They both snorted. 'And anyway, three is always a crowd.' He made for the kitchen door. 'I heard your sister's car. Now I think I'll leave you two to it and walk to the golf club. Gordon will be there and he's always good value.' He paused as if he'd only just remembered. 'David and the children okay?'

'Fine thanks, Dad. Just fine.'

As usual, Rachel came in like a whirlwind, her short dark hair sleek and sensibly pushed back from her face. Sarah handed her a mug of coffee, but she put it down firmly on the table without trying it and unpacked her carrier bag: two foil packs for the fridge in one-person-size portions, then dusters and rubber gloves, polish and wax.

'Dad,' she called down the corridor. 'Happy for us to start upstairs?'

Wilf came in, buttoning his coat, a red scarf round his neck and tweed flat cap on his head. 'Wherever ... And thank you, girls, for this. It can't be nice for you but you'll be better at it than me. I think there are some things I'd get all silly and sentimental about. Just throw away whatever you think isn't worth keeping.'

Sarah followed her sister's wide, jeaned bottom upstairs. 'Now, I think Mum's cupboards need going through first. We should have done it ages ago.'

'I know, Rach, but it would have been hard for Dad if we'd just swept in and whisked it all away too soon.' They passed the small table on the landing with pictures of her and Rachel's weddings. Sarah looked very young in the Princess Di meringue she'd chosen so carefully, her hair flicked back and Elnetted into submission. Her parents' bedroom – which it would always be to her – was the best in the house, with a view out over the back garden. The side her mother had slept on – and had ultimately died on – was crisp and untouched, whereas her father's pillow, though army-pristine, had wrinkles. On his bedside table was a thick biography and a glass of water. Her mother's side was empty save for a lamp.

'Do you remember Saturday mornings, Rach, and bouncing on the bed? Used to drive them nuts.' Rachel pulled open the wide wardrobe doors.

'I was the one who got the telling off. You could get away with anything.' She put her hands on her hips and surveyed the contents. 'Now, is there anything you want?'

Sarah knew Rachel well enough to know this was not a real question. That was plain by the way Rachel was already taking jumpers down off the shelves and loading them into a bin liner. The same little-sister contrariness came over her that had once made Sarah intentionally crash Rachel's bike so she wouldn't have to inherit that as well. 'Yes, as a matter of fact, there is. I've always loved her blue cashmere cardigan and that velvet coat.'

Rachel looked horrified. 'But isn't that a bit macabre, Sarah?'

'No it's not. She was our mum, Rach. What's wrong with wanting her clothes as a memory?'

Together they worked for an hour, sorting shoes into bags, throwing out old gardening clothes and tweed skirts that even the charity shop would turn their nose up at. At the back of the shelf above the wardrobe rail Rachel pulled out a fox stole and, after inspecting it for a moment, threw that too into the bag. 'God, where did that come from? Can't quite imagine her having worn it at one those fascinating-slides-from-my-walking-holiday-in-Peru evenings at the town hall, can you?'

'Oh, I don't know – even supermodels seem to be condoning it these days. Not much use with global warming, though.'

Sarah found her mother's nighties and underwear the hardest items to sort; not surprisingly, as the familiar waft of lily-of-the-valley filled her nostrils. Nothing in this drawer had been disturbed since last September when she had slipped away in her sleep, except for the addition of the nightie she had died in. It struck Sarah that her father must have laundered it and put it back in the drawer as if for another time.

'Are you and Colin happy?' Sarah asked as she folded each item up delicately and placed them in the bin liners: the bras and functional pants, the pink floral nighties and a rather incongruous bed-jacket.

'Happy?' Rachel snorted, now pulling jackets and skirts from hangers. 'Funny question. What do you mean?'

'You know what I mean. Do you look forward to him coming home at night? Do you want to spend time with him?'

Rachel stopped what she was doing. 'Well, it's a bit like the cat coming in really – predictable and sort of part of the day.' Rachel had described her husband as being like the cat. Dull, pompous Colin with his fascination for routes and journeys and miles eeked out per gallon.

Sarah pulled out tights and pop socks, something her mother had thought were fantastic and of which her daughter strongly disapproved. 'But what I mean is, does it still give you butterflies when you think about spending time with him? Do you still fancy him?'

'Oh Sarah, don't be ridiculous! We've been married for eons. It's comfortable' – she stressed the word heavily – 'and that can be nice. But fancy? Well, you can't really, can you, when you've squeezed a boil on their back or watched them put their toenails clippings on the bedside table.'

Sarah tried not to think about pustules on Colin's back. Dare she ask? She'd never really had this sort of conversation with her sister. 'Do you still have sex?'

Rachel spun round, a purple and black dog-tooth jacket in her hand. 'Sarah Lewis! That's a very personal question!'

'Maybe, but it's the one everyone is dying to ask each other, isn't it? And no one's ever honest with the answer.'

Rachel looked at her hard. 'You and David having problems?'

Sarah paused. 'Not really. And anyway, I'm asking the questions. Do you?'

'Well ... He likes to do it on holiday and occasionally if we've been out for dinner and he's had a couple of drinks. But otherwise ... Well, we both enjoy our books too much!'

Sarah looked at her sister, and tried to imagine her being sexy and abandoned. Poor Colin probably had to apply for permission to moor alongside.

'But, sister dear' – Rachel screwed up her eyes and pointed a warning finger – 'if you've got itchy feet, just remember the grass is never greener. They may be charming to begin with, but they all fart and they all pee around the loo seat in the end.'

David was halfway down the road before he realised just how cold it was. Although it wasn't windy, the damp in the air was bone-chilling and he briefly considered going back to the office for his jacket. Now he was on his way, though, he couldn't face turning back, particularly with the prospect of a pint and a quick lunch with Gerry and Phil ahead of him. The initiative meeting had been every bit as excruciating as he'd expected, with Barry handing out pointless print-outs and telling them to incentivise, to forward-face, to trend over, implement an oxygen move, so they could be major players. Someone – Clive, he rather thought – had made a suggestion, only to be told by Barry, 'It's not the long pole in my tent,' which had made David laugh out loud.

Barry had looked at him with ill-concealed disapproval. 'David,' he'd said, taking him to one side at the end of the meeting, 'you might just want to do something about that attitude of yours. I'm not the only one who's noticed it, you know. You're really starting to rub my rhubarb.'

David pushed open the door of The Rose and Crown and felt the welcome warmth and noise embrace him. He was the first there, so went straight to the bar and ordered the three pints of Theakstones from a barmaid he didn't recognise, wincing slightly as she splashed the bitter into the bottom of the glass, churning up a layer of foam that would take minutes to subside. She glanced up at him apologetically. Pretty. He smiled and shrugged.

'Sorry, I'm new. It always comes out faster than I expect. The beer, I mean.' She was blushing now, poor kid, and David felt a protective surge. She didn't look much older than the twins. She carefully poured the other two pints. David planted an elbow on the bar, linked his hands and turned to scan the room, more to avoid staring at her and making her any more nervous than out of interest. Everything was pleasingly familiar – none of the creeping gastropub tendencies that were sweeping town in here, thank you very much. He turned back and she pushed the first non-foamy pint towards him. He took a grateful swallow.

'Phew. That's better.'

'Tough morning?' She looked up at him questioningly

He shrugged, a little embarrassed. 'Yep! Incredibly tedious, actually. A two-hour meeting that could have been wrapped in an half and hour. Still, it brings home the bacon.'

A sudden punch on the shoulder made him slop a little beer onto the bar and he tutted as he turned to face Gerry and Phil, who had arrived together.

'Watch the amber nectar, you clumsy old sod.'

Gerry reached for the two other pints, and passed one to Phil. 'Cheers, mate. Yeah, can't have you spilling your precious fluids all over the shop.' He turned to the barmaid who was wiping up the puddle of bitter. 'Sorry, love. He's made a bit of a mess here. Can't take him anywhere. I'll get him out of your way. Can we order some food in a bit? We'll be over there. All right?'

Phil was making for a corner table and the others followed him. Once settled they each started on the beer in silence, sighing simultaneously in contentment. 'You got in fast with that new girl,' Phil remarked. 'Hope you don't imagine she fancies you, you old sod.'

'Nah – long past that. Besides I'm a married man.'

Gerry cackled, then stopped abruptly as the girl in question approached with notepad in hand. He looked round at the other two. 'Usual? Three sausage, egg and chips, please, love,' he went on. 'We'll be ready for another pint by then. Bring 'em over with the food, would you?' The others nodded in agreement and settled back in their chairs. This was more like it. The perfect antidote to a morning of Barry.

Once the food came, conversation – if you could call it that – tailed off and they sat in companionable silence as they ate. The official reason for them meeting like this, every Monday, was to discuss the progress of the Fat Dads, but there was not much to decide really. It had been going since their children were in primary school together. Dads had come and gone, and now David, Phil and Gerry were the senior members, supposedly responsible for organising the team. It was the perfect excuse for a regular dose of saturated fats and beer – all the more welcome after a whole weekend of putting up curtain rails, mowing lawns and enduring low-fat spread. And it was one of David's favourite rituals.

Gerry looked at his watch first and groaned. 'Ah well! No peace for the wicked. Come on, lads, let's go and settle up with the young lady. You first, David. Show us how it's done.'

They parted company and headed back to their respective offices. David shook his head and smiled. What a pair of old pillocks!

Suddenly the crisp afternoon seemed quite pleasant and he returned to his desk in a far better mood than he had left it. With any luck, he'd find time to firm up that package tour he'd found for their wedding anniversary. The idea had come to him from a feature in the weekend papers, and all women loved Rome, didn't they? All that ice cream and shopping and Audrey Hepburn nonsense. But he wouldn't spring it on Sarah until closer to the time – if he could resist. He was hopeless at keeping secrets – Sarah was always teasing him about it. But he'd really try this time. The look on her face would make it all worthwhile!

By the time Sarah got round to her mother's dressing table, Rachel was staging an assault on the bathroom with a frankly alarming vigour. The contents of the cupboard were being despatched into a bin liner with a speed and efficiency that would have impressed Field Marshall Montgomery.

Sitting on the little velvet stool, Sarah pulled open the drawers nervously. What if she found something embarrassing - the sort of things she knew people kept in private drawers. Ridiculous, of course, when her mother had been well into her seventies, but she'd been young once.

The drawer was surprisingly full and looked like it had been undisturbed for years. A trove of memorabilia, a statement of a life spent looking after a husband and a family. Had she grown as tired if it, as fed up of picking up dirty washing, as Sarah was now, following the same old routine until she wanted to throw her head back and scream? Crammed inside were old bottles of perfume, a couple still in their boxes, stuffed in next to old reading glasses, little packs of buttons and a travel sewing kit from a cracker. Sarah slipped the glasses onto her nose.

'What do you think, Rach?'

Rachel stuck her head round the door, rubber gloves on now, and snorted. 'God, you look just like her! Those were scary those specs.' And she disappeared again.

Sarah put them on the floor in the growing charity shop pile, and a bottle of paracetamol went in the rubbish bag. Though still in date, it didn't seem right to use pills of the dead. Sarah wondered if her mother had suffered headaches before her fatal stroke. If she had, she hadn't mentioned them. There were a couple of curled photographs of Rachel and Sarah on the beach – it looked like Wales – both children in shorts and T-shirts with spades and toothy grins. Sarah put them to one side, and opened the small jewellery box she'd made in woodwork at school, the word 'Mum' painstakingly burned out on the top. Inside were a couple of cheap brooches, their 'gold' tarnished now, and a string of faux pearls. The only vaguely valuable pieces of jewellery she possessed were her wedding ring and a small engagement ring bought with her father's meagre pay as a trainee draughtsman. She'd worn them both, alongside an equally modest eternity ring, all the time on her wedding finger; but on her other hand and at her wrists she'd been resplendent in cheap, colourful modern jewellery, rings with big glass stones, and chunky bangles that jangled as she gesticulated.

The rest of the drawer contents was rubbish – old tights and a pot of talc that must be well out of date. Sarah stuck her hand in to check the back and felt a small box. It was square and pale blue, with a crest in gold embossed on the top. Sarah flicked it open. Nestled in darker blue velvet was a delicate gold bracelet interspersed with tiny pearls. Sarah looked closer and ran her finger over the chain. The bracelet didn't look as though it had been worn – at least, Sarah had never seen her mother wear it. Probably another off-the-mark present from her father whose present-giving skills were, like David's, well meant but unspectacular. The name inside the lid, George Sutcliffe, EC1, offered no clues.

Sarah got up from the stool and was about to put the box on the To Keep and Distribute pile, but she hesitated and, checking that Rachel wasn't looking and, not quite sure why, she quickly slipped the box into her skirt pocket.

Chapter 6

David closed the spreadsheet he'd been yawning over and clicked on the Instant Messaging button at the bottom of the screen. He could see from his personal address book that Claire at least was online and smiled to himself. He typed a message to his daughter, leaned back in his chair and waited.

Claire heard the chirruping sound and looked up from her notes to see the orange message rectangle blinking at the bottom of her laptop screen. She unfolded her legs, and crossed the tiny room to her desk in a couple of steps. Sighing, she pulled out the wooden chair and sat down, then clicked.

At 3:45 p.m. Dad wrote:
Hi – anyone there? (And if so, why aren't you in the library?)

At 3.46 p.m. Claire wrote:
Hi dad. How r u? Slow day @ the office? It is poss 2 work in my room, you know! Me 'n' Tom r both fine and missing you and mum. How's granddad?

At 3.50 p.m. Dad wrote:
We're fine, thanks and granddad is managing surprisingly well. He's at the golf club most days. Mum and Rachel are there a lot, clearing stuff out. Wanted to ask – when are you planning to come back for w/e? Can we make a definite date so I can book restaurant for us all? Granddad would love to see you too. Are you horribly busy? I could come and collect you – that way you

28

can bring your dirty washing!

At 3.54 p.m. Claire wrote:
Maybe w/e after next? Will have 2 check with Tom. Not sure he
can hold out that long for washing! Will have to show him where
laundry room is – lol. It would be gr8 if u cld collect us. Sat a.m.?
Or r u playing footie?

At 3:58 p.m. Dad wrote:
Saturday would be better for me. I'll be there v early – ha ha!
Have fixed up a short break for me and mum for our anniversary
– Rome – but don't you dare tell her! Might spring it on her when
we're all out at lunch.

At 4:01 p.m. Claire wrote:
Inspired! That's more like it! She'll be thrilled. We won't breathe
a word. Promise! Maybe we could get her a guidebook for a
pressie too and give it to her at the same time so she can plan
your stay.

At 4:04 p.m. Dad wrote:
Do they do guidebooks without old churches in? If so, buy that
one!

At 4:06 .p.m Claire wrote:
Er – hate 2 tell u, that's all they have in Rome! Oh – and ice
cream. Will check with tom n msg u l8r – ok? I love secrets! Xx
Give our love to mum and the oldies. Xxxxx

Claire is offline.

Claire smiled to herself – Dad was never going to get the hang
of txtese – and turned back to her orderly pile of books, trying
to crank up what little enthusiasm she could find for her Culture

and Society essay. Her lecture notes didn't seem to make sense now and the internet was being no help at all. She shivered. The halls were either boiling hot or Arctic, and she pulled her chunky zip-up cardigan closer to her. A much nagged-for Christmas present, it felt like a hug from home and still smelled of the familiar fabric conditioner. She sighed heavily and picked up her pen. Bring it on, Marshall McLuhan. The medium is the message.

Sarah liked email. Those little messages that popped up were as if the postman came round several times a day, and as these days he only brought catalogues and bills anyway, it was the reinvention of the letter. Besides, email was a lifeline to the children – a way of finding out how they were without having to call, because Sarah always seemed to pick a time when they were busy or about to go out.

Most evenings, washing in, supper on and David due home, Sarah settled in front of the computer in the lounge. Tonight, she smiled as she saw there was a message from Nathalie, a couple of pictures of her new apartment in Sauzils attached. Sarah quickly opened them to see a room filled with sunlight and long windows overlooking trees and was that a building beyond? It was hard to tell. The floor was ceramic tile, as all French houses in the south seemed to be, and though it wasn't really Sarah's style, it looked comfortable enough.

What do you think of my new palace? Nathalie had written. *I'm so excited to have a place all of my own now – the bastard Stefan has moved to Lille with* la putain. *Can't wait to see how long it is until her bottle-brunette charms wear off and she's nagging him like a fishwife! Oh darling, can you escape your filthy winter and your philistine pupils and come and see me? It'll be so good for you. No excuses. All love N xx*

Sarah smiled at the thought. It would be fabulous to get away. Perhaps at Easter? She'd have to ask David. He certainly wouldn't want to come – he wasn't that fond of her old music college mate. 'She ought to grow up a bit and not try so damned hard with this free spirit thing,' he'd grumbled, though Sarah suspected he didn't trust her. Perhaps he was worried she might turn Sarah's head with her 'joys of the single life' propaganda. Well, maybe he'd like to go skiing again with the Fat Dads? He'd floated the idea already. Sarah quashed the feeling of relief that thought raised, and replied to Nathalie that she'd love to visit and would see what she could do.

'Are we still going to the Parkers' on Saturday?' David asked, as they cleared the supper trays later. 'Only, there's a bit of software Harry wanted to borrow.'

'Yup.' Sarah unwrapped a dishwasher tablet and then realised she'd put one in already. 'Stew and Pavlova again, I expect.'

David looked up, startled by her sharp tone. 'What do you mean?'

'Well, it's always stew and Pavlova with Sheila, isn't it?'

'I quite like Sheila's stew, as a matter of fact.'

'Bit of variety would be nice though, wouldn't it? She could go mad and open a cook book.' Sarah could hear the bitchy tone in her voice. What was the matter with her? 'I mean, don't you get bored with it all sometimes?' She turned to David who was peering closely at a bank statement. He needed his glasses.

'With what?'

'The same supper parties. The same routine.'

David dropped the hand holding the paper and thought. 'Sometimes it's fun to do something different. But that's the same with lots of things in life, isn't it?' He looked back at the statement and frowned. 'What was £340 for last month? Can you remember?'

'That new boiler part.'

'Of course. You wrote the cheque, didn't you? Hope we weren't ripped off.'

She saw him glance over at her. She didn't respond, but stood motionless, assessing her reflection in the kitchen window, black with the night behind, the washing-up brush held limply in her hand. Of course, it was inevitable he'd say that because she'd dealt with the plumber. It was the same whenever she dealt with anything on her own. He had a nasty habit of criticising first then asking questions.

'You're probably a bit low, love.' He was looking down at the statement again. 'What with your mum's death and Christmas and the weather. It's been a crap month weatherwise. You need something to look forward to.'

'Mmm, such as ...?' Sarah picked up the cloth, wiped the side and rinsed it out. She knew he didn't really deserve her mood but she was struggling to pull herself out of it.

'Well, what about planning to go away somewhere for our wedding anniversary? What's twenty years' good behaviour worth?' He smiled, a strange smugness in his eyes and she felt a flicker of worry. 'I was thinking about a weekend away? That might cheer you up. What do you say?'

Sarah looked at his familiar face and the old shirt she'd bought for him years ago when he was slimmer and which he'd almost worn to a thread. Yes, she wanted to see the Hermitage in St Petersburg, dance all night at the Mardi Gras, drink mojitos in Havana at sunset. In fact, she suddenly realised she wanted to see everything.

But why was it she didn't particularly want to do it with David?

Chapter 7

Claire checked her watch yet again. The lecture seemed to have been going on for hours and her stomach was rumbling. She hadn't gone for lunch because she hadn't seen anyone she knew in the queue and she couldn't face sitting on her own again. She'd walked briskly through the ref, hoping to see Tom's spiky blond hair among his usual gang of mates. They never minded if she tagged on, but they were nowhere to be seen and his phone was off, as usual. The Mars Bar grabbed from the buttery on the way over had hit the spot but she could have murdered a burger.

She looked up from her notepad, where she'd been doodling cartoon-style Swiss cheeses, and watched the lecturer as he shuffled his notes. She had no idea what he'd been on about for the last what-felt-like-three-hours-but-could-only-be-forty-five-minutes, but the way his dark jacket fell in folds when he lifted his arm to point at the interactive white board was really interesting, and she quickly sketched his pose on the page, bare of notes apart from a heading and the date. Next to her, a girl in a smock dress and woolly tights was writing diligently. She looked at her watch again. Not long now. She closed her folder in anticipation. She knew Tom didn't have lectures that afternoon – she had a copy of his timetable on the back of her door – so she'd pop over, just to make sure he was all right.

There was music coming from his room and she had to bang at the door before he heard and unlocked it. A shapeless band T-shirt was hanging off his body and his jeans, in dire need of a wash, were hanging low on his hips, the perennial sk8r-boy. 'Oh, wotcher. What are you doing here?'

She peered around. 'Just checking to see that you're okay. Have you been to the bank?'

Tom rolled his eyes, but stepped back to let her in. 'What a mess!' She wrinkled up her nose. 'Those transparent things in the wall – they do open you know.'

'Oh, ha, ha! Look, if you've just come to take the piss you can go right now. I've got an essay to do for tomorrow and I need to concentrate.'

She mooched over to his desk and looked at the notebook open by his laptop. 'Can you actually read your handwriting? Tell you what, if you want to dictate, I could help you with the typing. You know I'm faster than you.'

'Yes, yes. Rub it in, why don't you? You're better at everything, aren't you? Well, as a matter of fact, I do know what I'm doing, you know.' He tapped the mouse pad and the screen leaped into life, showing equations, diagrams and lines of text. 'See? I'm not quite as useless as you'd like to think.'

Claire shrugged. 'I never said that. You know I didn't. You're just being precious. Anyway, look – what time are you eating? Do you want to meet up and then maybe go for a drink after?' She looked hopefully at him. 'We could do our laundry too. I've got loads to do.'

Tom reached past her distractedly and tapped a correction into the keyboard. 'What's wrong? Your gang of little swots too dull even for you?'

She stared at him for a moment, stung by his lack of interest, his lack of need, then collected herself and gave him a dead arm with practised ease. 'I just thought, y'know – I've hardly seen you on our own this term. I thought it would be nice.'

He shot her a disbelieving sideways look and flicked back the pages of his notebook. 'Well, thanks for your concern but, er – no. Can't actually. I'm going into town to see a film with some mates. We'll get chips afterwards or a kebab or something. Wouldn't be your kind of thing. But I've really got to get on with this before we go, so …' He looked at her expectantly and gestured towards the door. 'Might see you tomorrow – okay?'

She hesitated for a moment, then left him staring at the screen and slipped out.

Of all the lamentable traits of humankind, Sarah rated petty-mindedness as her least favourite and their neighbour, Pauline Bayliss, Appalling Pauline, to whom they had been joined by a party wall for twenty years, had it in bucketfuls.

At times she was like the third person in their marriage, always just a brick-thickness away and shooting out of her front door like a ferret when there was a small 'issue' to discuss, or tutting at Sarah's child-rearing techniques. It might be their bins that had rolled over in the wind, Tom's bike left on the grass, or the height their hedge had reached. However insignificant its importance, the issue would be clucked over – Pauline's head jerking like a chicken's, the loose skin on her neck waggling as she strutted and her head shot forward is disgust. Every arrival home from work was a game of gauntlet-running to avoid her nosey interest.

'Sarah dear?' Damn, she'd been caught. Sarah could feel herself tense up as she opened the car door, the back seat hidden beneath supermarket carrier bags. Pauline emerged around her corner of the house and trotted over her small front lawn to the low fence. 'One small thing, dear. Oh, nice hair. Sorry to fuss, only there's a drainpipe which is dripping onto the roof of my conservatory.'

She used the word 'conservatory' in its loosest sense. It was, in fact, a simple glazed lean-to chock full of leggy plants and cacti crushed up against algaed glass.

'Right, Pauline,' Sarah said with a sigh, heaving a bag out of the back door. 'I'll ask David to take a look. How's your elbow?'

Sarah could feel the ridges the carrier bag handles had made in her fingers by the time she finally engineered an escape. 'She's lonely. She's a lonely old woman, and I know I should be more tolerant,' she muttered under her breath as she wearily unloaded the shopping into cupboards and the fridge, 'but aren't I due parole from having to put up with her?'

Time was running out – she was late after tacking on an extra lesson before she'd left school at lunchtime – so, shopping dispatched, Sarah picked up the box she'd pulled out of the last carrier bag, glanced at the clock, and headed into the hall. If her hairdresser hadn't the imagination to transform Sarah Lewis' life, then she'd have to do it herself. Picking up David's discarded old loafers like a reflex action and putting them back neatly under the chair, she took the stairs two at a time, then, once in the bathroom, opened the box cautiously, but not before looking long and hard at the glossy burnished locks of the model on the front. Sarah laid out the contents: plastic gloves, a tube of coloured gel and a sachet of conditioner. Breathing deeply, she began.

It was fiddly, the instructions sounding far more straightforward than the reality, but when the phone rang, she'd got as far as the plastic-cap-and-wait part of the ordeal, with the timer set for the recommended number of minutes.

'What's occurring?' Her friend Trish was clearly having another boring day at the office, though Sarah couldn't remember many that inspired her. Advertising sales on the local paper was hard slog, which Trish tolerated with very little fortitude.

'I'm giving my hair a bit of a tint, as a matter of fact.' Sarah sipped her tea.

'Crikey. That's a bit radical for you,' Trish chuckled, but then her own thick curly blonde mane was frequently highlighted in whatever shade matched her handbag.

'It's just a slight auburn tint. Thought it was about time I held back the alarming onslaught of grey.'

'Be careful. Those home dyes can be tricksy. You should come to my hairdresser. He'll take years off you. When I went blonde

Phil couldn't keep his hands off me!' Sarah flinched. She knew she wanted a life change, but perhaps not quite the treatment Trish had in mind, which might involve piercings or tattoos.

'What time will you be showing up for Ssheila's sshtew?' Trish put on her best Sean Connery 'Eshhh'. 'You can always rely on Sheila for a stew. Oops, gotta go. Call coming in from my big advertiser. See you later and can't wait to see the new hair.' And she promptly put down the phone.

The wait for the timer reminded Sarah of the pregnancy test she'd done when she was twenty-two, though, of course, the little blue line hadn't been able to impart the truly shocking news that it was twins. Being pregnant so soon had been one thing – they'd only been married a couple of months – but she hadn't been ready for the onslaught. Was anyone? Could any amount of reconnaissance prepare you for the reality of two small babies to care for? She had been so young, and, despite help from her mother, and often unwanted advice from the more experienced Rachel, Sarah was pretty sure the whole of their first year was wholly unaccounted for. In fact, it had totally passed her by. All she could recall was endless lactating, and taking so long to prepare to take the twins out that by the time she was ready the next feed was due and it was too late to go. Trish, who was on her third pregnancy at Sarah's first ante-natal class, still referred to that period as the Bermuda Triangle, and teased Sarah about the fact that she and David had eaten only pizza for ten months. Whole genres of music had passed her by – no time to listen to the radio – and there were still films she'd never heard of. It was not unlike having been in a coma.

At last the beeper went and Sarah cautiously removed the cap, dropping it in the bin, then she leaned over the bath and began to rinse out the dye with the hand shower.

The first moments of disquiet came when she saw the orange hue of the water running off her hair towards the plug hole. Of course that's normal, she assured herself. It's what stays on that matters. The dark stuff is bound to wash off. Quickly she shampooed then wrapped her hair in a towel, rubbing vigorously, her eyes fixed again on the model on the front of the box. Soft Autumn, it said clearly. *Soft Autumn.*

Standing in front of the mirror, she slowly pulled the towel away, the over-mirror light catching the colour in her damp tendrils. Soft Autumn? More Nuclear Attack.

'Oh shit,' Sarah gasped in horror, a smile of disbelief on her face. 'I look like Russ Abbott.' Then, dropping the towel on the floor, she crumpled, her body wracked with overwhelming sobs that made her ribs hurt with their violence.

Chapter 8

David glanced across the table. Despite the low lighting Sheila favoured, 'for atmosphere, you know', which made it almost impossible to see what was on his plate, Sarah's hair was like a beacon. A flaming Belisha beacon, actually. He could barely see her face, though, so he couldn't tell how she was doing now. All that effort, when he'd come in from work, and found her pacing around the house, grim-faced, in Claire's beanie. All that effort not to laugh, first of all, and then to reassure her that, no, it wasn't that awful and, no, it didn't look like an accident at Chernobyl. All that bloody effort gone to waste when Sheila opened the door and screeched, 'Oh Sarah, what the bloody hell have you done? You look like a clown!'

He'd never really seen the side of Sheila that Sarah objected to sometimes, but he did now. There was a point at which the frankness on which she prided herself veered into sheer rudeness, and Sheila had exceeded it tonight. As a result, he was being just a bit off with her, to show her he was annoyed. He wasn't sure she'd noticed, but it made him feel better.

She was onto skiing now. 'The conditions were so different depending on the altitude. Just skiing from one area to another, you could go from snow to sleet to rain within minutes. I don't even think there's any point going to lower down resorts these days. You might as well stay at home.'

Trish's Phil was concentrating on his stew, shovelling it in with enthusiasm, but he nodded in casual agreement, leaving the floor to David. 'Well, they say there isn't going to be any snow left worth skiing in twenty years, so you might as well learn waterskiing instead. You'll be able to do it over most of Norfolk and Suffolk, I reckon. No worries about altitude there.'

She tapped him playfully on the arm. 'Oh, very funny! You'll see, if you boys go off again. I told Harry, I said, "Go for glacier skiing. It's the only way you can guarantee really good snow," but of course you boys know best. I don't know why I waste my breath.'

'We all wonder that sometimes, Sheila,' David retorted with a big smile and turned deliberately away to the conversation at the other end of the table.

'I know when Sean went to Loughborough we didn't hear from him for three weeks. Trish was apoplectic – I had so stop her driving there to check he hadn't been lured into a drugs ring in Freshers' Week,' Phil said with a snort of laughter, and Sarah absentmindedly wiped a drip of stew off his chin. It was an oddly familiar action, she knew, but then she and David had been camping with Trish and Phil every summer for the last few years and, when there are four adults under canvas, there are few secrets left.

'Turns out he was shagging that Amy,' Trish interjected, putting her hand on her husband's arm. 'Still trying to shake her off, isn't he? Do you know' – she leaned forward conspiratorially – 'she even sent him a pair of her knickers for Christmas. That's just plain pushy!'

'Christ!' Harry's mouth fell open. Poor naïve Harry, pussy-whipped by Sheila and whose own sons were still at the GCSE stage and within his orbit – just. Sarah wanted to say that she was sure *her* children were fine – they had each other, didn't they? – but she bit back. Trish would only contradict her with a 'that's what you think' and a knowing glance over at Phil. It was what she always did – from the lofty position of Older Parent – whenever Sarah uttered some disquiet about anything to do with the twins. At least Trish had given her a supportive hug in sympathy with the hair-dye disaster, but still. What was it that made the been-there-done-that parent so insufferably smug?

She ran her fingers through her hair, hoping that she'd actually imagined the whole home-dye disaster, but the faintly strawy feeling of the strands between her fingers was a vicious reminder. Did hairdressers do emergency appointments, she wondered, like dentists and vets, or would she have to wait until next week?

'So, what about you two and the Big Anniversary?' Sheila silenced the table with her question. 'Come on, Tom and Claire are off your hands. Time you rediscovered the meaning of the dirty weekend after twenty years, and it's not the allotment *or*, David Lewis' – she looked hard at him – 'taking your wife to a classic car rally.'

Sarah shrugged and smiled weakly. 'Don't think we ever had time for dirty weekends, did we?' She looked over at her husband, who was fiddling with the stem of his wineglass.

'Well?' Sheila clasped her hands together. She wasn't going to let this go. 'Are you going to have a big party we can all come to and get pissed?'

Sarah glanced at David and was relieved to see he looked as unhappy about the idea as she felt.

'I doubt it. Just to keep you pissheads happy?' He smiled confidently. 'Nah, something a little more intimate, I think. It's all in hand.'

Sarah felt a wave of what she could only describe as dread.

They'd had the conversation – although it was really only a matter of form – on the way there. Sarah would drive so he could have a drink. Harry was unscrewing the cap of another bottle of Chardonnay and, as usual, was busy defending screwcaps over corks.

'I just can't get my head round it, though,' David protested as he knew he'd done before. 'I'd even rather have those plastic corks than a screw cap. There's just something nice about using the corkscrew and hearing the cork pop out. It's satisfying. It's all part of the experience.'

General shrugging round the table. It was really only he and Harry who seemed to care about this but he could usually rely on Sarah to back him up – just out of cussedness if nothing else. Sarah barely drank at the best of times – well, it went straight to her head – but even if she didn't share his passion for French wine, she was, like him, appreciative of tradition.

She hadn't been her normal chatty self tonight, mind you. The hair disaster had really got to her and David smiled warmly in her direction. She looked a little pale. Tired, possibly? He couldn't wait to spring the Rome trip on her. But that would come later.

She cleared her throat. 'I don't see the point, really. If screw caps are as good as you say. I mean, if it doesn't make any difference, why go to all the bother? Mind you, I feel sorry for those people who make those novelty bottle stoppers.' She stopped for a moment, took an alarmingly large gulp from her glass and he recognised that familiar, slightly dangerous glint appear in her eye. 'You know – those hideous silver-plated things you give to people you don't give a toss about for Christmas.'

There was an audible intake of breath and Sheila opened and closed her mouth several times.

'Oh, but I loved that sweet little set you gave us all last Christmas, Sheila,' Trish blurted. 'We use them all the time, don't we, Phil?'

'Er, er …'

Harry jumped to his feet. 'I'll get the trifle, shall I?'

David felt a flicker of hope. 'Trifle?' Sheila had recovered. 'Don't be silly, David! I know you wouldn't want to miss out on your Pav. I've made one of those as well – kiwi and raspberry this time. I'll come and help you, Harry.'

'You were out of order.'

42

It was the first time David had spoken since they had said their goodbyes. He'd taken the keys from her and got into the driver's seat but she'd barely noticed. She knew she'd drunk far more than him anyway.

'Was I?' She looked at the houses along the road as they drove by. She knew each one so well and must have walked, driven or pushed a buggy past them a million times. The Radcliffes with their new extension, the Greaves and their over-tall leylandii, Beryl and Sid Thomas and their tatty garden shed. She shut her eyes to block it out.

'You know perfectly well you were – that jibe about the bottle stoppers. Sheila must have been really hurt.'

Sarah shrugged, knowing she was being childish. 'Nothing hurts Sheils. She's got the hide of a rhino, and being pathologically right all the time must soften the blow.' The street lights flashed across the windscreen. She could feel a surge of resentment beginning in the pit of her stomach.

'I know she can be a bit overbearing, but she means well.'

'Means well?' Sarah turned to look at him, driving in the way he always did, his right arm held straight gripping the steering wheel, the other hand resting on the gear stick. Why did he do that when he didn't need to change gear? 'Means well? She can be a thoughtless bitch. No one knows me well enough to make some crack about my hair.'

'Oh, come on.' He frowned. 'She could hardly not say anything – it's sort of impossible to miss, let's face it!'

'She made me feel stupid.'

'You made her feel stupid. So who's in the right?'

'Oh fuck off.' Sarah folded her arms, not sure why she was being so over-sensitive. She'd have laughed it off another time – been the first to point out how ridiculous she looked and made a big story out of the whole rinsing-it-out event. But just now, just this minute, just today, it was unbearable. And she didn't even have her period.

43

'Are you having your period?' he asked without taking his eyes off the road.

'Oh David, don't be so bloody predictable!'

Well, what else was he supposed to say? It seemed impossible to get things right with Sarah at the moment. If he didn't ask, was it insensitive? Or was it worse to ask? He didn't have any idea any more – it had been quite a while since they'd had any action, and he'd lost track of her dates. And he certainly wouldn't be getting any tonight. Best to shut up and let her calm down.

Maybe if he told her about Rome, she'd feel better. It could spark a rapturous make-up session. They'd never really been ones for make-up sex, though. Never really been ones for arguing – until recently.

He glanced across at her. She'd closed her eyes but he could tell she wasn't asleep. Instead of that lovely, sexy relaxed look she got when she dropped off, her lips were pressed together and there was a little crease between her eyebrows. She was sulking.

As he pulled into the drive, she sat up and turned to look at him. In the dark, it was impossible to see her expression but, as he switched off the ignition, the interior lights came on. He turned to give her what he hoped would come over as a loving smile but he was shocked by the darkness in her eyes. Instantly, his irritation gave way to concern. It had all been too much for her – the children leaving, losing her mother, sorting out her dad, having to face middle age – probably menopause looming as well. Maybe the hair fiasco was a cry for help. And all he'd done was rub it in. 'Come on, love. Let's get inside and have a cup of something. You could probably do with drinking some water too, before you turn in.'

He opened the back door and waited for her. She seemed to be taking ages and he needed a slash, but he had to lock up the car. Eventually, she appeared, walking a bit too carefully. Shaking his head, he followed her indoors and went to the loo,

44

hoping she might make her way to the kitchen and the teabags. She really had drunk more than normal. She'd have a horrible head in the morning and would be mortified at what she'd said to Sheila. David zipped back up and washed his hands, then went to find her.

'All right, love? Did you put the kettle on?'

She was sitting at the kitchen table looking down at her nails. Clearly not.

He rather pointedly did it himself and got the cups down. 'Camomile? Rosehip?'

'Yes, fine. I don't mind. Whatever you're having.'

'But you don't like coffee at this time of night. Do you want that awful green stuff?'

'Look – anything. I just don't care. Just … anything.'

David raised his eyebrows and found her green tea, popping a teabag into the mug. She wasn't making any effort to mollify him – and he certainly wasn't going to make the first move. He placed the drink in front of her and sat down next to her, nursing his coffee. She glanced up quickly but dropped her eyes again and took a deep breath.

'I'm … I don't know what's wrong with me, David. I just don't feel right. Nothing seems comfortable any more: work, the house, my clothes, even my hair. I just … I want to change everything but I don't know where to start.'

Oh God, she wanted to talk. And at this time of night. He took a deep breath. 'Well, that's fair enough. I'm sure lots of people feel like that. There's nothing *wrong* with you, if that's what you're worried about. It's probably perfectly normal for your age. I bet if you asked any of your friends they'd say the same. Every area of your life can't be perfect. That's expecting too much.'

'But that's just it. I don't think it is expecting too much. I'm only forty. Surely there should be more to life than this?' She gestured irritably around at the kitchen.

Was that it? She wanted new units? They'd have to wait until after Rome!

'But there is more, isn't there? There's more than just the house and clothes and all that. There's family and friends. There's you and me and the kids. I mean, what more could you want?' A ridiculous thought suddenly occurred to him. He looked at her in alarm. 'You don't ... you don't want another baby, do you? I thought we'd agreed when I ...'

She looked at him as if he had two heads, then burst into a peal of almost hysterical laughter. 'No, David. That is something I most certainly don't want.'

'Well, good. Phew.' He laughed awkwardly. 'Anything else we can work on. Look, I know you've had a lot of changes lately, and it's a lot to get used to. But we'll work on it. We can start getting away more, now we don't have to be running round after the children. We can travel a bit. Go up to London for a weekend. Take in a show or something. You've always wanted to see places – so now we can! I wasn't going to tell you, actually. It was going to be a surprise, but—'

'I want out.'

'What?'

Her hands were partly covering her face and she was staring at the table.

'I want to go away. On my own. I have to.'

He put his hand out to her shoulder and she pulled away sharply. 'I don't understand. You mean you want to go on holiday separately this year?'

'No, David.' She dropped her hands to the table and turned her face so that she could look straight at him. 'I want to get away from here, from us. From everything.'

Chapter 9

Sarah hadn't realised that was what she was going to say until the words came out. It was as if someone else had spoken.

David simply looked at her without speaking, an expression of incomprehension and what looked terribly like fear in his eyes. What had she done? A wave of horror flooded her. It was as if she had sliced through the rope that secured her to everything: David, the kitchen they sat in, their lives. She hadn't even put the children's feelings into the equation. But mixed in with the sense of disbelief that she had uttered out loud something that had lain buried and unexplored, was the absolute conviction that she had spoken what she really felt.

In that moment had burst out the frustration of an unchanged life, where the landscape hadn't altered since before she could remember, and in which everything had moved around her and she had simply sat back and watched. The same town, the same street, the same house and curtains, the same conversations.

'You mean separate?' David's voice was a whisper; his eyes were wide.

She moved, turning in her chair and pushing her hands between her knees. Some noise to break the terrible tension where her words still hung in the air.

'Oh I don't know.' She fidgeted, aware that she had lobbed a hand grenade into their lives and she hadn't really formulated any answers to the questions that were bound to come.

David scraped back his chair and took his cup over to the sink. 'I do. I think you're drunk.'

'I'm not.' She shouted out the protest. 'Okay, so I've had a bit to drink,' she conceded when he turned back to look at her hard. 'But this isn't about the wine. This is about how I feel at the moment. David, I just haven't had time to find out who I am in all this.'

He sounded irritated. 'Is this from one of those magazines of yours? Who you are? What do you mean "who you are"? And in "all" what?'

Sarah waved her hand around. 'All this. All the things I haven't done ...' She tailed off, afraid she was going to cry.

He put his cup in the sink, the way he always did, without bothering to open the dishwasher, and went to the kitchen door. 'I don't think this is the right time to be discussing this, do you? I'm going to bed.' And he walked away.

In the silence, Sarah studied the backs of her hands. Why did they always show your age first? Then, finding no answers there, she looked around the room. The window blind with its motif of teacups and teapots, looked the same. The pine chairs they'd bought years ago, and which she desperately wanted to up-date, looked the same. But her inner landscape had irreparably changed.

She'd loved this house when they'd bought it. Their first real home after the tiny-one-up-two-down they'd rented when they were first married. It had been way too expensive, of course, bought on a wave of excitement at David's pay rise and with a small injection of money from her grandmother's will. The first morning they were there she'd woken at dawn and padded about, wrapped in the counterpane, marvelling that it was *theirs*.

Well, almost theirs. David's parents had chipped in to help them, persuaded by the need for somewhere bigger thanks to the impending arrival of twins – a concept that had appalled David's mother, Heather, who seemed to consider the idea of producing two children at once as vaguely obscene or self-indulgent. She'd always been draconian with children, organised down to the fin-est detail whenever she'd been called upon to have the twins for the afternoon and, while Sarah's own mother would return them covered in paint and chocolate, broad grins on their faces, they would come back from Heather's house crisper and cleaner then they had been delivered. Gifts too were always worthy, clearly thought out but boring. David would laugh and say 'twas ever thus. Whatever he wanted he'd always been given the cheaper brand or nothing at all. Perhaps that accounted for his irritatingly anal obsession with scouring *Which?* Magazine reports for hours before choosing the gadget, domestic machine, lawn mower that was just right.

The sound of David moving about upstairs ceased. Sarah knew he would have taken off his watch and placed it on the bedside table; he would have thrown his shirt onto the floor by the door, as always, followed by his socks, still rolled in a ball. Then, after cleaning his teeth for almost exactly one minute, he would splash water on his face, dry it on her towel and, pyjama bottoms on, get into bed and open his book. Though perhaps not tonight.

Sarah ran her hands over the kitchen table wonderingly. She had always been so impetuous about things. Taking action without thinking things through and then laughing it off when it went wrong. At first David had indulged her, but for years he'd put his foot down whenever she started one of her 'Why don't we ...?' conversations. He'd almost always been right. This table was far more practical than the glass one she'd had her eye on, but where was the fun? Where was the spontaneity? The aesthetic?

She pulled herself up and wobbled slightly, then, suddenly irritated, picked up his cup and banged it down hard on the *Kitchen Magazine*-recommended Best Buy granite. She heard the impact and peered into the cup to see the hairline crack run from the base right up to the rim. Damn. One of her favourites too. She lifted the lid of the bin and dropped the cup inside, and turned to the door to go upstairs, her hand on the light switch. Then, turning back to the bin, she lifted the lid again and pushed

49

the broken cup further down inside and covered it with an old wrapper.

David woke up suddenly. It was getting light outside and, for a moment, he wasn't sure what day it was. Had he slept in? No – he remembered now. Slowly, he shook his head in surprise at how late he'd slept. He hadn't managed to get to sleep for ages the previous night. Even though he'd gone up first – no point prolonging that ridiculous conversation with Sarah when she clearly wasn't thinking straight – but had lain awake, trying hard not to go over what she's said. She'd come up about half an hour after him and he'd felt her looking at him, trying to work out if he was asleep. He didn't stir. And when he'd felt her get quietly into bed beside him, he'd kept up the pretence. Infuriatingly, she'd fallen asleep straight away, confirming his theory about the drink. How could she say something so bloody stupid then drop off to sleep as though nothing had happened? She'd regret it and have a hell of a head this morning, though. He'd certainly get a cuppa in bed out of it and maybe even ...

Hmmm. He turned his head to see how deeply asleep she was. But her eyes were open and she was staring at the ceiling, completely still. He waited. She could bloody well make the first move. Silence. She must have realised he was looking at her. She looked a bit pale. Probably hung over. Still nothing. David began to feel a twinge of irritation. This wasn't how it was supposed to work! He cleared his throat, turning it into a bit of a cough. Blimey – a cup of tea was the least he could expect after everything – the supper as well as what came after. Still nothing. Oh well. At least he could act like an adult!

'Morning.' That was it – a bit curt, a bit chilly. She'd have to work to win him round. 'Sleep all right?'

She turned to look at him briefly, almost irritated, as if he'd interrupted a train of thought. 'Yes, fine,' she replied quietly.

Huh – how about that? She hadn't even asked him how he felt. Looked like he was going to get some sort of silent treatment, although what possible reason she could have for being angry with *him*, he couldn't even being to imagine. Sod her, then. He'd make his own tea.

He rolled over and stood up, flexing his shoulders. 'I said I'd pop over to see Phil later. Do you have any plans? You'll have to ring Sheila at some point.'

'What?' The hostility in her tone was the last thing he was expecting.

'I said, you'll have to ring Sheila to apologise about last night. Everyone saw you'd had too much to drink, so you'd better blame it on that.'

'Is that what you think this is about?' She sat up quickly, tilting her head challengingly to look at him. 'Are you trying to blame all this on me having had too much to drink?'

'You can't just insult one of our oldest friends, wreck a dinner party, have a go at me – completely unprovoked – and then spout some nonsense about "wanting out" and not expect me to try to find some reason behind it. Of course you'd had too much to drink. It was perfectly obvious. And after we'd agreed that you would drive! Just as well I didn't decide to be completely selfish too, isn't it? Or we'd have ended up having to get a taxi.'

She stepped out of bed and, against the light from the curtains, David could see her hips and waist through her nightdress. In spite of his anger, he could feel himself start to want her. Maybe even because of his anger.

She held his eyes angrily, and reached out for her dressing gown, pulling it on and tying the belt with a grim finality. 'Nonsense? So that's what you've decided this is – nonsense. What do I have to do to make you take me seriously?' She shook her head and looked suddenly tired. When she spoke again, her voice was softer. 'Look – go and have a shower, or whatever you want to do. I'll make us some tea. We have to talk.'

David pulled a towel from the stand and left the room without speaking. That would show her. Hah – he knew she'd make the tea eventually.

Chapter 10

The reply to her email from Nathalie in the South of France had come back very quickly – within an hour of Sarah sending it last Sunday morning – but she'd ignored it. Ignored the invitation that hung in the air: *Yes come, do! What liberation for you, darling! Can't wait.*

The week had not been a liberation, though. In many ways it was the worst Sarah could remember. Worse even than that surreal few days between her mother's death and the funeral. At least there had been a shared grief then, and plans for the service had been interspersed with memories and anecdotes about her mother's life. There had even been laughter with the Dickensian-looking undertaker with the long grey sideburns and down-turned mouth, which had broken into a smile when her father had asked if there was an increased charge for dying on a Bank Holiday. A weak joke but it had broken the ice of despair.

She couldn't even bring herself to face the hairdresser, using a scarf when she was out to cover up the diabolical hair colour, rather than have to face explanations and trite conversation. The expression on her face must have been enough to deflect questions, and colleagues at school didn't pry. Every day brought analysis and questioning from David, and the only thing they shared was an agreement not to tell anyone else until the children knew. This created a schizophrenic existence. She'd smile sweetly at school when colleagues asked if she and David planned anything over half term, or lie that they were busy when mates called up and asked them if they were free for dinner a month or so hence.

Then she'd come home, or had put down the phone, and been faced with his questions.

They came as texts from work, or broke the deafening silence as they each played with their supper at the kitchen table.

'Why, Sarah? I don't understand. Twenty years, for God's sake. We've been happy, haven't we?' His eyes were searching.

'Yes, yes we have,' she'd answer, 'but I've never known anything else. It's as if there wasn't a time in my life when there wasn't an *us*. When I could think independently. Just worry about myself. I mean, I haven't even travelled on a plane on my own, or been able to ... I don't know, get up in the morning and go somewhere without telling anyone or having to be back at a certain time.'

'But you can do that,' he said over and over again. 'I'd let you. I mean, I've never stopped you. You only had to say that's what you wanted.' Sarah nodded slowly, knowing he didn't really understand.

Then, after a glass or two of wine on Wednesday night, he'd got angry and called her selfish and a hard bitch, and it was then that she felt she could be more honest.

'David, this life is stultifying! I'm being buried before I've even started to discover things. You seem happy with settling – just having everything the same old way. Me here cooking for you, your underpants clean and ironed, our social life organised as if I was your diary secretary – the same old routine—'

'What the hell is wrong with that?'

At this point she tossed down the fork she was holding and threw her arms out in despair. 'It's boring. I'm *bored*, David. Bored of all this; bored of who I am, and bored of just seeing the world via the Discovery Channel.' She knew she was going to be cruel but she couldn't stop herself. 'I don't want a life where the most exciting thing that happens is that we get Sky or decide to go mad and buy a new car.' The brochures were there at the other end of the table looking innocently at them both.

David pushed back his chair noisily and, casting out his arm, knocked the brochures flying onto the floor. 'Okay, so forget a sodding car. I thought you'd be pleased. Because that's what people do, Sarah. That's life. You earn a living, you have a nice house, you go on holiday. You better yourself!'

'That's exactly it!' Somehow he'd put his finger on it. 'Who's bettering themselves here? You're doing great, David, because you can. You earn three times as much as you used to, you get better perks; but what about me? I'm still teaching like I've been doing since the children went to school. Endless days of diabolical fiddle playing, and where's the satisfaction in that?' She could feel the tears hurting the back of her eyes.

'You could have done something else!' He faltered, flailing about for an example, but she knew he wouldn't find one.

'What exactly? I didn't spend three years at music college to have to drop it for ever because of the twins and raising a family. I love my music. It's in my bones, but how could I have done more with it, David? Play in orchestras every night at the theatre? How would you have liked that? Me never here, you having to see to the children. Worse.' She really warmed to her subject now and leaned over the table towards him, unaware her cardigan was trailing in the discarded macaroni cheese. 'I could have gone on tour. Weeks on end. One of us had to make the sacrifice and naturally it had to be me. I'm a woman and that's what women do—'

'Don't give me that woe-is-me crap.' David's face was dark and he thrust his hands in his pockets, a gesture of defence she'd seen him do many times over the years.

'I wouldn't have changed a moment,' Sarah burst back, 'but you have to recognise what it's done to me as a person. We've lost sight of our dreams. You don't even touch that bloody Alvis in the garage and after you saved up so long to buy it.'

'Oh Christ, not that again. If you hadn't noticed I've been

working my balls off providing for you and the kids and putting up with Barry's crap.'

'And I haven't been working? Of course you've had time. You just haven't bothered. It's like everything else.'

'I've had enough of this,' he shouted and stormed from the room.

After tidying the kitchen and taking perverse pleasure in banging the pans, she followed him out and, tripping over his discarded shoes in the hall, kicked them hard down the corridor.

For the next two days they shadow-boxed each other. He left for work early without breakfast, something he had never done, and came back late on Thursday evening after his regular five-a-side game and a couple of pints. Sarah could only speculate what that pub session had been like – an evening of thin conversation as it so often was with men – but she could tell by the way he snored when he fell asleep that he shouldn't have driven home.

On Friday she finished lessons at lunchtime – a speaker had come into school so all the pupils were busy – but instead of going home to the ironing or the dusting, she wrapped up warm and walked up to the obelisk on the Welcombe Hills that looked out across the River Avon towards the Cotswold Hills. There were only been a few people about – an old man with a fat dachshund panting up the hill and a couple with a pair of Highland terriers – but they ignored her. She sat alone on a graffitied bench in the watery winter sunshine and looked out at the patchwork quilt of fields, the hills with their clumps of dark trees and the roofs of barns on the farms. She and David had come up here many times when the children were small, a habit that had died off when they became teenagers and considered walks to be 'pants'. They'd always marvelled at the view and thought how lucky they were not to be holed up in a city. It had become a sort of family cliché.

'Lovely, isn't it?' Sarah jumped when a lady joined her on

the bench. She hadn't heard her approach but she perched on the other end as her spaniel shot frantically from rabbit hole to rabbit hole, sniffing excitedly.

Sarah hunched her shoulders against the bracing wind. 'Yes, it is, especially on a day like today.'

'I never get bored of it. Makes me realise why I've never moved away. It's sort of part of your landscape isn't it, a view like that?' She turned and smiled at Sarah. 'You local?'

'Yes, all my life.'

'Well, you'll know what I mean then.' She paused and looked at Sarah more closely. 'Are you Mary's girl, the violinist?'

'Yes, I am.'

The woman folded her gloved hands in her lap. 'Well I never! I don't suppose you remember me. I'm Pamela Morris. We used to live close by when you were – gosh, you can't have been more than five – then we moved to Old Town.' She smiled. 'I remember your first day at school. You were adamant you weren't wearing the shoes your mum had bought you and you went off in your socks down the road!'

'Crikey, I'd forgotten that!' Sarah laughed, though she didn't remember Pamela at all, and felt a wave of love for her mother.

'I didn't know Mary well – just to say hello to when we passed – but I was so sorry to hear about her death. How is your father coping?'

Sarah shrugged, trying to fight back the tears that were threatening. 'He's been very strong but it's been hard for him. He's moving into town soon, a flat in Linden Gardens. It'll be easier for him then.'

'He must get lonely,' she said, squinting into the distance. 'But don't bury your own grief in concern for him, will you?'

Sarah turned to look at her. Such a direct piece of advice from a stranger. 'What do you mean?'

'Well, just because you are older when you lose a parent doesn't make it any less painful. You'll find you grieve not only

57

for them, but for the order of things. The place we called home has disappeared and suddenly there is nothing between us and the grave.' She laughed wryly. 'It's not unlike going to the front of a plane and finding there is no one at the controls. People seem to believe that the older you are the less you are expected, or allowed, to mourn. "She had a good innings", they say, or "was it expected?" Crass and stupid remarks, don't you think?'

The woman stood up and whistled to her dog who had wandered off. 'She was a lovely woman, your mother. So much more to her than perhaps she ever showed. Creatively, I mean. You look just like her. So long.' She waved as she moved away. 'And take care of yourself, won't you?'

Sarah knew she'd have to face David that evening, and, idling in front of the computer, she waited for his car lights to swing into the drive, aware that she was starting every time she hear a sound. She sent a silly message to the children, in some sort of subconscious attempt to allay any fears they couldn't possibly have yet anyway. Then she replied to Nathalie in France, explaining in more detail how her visit to the new flat might be a bit more than a holiday – it would be a bolthole – and did she mind?

For David the rest of the week passed in a blur. No one at work seemed to have noticed anything was wrong, apart from Doreen, of course, whose gaze he could feel uncomfortably between his shoulder blades when he breezed past her to the stairs, but she was far too discreet to ask. He'd called off drinks with the lads, got out of footie on Thursday by lying that he had to take something – he couldn't even remember what he'd said now – to his father-in-law's. The mild abuse he'd got from Phil reassured him, at least, that he'd managed to cover it up. He couldn't have faced the the pub afterwards and the inane banter and, at the last minute, he couldn't bear to go home either and had spent too long in another pub on the other side of town, one so grotty he was certain no one he knew would be there.

But the artifice wouldn't last. And every time David thought about having to tell everyone, and what they would say about it, both to his face and behind his back, he felt sick. And yet Sarah didn't seem bothered by it at all. He'd even tried talking to her about it. 'What will everyone say?' he'd asked, aware, as the words left his lips, of how pathetic it sounded.

She had looked at him as if he were mad. 'What does it matter what anyone says?' she'd demanded shrilly. 'This isn't to do with them. It's to do with you and me.'

Except it wasn't. Not really. As far as David could see, it was nothing to do with him at all. Sarah had decided and that was that. No room for discussion. And if Sarah had decided, she could bloody well explain herself to everyone. Except ... Except if he was there with her, at least he could say it was a mutual decision. At least it wouldn't look as though she was leaving just because of him. But how could she claim to have been so unhappy all this time? Wouldn't he have known? Shouldn't she have told him? All those times when he'd felt happy – well, content anyway – and thought she felt the same. Had she been planning this for years? Hating every moment of their life together? Just waiting for the twins to leave home so she could make her escape?

Oh God! David looked up at the computer screen on his desk, almost surprised to see it was still there. Would it be easier if there was somebody else? Maybe there was, and she just wasn't saying. No – there couldn't be. Or could there? He sat back in his chair and rubbed the back of his neck. The look of surprise on her face when he had asked her outright suggested there wasn't – she'd always been crap at lying, unable even to cover up when she'd dented the car – but there was always a first time, wasn't there? These thoughts had been chasing round and round in his head for days now, like a *Tom and Jerry* cartoon. He'd barely achieved any work, and it was bound to show sooner or later. He stood up and went to pour himself a coffee, surprised to notice another full cup, still hot, on his desk when he returned. He rubbed his eyes. He was losing his grip.

'Oh, a trashy magazine,' Lydia gasped with enthusiasm and grabbed it from the floor by Claire's bed. 'Can I read it?'

'Sure.' Claire turned on the kettle and, looking suspiciously into the mugs to check there wasn't any actual fur in them, spooned in some coffee and powdered milk. Odd how she'd managed to acquire a taste for the stuff, but needs must when she always forgot to buy milk. In fact, since starting here she'd managed to cope with a whole raft of new experiences – Pot Noodles, cold pizza from the night before, warm wine and cold tea and eeking out a pair of jeans for five days. Perhaps this is what everyone meant by growing up. Whatever, Claire was fairly certain that her immune system was now as strong as an ox's.

Lydia was bent over the pages now, unconsciously twiddling her hair between her fingers. 'Isn't it fantastic that this kind of trash is required reading?' she giggled. 'Who'd have thought you could do a degree in reading about celebrity cellulite and exclusive wedding scoops!'

'Is that why you chose the course?' Claire enquired. 'You shallow thing you.'

Lydia looked up, her eyes sparkling. 'Only sort of. Actually, it's always been my dream to work in the media. I used to make pretend newspapers when I was little, and then go around the house with a wooden spoon as a microphone interviewing everyone. The editor of our local rag at home gave me work experience after GCSEs and I loved it.' She paused. 'I might see if he wants me again over the long vac.'

Claire couldn't imagine anything she'd enjoy less. Sitting on the phone asking people about how much they made at the village fete. But then she couldn't imagine a course she'd enjoy less either. Nuclear physics, maybe, or geography like Tom. She kept reminding herself as she crawled out of bed each morning that there were only seven and three-quarter terms left, but somehow the prospect did not fill her with joy.

'Did your parents want you to have a degree, then?' she went on. 'I mean, couldn't you have stayed at the paper and learned on the job?'

Lydia dragged herself away from Jordan's tits and thought for a moment. 'Oh no, I was always going to do a degree. You sort of have to, don't you?'

'Well, my parents certainly think so.'

She put a mug of disgusting-looking coffee down next to Lydia and watched the milk powder spiral lazily on the top. Then, pulling out her hard desk chair, she sat down and rested her socked feet on the bed. Lydia was now pulling her gum out of her mouth, wrapping it around her finger and putting it back in again. The light from the bedside lamp threw half her face into darkness and her curls left a shadow on her cheek. It was her quirky clothes that had made Claire earmark her as a potential friend – someone after her own heart who didn't have a problem with striped tights and shorts – but though it soon became clear that Lydia's irrepressible enthusiasm was grating in the extreme, she could be good company, and there wasn't really anyone else that seemed worth knowing. She felt a surge of homesickness, realising how much she missed her old friends from home, Jess in particular; missed the ease with which she and Jess just got on without having to try too hard.

This evening Lydia was wearing a ripped lime-green T-shirt that hung off her shoulder, and a ropey grey cardigan. The colour contrast was striking and, for want of anything else to do, Claire pulled out her pad from under a pile of books, her pastels from her drawer and, pulling up her knees to act as a rest for the pad, began slowly to sketch out the girl sitting on her bed. Space out the proportions, her art teacher had always said, in those delicious all-too-short lessons she'd absorbed herself in until she'd been advised it was sensible to drop in place of more 'valuable

A level choices'. Gently, her hand resting lightly on the pad, she sketched Lydia, the rough lines on the page slowly and magically taking shape. The shoulder wasn't right so, with a sweep of lines, she adjusted it.

'Don't move!' she snapped, as Lydia adjusted her body to get more comfortable.

Lydia looked up, surprised. 'What are you doing?'

'Just having a bit of fun. Can you hold it just a second longer?'

Lydia shrugged and went back to the magazine. 'Have you seen this?' she said after long minutes. 'That daft cow off *Big Brother* has been shooting her mouth off again.'

'Never watch it,' Claire mumbled, deep in concentration on Lydia's ear. 'Too much of a freak show.'

'Ooh Claire, you're going to have to up your crap TV viewing, you know. It's all part of course requirements.'

'Mmm. I'm gathering that. There.' She held the pad away from herself. Not bad. Not great – the angle of Lydia's leg needed some work, but for a quick sketch she'd done worse.

'Can I see?' Lydia slipped off the bed, stretching out her stiffness.

'If you must. It's nothing really. Silly.'

Lydia came and looked over her shoulder. 'Oh Claire, that's really good.' Claire blushed. Lydia would say that. She'd have said it if Claire had drawn her as a stick man.

'No, it's really good,' she breathed. 'Can I keep it?'

Claire flushed with surprise and pride. 'Well yes, if you really want it.' Carefully she tore out the page.

Lydia held it up and tilted her head to one side. 'I'm going to get it framed and give it to my mum for her birthday. You can get those clip frames from the shop, can't you? Oh, but you'd better sign it.'

Claire snorted. 'Don't be ridiculous.'

'Nah.' She shoved Claire. 'You might be famous one day.'

Chapter 11

Sarah looked at the clock again. He was later than usual, and she began to feel mild concern. Ridiculous, and just symptomatic of the rut they had got in to that she could set her watch by what time he pulled into the drive.

Irritated with herself, she began to search the internet for trains to the South of France. The reality was, of course, that she barely earned enough to cover the fare, let alone the living costs when she was there, but she knew she had a very small buffer from her mother's will to tide her over. Naturally, she'd have to get a job – that was obvious – and who knew how long she'd be with Nathalie anyway? Sarah started to feel a bit uneasy at the thought but brushed it aside.

'We will find it very difficult without you,' the tart little woman at the Community Music Service had tutted when she'd called the office to say she was leaving. 'And such a shame you couldn't have given us a bit more notice, but your relative's ill health can't be helped, I suppose, though I can't be sure how long we could keep an opening for you.'

Sarah was relieved the woman couldn't see her blush at the fib, but the Music Service would have made her see out the term if she'd simply said she wanted to leave, and the sense of freedom she felt at waving goodbye to those tedious lessons was almost overwhelming. Using her pidgin French, she began to search Google for orchestras close to Nathalie's town, glancing at her watch in spite of herself every now and then.

As soon as Wilf opened the door, David could sense something was up. The old man had called him at work to ask him to lift down a heavy box from the loft and David had turned up, as he always did when summoned. Good old reliable, not-good-enough-to-be-a-husband David. When the usual smiley greeting was missing, David wondered if Sarah had told him. Nice of her to let David know – but it was beginning to look as is he was always last to know.

Manly handshake, nothing said. He followed his father-in-law upstairs and manoeuvred the box through the loft hatch into the spare room, now almost empty of its contents. Then they started on the usual ritual of Wilf offering David a glass of Scotch, him refusing at first, then a little joke about the yardarm, and then there would usually be some comment about Sarah and what she would say. This time, the silence stretched out between them as they sat in the darkened sitting room. It was lit by one standard lamp, and the pictures removed from the walls for packing had left a mark where they'd hung.

Wilf broke the silence. 'Anyway, very nice of you to come, David, and at such short notice.'

'No problem. I was coming over this way anyway.'

Wilf paused significantly. 'I know that you weren't, David, but I do appreciate it.'

Before Wilf could say any more, David drained his Scotch and stood up. 'I'll just take this through to the kitchen.' Looking round at the familiar chairs, framed photographs of much-loved dogs, ornaments ready to pack now coated with dust, David felt as though he was seeing the room for the first time. And maybe the last. Would it come down to taking sides? Would he simply stop seeing this tall, elderly man, who had been a part of his life for the past twenty-three years? No, it couldn't be. When David looked round, he saw, in his memory, the images of so many meals shared, birthdays, Christmasses, the first awkward meetings when he and Sarah were dating, bringing his parents over to meet hers, the twins as babies and the centre of everyone's attention, the twins as tiny laughing children and tall, gawky adolescents. He couldn't bear it. And yet that must be what it was like for Wilf, here alone with his memories.

David turned as he heard Wilf in the kitchen doorway behind him.

'David, is something wrong?'

David shrugged and shook his head. 'No, no. Nothing at all.'

Wilf frowned. 'Please, David, don't hide things from me. I could tell something was up when Sarah popped over the other day. And you sounded so low when you answered the phone earlier. Is one of you ill? Is it the twins?'

David felt his shoulders sag. He couldn't leave Wilf fretting. 'Well, yes, actually. There is something, but I don't know if I should ... oh, to hell with it. You'll have to find out sooner or later. Sarah's leaving me.' He couldn't bring himself to look at his father-in-law, and examined his nails carefully, not even looking up when he heard the sharp intake of breath. 'She announced it the other night. We still haven't sorted it out properly. I don't even know what's behind it really, except she says she wants to "find herself" or some such crap.'

'I'm so sorry,' Wilf whispered.

'I probably shouldn't even be talking about it, and not to you certainly, but ... well, I mean, it's nothing like you were thinking. Nothing life threatening or anything.' He paused, then couldn't stop himself. 'She says I don't understand her – and she's right. I don't. I don't understand any of it.' He looked up and shrugged. 'That's it really.'

Wilf's face was wrinkled in concern. 'Oh David, I *am* sorry. You must be feeling as though you've had your guts ripped out.'

'Actually, that's just what it does feel like.' David sighed, amazed at how relieved he felt to have told someone – even though Wilf was the last person he'd have considered as a confidante. 'The thing is, this came totally out of the blue, you know …' David trailed off. Was that disloyal?

Wilf rinsed the two glasses quickly under the tap and turned them upside down to drain. Oh God, was this what David would become? Rattling round the house, paring domestic tasks down to a minimum, eating ready meals for one, while Sarah …? David felt a surge of anger.

'I just don't know what I've done. She won't explain. And why can't she "find herself" at home? Why does she have to leave everything behind? Why does she have to …?'

Wilf stood for a moment without moving, then as if making a decision, shook the water from the glasses and picked up the bottle again, then indicated for David to pull out the kitchen chairs. Another drink? This was unprecedented and David started to protest, then gave in, willingly.

Mostly Wilf talked and David listened. As the pungent, peaty liquid in the bottle started to dwindle, Wilf probably said more than he had in the entire time David had known him. He talked about Sarah, about how she'd been as a child, about how she'd fallen off a gate and cut her knee and wouldn't be comforted, about their excitement at her growing skill with the violin, about how she'd put posters on her ceiling as a teenager, about how she used to come over to see them with the twins when they were tiny. He described a Sarah that David sometimes didn't recognise. Not his Sarah, a different one. One that he'd never known.

'The thing is, David' – Wilf leaned towards him, frowning slightly – 'you can't force her to stay, can you? Not really. And what if you did? Just say you gave her an ultimatum, or something. What would that do to the way she feels about you? What would it mean for your relationship?'

It all seemed to make a sort of sense. At least, after a few glasses of Scotch it did. Maybe that was the solution, David thought to himself, lose himself in drink, and he reached for the bottle again, topping up both glasses. 'But why do I have to agree to something I hate? What am I supposed to do here?'

Wilf lifted his glass, studying the colour against the lightbulbs in the ceiling fitting. One of them had gone, leaving it looking lop-sided. 'I've known my daughter all her life. She's very like her mother in many way. If Sarah is doing this, it's because she feels so strongly about it that she really can't prevent herself. She's not going to drop it and just go back to how it was before. You have to let her go, David. And you have to make her feel safe to do it. Otherwise you will lose her for ever.'

He drained his glass, set it down resolutely, and studied the backs of his hands. 'You have no choice, David. No choice in the matter at all. If she loves you, she'll come back. But you can't make her love you. And you can't make her stay if she wants to go. Now, pour me another. I think you'd better stay here tonight, don't you? Better call Sarah first though, eh?'

Chapter 12

The phone breaking the silence made Sarah leap and her heart pound. She hadn't realised how quiet it was in the house.

'It's me.' David was trying to sound brisk but was clearly slurring. 'Look, I'm at your dad's – he asked me to help with that book box in the loft – and we've hit the Laphroaig a bit hard. I'm going to bed down here.'

Sarah was confused. David drinking with her dad? For a moment she felt a stab of jealousy that he'd be the last one of the two of them to stay in her childhood home before it was sold. That should have been her privilege.

'Why?' was all she could think of to say.

'We've been talking.' She knew then he'd told Wilf about the separation and her anger rose.

'You've told him, haven't you?'

'Yup.' David's voice sounded bold and defiant. 'And why shouldn't I?

'Because he's my dad.'

'And he's been my father-in-law for twenty years. Nearly. I'll see you in the morning.' And he put down the phone.

Sarah drummed her fingers on the desk, then, still angry, stood up abruptly and headed towards the stairs. Damn him. If he was going to be like that, she'd have a long bath, with a violin concerto on very loud, both of which he hated, and go to bed sleeping across-ways to take up as much room as she could! When was the last time she had been able to do that?

Emptying too much jasmine oil under the running water, Sarah lit some candles – a romantic touch she'd read about somewhere but one that hadn't impressed David at all; he couldn't see the point and had asked if there was a power cut. She put the phone handset on the edge of the bath in case anyone tried to spoil her moment of heaven. Then she tied up her hair, avoiding looking in the mirror at the appalling colour, slipped off her dressing gown and slid into the water. As she lay down, she had a good view down her body. If she bent her knees up her thighs didn't look so fat, their size distorted by the water. When they'd first met, David had always admired her legs, which were quite slim around the ankles, but she'd learned long ago not to wear shorts. She didn't quite trust how her thighs looked from behind now. From here she couldn't see the seersucker stretch marks – a legacy of the twins – under the swell of her belly, and if she lay flat, her stomach did too, so she fantasised that it was always this shape.

Pah! She squeezed the sponge so tightly that water spurted out over her skin and the side of the bath. The days of a neat little waist and flat tummy like Claire's were long gone, and besides, who the hell took any notice these days? She slid further down, the water now level with her lips, and absorbed herself in the music.

The phone bellowed halfway through the slow movement. Sarah had been dozing off and, as she reached for the receiver, the bath water felt cooler on her skin. She shivered.

'Sarah, sorry to bother you so late.' It was the unmistakable voice of her mother-in-law, who always made an apology for calling, but always ploughed on regardless. 'Has David finished with the patio pressure hose? Only we need it. I want Anthony to clean off the garden furniture before the spring.'

Sarah sat up in the bath. The little tea light candles has burned low now and were a pool of wax. 'I'd ask him, only he's not here.'

There was a pause. 'Oh.' Heather sounded amazed at anything so irregular, disgruntled that she didn't know exactly where her son was at any given time. 'It's not his football night. Where is he?'

'Out.'

'Oh.'

Sarah could feel the goosebumps on her arms and stood up precariously, the bottom of the bath slippery with the oil. With one hand she reached for the towel and tucked the phone under her chin. A vision of David, chatting cosily with her father over Scotch, came into her head. Well, if he could, so could she.

'Actually, Heather, I've something to tell you. David and I have decided to separate.'

The pause was even longer. 'Whatever for?' she spluttered eventually.

Sarah tottered over to pull the light switch, water dripping from her body onto the cold tiled floor, and the room was suddenly flooded with hard, bright light. 'Because we need a break from each other, Heather.'

'Good grief! A *break*? Marriage isn't like ITV, you know, dear, with the occasional bit of time off. Your generation have no staying power. The slightest problem and you cut and run.' Sarah held the phone slightly away from her ear; the pitch of her mother-in-law's voice was hurting her ear drum. 'Marriage isn't disposable like ... like some kind of razor. Whose idea was this?'

Sarah paused. Could she face the inevitable diatribe if she told the truth, from a woman who never held back what she thought of anyone, least of all Sarah? 'It was me actually.'

The silence down the phone went on for so long that Sarah wondered if they had been cut off. 'Well, I knew it wouldn't be David.' Sarah smiled to herself. Golden boy who could do no wrong. 'Like mother, like daughter, I suppose.' Heather sighed.

'Sorry?'

'I said you're just like your mother.' There was a cynical edge to her voice.

Sarah was confused. Heather had never been particularly

warm towards her mother – in fact, for many years, family get-togethers had been minimal – too complicated it seemed to get everyone together - so the two women had barely crossed paths. But Heather sounded harsh now.

'I don't know what you mean.'

'I mean, dear, and I'm sorry to tell you this, but your mother's approach to her marriage was equally, shall we say, uncommitted.'

'Meaning what exactly, Heather?' Sarah sat on the side of the bath, pulling the towel further round her, her arms now really cold.

'She made your father look quite stupid, frankly, but then he was always a weak man. Flirting and batting her eyelids. And she didn't stop there. Oh no.' Sarah could feel a pain in her stomach. 'Of course, people talk and I wouldn't want to tell you some of the things they said.'

'Oh Heather, I'm quite sure you would.' Sarah felt breathless with anger and fear. 'But I don't want to hear them or any more of your lies.'

'You might not, dear, but I won't have my son made a fool of too—'

'Our marriage is between myself and David,' Sarah bit out. 'Now you seem suddenly very keen to spread gossip, but I'd be grateful if you could refrain from expressing your opinions until we have talked to the children – your *grandchildren*. Goodbye, Heather. I'll pass on your message to David.' And she turned off the phone, her heart pounding fast.

The first of the only two remarkable events over the next couple of days, which punctuated hours spent alternately pondering Heather's remarks and getting her head around the impending weekend with the twins, was her return visit eventually to the hairdresser.

Andre, sensing the seriousness of her tone when she'd called,

71

had promised to squeeze her in between a half head of highlights and a cut and blow dry, and he was just putting the finishing touches to a client when she walked in and pulled off her beanie. Not recognising her for a moment, he looked blankly at her, then his mouth fell open.

'Mother of God, what have you done?' His outburst brought the whole salon to a standstill and Sarah blushed furiously.

'Er ... it was an experiment.'

'No shit, Sherlock. And what exactly was the experiment? To find an alternative power source?'

Sarah moved closer and whispered urgently, 'Andre, I've been coming to see you for fifteen years. Now do me a favour. Don't make me feel more of an arse than I do already and just do something, will you?'

It all seemed to take ages, and by the time he had faffed about, the new colour was only a debatable improvement on the Russ Abbott orange. 'Well, it's the best I can do,' he said with a shrug, 'short of giving you a number two all over. But then you'd look like Sinead O'Connor.'

'That might be preferable to this Pamela Anderson blonde.'

Cramming the beanie back on her head, she bolted out of the door, her wallet and her hair several shades lighter.

The second event had even more unexpected results. The following Thursday night, after an evening conducted almost completely in silence, Sarah had a nightmare that woke her, the sobs wracking her body and the hot tears pouring down her face. She'd been visiting David who lived in a house she didn't recognise but somehow she'd walked in and was starting to make him a fish pie. He'd seemed happy enough to see her, though he had a small dog which she didn't recognise, then, just as she was about to put the pie on the table, a tall dark-haired woman, wearing a red cardigan, walked in and sat down in his place. Sarah shouted at her but she wouldn't move, just picked up her fork and started eating.

Sarah must have shouted out loud because as she sobbed she felt David's arms go round her and his voice murmuring comforting words. He'd done this before when she had bad dreams but this one had made her feel so desolate and so desperately sad, that she'd clung to him though even in her semi-sleeping state she knew it was the wrong thing to do.

'It's okay, darling,' he whispered in the darkness, wiping the tears from her cheeks and kissing her forehead and down her face, and before she could stop herself she was kissing him back, half asleep and in desperate need of comfort. His hands moved down to her waist, and over her hips. She froze.

'Oh God, let me, Sarah, just one last time,' he said into her hair. 'I can't bear not to touch you again.'

Sarah put her hands on his chest and pushed him away, livid with herself for allowing her body to respond to him. But it wasn't right. She'd be pulled right back in and he'd expect her to stay. 'No it's not right, I don't want to.'

She swung her legs out of the bed and pushed the hair off her hot wet face. It was pitch black, the room lit only by the digital clock, which read three twenty-five. She made her way to the bathroom to splash her face with water. When she came back in she could just about make out David's shape in the bed and she made her way over instinctively to her side, so familiar with the lay-out of room, and slipped under the duvet. She rested her arm behind her head.

'How did we come to this?' David asked quietly after a while. Sarah didn't answer, and he propped himself upright on his arm. 'How did we get from being parents and friends to being strangers?'

'I don't know,' she sighed. 'Perhaps it's a change in me. People do change, you know. We can't just stay the same for ever. Things change us, circumstances. The children don't need me like they used to and now I have to find another role for myself. Another identity, if you like. I'm all nurtured out. It's as if I've been sucked dry and I've forgotten who I am.'

David fell back on his pillows and sighed. 'I just don't see why it has to be forever.'

They lay in silence side by side for some time. She knew he wasn't sleeping because his breathing was too deep and he always twitched as he fell asleep.

'What if ...?' Her voice broke the silence in the darkness of the room. 'What if I went away for just a while. A sort of sabbatical. A sort of gap year.'

He didn't answer at first, considering the idea. 'And what would that mean?'

'It would mean that we'd do our own thing. No questions. No explanation. Then after, say, a few months, I'll come back and we'll see how things stand.'

'All on your terms, then?' His voice sounded bitter.

'You don't get it, do you? I need some space. I can't leave Dad for long – it wouldn't be fair on Rachel, for one thing – and I can't bear to be too far from the children, but I have to get out from this oppression. I love you and I don't want to get to the stage when I hate you. Let me go, David, or I will go permanently.'

Her words hung in the air, then David turned on his side, his back to her. 'Whatever.'

Chapter 13

Relieved was the last thing David had expected to feel when they pulled into the hotel car park. Sarah was there already, as they'd agreed, and had brought her dad with her. When she had made the reservation she'd asked for a table for five. She hadn't added that it should be large enough to drop a bombshell on.

As he got out and stretched, he was aware of the twins whispering behind his back and deliberately didn't turn round. They must have sussed that something was wrong from the moment he'd picked them and their laundry up from the campus. He was pleased to see them, of course, but he'd had to fight the urge to blurt out everything that was going on. He'd agreed with Sarah – among all the other things he'd agreed with Sarah – that they would wait until everyone was together before they explained. And so he'd fiddled with the radio, asked endless questions he already knew the answers to, talked about work – anything to avoid raising their suspicions. Yet that was clearly exactly what he'd done.

He rubbed his hands together with forced jollity. 'Well, let's get inside, shall we? I expect you're hungry.' He walked off briskly towards the reception, feeling them dawdling behind him.

Inside he led the way to the panelled dining room. How many times had they come here over the years? Mothers' Days, birthdays, anniversaries. And now 'sabbatical' announcement day. Did Hallmark do a card? David suppressed a sardonic laugh as the head waiter approached. 'We're meeting my wife and her father. Table for five. Lewis. I think they're waiting for us.'

The waiter smiled smoothly and led them through to a table

near the window where Sarah and Wilf were already seated, both drinking a glass of white wine. Sarah had left the chairs free on either side of her father, as they had always done before her mother had died, so that the children could sit and chat more easily with their grandparents. At the sight of Wilf on his own, David felt his throat tighten, whether through sympathy or self-pity, he couldn't be sure. Sarah had her back to him, and the back of her head, though the hair was now bleached blonde, looked sleek and sweet and, just for a moment, everything seemed just like before.

Then Wilf caught sight of them across the room and smiled, his face lighting up, as always, at the sight of his grandchildren. Sarah turned round and stood up, and the expression of tenderness on her face nearly took the legs from under him. Until he realised that she, too, was focused on the twins, who now brushed past him and rushed to the table. He hung back, listening to the greetings and exclamations about her hair being as tarty as she'd described, as though they were nothing to do with him. He closed his eyes. He felt like an eavesdropper. She could do the talking.

On the face of it, everything seemed so normal. Sarah ordered fish, as she always did, Tom a steak and chips, Claire mushroom risotto. Wilf had taken ages considering every single dish on offer. Everything was exactly as always. David frowned at the menu.

'Sea bass. I'll have the sea bass, please.'

'Whoa, Dad! Way to branch out,' laughed Tom. 'Ten to one he sends it back and asks for mixed grill instead.'

'That's great, Dad. Fish is far lower in fat,' Claire said, nodding approvingly. 'Can I try a little bit please? Swap you for some risotto.'

'Thanks, but no thanks, love. I just felt like a bit of a change.' He looked hard at Sarah. 'People do. Apparently.'

Sarah glared back at him. She'd made it very clear, in a terse conversation that morning, that she didn't want to spill the beans until they'd all settled in. It was a puerile enough gesture of resistance, and maybe he'd hate sea bass after all. But it made him feel obscurely better. The twins were exchanging glances. They must have caught on to the fact that something wasn't being said. Had Sarah noticed? It was hard to tell. She seemed unsettlingly normal but wasn't really meeting his eyes. There was plenty to talk about, though, with all the twins' news – lecturers, libraries, new friends, parties and clubbing. Tom dominated, regaling them with stories; Claire seemed more reticent. The banter, though, was not quite enough to keep the gnawing feeling of tension from David's stomach – or maybe that was down to the sea bass. Eventually, they ordered pudding – or at least the twins and Wilf did. David now felt slightly nauseous.

Claire chopped a profiterole in half with her fork. 'So? Dad? Is there anything going on with you?' she asked in a leading tone. 'Got any plans to, oh, I don't know, go away?'

David stared at her and could feel himself start to bluster. 'What? Me? Oh no – nothing, er, nothing planned.'

She was staring at him in a most peculiar way. 'Any plans for your anniversary?'

Oh God. He'd forgotten that he'd told them about the Rome thing. Shit! He shook his head minutely and saw her brows crinkle up as she tried to work out what he meant. Tom hadn't noticed and was rummaging under the table.

'Well, here's a little something you might find useful,' he said, emerging triumphant with a small gift-wrapped parcel, which he handed to Sarah with a flourish.

'Oh! For me? What's this in aid of?' She smiled uncertainly and opened it. 'Rome? Oh. That's lovely. I—'

'Go on, Dad. Tell her!' Tom was grinning at him.

'Oh, I er … There's been a change of plan, actually. I forgot to mention …'

Wilf's hands had come up to cover his face. Sarah was staring at him with a mix of emotions he couldn't untangle.

'Thing is, I booked a trip to Rome for our anniversary, and I must have mentioned it to the kids before ...'

'Before what, Dad?' Claire pulled at his arm, her voice getting louder. 'What aren't you telling us? What is it?' She was starting to sound tearful, and he put his arm out to comfort her. People at other tables were beginning to stare.

'Well, your mother ...'

'We've decided to ...'

Both he and Sarah started to speak at the same time, then he trailed off, leaving her to take over.

'Your father and I have decided to take a little break apart. Just a chance for me to go abroad and see an old friend. I didn't know anything about the trip to Rome, I'm afraid.' She stared at him accusingly. 'It was a lovely thought to get a guidebook, though. Thank you, both, so much.'

The questions started immediately, mostly from Claire. Where, when, why, how long for? Sarah answered almost everything calmly, as though it had been a reasoned, joint decision: her going away a gift to herself for twenty years of hard labour, rather than something she was wrenching from him and flinging in his face.

The only answer she faltered over was to the question 'How long?'

'Oh, I'm not sure yet. I'll see how things pan out. I'll be staying with Nathalie and if I can get any work out there, it might be ... oh well, I can't possibly say. But you do see, don't you ...?' Her eyes were almost pleading as she leaned across the table towards the twins. 'It's what I always wanted to do, and now seems the logical time. I just feel as if it's what I *have* to do.'

There was a brief silence, then Tom spoke for the first time. 'And what about Dad?'

All eyes turned to David. It was time for him to make up his mind. What he felt like doing was howling that it was unfair, that he couldn't bear for anything to change. That he had no idea what was going on.

'I think,' he started slowly, 'that it's a bit like a gap year for your mother. It's a chance for her to go and see new places and have an adventure.' He could see her visibly relax and he continued. 'It's the perfect time to do it, in a way, with you two off conquering the world. And I'm busy at work and I can't get away, so I'll still be around if you need anything. Anyway, I should think your mother'll be pleased to see the back of me.'

Their eyes met and, for the first time in what felt like forever, she smiled at him. A little tentatively, but a smile nonetheless.

Claire saw Lydia's spotted tights appear in her line of vision but could only lip read what she said.

'Uh?' She pulled the ear plugs for her MP3 player out of her ears.

'I said do you fancy a coffee, Mrs Sociable?' Lydia put her hands on her hips.

'Nah, I'm all coffeed out, thanks. I'm starting to get latte-overload.'

Lydia sat down on the stool facing Claire and looked around the Union coffee bar, pulling her ponytail between her hands and chewing her gum with her mouth open. 'Anyone here worth looking at?'

Claire hadn't noticed, though she had been sitting there for over an hour. Her ears had been full of The Mission, and her eyes had been on her textbook without seeing anything. Her thoughts had drifted to home.

'That bloke we saw at the film the other night is over there,' Lydia whispered loudly. 'And he hasn't got that blonde cow on his arm. Shall I schmooze over and charm the pants off him?'

Claire shrugged.

'What's with you? How was the weekend, by the way? Where did you say you lived?'

'Stratford-upon-Avon, and it was crap, thanks.'

'Oh?' Lydia looked round furtively again at the boy on the other side of the crowded room. Her thin legs were crossed, her foot hooked again around her calf and she looked as if she'd spin out of control if she unravelled too fast.

'My parents announced they are separating.' The words still amazed Claire and she could hardly bear to say them aloud.

'That's a bummer.' Lydia picked up a plastic coffee stirrer and fiddled with it, wrapping an empty sugar sachet around it. 'Mine did ages ago and my mum's on her umpteenth boyfriend and each one's worse than the last.'

'How did you feel when they told you?'

Lydia shrugged and looked round at the bloke again, who'd now been joined by some mates. 'I don't remember. I was only about thirteen. It was all pretty messy, though. You coming to Boring Bolton's lecture, then?' She glanced at the garish pink watch on her wrist and, unwrapping herself carefully, picked up her canvas bag of files. '"The Media – Moral or Amoral?" Unmissable.'

'Oh, I don't think so.' Claire sighed. She couldn't face it.

'Hey, girlfriend, you haven't been to anything so far this week. Well, for ages, come to think of it. You'll have the department on your back.' Lydia stood up and smoothed down her ridiculously short skirt for the benefit of the group behind her.

'Yeah well. The media *is* amoral. I don't need to sit for an hour being bored senseless to be told that.' Claire waved her off. 'Have fun!' She pushed down the strong sense of guilt, the knowledge of how cross Mum and Dad would be if they knew how often she was bunking off. She'd kept well out of Tom's way too when she'd spotted him, usually surrounded by mates and on his way to kick a ball about or off to the faculty.

Since the weekend she hadn't seen him at all. They'd travelled back on Sunday in virtual silence, Claire curled up in the back of the car, after an awkward and tearful farewell to her mother.

'I'll get you both a ticket to come and see me at Easter, shall I? It'll be lovely down there then. Really warm.' There had been a pleading look in her eye that Claire had never seen before and which made her feel uncomfortable.

Now she felt guilty for brushing her off with a 'Yeah, maybe. I'll see. We've got exams.' Sarah's hands had dropped.

'Okay,' she'd said quietly. 'Take care, won't you? I'll call with Nathalie's email address ...'

Claire hadn't trusted herself to speak as she'd hugged David goodbye outside the halls of residence.

'Will you be okay?' she'd muttered eventually into his jacket.

'Course I will!' He'd laughed, his eyes bright with tears. 'Come home again soon, though, won't you? I might be struggling with the workings of a can opener!'

Tom had hugged him awkwardly too and waited until the car tail lights disappeared round the corner by the Arts Centre.

'Hey, sis, it'll be okay.' Tom had picked up his holdall.

'Will it?' She'd felt the tears pouring down her face. 'Christ, I'm so angry with Mum I could kill her.'

'Yeah, well, see you later.' And he'd walked away, leaving her standing by the door looking out into the night.

Events seemed to go at an alarming pace over the next two weeks, and by the following Thursday night Sarah had lost count of the times she'd told friends they were separating and given the 'It's only a sabbatical' spiel. Imparting the news became easier and easier once she had told the important people – whose reaction varied between disapproval and incredulity – and besides, the word got round so quickly that most people were approaching her about it before she could say a word.

It reminded her of the days just after her mother's death. The most unexpected people – friends you had imagined would be supportive – were surprisingly reticent, and others, colleagues from work or even the lady behind the counter in the small newsagent who'd known them for years, rose to the occasion offering a cup of tea and an ear if Sarah wanted it.

She didn't. In fact, as the days went on she wanted to talk about it less and less, especially to the third-division acquaintances who phoned up on a pretext out of the blue, and pried for the gory details, hoping Sarah would burst out with lurid stories of rows or David's violence, and then they proceeded to tell her the gory details of their own marriages and how long it had been since they had had sex. Why on earth did they think she cared?

Sheila had arrived on the doorstep unannounced and armed with a packet of biscuits as if she were in for a siege, then launched into an aggressive defence of David.

'What on earth do you think you are doing?' She'd proclaimed in exasperation, as if Sarah must be mentally ill and had momentarily lost her marbles. 'And what about the children?'

She had not listened to any attempts by Sarah to explain how a happy mother was better than a stifled one, and continued mumbling to herself in between biscuits, pushing her coffee mug forwards towards Sarah for a refill.

Pauline next door had also taken the news with her normal incredulity. 'Well, I don't know what to think,' she'd clucked, as if her opinion had been sought, but at least Sarah's news stopped her in her tracks from a diatribe about the temporary traffic lights on the road into town. Trish, for once not the first in line for a life experience, was shocked to silence. 'I don't know what to say,' she muttered eventually, with refreshing honesty, then, 'I think you are very brave,' a statement with two possible meanings.

But it was Claire's words and the startled expression on Tom's face at that excruciating lunch that were in the forefront of her mind all day, every day. Claire had replied to her subsequent texts in a very cool manner, and Tom had called her but had discussed everything except the elephant in the corner.

The meeting with her father was more complicated. Sarah had

been torn between wanting to see him alone to discuss Heather's extraordinary revelations, and avoiding him for fear of his disappointment in her. She knew he wouldn't be angry – he never was – it was his 'disappointment' that had always managed to floor her. 'Wilf, you tell her!' her mother would shriek when Sarah hadn't come in until three in the morning or had refused to tidy her room or do homework. But he would just shake his head.

'If you feel you must go, then you must go,' he said quietly as he made her coffee in the kitchen, surrounding by packing cases.

'So you understand, then?' she answered, a little confused. This was not the reaction she had expected.

'No, darling, I don't understand.' He sighed and sat down opposite her, stirring sugar into the hot liquid. 'But I do know that you're like your mother and it was pointless ever trying to hold her back. You have always pulled hard at the leash – when you were determined to go to music college, even that time you wanted to learn to skate and fell and broke your ankle – but it's the only way to find what you want in life, to go out and look.'

'So you aren't cross?'

Her father smiled. 'No, Sarah, not cross. It's not my place to be cross. That's David's prerogative and you'll have to understand that he is. And as you know, I don't do anger very well. Your mother used to call it a weakness.'

'Yes. Mum …' Sarah looked down at her hands and fiddled with the seam of her jeans for a moment. 'Heather called the other night.' Her father shifted – was it uncomfortably? – in his chair. 'She said some … some things about Mum.'

'Did she now?'

'She suggested she'd … behaved badly.' Sarah looked hard at her father. 'Did she, Dad? Was she unfaithful?'

Her father picked up his spoon and rubbed it between his fingers. 'It depends what you call unfaithful. She never left me, no, but somehow I wasn't always enough for her. Your mother

83

had a massive love of life. I don't think a small place like this could contain her and yes, I suppose you could say she enjoyed the company of other men.'

Sarah frowned, terrified that the perception of her world and her parents was suddenly and extraordinarily being turned on its head. 'What do you mean?'

'Well, she had some very deep friendships with a few men over the years.'

'Oh come on, Dad, what are you saying?' The image of her mother in her head seemed to recede. 'Did she sleep with them?' Her father winced and visibly shrivelled.

'I didn't question her, Sarah. I didn't really want to know; it was her business and no one else's.'

Sarah felt anger rise. 'It bloody wasn't just her business. It was very much yours! She was your wife, for God's sake. Why did you put up with it, Dad?'

Wilf shrugged and smiled ruefully, as if amused by his daughter's indignation on his behalf. 'Because there was one part of her I had that no one else did. She was the mother of my children. We had you two and that was more precious than anything.'

Sarah shook her head, desperate to ask more but sensing strongly that her questions were not welcome. 'Dad, I found a bracelet in among her things. Gold with pearls. I'd never seen it before – did you give it to her?'

'Did you?' he didn't sound surprised. 'I might have done. You know how hopeless I am with presents. Is it one of my worse efforts? Christmas morning used to be a tyranny with you girls laughing at my pathetic efforts. Do you remember the grey knitted dress? I don't think I'll ever live that one down.' He patted Sarah's knee lovingly. 'Your mother must have hidden it, hoping I'd forget about it. You keep hold of it if you like, if it's not too ghastly. Keep it for Claire. She might like it one day.'

When she left, he gave her a huge bear hug. 'I always loved her, you know, and she was always mine really.'

'I know, Dad.' Sarah rubbed his back. 'You are the best.'

When she got home, there was another email from Nathalie, one of many over the last few days, with train times and plans she had for her, and what they would do when she arrived: how they'd sit in the sun and paint their nails and do girlie things together.

Just think, she finished, *no more loo seats left upright and footie talk.*

Chapter 14

At the leisure centre a light drizzle was falling, visible in the glare of the arc-lights. David left his wallet and holdall in the car, taking out his towel and water bottle, then jogged slowly over to the outdoor pitch. Phil was there already, talking to a couple of blokes David hadn't seen before. At his approach, Phil detached himself and walked over. David wondered, in passing, if they'd been talking about him.

'All right, mate?' Phil asked, looking at him a bit too carefully. Presumably for signs of neglect or rust or leprosy, which might be setting in with Sarah's imminent departure. David shook himself. He'd have to get a handle on the weird thoughts that kept bubbling up. He smiled, maybe a little too broadly, then stopped abruptly. Shit, he seemed to have lost control of his face.

'Yeah, fine. You know.'

'Yeah. Well, no I don't actually. But, well, y'know ...'

'Yeah.'

'I mean. If there's anything ... y'know.'

'Yeah. Well ... thanks, mate. Anyway ...'

'Yeah. Right. Okay.'

Phew. That had been a bit too intimate. David jogged over to the side and put his stuff next to the chain-link fence. On the court next to them a group of women were warming up for their regular game of netball and, although he couldn't see them through the dense green plastic fabric, he could hear them talking.

'... so I don't really know what to do next. I mean, I'm sure Gavin does want children. Well, he says he does. And he's been for all the tests – quite willingly too – you know how hard that is for some men.'

'Hmm, yes,' came the reply. 'A friend of mine went through all that last year. Mind you, it helped that she's a teacher so she could arrange the appointments for the school holidays. What do you do? Oh, my name's Kate, by the way ...'

How did women do that? Get from nought to talking about their husbands' bollocks within seconds of meeting each other. He shook his head in wonder and moved swiftly away from the fence, before they got into details.

The new blokes were kicking around already. Showing off, really, rather than warming up. They were from Gerry's work, he seemed to remember, and played in a league somewhere. David sighed. The others were trickling in now. Gerry, Harry, Paul, Mike and the rest. All the regulars. And they'd all heard about him and Sarah. That much was clear from the sympathetic nods, the smiles that were sort of just pressing the lips together, the lack of eye contact, and the lack of usual insults.

He knew he should say something to break the ice but, just at that moment, he absolutely couldn't. So he fussed with his shin pads, bending over to adjust the Velcro tabs until they all went to the centre to get started.

From the netball court he could hear laughing. It was the same every week. That and, 'Oh sorry!', 'Are you all right?', 'Yessss!', 'Nice shot!', 'Oh bugger! Oops – sorry'. And laughing. He'd seen them arriving and leaving some weeks, too. Women in their thirties and forties. He didn't know any of them, but he'd begun to recognise some of the more distinctive ones. There were a couple of tall ones who looked like sisters. One very short one with a loud voice. A couple who could lose a few pounds. They were relentlessly amateurish, almost proudly so – he wasn't sure they even kept score. A wave of something that felt like vertigo swept over him and he stood up, taking a deep breath.

'Come on! Let's get warmed up.'

The rest of the lads had started jogging round the perimeter of the pitch and he tagged on, settling into the rhythm that gathered them all in.

'Change!'

They turned and jogged the other way for a while, and he felt his heart rate start to pick up just a little. It felt good to be doing something so familiar after days when everything he thought he knew had been demolished. He picked up the pace, just a little, pushing past a few of the others, and felt the rush of blood through his thighs. This was what he needed.

'Right, let's get started or we'll never get to the pub. C'mon, you lazy bastards.'

This was more like it. They took up their positions with the customary argy bargy. The new blokes were together on the other side, and they were a man short on David's side. Ross was usually late, but his wife had just had a baby and it was hard for him to get out. He'd make up for it in speed when he got there.

The game followed its usual pattern, with plenty of near misses, flukes, rank incompetence. Their breath clouded in the air and their yells mixed with the more ladylike cries of the women.

'Jammy bastard!'

'Oops, sorry! My fault!'

'Out the way, shit head!'

'Ooh! Nice one, Lucy.'

'Ha ha ha! You're crap and you know you are.'

'Are you all right, Kate?'

The two new lads – Matt and Greg? – were slotting in well. A bit pushy, maybe, and they weren't passing much, but they looked like sound players. David concentrated on the game. The other side had the ball and were looking for an opening but David was marking Gerry as closely as he could, so Matt passed to Mike who got into position and wellied it at the goal. Harry got there in time and a groan went up from the other team.

'Awww, you stupid fucker! What's wrong with you?'

David turned to look at Matt, the new boy, whose voice carried, angry and accusatory, through the cold evening air. Mike shrugged and muttered something, turning away, panting, to continue the game.

'It was wide open. Jesus! One of them lot could have scored.' Matt gestured at the netball court next to them.

'All right, all right. Leave it out, Matt.' Phil puffed up to the two younger men and David, in his capacity as the other senior member, walked over in silent support, making sure to place himself between Matt and Mike, who was beginning to look angry.

'Get off! It was an easy shot and you know it. And he knows it too.' Matt raised his voice again and peered round Phil's bulky form at Mike.

David raised his hands in front of himself in a calming gesture. 'Look, mate, this is a friendly game, all right? No one here takes it too seriously and if that doesn't suit you, then maybe this isn't the team for you, eh? Now, we can play on and keep it friendly, or you can sit out for a bit, even the teams up. What do you say?'

Greg had joined Matt now, and put a hand on his arm. 'Come on, Matt. Leave it.'

Matt shook him off angrily, and stepped up to David. 'Are you trying to send me off? Are you? Who the fuck do you think you are? Send him off. Or fuck off yerself.'

It happened in a split second. When he thought about it later, David remembered literally seeing red. He'd never understood the phrase before then, but suddenly a rage swept over him and he launched himself at Matt and sent him crashing to the ground. He managed to land at least two punches on Matt's astonished face before Phil dragged him off. The others closed round in a horrified circle as Greg helped his friend up.

David was panting, the adrenalin rush over, and all he could feel was a deep throb in his back, the pain of his bruised knuckles and a feeling of total disbelief.

Matt's voice, shocked and indignant, floated over the heads between them. 'Stupid tosser! Prick! You're mental, you are!'

He could hear the rest of his friends coping, closing ranks as they sent the two newcomers off. 'Go on, Greg, take him for a drink. Calm him down a bit. He was out of order ... No harm done.'

The two younger men left, Matt still protesting and being shushed by Greg all the way to the car park.

Back on pitch, there was an awkward silence. David, humiliatingly, could feel tears start to sting his lower lids. He breathed out hard, rubbing his face with his hands. How the hell had that happened?

'What a tosser!' Mike laughed and everyone laughed their agreement.

'Yeah, you showed him, David. Little prick.'

'Mind you, we're all going to be giving you a wide berth now, mate. You've got a mean right hook there.'

So this was how it was going to go. David felt relief ripple through the rest of his mates as they started to fit this latest, shocking event into their group story. It would become 'that night David showed that idiot'. They would joke about it for years. David's temper would become a legend and his loss of control would perversely earn him some respect. And they'd all go home and tell their wives, who'd say it was because of Sarah leaving him. Or they'd say it was why Sarah was leaving maybe. Because women think like that. And they'd all discuss it and all nod knowingly.

And David couldn't bear it.

'Come on,' he called, looking round at the rest of them and scowling. 'Are we going to finish this game or what? Look, here comes Ross. Just in time, mate. Hurry up. Get yourself warmed up or I may need to punch your lights out.'

The rest of them missed a beat, then laughed and went back to their positions. Everything was back to normal.

Chapter 15

Sarah looked nervously around the Gare de Lyon and slipped her hand inside her bag once again to check she had her tickets and passport. She knew she did, of course, because she'd checked three times already but, she realised with disgust, she was only doing it because David always kept hold of any documents when they travelled and the responsibility was a new one.

He was the French speaker too and, though the staff at the information desk would have talked back to her in English even if she'd been fluent – a particularly irritating trait in the French – it galled her that her attempts had been so faltering. The man at the coffee booth, however, had taken the opposite tack and had feigned complete incomprehension when she knew her '*un grand crème s'il vous plait*' was perfectly acceptable. Perched on her suitcase now, she sipped at the hot milky liquid sulkily, her eyes returning constantly to the departures board in case she missed the announcement of the '*quai*' for her train heading south.

'Why in God's name are you going by train?' Claire had asked, lounging on Sarah's bed watching her pack two nights earlier. 'I mean, you could be in Perpignan in the time it'll take you to get to Waterloo.' She was right, of course. David hadn't failed to point out the stupidity either, and just shrugged and turned away, but they didn't understand.

'Because I never did the backpack-across-Europe thing, darling, and to fly is just a cop-out. I'll miss all the scenery if I'm stuck in a plane. I want to get a feel for it all. Immerse myself in it.'

'Oh God, Mum,' Claire had exclaimed and, rolling off the

bed, had stomped out of the room. She'd done a lot of stomping since arriving at home at an hour's notice the night before, explaining she wanted to say goodbye again. Both Sarah and David had asked about the lectures and tutorials she must be missing but Claire had just shrugged at that, and they didn't push it. Besides, the atmosphere in the house had been hideous and having someone else there had been a good thing. Missed lectures seemed unimportant.

Sitting here now, around her a mass of purposeful-looking French people walking across the concourse and a handful of students with neatly packed backpacks, Sarah realised how ridiculous she must look in her sensible fleece and jeans against the Paris wind, her Samsonite suitcase packed with equally sensible skirts and T-shirts that had been at the back of the wardrobe since last summer. The only thing that made her appear less than totally boring was her violin case, tucked protectively behind her feet.

Settled into her seat on the train, though, watching the unromantic suburbs of Paris slip away beside her, she began to feel something approaching the excitement she had promised herself. Yes, going by train had been a good idea. It was an important transition from the old life to something new with endless possibilities. She'd left her packed suitcase in the hall last night so its presence in their bedroom wouldn't make her departure so obvious, but David had left ridiculously early for work anyway without so much as a cup of coffee, so it had hardly mattered. They had agreed he would not stick around until she left and she'd briefly kissed him on the cheek before he turned away and slammed the front door, leaving only a blast of icy air behind him in the hall. Sarah had left the house immaculately tidy, took out of the freezer a cottage pie, one of a batch of single-portion meals she'd made for David a few days earlier in some pathetic gesture of apology, and had been in a taxi to the station by seven thirty.

Who knew now what was going to happen? All that absorbed her at the moment was the overwhelming sense that a massive burden had been lifted from her shoulders and, for once, for longer than she could remember, she could open her eyes and see the whole picture.

She dozed off a few times and woke as the landscape began to change. Curious how French towns all blended in to each other, with their roof tiles and shuttered windows, she mused. You so rarely saw into the heart of people's lives from a train, except for those wonderful gardens you can see on the way into London, but she knew from driving tours she had taken with David that French towns were often disappointingly the same.

With David.

With David holidays had always been companionable enough – subjugating their own desires to the children's for years and tolerating bucket-and-spade affairs on the south coast, though Sarah had lusted after adventure as she collected shells and kept sand out of ice creams. But, as the twins grew older and turned up their noses at coming with their parents, preferring cheap apartments in Mallorca with friends, and days that started at noon and ended as they fell out of a club at four in the morning, Sarah and David had found themselves camping with Trish and Phil or 'touring' from the safety of their car with its roof rack and GB sticker. When she'd showed an interest in discovering an Eastern Bloc country, even wildly suggesting Vietnam, David had made some lame excuse and turned to the see-the-world-in-comfort type features of the Sunday supplements, with a 'that looks nice' at hotels in Tuscany or Provence. Years of scrimping had made him tight and he still couldn't break free. Inevitably, Sarah had done the organising – he'd just assumed she would – and then at the last minute he would begin to question why she'd picked that ferry crossing or that *pension* to stop the night in.

Sarah leaned her head now against the train window and smiled. All right, she wasn't on her way to Vietnam, but it was a start and she could do what she pleased, without explanation or fear of criticism. In an act of defiance, she picked up her handbag and headed for the buffet car to get herself a drink and a train sandwich – always deemed by David to be 'too expensive and too disgusting to waste your money on'.

Her phoned beeped twice as they pulled into Toulouse station. *I've put the wine in the fridge and I'm on my way. Itching to see you x*, wrote Nathalie.

Time for a coffee before you launch off or have I got my dates wrong? asked Trish.

Me too. On time and *Too late. I'm on my way. I'll send a postcard,* Sarah replied respectively. She snapped her phone shut, comforted in some way by the fact that she knew exactly what Trish would be doing today – the gym then her Pilates class then coffee at Costa – and wanted no part of it. Instead, the sun was shining, she was about to pull into Perpignan and head for Nathalie's and drink wine until the small hours. After that, who knew? She felt a ripple of excitement in her stomach.

Chapter 16

David parked the car in the drive and turned off the ignition, but he didn't open the door. They'd agreed it would be better this way. Well, Sarah had decided it and David had agreed, as with so many things in the last few weeks. She would just go – no messy goodbyes – while he was out at work. Nice and clean and painless.

The last twelve hours had been unreal. Very much business as usual. So much so, in fact, that it was hard to believe she was going, except for the suitcase in the hall. They'd stepped round it the night before, ignored it, while she'd made him tea, so solicitous, and asked him about his work. And he'd gone along with it – well, what choice did he have? As he'd left for the office this morning, as early as he could, she hadn't met his eye, but had kissed his cheek as he'd pulled her into an awkward hug and muttered, 'Take care. Call me when you get there ... if you feel like it.' He'd left without turning back, but the feeling of her in his arms was still there like a bruise.

He'd thought about it all day, her journey and where he might be as the day wore on. She hadn't told him much about it, despite his questions both direct and subtle. She'd guarded the details as though they were a secret, precious to her. And maybe they were, in a way. Trying to follow Wilf's advice, he'd forced himself not to keep asking, but after twenty years, for God's sake, was he supposed to just switch it off. Like she had?

He'd stayed at work for as long as he decently could although, as usual for the past couple of weeks, he'd simply stared at the screen and pretended to be looking through files when anyone hovered nearby. He'd turned his CD player up far too loudly in the car on the way home, blasting any thoughts from his head, and unable to listen to the evening news. Life had no right to carry on as normal.

He ran his hands through his hair and loosened his tie, then got out of the car, locked it with the remote and went in. The silence when he opened the front door hit him with a physical pain.

Of course, he'd often let himself into the empty house before, when she was out at concerts or with her friends or over at her parents' place. But this was a different feeling altogether. And the house knew it too. He could hear the quiet hum of the central heating, yet the air felt cold. He shivered and put down his briefcase next to the hall table. As he always did.

'Right! Better get on.' His voice sounded too loud in the still house and he rubbed his hands together. He'd been meaning to fix the catch on the window in their bedroom for ages and he'd made a whole list of other jobs he'd been putting off too. Earlier in the week he'd stopped at B&Q to get the right screws. They had to be brass to match. He went out to the garage to get his screwdriver. His old Alvis, still with the engine in pieces on his work bench, was standing there, abandoned. He hadn't worked on it for years and it had become a bit of a sour joke between them, but he patted it protectively, then turned to look at the dust-sheeted form parked neatly just inside the door. Sarah must have covered her car up before she left, and the sight of it, shroud-like, sent a wave of panic sweeping through him.

His tools were all as he'd left them, each in its place on the pegboard he and Wilf had attached to the wall years ago, when he and Sarah had first moved in. Everything in its place. He took the screwdriver down and sighed. The plans he'd had! To buy old cars and fix them up again, just as a sideline. And here was the Alvis, its head lamps staring at him to make him feel guilty, untouched for so long. Well, with the kids and everything, there had never been time. He shook his head and looked around. He'd have a bit of clear-out in here at the weekend, maybe. Add it to the list.

Going into the kitchen, squeaky clean and lifeless, he saw the meal for one defrosted in its foil container, the words Cottage Pie written in her neat hand on the lid. Putting his foot down on the pedal, he opened the bin and dropped it in.

Up in the bedroom, everything was as neat and clean. Even the chair beside her bed, which usually had a blouse or a bra or something hanging on the back, was empty. Suddenly fearful, David opened her wardrobe doors. Then let out the breath he must have been holding. It was depleted, certainly. But not empty, the dresses and skirts a vestige of hope that maybe she would come back.

Before he could stop himself he pulled out a cardigan, the blue one she often wore for work, and buried his face in it, inhaling the smell of her, then he sat down heavily on the bed, and sobbed into it.

Claire heard her phone bleep a message. She had a good idea who it was from, but she finished brushing her teeth and getting ready for bed before she looked at it.

Got here safely, it read, *& enjoying the local plonk with N. Hope u r well darlio, Speak tomorrow.*

Claire slowly deleted the message and dropped the phone into her lap. Her mother had clearly sampled a skinful of the local plonk, though her texting had always been pretty crap. The tone of her conversation with her dad earlier in the evening hadn't been quite so upbeat. Claire could hear the tension in his voice, though he'd done his best to sound positive. She'd even asked him what he'd had for supper and he said he'd made an omelette.

'Mum hates those,' she'd said before she could stop herself.

'Yes, well,' he'd replied. 'That doesn't matter now, does it?'

Claire was about to blurt how selfish Sarah had been not to leave anything for him, but stopped herself. She'd probably been too busy packing her sun cream to think about Dad getting home from work to an empty house. Claire lobbed her phone into her canvas bag of files on the floor and slid down the pillows.

So it had finally happened. She hadn't really believed it would, even after Mum and Dad had explained that she was going away over that nightmare lunch. Claire had really thought until yesterday that Sarah would change her mind. But the text was emphatic proof. Claire took in her pokey little room: the narrow single bed, thin curtains, a tiny desk hidden beneath piles of books, an empty bottle of water and clothes that hadn't made it to the cheap built-in drawers.

What a shit pit. Even the posters she'd put up couldn't disguise the fact that it was little better than a rabbit hutch. A rabbit hutch in a warren of rabbit hutches, in a crap university in a crap town.

Claire turned to face the wall and, pulling the duvet over herself, sobbed herself to sleep.

How many times had he and Sarah driven along this road? It must be hundreds. Almost twenty years of visits to his parents, first in their weekend cottage in a Cotswold village, then in the town house they'd bought in Chipping Campden when his dad had finally retired from the City. David swung off the roundabout and onto the Fosse Way, that long Roman road that carved, brutally direct, through valleys and over hills from Cirencester in the south all the way to Leicester. You could still follow its arrogant line on the map, although modern roads tended to more doubt and prevarication, veering off for a by-pass then returning, shame-faced, to join it once again. How certain those Romans must have been. They'd known exactly where they were going and what they'd wanted to achieve. No wonder they'd walked all over the poor old Anglo-Saxons, with their twisting paths and by-ways, dictated by the lie of the land. David sighed. The road forged ahead of him, boldly visible until the crest of the next hill. He took the next right, onto a more comfortable meander. A bit like him and Sarah, really. Her, forging ahead so fast and certain, and already out of sight; him, still ambling along. But where was he going now?

He pulled his attention back as the road veered sharply left, the waterlogged fields on either side only partially visible through the bare, severely laid hawthorn hedges. Ahead, he could see the hills that embraced Chipping Campden on the far side, the town tucked neatly into the valley. He was anticipating a bit of an awkward time with his parents. It would be the first time he'd been to see them since Sarah had left – he'd managed to fend off several invitations – and he knew Heather wouldn't be able to resist raking over the facts. It was a bit of a hobby of hers, although his father would resolutely refuse to join in, fixing his gaze on the middle distance instead, and affecting not to hear. Without the twins there to act as a distraction, it was going to be a bit intense.

The sight of the Jacobean Banqueting Hall, so incongruous in the fields behind St James' Church, never failed to arrest him. Part of the remains of what must have been a sumptuous manor house ravaged by fire, it stood alone, its Cotswold stone glowing in the feeble sunlight. He took the one-way dog-leg onto the High Street with practised ease then started the search for a parking space. Saturdays were always busy in Campden, even at this time of year, with visitors ambling along, heads swivelling as honey-coloured buildings, each more elegant than the last, jostled for attention. Sarah had always said that so much beauty in one place wasn't fair. It really should have been diluted and spread through the country, just to even things up a bit.

He fronted into a space outside an antique shop – one of many – then took a quick mental scan of how he felt. He kept doing that lately. Deliberately thinking of Sarah, then testing himself for a reaction, a bit like prodding a painful tooth. Nothing. He felt nothing. Maybe that was a bad thing. He just didn't know any more.

Slowly, he got out of the car and shivered in the bitterly cold air. Then crossed the road and climbed the short flight of steps to the pavement on the other side to his parents' front door, standing back to let a group of sightseers pass before he knocked with the dazzlingly polished brass knocker.

His mother, equally well polished as always, answered almost immediately and folded him into a taut embrace then stepped back and held him at arms' length.

'Darling! Let me have a look at you. Oh, that wretched girl. You're looking pale. Come on. Your father will pour you a drink. Lunch is nearly ready.'

His father had been doing *The Times* crossword, as usual on a Saturday, and it lay folded on the armchair he had just vacated. With his spectacles on a new cord round his neck, he looked more an academic than the retired City man he was.

They shook hands and David indicated the specs with a smile. 'That's new, Dad. Get fed up of losing them, did you?'

The tall man shrugged ruefully. 'Your mother got them at the optician. Said she'd had enough of me borrowing hers in restaurants. I think it makes me look old but she insisted.'

'You *are* old, you silly fool!' his mother exclaimed from the kitchen door, popping her head out, a steaming saucepan in one hand. 'Anyway, you looked ridiculous wearing mine. You were the only person who couldn't see yourself.'

David and his father exchanged amused and resigned glances and sat down together. Heather's comments were often acerbic and usually amusing, but she always had the last word. The age difference between his parents, only ten years, had been an endless source of material for her, and from about the time Anthony had retired and they'd moved to this house, she never missed an opportunity to remind him of it. In fact, to David's eyes they looked very much of an age, although his father had, over the last few years, started to look rather more stooped, but that might have been a result of the low ceilings in the house.

He looked around the comfortable, familiar sitting room, with its beams and book-lined shelves, the large lamps on the polished side-tables and floral-covered sofas, and began to relax. His father was looking at him intently. 'How are things, son?'

'Oh fine. You know. Kids seem to be doing all right. They barely need us ... me now. I only expect to hear when they need money.'

It was a feeble enough joke and Anthony didn't laugh. 'No. I mean, how are things really?'

David glanced towards the kitchen, then met his father's eyes. 'I don't know, Dad. I don't know anything. I don't know where any of this came from. One minute everything was fine. The next, she tells me she's been frustrated ... thwarted ... I don't even know what. But she says she's been feeling that way for years. I mean, I didn't even know. She never said. Am I supposed to be a mind reader? But, of course, it's all my fault. And off she goes.'

His father took a sip of his whisky without taking his eyes from David's. 'Is there someone else?'

'No. Well, she didn't say so. I mean, how could there be? She's gone to France to stay with that awful Nathalie – do you remember her? She's been to stay a couple of times. Complete ballbreaker. So ... No, I really don't think there is. In a way, it would be easier to understand if there was.'

'Has she been in touch? Is she all right? She's very ... she's naïve in many ways, I've always thought. Do you know she's safe?'

David shrugged uncomfortably. 'She sent a text, as agreed, to say she'd got there, but that's all I've had. We agreed ... well, I said, really, that I didn't think we should contact each other. I mean, it was her decision to just leave. She refused to discuss things properly before she went. I don't see any point ...'

'She's still your wife, though, isn't she?' His father was holding his glass up and examining it in the light as he slowly rotated it.

'Dad, I don't particularly want to discuss this now.' His eyes flicked once again towards the kitchen. 'I think the best thing I can do is let her get this out of her system – whatever it is – and just keep on with my life. She hasn't given me much choice, has she?'

'As you wish. It's just that' – he lowered his voice – 'well, I've always had a soft spot for Sarah. I just hope she's safe.' His father stood up, pressing hard on the arms of the chair to lever himself upright. 'Come on, let's go and eat.'

At the table in the tiny dining room, rather formally laid out, the joint was as tender as ever, but his mother brushed aside any compliments. 'The butcher's really very good, that's all. You can't go wrong with decent meat. Now, have some more carrots. And pass the gravy, would you, darling? David needs feeding up. I don't see how a man holding down a full-time job can be expected to look after himself. It's ridiculous.'

David accepted the food gratefully and braced himself for the onslaught. Heather had been dropping in little digs here and there already and seemed to be gearing herself up for a tirade.

She scraped the rest of the cabbage onto his plate without asking, and went on, 'I mean, what kind of woman would leave her husband just when he needed her most? With the children gone, you're all alone. But some women are entirely selfish, only thinking about their own needs. That's not marriage, in my opinion.'

'Quite. I didn't think it was either.' David played with the cabbage, and experienced a surge of self-pity. He felt comforted by his mother's validation.

When they finished, Heather stacked the plates more noisily than was strictly necessary. 'She'll be back, you mark my words. Tail between her legs. That'll change things.'

David noticed her glancing over at his father, as though

checking his reaction, but Anthony was examining his nails with close attention. 'Let me help you with the plates, Mum. I'll put them in the dishwasher.'

'Certainly not! Your father can do that later. He's spent all morning tweaking a couple of tubs in the garden then far too long on the crossword, after all.'

'Well, with sod-all garden, what else am I supposed to do?' Anthony muttered.

Heather rolled her eyes. 'You sit down, my love. I've done bread and butter pudding for you. Your favourite!'

She bustled out to the kitchen and Anthony raised his eyes and smiled, a little wearily, David thought.

'The thing is, David,' he sighed, 'it's far too easy not to say what you really mean, even when you're talking to someone. Even when you're with them all the time. What hope is there if you're not talking at all?'

David looked at his father in astonishment. What did he mean by that? But his mother returned before he had a chance to ask.

Sarah watched as the waiter took the order from Nathalie, nonchalantly wiped the table and, tray aloft, sashayed back to the bar. Nathalie leaned forward conspiratorially. 'That,' she emphasised, jerking her head towards the waiter, 'is Pascal. Very cute arse.' She said the last word with the flat vowel of a totally fluent English speaker. 'But no brain.'

'Not him too!' Sarah was shocked but amused. Pascal was the third man that Nathalie had pointed out since she'd arrived in Sauzils and the other two she'd announced she'd had an affair with.

'Nah!' Nathalie sat back on her chair. 'Delicious body is one thing, but you have to have something to talk about afterwards!'

Sarah nodded as if she understood, then closed her eyes and put her face up to the warm sun, which was pushing its way through the gaps in the leaves overhead. In the summer, no doubt, the towering plane trees, with their mottled bark so perfect it looked as though it had been painted on, would provide valuable shade, but on this early spring morning Sarah wanted to absorb it all, just like she did everything around her. The first night she'd arrived, Nathalie had plied her with wine, and had then talked and talked, mainly about her erstwhile lover and her new life in Sauzils, until Sarah had begged for mercy and crawled off to her room in the little flat. She was so tired she barely acknowledged her surroundings and it wasn't until she opened the shutters the following morning and revealed the sunlit square below with its little fountain, that she realised how enchanting the place was.

Nathalie's incessant chat had continued all the next day as she'd taken Sarah on a whistle-stop tour of the town and its environs in her battered Renault – so clichéd, so French, so reassuring. Nathalie had pointed out her favourite club or restaurant, shoe shop or bar, every now and then (and usually after Sarah had prompted) a museum or church.

'Oh Picasso found his muse here,' she said, waving her hand loftily. 'The tourists flood in in the summer like lemmings but you'll be a native here by then and totally blasé. Now, let's have *un demie.*'

But already Sarah was captivated by this compact little town tucked beneath the foothills, the massive peaks of the Pyrenees dominating the horizon. And while Nathalie stopped to talk to a friend, a wizened little woman with a hunched back and a small dog, Sarah had carried on walking, taking in the balconies and the roof terraces just visible if she craned her neck; and churches, tucked away in the corner of squares which appeared suddenly as she turned the corner of a narrow little street. Dodging dog shit and the shallow gutters that ran on either side of the cobbled streets – a curious controlled system, Nathalie had explained, which transported water down from the mountains in rivulets – Sarah peered in at shop windows and through any shutters open in the sunshine to the dark kitchens within. It was still too early in the season for all the restaurants to be open – what did the owners do in the colder months? – but the winter was being sloughed off and the squares were beginning to fill with tables outside the cafés.

Pascal came back now with their coffees, slipping the bill on to its ridiculous little plate, with almost balletic panache, all the while looking around him.

'This is my best friend from England, Pascal. *Elle s'appelle* Sarah.'

'*Enchanté*,' he replied, looking at Sarah for the first time, but without really looking at all.

'She's escaped a dreadful marriage,' Nathalie continued expansively and giggled. Pascal smiled weakly and moved off to serve a couple who had sat down at a table further away.

'Oh Nathalie, don't say that.' Sarah frowned in annoyance. 'It makes me sound like some kind of victim, which I'm not. It wasn't like that.'

'Darling, you are!' Nathalie shrieked. 'You are typical of women who realise after years of wiping bottoms and pandering to their husbands' stupid little egos and desires that there is another life. You're finally seeing all men are bastards!'

Sarah snorted with amusement at the characteristic melodrama, and stirred her coffee, a part of her reassured. It was some sort of comfort that, even though she and Nathalie had wholly different experiences of life – Nathalie with all the glorious selfishness of the single, childless woman – it was being affirmed by someone else that her life until now had been put on hold, and this was her chance at last to unfurl her wings.

'Come on, then.' Nathalie rested her chin in her elegant, ringed hand. 'Cough it out. When did you suddenly see the light?'

Sarah stirred her coffee. 'It wasn't really like that. It was a sort of creeping realisation that I couldn't face another twenty years. It's about the little things … oh, I don't know. You might not get it really, but the everyday things. The way we've got stuck in a rut.'

'Oh I know, darling.' Nathalie threw her head back and laughed. 'In the end it's not the big things that make you want to bury their heads in a bucket.' She pronounced it boo-ket. 'With Stefan it was the way he drank his coffee that finally did it for me. A sort of deesgusting slurp, like this.' She picked up her cup to demonstrate.

Sarah laughed. 'Mine was the cling film. How he'd never use the serrated edge of the box to tear it off. He'd just tear it so it got all tangled!'

'Eek!' Nathalie put her hand to her mouth, her eyes gleeful. 'Stefan would wear his boxers hanging off his arse. Such a sight in the morning. Good God!'

'David—' Sarah realised it was the first time she'd actually mentioned him by name. 'David would do the washing-up and just leave the water in, with a scum on the top, until it went cold and it was me who had to put my hand in and pull out the plug.'

Nathalie leaned forward. 'Be grateful he did the bloody washing-up at all, darling.' She then turned to gaze at the backside of a young tourist who had just passed close to their table. Sarah realised how petty she sounded. This wasn't what she meant to be communicating at all.

'But it's about more than just those habits. It's the big things, really, that I've just lived with for too long. I want to find out who I am other than someone who's great at ironing and knows the layout of Tesco like the back of my hand.'

Nathalie plonked her elbows on the table decisively, her bracelets jingling and her long earrings wiggling at her ears. Sarah thought her the most complicated dresser she had ever known. When they had first met at music college, she had been a riot of colour and accessories. Even her shoes were never simple and plain – though Sarah's in those days had been Doc Martens.

Today, Nathalie's were leopard skin, her trousers wide and pink topped with a patterned cardigan, all covering up a voluptuous figure, except for her deep, deep cleavage pushed forward and tumbling over the tight brocade top.

'Well, for a start, girlfriend, we need to take you in hand. If you are beginning a new life, we need to create a new Sarah. Make the most of that fab figure, for example.' Sarah blushed despite the ridiculousness of Nathalie's gush. 'And that hair! Christ, woman, what have you done to it?'

'It's a long story.'

'It's a fucking tragedy, that's what it is. I'm thinking a gamine bob and tone down that colour. You look like that Jordan woman who's all over your papers. I know just the person to help out. Thierry – dreadful old queen but quite a genius. Left Paris cos he couldn't bear the gay scene there. Lives down here now with his boyfriend who's a loser. Sucks him dry.' Nathalie paused then shrieked at her disgusting pun and, pulling out her phone, punched in some numbers.

'Hang on—'

Nathalie held up her hand to Sarah's interruption. She gabbled fast in French then snapped her phone shut.

'Sorted. Tomorrow afternoon. Meanwhile' – she pushed back her chair – 'drink up because we are off to see Sylvie.'

'Sylvie?' Sarah gulped down the last mouthful.

'Runs the most beautiful shop in the Rue de Bac. Bit expensive but she was a model for an artist – very celebrated – and her taste is impeccable.'

Sylvie was seated behind a wide desk, tucked away to the side of a long thin shop around the corner from the café. It was quite dark inside after the bright sunshine and, like most of the shops in town, made even darker by the tall buildings and trees that blocked out the sky. The murk was dispelled by table lamps which threw light on to the mobiles of crystals hanging from the ceiling beams. The clothes Sarah had expected to find were on shelves and hangers on the back wall but, in front, round tables were laid out with an eclectic mixture of antique boxes, jewel-coloured notebooks, necklaces made of pearls and coloured glass. There were candlesticks beneath candelabra, scarves draped over small decorative chairs. Even books were laid out with titles Sarah couldn't understand. Everywhere she looked was something beautiful to covet; she could almost feel her mouth water.

'Sylvie, *bonjour ma chérie.*' Nathalie greeted the handsome woman with a kiss on both cheeks, and explained Sarah's dilemma in rapid French. From the odd word and the expansive arm movements, Sarah could work out that some sort of dramatic life story was being explained, and Sylvie nodded with sympathy and glanced over at Sarah as if she was some tragic heroine who needed careful handling.

'*Alors.*' She came forward, and, shaking hands with a long cool hand, smiled at Sarah, assessing her body with an analytical look. '*Venez.*' And she moved gracefully through the tables to the back of the shop.

Half an hour later, having taken off and tried on a vast array of clothes, popping out of the curtained cubicle to be approved or rejected by her audience of two (Nathalie and Sylvie gasped at her dreadful underwear), Sarah watched helplessly as Sylvie wrapped two skirts, three tops, a delicious floating velvet jacket and matching scarf in pink tissue. Frantically, she tried to calculate in her head how much it was all going to cost. She had barely had a handle on francs, and Euros floored her totally, but she had a horrible feeling that she was waving goodbye to about three hundred quid.

'You will be beautiful,' Sylvie managed in very broken English. 'Come back to see me again, yes? And, Sarah, the bra. It simply must match *les culottes!*'

Despite the nausea as she punched in her credit card pin number, still not quite sure how much she was spending, Sarah felt suddenly elated and feminine. It had been years, if ever, since she'd shopped with women like this. With Claire it was usually a stroppy row around Birmingham as she pushed for low, low-cut jeans and Sarah refused on the grounds of decency. What would Claire make of this? Sarah quashed a surge of massive homesickness and left the shop, stiff and shiny carrier bag over her arm.

The result of Thierry's ministrations the following day was even more of a transformation. He was utterly entertaining, mincing about his little salon in tight white trousers and silk shirt, regaling her in perfect English with details of his life that made Sarah almost gasp with disbelief – did men really do that to each other? – but Nathalie had been right. He was a genius, and she came out after three hours of intensive care barely able to recognise herself or wipe the smile off her face. Gone was the safe straight look; instead her hair, toned down now to a rich honey blonde, clung to her head in a neat, layered crop. She could feel the air around the back of her neck and couldn't stop herself from putting her hands up to her head. Nor could she wait to text Claire and Tom about her new image.

'Leave it,' pleaded Nathalie, as she prepared a salad for their lunch. 'You look stunning, like a woman ready to be treated like a woman. You know' – she stopped and waved the salad servers at Sarah – 'you can tell that David never made you feel sexy. Men get so lazy about their women. You need to feel good from within.'

'Oh shut up, you silly Frenchwoman, with your lurve nonsense!' Sarah laughed as Nathalie shrugged with a maybe-but-you'll-see-I'm-right expression, but deep down she felt warm.

'And once we have eaten this,' Nathalie continued, carrying a bowl brimming with leaves, artichokes hearts and neat little plum tomatoes over to the table by the window, 'we move on to stage three.'

'And what exactly is stage three?' Sarah took a sip of the chilled wine.

'Getting you a job.'

The phone ringing startled David. He was watching *Newsnight* and eating a microwaved meal that Sarah had prepared and left in the freezer. Some kind of risotto, but it was all right. There were only a few things left in there now. At first, he'd sulkily ignored her offerings with their neatly written labels, as he had that first night, but the thought of the supermarket was too much and he'd eventually caved-in and plundered the freezer.

He'd given footie a miss tonight and had been sorting through some old magazines until about half an hour ago. Amazing how the evenings went by. Normally, he and Sarah would have eaten hours ago. He put his tray on the floor and reached for the hand-set, turning down the volume on Jeremy Paxman.

'Hello?' He hurried to swallow before he had to speak again.

'Dad? Is that you?' Not Sarah, then.

'Tom! Hello, there. How's things?'

'Fine. Great, in fact. I've been really busy.' His son's voice sounded ebullient.

'That's what I like to hear. Lectures, I hope.'

'Yeah, yeah. Don't worry about that. I'm sorted. I've been going out a fair bit too. And using the climbing wall. It's great. You should come up and give it a try sometime. Do you remember when you took us climbing in Wales years ago?'

'Course I do. You didn't like it much at the time, though, did you? Fancy you taking it up again.'

'Well, I was a bit small. And Mum didn't like me doing it, did she? And Claire freaked out completely. And you had to climb up – do you remember? – and help her get down. What a performance! Anyway, there's a really good club here and it hardly costs anything. They've got all the equipment ...'

David was barely listening. He was remembering that summer's day when he'd climbed up to reach Claire, crying halfway up the rock face. She'd never been in any danger but Sarah had been so angry, turning away from him and holding Claire close, as if he'd upset her on purpose. They'd never discussed it, but he had not suggested going again. He hadn't even gone again himself.

'... and she's really good. Been doing for years. So if she plans another trip, I thought I might go too. If I can get enough practice in to keep up with her.'

'Sorry? What was that? You're going away?'

'Yes – a whole crowd of us. Not just me and Gemma.'

David frowned and stared into his rapidly cooling dish. 'Gemma – right. So how long have you known her?'

He could hear the smile in Tom's voice. 'It's all right, Dad. You don't have to give me the third degree. But the thing is, they might be going in March and I need to pay a deposit. Could you bung us fifty quid?'

David smiled. Children were so transparent. 'Course I can, you sponger.' There was a pause. He couldn't stop himself but he tried to make it sound light. 'Er ... have you spoken to your mother at all?'

Tom faltered. 'Well, it's expensive calling abroad, isn't it? So we've just emailed each other a few times. She sounds like she's having a great time, and says she's doing loads of new things. Have you?'

'Er, no. Not since she arrived.' He could hear how phoney his voice sounded, and coughed as if to clear his throat.

There was a pause. 'What about you, Dad? Aren't there loads of things you want to do now?'

Just be with her again. Just feel her in my arms again. Just go back to normal. 'Oh, well. You know me. I've got plenty on. Usual stuff, you know.'

'You should be trying out new stuff too, though. I mean, like this climbing thing ...'

David could hear the happiness in Tom's voice and suddenly understood. He was in love. For the first time. 'Listen, Tom, don't use up all your credit on me. Tell you what. I'll call you sometime this week – all right? And I'll put that money in your account. Now take care with that climbing, remember? Keep your mind on what you're doing. Give my love to your sister. I haven't heard from her in ages. I left her an answerphone message the other day, but I'll try to email her from work tomorrow. Okay. Goodnight, son.'

His supper was cold now and he threw it in the bin. He wasn't really hungry anyway. Dropping the dirty plate into the sink, he flicked off the kitchen light. It could all wait till tomorrow.

Chapter 17

Five days later and Sarah was standing on the wrong side of a very closed door with a large imposing knocker and no obvious means of working out if she was at the right place. She looked again at the paper in her hand on which Nathalie had written M Flocourt, 7 Rue des Cerises. Next door was number six, but what was to say it wasn't like England – odd numbers one side and even on the other?

Her stomach ached with tension. She was wearing one of her new skirts and tops to give her courage, but hadn't felt this nervous since her interview for music college. She shook herself. This was just stupid. She was a more than capable musician and this wasn't the LSO, for God's sake. Nathalie hadn't been too specific with the details of the person she'd lined up for Sarah to meet. Only that he was a 'celebrated' musician in the area – according to Nathalie every one was *très connu* – and that he directed the Ensemble de Roussillon and there was a chance he might need her. It all sounded a bit haphazard. Sarah sighed.

Claire had been cool on the phone last night, just as she had been every time Sarah had been in touch. Sarah had tried to make her laugh with her stories about Thierry or the bar Nathalie had taken her to where they'd been flirted with by two off-duty policemen, but Claire had remained silent. She hadn't even commented on the picture message of her new hair that Sarah had sent over, wincing at what it must have cost to send, and she just muttered 'whatever' when Sarah told her about today's interview. Oh well, she'd face that one later. Right now she had to work out where this man lived. She stepped back from the doorway and was glancing up the street when the door was ripped open and there stood a small man in beige cotton trousers and a blue striped shirt, the sleeves rolled up. His hair was grey and wiry, receding from the front of his head, to reveal a large shiny forehead, but longer at the back to his collar. In his hand he had a leather portfolio case and he frowned at Sarah from over his glasses. '*Madame?*'

'*Je cherche*' – she looked at the paper – 'Monsieur Flocourt?'

'*Oui, c'est moi. Et vous êtes?*'

'Sarah. Sarah Lewis.' She was going to remind him that Nathalie had called but couldn't remember the word for 'called' let alone in the past tense.

'Of course!' He slapped his forehead dramatically and smiled broadly at her now. '*La violiniste Anglaise.* I had completely forgotten. Come with me, come with me.' And beckoning her in, he turned back inside. Sarah entered the cool, musty-smelling hallway with its marble floor and followed him as he scurried up a curving stone staircase, disappearing through a doorway on the landing. The room he had entered was large, high ceilinged and utterly chaotic. There were piles of papers and scores everywhere. Books were teetering on top of each other on the floor and an old-fashioned music stand groaned under the scores balanced on it. A vast glass-fronted bookcase covered one entire wall and Sarah could see papers shoved on top of serried lines of books which must once, years ago, have been neatly ordered. Everything seemed pale grey or worn and, in the shaft of sunlight coming in through the shutters, dust particles danced. In the corner stood a grand piano. The scene was so archaic and comical, Sarah fully expected to see Beethoven seated somewhere composing.

'Gosh,' she breathed before she could stop herself.

'Oh, please don't!' Monsieur Flocourt looked sheepish as he dropped his portfolio on top of a pile on the desk. 'There is never any time to tidy up and then more papers and music arrives. I need a secretary, that's what I need. You see there?' He pointed to a box pushed against a bureau, its open top revealing it was filled with scores. 'All the orchestra parts for *La Mer*, just arrived and more to come tomorrow. Now' – he started to rifle through the papers on his desk – 'where is the résumé she sent over?'

'Debussy. I've never played that. Beautiful piece but fearfully complicated violin part, I'm told.'

Monsieur Flocourt looked up. 'Indeed it is. Half my musicians are having vapours about it. We start it at the end of the month. *Voilà!*' Amazingly, he pulled out the sheet Sarah had put together on Nathalie's computer a few night's earlier.

'It's impressive certainly.' Monsieur Flocourt looked at it as if for the first time, his fingers to his mouth. 'It looks like you've been very innovative with your little charges.' Sarah smiled bashfully. It was pleasing to get some acknowledgement of the hours spent rehearsing the excruciating school orchestra. Monsieur Flocourt went on, 'But perhaps too long teaching children and not enough recent orchestral experience. Are you sure you haven't atrophied to "Twinkle Twinkle" or whatever that ghastly little tune is called?' He looked circumspect over his glasses at her again, a sparkle in his eye.

'Possibly,' she laughed.

'*Alors.*' He dropped her résumé on the desk and pulled off his specs. 'As it happens, one of the women in the second desk has got herself – what is it you so delightfully say? – a bread in the oven, and is unavailable for our concert. We're playing a repertoire including *La Mer* at the *Festival du Printemps*, which begins' – he looked at the calendar by the phone – 'exactly three months from today. The only available alternative I know is a grisly little man with the most terrible body odour and I think half the second fiddles will resign if I draft him in. So, Sarah Lewis, you may be able to help me. Let's see what you are capable of, shall we?' And he nodded at the violin case in her hand.

He went over the piano, and lifted the lid, playing a little Chopin as she fumbled with her violin, tightening the bow and getting ready. Without asking, he played her an A and she tuned up, her fingers fumbling in her nervousness.

'Relax, Sarah,' he said, looking out of the window at the square below, idly tinkling on the keys with his right hand. 'I once had a trombone audition the whole of *Schéhérazade* in the wrong clef – and now he's the finest trombonist in the whole of France! Now, give me something you love and that makes you feel clever and inspired!'

Sarah let her shoulders drop, breathed deeply and tucked her beloved fiddle under her chin. Then she closed her eyes and began. It had been an age since she'd had the freedom to play what she wanted; to let the music flow from her and not to be restrained by playing with children. She couldn't even remember the last time she'd played for herself, all her time spent arranging the piano parts for school concerts not just picking up the fiddle and playing for the hell of it. But as she bowed the strings, completely unaware now of Monsieur Flocourt listening, she felt something give inside her head. Something that had been tightened firmly until this moment. David's face as he'd left the house that morning. Claire's disbelief when they'd told her the news. Tom laughing in the garden at home. Sarah could feel the tears pouring down her face – tears she couldn't stop even though she was standing in front of a man she'd only met a few moments before.

She played the final cord and, dropping her head, wiped her nose on her sleeve. There was silence in the room, save for the sound of a child calling in the street below.

'Why are you here?' Monsieur Flocourt asked quietly.

'Because I need a job.' She sniffed, getting a hold of herself.

'No, I mean why are you here in France. Have you run away?'

'I hope not.' She looked up at his open face. 'I was rather hoping I'd come to find something.'

Flocourt looked hard at her. 'I hope you find it.' Then he

slapped his hands on his knees. 'I don't think I need to hear any more.' Sarah felt a panic rise.

'Shouldn't I at least sight read for you?' she asked anxiously. Had the tears made him think she was unhinged or something?

'No, I am quite sure your sight reading is exemplary. Besides, you will cope with *La Mer*. Debussy wrote it in one of your ghastly seaside resorts, Eastbourne or some such place, in 1905 at the Grand Hotel, so it's the water that side of the Channel he must have had in mind. Now, I must get off to this meeting. They will wonder where I am and the officials at the Mairie don't like to be kept waiting. Idiots!' He picked up his portfolio again and Sarah quickly packed away her fiddle, not quite sure what was going on.

He made for the door slowly, then turned back to her. 'We don't pay much, you know. You will have to do something else as well.' Sarah frowned. Did that mean she'd got the job?

'I suppose ... I suppose I could try to get a post in a school ...? My friend Nathalie might be able to help.'

Flocourt rubbed his hand over his forehead in thought. 'I think you English have an expression: out of the pot into the fire?'

Sarah smiled. 'Frying pan.'

He waved his hand as if it were unimportant. 'Whatever. But it is a good sentiment, isn't it? No, I don't think little French violinists would be any more rewarding than your little English ones. A shop perhaps? Could you find a job there?'

Sarah knew her French wasn't good enough for that. The opportunities for disaster were too great. She looked around the room, an idea forming. 'I don't know if it would help but I'm quite an organised person.' Monsieur Flocourt looked questioning. 'You said ...' she went on '... you said you needed a secretary. Could I perhaps help you get a bit more organised here? At least try to create some kind of order?'

He thought for a moment then a smile spread across his face. 'Genius! Can you start tomorrow?'

Sarah wandered slowly back to the flat, letting the sunshine warm her back after the coolness of Monsieur Flocourt's study. She'd have to make sure she took a cardi when she was in there. She smiled at an old lady who passed her, and got a toothy grin in response. Two jobs in one afternoon – not bad going, Sarah old girl. That called for a coffee to celebrate. Nathalie wouldn't be back from work for a while, so Sarah headed for their favourite café, swinging her fiddle case as she walked.

'*Bonjour, Madame.*' Pascal came to stand by her table. '*Un crème, comme d'habitude?*' Sarah smiled at him and nodded and he waltzed off.

While she waited she watched the people passing; the shoe shop owner opposite pulling up the shutters and opening up for the afternoon, putting a display of sandals out at the front of his shop. The old stooped lady with the small dog passed and, recognising Sarah, raised her hand in greeting. Sarah waved back, then texted Claire, Tom and Rachel with the news about the jobs. How amazed her sister would be! Of all the reactions to Sarah's 'sabbatical' as she'd referred to it with curled lip, Rachel's had been the most extreme.

'For God's sake – bloody ridiculous – what are you thinking of? You are perfectly fine.' She had fidgeted with her scarf as she spoke, folding it and unfolding it agitatedly. To Sarah, she seemed more distressed than she had been when their mother had died, an event she'd taken with alarming sangfroid. She'd continued for ages to berate her and then warned darkly, 'You'll be bored within a week and realise what you're missing. You'll see. Like I told you, it won't be any better anywhere else.'

'*Voilà, un crème!*' Pascal placed it on the table with a flourish. '*Mais dites-donc, vous avez bronzé,*' he said, and she frowned, not really understanding. 'Your face.' He faltered, indicating his own skin. 'Good *couleur*.'

'Er … *merci.*' Sarah blushed.

'*Oui. Une vraie femme du Sud.*'

Sarah hadn't a clue what he said but she smiled broadly all the same.

Chapter 18

In the rear-view mirror, David could only see a little of his face at a time, but he turned his head slowly from side to side. He looked like shit. Doreen had been too kind when she'd haltingly commented that he wasn't looking too well. He was pale – well, grey was closer to the mark. His eyes were bloodshot and there were purple shadows underneath them. He knew he'd put on weight with his re-tox diet of lager and takeaways because all his trousers were too tight and even his hair looked more dishevelled than usual. What a cliché he was: the abandoned husband gone to seed.

Suddenly disgusted with himself, he left his briefcase on the seat – it wasn't as if he was going to do any work – and picked up his fish supper. It might be junk food but, frankly, he couldn't give a toss. The smell of grease and vinegar was making his mouth water and he kicked the car door shut behind him, trying to hold the scorching, paper-wrapped parcel away from his jacket. It was hard enough keeping shirts clean without having to go to the dry cleaner's too. He fumbled with his keys, shouldered open the front door and headed for the kitchen. That wasn't looking too pretty either. He'd forgotten to put the bins out again, and several days' worth of plates were stacked on the table. He found a clean one and, abandoning the outer layers of paper, dumped the near-solid mass of soggy chips and brittle batter enclosing the flaky cod morsel onto it, picking off the saturated greaseproof paper bag. He reached for the ketchup, still on the table from last night, as the phone began to ring.

Shit. He reached it just before the answerphone clicked on,

banging his knee on the doorframe in his haste to get there. But instead of the voice the wanted to hear, he heard Sheila's over-solicitous tone.

'David? How *are* you?'

He tried to keep his sigh inaudible and leaned back against the wall. 'Fine, thanks, Sheila. Well, you know.'

'Hmmm,' she crooned knowingly. 'I've been thinking about you such a lot. Well, we all have. Is there any news? Have you heard anything?'

'You mean from Sarah?' David shut his eyes tight and tried to inject the right amount of warmth into his voice. 'Well, she's arrived safely. She's with her friend. She seems to be settling in, according to Tom.'

He could feel Sheila weighing up his words, picking them over for hidden meaning. 'Yes, but, David, has she said what her plans are? I mean, it all sounds very vague. Hasn't she at least told you when she'll be back?'

'We've left it open, you know. Like we said when we told you about it. It's up to her really. She's got a lot of things she wants to do.'

David screwed his eyes up tight. He could almost convince himself if he said it often enough. And instead of this awful nothingness opening up in front of him, he could picture a nice neat future with Sarah back at home, wanderlust spent, and everything as it was before. He nodded to himself. It was vital to keep that image in mind.

Sheila didn't sound quite so convinced. 'Well, I think you're being marvellous about it. I don't think my Phil would be quite so accommodating! Mind you, he'd be hopeless on his own. Can you imagine?' Incredulous laughter. 'Anyway, I was thinking, why don't you come over for supper on Thursday?'

'Oh – that's kind of you. I'd love to but … er … that won't work, I'm afraid.' He cast around desperately for an alibi. 'I've got this work thing. A meeting.'

'What? All evening? Well, that's very unusual for you.'

He could hear the disbelief in her voice and was seized by a surge of annoyance for being so transparent. And predictable. 'Yes, I know, but it's a new drive, you know. Productivity targets. That sort of thing.'

'Well, if you're sure. Only we were thinking, we didn't want things to change, you know, just because Sarah's gone. I haven't asked before because, well, I thought you might feel a bit upset at being with us all but, really, there's no reason for anything to be any different and ...'

David shut his eyes and let Sheila's voice fade into the background, making the occasional non-committal grunt in a way that would, he hoped, give the impression that he was listening. Perhaps it would be comforting, after all, to go along and join in the usual banter. At least he'd get fed. But the idea of everyone carefully side-stepping the issue of Sarah, and of the women watching him for signs of neglect, was unbearable. And could he cope with the close questioning that Sheila specialised in? Even now, she was going on and on and on. 'Hmmm, yes. OK.'

'Oh that's wonderful! You know, Phil said I shouldn't mention it. Well, not yet, anyway. But I said to him, "Oh, David won't take it the wrong way". I don't mean anything by it – good heavens, no! It's been no time at all since Sarah left after all, but she's a nice woman and she needs taking out of herself. I know I was right. You can't live in a vacuum, after all.'

David tried to catch up without appearing to. 'Er, no. Quite. Sorry? What?'

'So is next week any good? Have you got your diary there?'

'No,' he said hastily. 'I've left it a work. Can I call you later on in the week?'

'Yes!' Sheila crooned, sounding thoroughly satisfied. 'Of course you can. Got to get on. I've got a casserole on the hob and I've just got to pop in the garlic.'

'Mmm. Well, don't let me keep you. Thanks for calling and tell Phil I'll give him a ring. Bye.'

He replaced the handset then stuck his cooling supper into the microwave for a blast. What the hell had he just agreed to?

Claire knew she couldn't really afford the train fair to London, but what the hell? The sense of relief as she took the bus out of campus was immense and she watched the countryside speed by as the train whisked her towards St Pancras. She'd asked Lydia if she'd like to come too, but she'd been more interested in the advances of a member of the rugby first XV and had squealed 'No way!' as if Claire had suggested a trip to an abattoir.

Anyway, Claire thought as she rested her feet on the seat opposite, it was better on her own. She could spend as long as she wanted in the gallery without feeling hassled. Squinting at the Tube map, she realised this was the first time she'd handled London on her own, but hey. Everyone else managed it, didn't they, and she faked a nonchalance, trying to glance at it as quickly as she could as if she was an old hand who just needed reminding.

After the chilled London air and the bustle of Trafalgar Square, the gallery felt warm and quiet. She flashed her student card and paid the concessionary rate then moved into the exhibition, a thrill of excitement going through her body as she caught her first glimpses of the canvases. Her eyes were greedy and she had to make herself slow down and take each picture one by one, drinking in the details. The oils were thick and lush, the charcoal sketches light and clever.

This was what she loved. This was where she wanted to be. She turned round, wanting to share it with someone, to point out the richness of the tones and shadows, but there was no one there, of course. All she could see was the disinterested figure of the guard by the door, and her heart shrivelled with disappointment.

*

David was late again. He'd slept through the alarm and woken, with a start, at eight o'clock. Even speeding through his usual routine, to the extent that he'd cut himself shaving and had to leave the house with loo paper stuck to his face, hadn't made up the lost time. His usual parking space was, unbelievably, taken, and he'd had to leave the car in the overspill. It was a quarter past nine when he reached his desk. He called up his emails and scanned them for anything crucial, then sat back and looked around.

No one had noticed. Why had he bothered hurrying? Taking in the grey partitions beside each desk, laid out in ranks, he wondered if anyone would even notice if he'd turned up with a pink Mohican and dressed in a hula skirt. All the years he'd spent at that desk, doing more or less the same thing – and for what? At the time, it had seemed as though he was working to-wards something worthwhile. But now? He stood up and looked around, suddenly feeling uncomfortable and awkward. So many people with their heads bent over their keyboards or muttering earnestly into their phones. His own phone rang – a client with a query he'd said he would look into last week . And he hadn't. He hadn't done anything about it. In fact, he'd forgotten all about it. He made a vague excuse and sat down again, slightly shaken. That wasn't like him. If there was one thing David prided himself on it was being a safe pair of hands. Good old reliable David. Provider. Husband. Father. He rubbed his face with both hands. He thought he was a cog in a machine, but he had the disconcerting feeling now that he was more like a hamster on a wheel. Going sodding nowhere, and all alone in his cage.

Chapter 19

'Enough for today. Monday, same time.' Flocourt – or Maurice as he now insisted she call him – put his baton back on the stand and began to tidy up his papers. There was a communal sigh of relief among the orchestra as people began to push back their chairs, pick up scores and head for the back of the room and their instrument cases. Two and a half hours of Debussy's fearfully difficult passages had rendered them all exhausted. Sarah had watched the sunshine pour through the high windows for the last hour and was now desperate for a cup of tea – and the proper PG Tips she'd asked her dad to post from home. The choice in the small selection of British goods at the local supermarket somehow didn't taste the same. Her neck ached and she hadn't realised how tense she had been.

'Very gooood.' The girl next to her, in her early twenties and exotically beautiful, leaned over. 'You are enjoying it with us?'

'Oh very much, though that last page has some terribly difficult bits, don't you think?' The girl frowned in incomprehension. 'Hard bits. *Difficile?*'

'Ah, *oui oui.*' She laughed at last and rolled her eyes in agreement then wandered off with her friends. Yes Sarah was enjoying it, despite the fact that she was putting in an hour or so each evening at the flat or when Maurice was away from his house at a meeting to go over and over the harder parts. Everyone in the desks around her seemed awesomely accomplished and, during the first rehearsal, she had cowered, feeling every bit the primary-school violin teacher that she was, trying to listen out to everyone else, until Maurice had tapped his stand and gently encouraged her with a '*Courage, petite Anglaise*', which had brought a titter from the rest of the orchestra.

Outside, the afternoon sunshine was pushing through the trees and spreading patterns on the ground. Her skirt swung softly around her legs which, she'd noticed last night in the shower, were getting nicely brown too. Nathalie and she had driven out to the coast at Collioure and sat in the Spring sunshine with a bottle of wine last Sunday, shooting the breeze, and the results were looking good. It was over the second glass that Nathalie had come up with the plan for tonight's dinner party. Sarah had groaned.

'What's the problem?' Nathalie had pushed her sunglasses up onto her head, her eyes excited at the thought.

'Oh Nathalie, I won't know any of them, and they'll all gabble on in French and I won't understand a word.'

'All my friends speak English beautifully and you know they do. Unlike you English people, we make the effort, whereas you lot just shout louder to make yourself understood. No, it's about time you met a few more people. If you are going to live here, we need to make that new life for you!'

So Nathalie was resolved and, when they had finally wound their way back along the coast, the Mediterranean slowly slipping away behind them, she had spent the remainder of the evening on the phone amassing a group of eight people available on Friday night, including the man she'd met at a jazz club and was trying to bed. 'Oh I love spontaneity!' She had clapped her hands in delight. 'You will love them all, Sarah. You'll remember my mate Marie-Laure – we met her in the street – and she'll be bringing her husband Pierre who is dull but teaches English at the University so you'll be fine. The rest – well, wait and see! There's one in particular I just know you are going to like.'

Alarm bells ringing loudly, Sarah looked at her watch now. Four thirty – she would have enough time to go and finish the filing she had started that morning at Maurice's before picking up the fish for Nathalie as she had promised she would. Nathalie was going to handle the salad, not trusting Sarah's nose for quality control, considering the English idea of leaf variety was a 'bag of iceberg rubbish with carrot shavings'. Sarah smiled to herself as she headed towards Maurice's apartment. Nathalie would probably have bunked off work already to start the preparations. Her work ethic, as it was when they were twenty and sharing freezing digs in Didsbury, was slack to say the least. After college she'd moved home to France and, like Sarah, she'd taught music for a while but, unable to cope with the occupational hazard of the children it involved, had quickly transferred to an administrative role in the music sector of the education department – hence her knowledge of Maurice and the orchestra. The role, which gave her the opportunity to escape from her desk on the pretext of 'visiting schools', suited her lazy hide well. She certainly hadn't picked up her flute for ten years or more.

Sarah made her way across town, pleased with how well she'd got her bearings now. She'd even directed a tourist yesterday to the *Musée* and felt herself grow taller with pride. Passing Sylvie's shop, she was sorely temped to go inside and see if she had anything she could buy to wear tonight but checked herself. The orchestra pay would be small when it eventually came in, and what Maurice was giving her barely covered buying food, so nominal rent for Nathalie and all her other expenses were going on the debit card. She could eek out her mother's legacy a bit more but she wanted to keep enough for tickets for Tom and Claire to come out and for emergencies. David was not going to appreciate it if she just relied on their shared bank account all the time.

What would David be doing now? she wondered. During the day she tried not to think about him, positively revelling in the growing sense of freedom as the days went by, of being herself. Getting into bed alone and waking up alone, however, still felt weird, even though he'd never been in that bed with her. It was silly, of course, but after waking up every morning to see his head on the pillow beside her, and for there suddenly to be nothing seemed … odd. She thought about their deal not to contact each other, and neither Claire nor Tom were giving away anything but, suddenly gripped by curiosity, she stopped in front of the art shop in the square opposite Pascale's café. She'd send David a postcard. And, before she could change her mind, she picked out one of the town's famous medieval arches, and took it inside the shop to pay. Like all the shops on that side of the street, it was set slightly lower than ground level, but unlike Sylvie's, this one was well lit and packed with racks of art prints in white crate-like boxes. In the background she could make out Schubert's *Trout Quintet* coming out of speakers somewhere, and on the whitewashed walls hung a variety of large canvases, some reproductions of famous paintings by Picasso, Chagall and Matisse, others originals, the tickets beside them, as Sarah peered closer, revealing they were by local Catalan artists. The colours were stark and brassy on some, on others smudged and brooding, but all were contemporary and exciting.

'*Vous les aimez?*'

Sarah turned at the deep voice behind her. Standing behind the desk was a tall, impossibly good-looking man, with dark hair that looked scruffy but clean. His hands were in the pockets of jeans and over his white T-shirt he wore a dark blue waistcoat of some soft material.

'Yes. Yes, very much.'

He put a hand briefly on her arm. 'Oh, pardon. I thought you were French.'

She smiled, flattered. 'They aren't the sort of thing I'd usually like, to be honest, but …' She looked away quickly and stepped back to look at the pictures again. 'Really striking.'

He came round the desk and stood close beside her. She could smell a light cologne and, a bit uncomfortable at his proximity, moved away slightly. 'This one here' – he pointed to a large canvas in oils, perhaps a metre wide, which was a mass of olive greens and pinks, with small splashes of whites and pale blues – 'is by a man who lives here in Sauzils. I was the first to exhibit him.' He said the word 'exhibit' without the bitten British pronunciation. He must be French then. 'But he has just been taken on by galleries in Paris and Nice so his value will go through the ceiling. Brilliant, isn't it?' Sarah nodded. 'You are staying here in Sauzils?'

'Yes, well, kind of.' Sarah scuffed her sandal on the floor. 'I'm sort of living here with my friend for a while.' The man stood back and looked at her face thoroughly with his dark eyes.

'You're not Nathalie's friend, are you?'

'You know her?'

He threw back his head and laughed. 'Nathalie is hard not to know! And not only is she a great friend of mine, I am going to dinner with her tonight.'

Back in the safety of Maurice's study fifteen minutes later, Sarah realised why alarm bells had rung when Nathalie had said 'wait and see'. A very unsubtle bit of matchmaking, my friend, she thought, then began to explore the tingle of anticipation she felt at the prospect of the evening ahead. It had nothing to do with the way he had held her hand a moment too long when he said goodbye, or with the way he'd said how much he was looking forward to seeing her later. No, she told herself, as she pulled down a pile of papers from on top of a box, she was probably just hungry.

Chapter 20

Before he left the house, David picked up the morning's mail from where he'd left it, stuffed behind the phone. A couple of circulars went straight into the bin. The classic car newsletter he'd look at later, but he tore open the bank statement for a quick look. He'd reconcile it with the cheques later but he scanned the usual outgoings, noticing that the weekly trips to the supermarket had been replaced with the odd transaction from France. He scanned them uncomfortably – it seemed too odd to be monitoring her movements this way and he turned the page quickly, then stopped. A single payment of nearly three hundred pounds to a shop in a Sauzils, where Nathalie lived. He frowned, and ran his finger down the rest of the page. Nothing further.

He put the statement down thoughtfully and checked the time, then glanced in the mirror to ensure that he'd got all the creases out of his shirt. He wasn't about to waste any more time worrying about Sarah. He had a dinner party to go to.

Pulling the door closed behind him, he scuttled head down to the car, aware that Appalling Pauline was hovering near her bins. She'd already pinned him to the fence yesterday, grilling him about Sarah's departure, and he couldn't face another interrogation. Relieved to have escaped and heading down the Banbury Road and over the Clopton Bridge, David felt the first stirring of anticipation. He was fully aware that he was being set up, although he had no intention of following through – even if Sheila had thoughtfully provided Keira Knightley for his delectation. But it might be interesting to meet someone new. And at least it'd be a change from chips. He turned left along Waterside, past the theatre, and started whistling a little tune.

Sarah looked at herself in the bathroom mirror, running her fingers slowly through her short crop. With her lightly tanned skin and smattering of freckles on her nose, she was quite pleased with what looked back at her. Around her neck was her new necklace, glass leaves of blue and aquamarine. It matched her top and had been a moment of weakness she'd succumbed to when she saw it in the window of the shop next to the *poissonnerie*. Outside in the hallway, she could hear Nathalie greeting her guests, but Sarah just wanted to steal some time to – to what? Prepare herself?

With a squirt of Nathalie's Guerlain, and a light coat of pale pink lipstick, she breathed deeply. 'Now don't get carried away,' she warned her reflection and went out to join the others.

Sheila had taken more care than usual with the table. A pungent bowl of freesias occupied pride of place in the centre and threatened to spill over at any moment. He and Debbie, the predicted other sad single, had been ushered to the far end of the table, although he'd started to run out of conversation with her over the drinks in the sitting room. Fortunately, though, Debbie still had plenty to say. And, boy, was she busy saying it. Under the scrutiny of four pairs of very familiar eyes, David went on nodding politely, as he had from the moment Debbie had started explaining the history of the Tarot.

With her usual vigour, Sheila thumped the plates down and tried, rather archly David thought, to big him up. 'Has David told you about his old car? He's got a smashing old Alvis hidden away in the garage. Are you going to use it this summer? It would be lovely for picnics, wouldn't it?'

Debbie smiled toothily. 'Mmmm, yes. I can't wait for summer. I'm going down to a crystal healing workshop in Devon. Have you ever been to Devon, David?'

Sheila came unexpectedly to the rescue, lugging in the good old blue Le Creuset casserole from the kitchen. A farmer's daughter to her sturdy fingertips, she had, according to Sarah, honed her domestic skills at agricultural college. David recalled how he'd always tutted disapprovingly at these sort of catty comments of Sarah's but, looking now at the greyish mess of stew and pasta she'd ladled onto his plate, he realised it closely resembled something you'd serve up as a delicacy to a sty of Gloucester Old-Spots.

And the only person who would possibly get that joke was in another country.

Sarah feasted her eyes on the plate Nathalie had placed carefully in front of her. The delicate fragrance of the fish and the sauce filled her nostrils, doing battle a bit with Fabien's cologne, which was stronger tonight. Somehow hearing his name made him seem more Mediterranean and exotic, but in his impeccable English he had taken her hand after Nathalie's introduction with a 'Yes, we are old friends already'. There was a twinkle in his eye. 'She spent a fortune in my shop this afternoon. A massive forty Eurocents, I think it was?' The others all tittered at this, and Sarah was aware of being the protagonist in a contrived little performance engineered by Nathalie, with everyone else in the room in on the joke. But what the hell? The attention and Fabien's warm hand were really quite enjoyable.

'It's called Zarzuela,' he said quietly now. 'It's a seafood – what do you call it? – a seafood stew, mixed with prawns, clams and mussels, cooked with tomatoes and chilli. Doesn't it look and smell divine?' He leaned over her plate and breathed in, closing his eyes.

'Mmm, it sure does.' She smiled, not able to think of a single Englishman she knew who would do that, or who wouldn't look a right prat for doing it. 'Where does it come from? It doesn't sound very French.'

'It's a local dish – so much in this part of France is a magical mix of Spanish and French. It's named after a Spanish operatic genre – a sort of operetta named after a royal hunting lodge, the Palacio de la Zarzuela in the El Prado woods near Madrid.'

Sarah was intrigued, and put her head to one side. 'I ought to know that.'

'It is very particular to Spain. The story goes that back in the seventeenth century when the King's court moved to the palace for hunting, coach-loads of entertainers and musicians came with them, and the royal party was offered a new musical comedy, a mixture of classical opera and – what do you call it? – slapstick and folksong. And that became Zarzuela.'

'So what has that got to do with fish?'

'Something to do with the exciting mixture of ingredients, I think. And the Palace, Zarzuela, is so named because it is sur-rounded by thick brambles, *zarzas* in Spanish.'

'Ooh, brambles. They can be nasty.'

'Indeed.' Fabien paused. 'Sometimes you can get hooked on them and you can't get away.' He looked at her closely then threw back his head and roared with laughter.

'Mmm! That's delicious, Sheila. Really tasty. You must give me the recipe.'

David looked sideways at Debbie, gushing beside him. She'd certainly put the stew away. Her plate was empty already. David pushed a mushroom round, making patterns in the gravy. Debbie leaned across, the long ropes of beads around her neck threatening to dip into the butter on her side plate. 'You've barely touched yours, David. What's wrong? Lost your appetite?'

'Er, no. I mean, yes. Well, you know. It's been a tiring week.' David could feel himself shrinking back slightly under the assault of this – what was it? Flirtation? If so, he didn't like it much.

She tilted her head thoughtfully to one side and frowned a little. She was very much the wrong side of thirty-five, and catching her hair back with a ribbon, with odd curly bits sticking out, wasn't really the best look.

'This can be quite a tiring time of year,' she sighed. 'When the seasons change, your energy can really get depleted. Tell me, what sign are you?'

David had, in desperation, shovelled a forkful of pasta into his mouth. 'Eh?' he mumbled.

Someone had probably once told Debbie she had a musical laugh. She was certainly giving it plenty tonight. 'Your star sign, silly.' She playfully cuffed his arm and he winced in irritation.

'My star sign? Christ! I don't know. Probably Taurus, the bullshit.'

'Oh, David!' Sheila huffed, giving him a warning look. 'Play nice. Debbie's amazing. She's absolutely uncanny, in fact. No – you are, Debbie, don't be so modest. You should see what she can do with her dowsing rods. She'd convince even you. Would you show us, Debbie, after dinner?'

Debbie bowed her head and played with her ringlets and with the frills on the front of her white linen shirt. There was plenty going on down there, but most of it, from what David could see, stage dressing. 'I can't do readings to order, I'm afraid,' she said softly. 'I take it far too seriously.'

Sheila nodded understandingly and returned to her conversation with Harry. David made very little effort to disguise a snort and took a long slug of white wine as Debbie leaned towards him confidingly. 'I don't usually do this, David, but I just wanted to say that your aura – well, I was bowled over by it as soon as I saw you. I can see immense strength in you, David, and passion.' She looked up at him through her lashes which, David noticed with amazement, seemed to be purple at the tips. 'But I'm also getting tremendous pain. I think you've been hurt very deeply. I think you need healing. That aura – I'm getting charcoal.' She squinted at him and laid her hand on his arm. 'With touches of viridian!' She shook her head sadly.

'Eh, Fabien, what's so funny?' Nathalie enquired. Sarah was aware she had been watching their close exchange from her end of the table.

'Oh nothing. I've just been explaining to Sarah the origins of Zarzuela. It smells delicious, darling. As always. So how is *Le Salaud*?'

Nathalie shot him a disapproving look, indicating, as discreetly as she could, the man beside her, in conversation with Nathalie's friend Marie-Laure. This dark, chubby little man was Christian, the one she'd flirted with all evening at that jazz club and she had been on full charm offensive.

'Oops, have I said the wrong thing?' Fabien turned back to Sarah and whispered theatrically.

'I don't know. What did you ask her? I didn't understand.'

'I was asking about the erstwhile lover – we call him *Le Salaud*, bastard in other words. Did you ever meet him?'

Sarah smiled. 'Stefan? Er … no but after the last few weeks with Nathalie I feel I know so much about him, I'd find him even in a darkened room.' Fabien laughed again and she felt witty and clever. It had been an age since she had done this, consciously flirted with a good-looking man, and, revelling in it, she leaned forward conspiratorially. 'I think she's still mad about him, to be honest, but she's also trying to make an impression on the man beside her, and I don't think she wants to look like she's just come out of a bad relationship.'

Fabien slapped his own hand theatrically. 'I shall behave.' Sarah watched him dollop on the garlic mayonnaise which he then handed on to her, then took a mouthful of the Zarzuela, dipping the crusty bread into the juices. Sarah did the same. The flavour was immense over her tongue.

'Good, huh?' he asked, taking a sip of wine. 'And what of you, Sarah? Have you come out of a bad relationship that has brought you here to Sauzils?'

Sarah quickly put some more bread in her mouth, not really sure how to reply. Did she want to talk to this man about why she was here? And if not, why didn't she? Mercifully, Marie-Laure came to her rescue before she had time to explore that one.

'How are the rehearsals going, Sarah?'

'Rehearsals?' Christian, the jazz man's, head shot up. 'What are you rehearsing?' His accent was strong and Catalan.

'Oh, it's nothing.' Sarah looked down, feeling foolish, some English fraud who'd somehow levered herself into town life.

'It's not nothing at all,' replied Pierre, Marie-Laure's husband and the English teacher, a tall earnest man with a mop of dark hair and a face saved from mediocrity by designer glasses. 'She is playing in the Festival orchestra, and very good she is too!'

Sarah blushed stupidly. 'Oh Pierre, you are kind, but how can you possibly know?'

'Because this is a very small town, *cherie*, and I know Maurice Flocourt very well. He says you are getting along brilliantly. Not to mention organising his life and keeping him sane.'

'He has been wonderful,' Sarah genuinely enthused. 'And I'm just loving making some order out of his dusty chaos.'

Pierre waved his hand dismissively. 'It is chaotic, you are right, but there are no flies on Maurice. He is a brilliant musician and conductor and other orchestras are always trying to poach him, but I don't think he will ever leave his beloved Sauzils.'

'So you are an artist too?' Fabien changed the subject, putting in another forkful of the stew.

'No, a musician.'

He swallowed his mouthful. 'Same difference. Paintbrush, pen, piano, we are all artists and we feel things very deeply.'

Sarah watched with glee as the charm chariot came hurtling over the hill. She was loving every minute of it.

'Let me get that for you.' David reached over for the jug of cream, taking the opportunity to shoot another surreptitious look at his watch. God! The evening was crawling past and yet he already knew so much about Debbie's spiritual journey.

'Thank you,' she simpered. 'It's so nice to be looked after. You're a very considerate person, David. I could tell that at once.'

So many things she could tell at once. Strange, then, that she couldn't tell he was bored to bloody tears. Once Sheila had finished her coffee, he promised himself, he'd be out of there. He glanced over to see her draining her cup and pushed his chair back.

'So sorry.' He shrugged. 'I've got to get over to see the twins tomorrow, early. I'll have to be heading off.' He hoped his aura wasn't flashing a neon 'LIAR' sign. Debbie had dived under the table. Strangely, she hadn't predicted this.

She reappeared and slipped a square of card into his hand. 'My card. I feel sure I could help you, David, if you'd only let me. Do call me, any time.'

David bent and gave her a quick kiss on the cheek, judging it the quickest way to disentangle himself, then moved on to bid goodnight to the others. Outside, he breathed in the cold air, mercifully not scented with patchouli, and crumpled up the card without a glance. One consultation with her wasn't going to help his shit-coloured aura, thank you.

'It's been a pleasure.' Both Pierre and Christian gave Sarah a warm embrace as everyone got up to leave. It was two a.m., according to Sarah's watch, but they were all full of wine and had laughed and chatted for hours.

Marie-Laure too took her into her arms. 'Isn't he gorgeous?' she whispered, a wicked giggle in her voice. 'I think you've made a bit of a hit there.'

'Oh,' Sarah said quickly. 'I didn't mean to ... I mean I—'

'No woman means to make a man fall in love with her. Well, not unless you are Nathalie, of course!'

Sarah snorted with laughter and they both turned to Nathalie who, fuelled by a bottle and a half of wine, was making overtures to Christian that were so unsubtle a wheelie bin would have got the message.

'I'll call you,' he demurred, wrapping a scarf around his neck and backing away hastily.

'I wonder if that means the same in French as it does in English?' Sarah asked Marie-Laure out of the corner of her mouth.

'Oh, I think so!'

'And may I call you?' came a voice behind Sarah. She turned to Fabien who was shrugging on a soft leather jacket, turning up the collar. 'There's an exhibition of photography in Perpignan. I wondered if you'd like to come with me.'

Marie-Laure smiled encouragingly. Nathalie smiled encouragingly. Even Christian looked enthusiastic as he reversed out the door as fast as he could.

Sarah nodded her assent. It couldn't do any harm, could it?

Chapter 21

Claire placed her mobile carefully on its side on her desk and shuffled her papers into a pile. She'd be able to hear if Dad answered, and doing two things at once gave her, at least, the illusion that she was achieving something. She quickly tucked the still unopened notes from her tutor right at the bottom of the pile and peered at the page on top. It was a list of essay topics given out at another lecture she'd missed, and that Lydia had dropped round last week. She'd only stayed a minute, friendly enough but they didn't really seem to have much to say. Claire frowned at the titles, and put them to one side.

On the pad in front of her, she'd sketched an interlacing web of tiny figures, some flying, some dragged down by sorrow and barely able to crawl along the page, some skipping or running. Some hand in hand, others alone. She picked up her pencil and added a few more. Where did she fit in?

She glanced at her phone. Where was he? She tried to picture Dad at home, all on his own, and her throat felt swollen with pity. Why was everything so awful? What was wrong with her?

She tried his mobile number instead. Maybe he was out somewhere, shopping for himself, getting in meals for one, blinking in the harsh lights of the supermarket and getting all confused. She was getting ready to leave a voicemail when he answered abruptly.

'Yep? Hello?'

'Dad? Are you all right? Are you in the middle of something?'

'Oh, hello darling.' His voice warmed and she felt herself relax a little. 'Sorry, I was under the Alvis. I'm replacing the starter motor and it's a bit of a fiddle.'

'Oh – you're working on the car. Wow!'

He laughed shortly. Sarah would have been amazed. She'd been nagging him about it for long enough. 'Well, it's about time, isn't it? I've been meaning to get on with it for ages. And it gives me something to do, you know.'

She closed her eyes and pictured him, probably covered in oil in the empty house, whistling. 'Dad, can I come home?' She'd voiced the question before she'd even had the thought. But there it was, the perfect solution. She could leave behind the whole catastrophe this course was turning into. Look after Dad. Keep him company. Be back with Jess and her other friends from home. Do some painting. She could cook for them both in the evenings. She looked around. She'd never have to spend another gut-wrenchingly lonely evening in this little breeze-blocked room again.

'What's that, love? Come home? Don't be daft. I'm fine. In fact, I'm doing pretty well. I think you'd be quite proud of how I'm coping. I'm doing things – you know. Obviously, I'm missing Mum, but I'm managing fine – I've worked out the fan oven.'

He laughed again, seeming amazed at himself, and Claire felt herself shrivel up a little more. No one needed her. 'Anyway,' he went on, 'I'm going to see you both next weekend for Grandpa's party, aren't I? Let me know what time your train gets in, won't you? Tell Tom he'll have to wear my old dinner jacket. That's a thought – I hope mine still fits me, I'm getting so fat. But that's enough about me. What are you up to? Working hard, I hope.'

Claire swivelled her chair away from the desk and pressed her hand hard against her forehead. 'Yeah, fine. You know.' She struggled to keep her voice steady as tears started to pour down her cheeks. 'Pretty busy. Lots of new friends.'

'It's a wonderful opportunity, Claire. I'm so envious of you, and all the fantastic new experiences you must be having. Well you and Tom, of course. How is he? Keeping out of mischief? Not drinking too much, I hope? What about this new girl, hey? Hope she lasts longer than his average five minutes.'

Claire thought of the last time she'd seen Tom, laughing, surrounded by mates from his course, arm draped round his new girlfriend. He'd waved at her and she'd pretended not to notice him and had gone to hide in the recesses of the library. She covered the mouthpiece, took a shuddering breath and gritted her teeth. 'No, he's fine. Er, Dad, I've got to go. Someone at the door – yes. A bunch of us going out. I'll call you later. Yeah – love you.'

She hung up quickly and put the phone down on her desk. The evening stretched ahead, long, silent and empty.

'No, really, David. It's no trouble at all. We only ever take one car. Think of the emissions, after all. And it gives us more of a chance to really chat. Maybe you can drive next time.'

'But isn't it terribly out of your way?' David was floundering and he knew it.

'Not at all!' Richard went on heartily. He had thought this one through well in advance. 'I'll pick up Malcolm first then I wanted to pop over to that aquatics centre near you anyway, to get some barley straw for the pond. You haven't seen the new pond, have you? Honestly, what are we like? It's been far too long since we last met up. Just a reminder, don't forget to bring lunch. We usually end up swapping around. Oh, but just to remind you, Malcolm can't be doing with chutney – okay?'

David weakly agreed to a good early start on Saturday and put down the phone. He'd been fatally diverted by that question, 'What are we like?' He'd never really got that, yet people said it so often. Rhetorical, obviously, but with his rather literal mind, he could never resist framing an answer. What are we like, Richard? We're like two slight acquaintances from college who never make any effort to see each other. So why all the attention now?

As if he didn't know.

Bad news travels faster than shit off a shovel. And David had been fending off the kindly, the curious and the downright morbid ever since he and Sarah had announced the split. This sudden invitation to walk up the Malvern Hills with Richard and Malcolm, another slight acquaintance from the Jurassic period that was college, could only have been motivated by them having heard. Still, he reflected, it was kind of them to think of him. But he was going to have to stock up on emergency excuses in future.

On Saturday morning, slightly hung over from another solitary bender, David fervently wished he'd thought of a decent excuse to get him out of this one. Richard and Malcolm turned up right on time, kitted out as though for an expedition to the Arctic, all neatly pressed Rohan trousers and serious high-performance boots. In his trainers and jeans, David felt every bit the poor relation and, hunched up in the meagre space in the back of Richard's low-emission hatchback, he probably looked like one, with his unshaven face and queasy pallor.

Malcolm, divorced, had greeted David with an especially sincere two-handed handshake and a sympathetic and brotherly smile, which had been worrying because Sarah had always dismissed Malcolm as a 'sad sack'. Richard, who was the hearty sort, and had a wife who earned three times what he did and was always away on business, was clearly the moving force behind these regular walks. Did he now see David as a sad sack too?

Fortunately, sitting in the back meant that David could avoid the conversation and he managed to doze off for a while – no more uncomfortable than falling asleep on the sofa, as he'd taken to doing lately, with the telly on quietly in the background. By the time he woke up, they were bumping up a track towards the car park.

'You can't carry your lunch in a plastic bag, David!' Richard exclaimed with concern. 'I'll put it in my day pack. You should get one of these. They're marvellous.'

David handed over the offending bag and noticed, with sly amusement, Richard folding it over with distaste. 'Sure you've got room? You seem to have a lot of stuff in there.'

'Well, if I haven't, I'm sure Malcolm will help out, won't you, Malc?'

Malcolm was struggling with an identical backpack, pushing loose bananas in around the sides of a large waterproof. 'Er, yes. No problem. I could just put on my jacket then I'd have plenty of space. Have you got the map there?'

Richard produced a neatly folded map in a plastic pouch with a cord to go round his neck. 'All in order. Shall we?'

Richard paused for a moment for some unnecessary consultation of his compass, also neatly dangling round his neck. David sighed quietly to himself. Christ! This was the Malverns not the freakin' Himalayas. He'd be roping them together next. Eventually they set off up a path, climbing steadily towards a ridge. In spite of himself, David started to enjoy the cool air on his face and the slight tiredness in his thighs as the path led uphill. Though he hadn't been walking like this in years – not since that holiday with the kids in Austria – he had no trouble keeping up with the others, and noticed that Malcolm was certainly breathing harder than he was. All thanks to the footie, not that he'd done that too regularly lately.

As the path widened, David moved up alongside the other two. Richard always managed to look tidy, with his neatly-clipped beard and little boy's haircut. Even the way he walked was measured and economical, everything thought out. He gave the impression of being someone who never acted spontaneously and was an expert of everything. Even now he was pointing out birds and stopping occasionally to look through a pair of compact binoculars, also hanging round his neck.

Malcolm was a different specimen. Tall and awkward with a pale, flabby, high-domed head and terrible teeth, he had the look of a sad Humpty Dumpty. He wore a perpetual expression of worry and seemed to be anxious not to be the last in their procession. Whenever one of the others pulled ahead, he'd give a little skip to catch up. David toyed with the idea of upping the pace a bit, just for the fun of watching him rush, but dismissed it as mean. Looking at them now, David couldn't imagine what he had ever had in common with these two middle-aged men. Sure they'd both been swottish – it came with the territory of being an engineer, after all – but so does a reputation for putting away the pints and he certainly remembered Saturday nights at the Union bar until they all fell over. Had they all changed so much? They seemed so staid and, well, boring. He glanced down at himself suddenly shocked. Shit, is that how *he* looked to other people?

Conversation was scant, as the slope grew steeper. It really was beautiful, seeing Worcestershire open up behind them and the view over fields, orchards, towns and villages, threaded with tiny, narrow roads, stretching further and further until it blended with the misty sky.

On a ridge at last, they stopped to gaze around them, all panting now and hot in the spring sunshine. Richard consulted his watch. 'Bit early for lunch, I think. Shall we press on and find a bit of grass to camp on?'

David eased his back. 'You couldn't find a better view, though. I mean, you can see for ever from here.'

Richard preened as though he'd created it himself. 'Well, Worcestershire, obviously, and Herefordshire and Gloucestershire. That's Wales over there, of course. It is a wonderful sight. Here – have a look at the guidebook.'

David took a cursory look, then closed it. 'Why read about it when you can look? It's amazing.' He stretched luxuriously. 'You know, I think I could get into walking. I always thought it was a bit middle-aged but – well, I suppose I'm growing into it.' He laughed.

Malcolm was hovering, having taken off his pack, and was looking anxiously at Richard for approval.

'Oh well. Why not stop here?' Richard sighed. 'After all, it is your first time, David, and we don't want to wear you out.'

They all sat down on the waterproof rug Malcom tugged from his pack. Richard handed David's plastic bag over, then produced a thermos, teabags and a china mug wrapped in a tea towel, then sandwiches wrapped in greaseproof paper, a Tupperware box of cherry tomatoes and, curiously, a small leather-bound book, which he placed carefully beside him with a loving pat. David's own contribution of pork pies, a can of diet coke and a bag of tortillas looked a bit out of place, but he offered them around and swapped with Malcolm for a pickle-free ham sandwich. He lay back in the sunshine and could feel his body tingling with the unaccustomed exercise. Despite the Scotch he'd put away the night before, he felt fantastic. Not such a bad way to spend a Saturday after all.

Richard efficiently screwed the lid back on his thermos and cleared his throat. 'Now, David, as a new member to our little club, I ought to tell you we take it in turns to read out loud to each other after we've eaten.' David felt his stomach shrivel. Holy fuck. 'We find it so relaxing outside, with your mind clear and nothing but the sky above! Today we've selected Yeats.'

David swallowed hard. The pork pie had stuck somewhere around his collar bone, and tried to block out Malcolm's portentous tones as he launched in to '*No Second Troy*'. 'Why,' he intoned, 'should I blame her that she filled my days/ With misery ...' David winced. Must have been a messy divorce, then.

There was a respectful pause for contemplation after Malcolm said the last line and Richard nodded his head slowly and stroked his beard.

'Lovely. Now here, David. You pick something.' Malcolm

solemnly handed over the book and watched as David flicked through the pages.

'Must I? I hate reading aloud.'

'Oh do, David.' Malcolm was insistent. 'You'd be amazed how much more meaning your favourite poetry has when you share it with your friends.'

David suppressed a sigh and looked for something he recognised even vaguely. 'Here we are. "He Wishes for the Cloths of Heaven".' It had been one of Sarah's favourites, but he couldn't remember how it went. It was short, at least.

When he'd finished, Malcolm drew a shuddering breath. '"Tread softly because you tread on my dreams",' he echoed. 'Oh David, that's so touching and such a brave choice.'

Richard squeezed his arm and nodded, seemingly robbed of the power of speech. 'Very moving and beautifully read. You know, David, I think I speak for Malcolm when I say I hope you'll join us regularly on our little outings. And, now you're on your own, you know you can call on us whenever you like. Hilary and I would love to have you over, you know that. I think there's a lot of feeling in you, and you shouldn't be ashamed to let it out. I can tell you're a kindred spirit. I'm right, aren't I, Malcolm?'

David looked at the two well-meaning faces, smiling encouragingly at him. Not bloody likely, he thought, smiling back.

Chapter 22

'Hi, Mum.' Sarah could hear a dispiriting sigh in Claire's voice, and she knew the forced jollity of her chirpy 'Hello, darling' must sound fake and contrived.

'How are you?'

'Fine.'

'What's new, then?' This shouldn't be so difficult. Sarah battled with the guilt demon never far from the surface of motherhood, which told her it was all her fault Claire was being so difficult, and what did she expect when she had upped and gone. Rubbish, said the other voice in her head. The girl is nineteen, you were nearly married with twins by then and, besides, you have given everything for them – this is your time, girlfriend, so make the most of it.

'Are you working?' she tried again.

'God, you're just like Dad. Not much. It's all so dull.'

'Well, it's bound to be.' Sarah tried to remember what her own college days had been like, but she'd loved them. Loved being surrounded by music and enthusiasts and the opportunity to explore deeply what she had always enjoyed so much. It had been worth the months of battle and slammed doors it had taken with Mary and Wilf to allow her to go. They'd have preferred teacher training – even secretarial – instead of the vagaries of a life eeked out on a salary of peanuts. 'They have to teach you the dull bits as well as the good bits!'

Claire sighed again, and Sarah could hear her moving around her little room. The size of it had alarmed both her and David when they'd delivered the twins at the beginning of Freshers'

Week last September. There was barely room to swing a cat, and the window looked out onto another student block, an uninspiring edifice of plain red brick and metal windows. Tom, who would have been happy in a broom cupboard so long as he had his beloved bass guitar by his side, had just dumped his stuff and gone to explore. Claire, usually such a nester, had tried to smile and joked that she'd need her old doll's house furniture, but all the way back home, Sarah had fretted.

'Yeah, well maybe it will get better,' Claire went on now. 'They are organising some work experience days with a city paper so who knows . . .' There was a long pause. 'How are you, then?'

Sarah babbled on about Maurice and the mess, exaggerating for effect, and about the orchestra and how her fingers ached from practising. She talked about Amélie-les-Bains, the beautiful little spa town up the valley that Maurice had sent her to explore yesterday and where she'd sat by the river for hours reading her book. She talked about the dinner party and the Zarzuela, the weather, the market. She talked about everything except Fabien, with whom she was going to spend the following day, a prospect that made her stomach ache with anxiety and anticipation.

'How's Dad?' she found herself asking instead.

'As well as can be expected,' Claire replied defiantly, her blind loyalty to her father even more entrenched. She doesn't get it, Sarah thought to herself, and she won't get it either while she has the arrogance of youth and the expectation of a life ahead of her that will be just the way she wants to live it. 'We're off to Grandpa's seventy-fifth on Saturday.'

Sarah could imagine it. Heather in her element, hopping about like a sparrow, displaying her skills as hostess to their friends to whom those sort of talents mattered. Anthony would be aloof and debonair in his dinner jacket – he was the sort of man who was made for one, his hair slicked back, a silk handkerchief in his pocket and his familiar crisp lemony aftershave bought from Penhaligon as it had been for ever. In a way she would like to have been there – she'd always loved Anthony and wanted to celebrate with him – but she'd done so many family parties, and witnessed so many of Heather's displays of flowers and folded napkins (never serviettes, dear), that she felt weary even thinking about it.

'Oh, how lovely. Granny will love it. What are you going to wear?' Sarah would like to have chosen with her, and made her daughter look beautiful.

'Haven't decided.' The conversation flagged again, and, after Sarah had proposed a couple of dates for the twins to come out to Sauzils, she admitted defeat and said goodbye.

Her own father would have enjoyed the party, but he hadn't mentioned it when she'd spoken to him a couple of days before. Perhaps he wasn't invited. He sounded happy and settled, even joked about a lady in the flat next door who'd invited him over for tea, and reassured her that Rachel was being more than attentive, but Sarah worried that old friends had forgotten him and carried on with their lives, lazy as people so often are about contacting the bereaved. Things can change so suddenly, she thought the next morning as she finished collating the scores for a string ensemble that Maurice needed, finally locating the viola part behind a cabinet. So much had happened over the last few months: her mother's death, the children leaving for university, the hideous months that followed, and finally facing the growing unhappiness in her own life. It had felt as though the sands had shifted beneath her feet. Everything that had been her normality had changed or come into question, not least the discovery from Wilf about her mother.

She looked at her watch. She was due in the square in half an hour, to spend the day with an attractive man who wasn't her husband when, despite the wedding band she had tucked away in a box in her room, she was still married. The word adultery rang loudly in her head. Had her mother behaved like this? And was Sarah any less culpable just because she'd walked away from her husband first? She tried to imagine her mother, so pretty even in old age, so effervescent with her colourful scarves and necklaces, giving that love and attention to someone other than Wilf. And what did she feel about David right now? She pushed into the back of her mind the comfortable routine they'd established after so long and, instead, thought about the stultifying boredom. When was the last time she'd tingled like she was now? Had she ever?

Emptying the contents of the dustpan – alarmingly full after just one foray behind the piano – Sarah brushed her hair in the mirror, applied a bit more lipstick – too much? – and grabbed her cardigan and her bag. Her dress swung around her bare legs, its pink matching the little pumps on her feet (well, they had only been cheap at the market), and for a stupid, embarrassing moment she felt like the heroine in a French film. Silly woman, she smiled at her reflection, and let herself out of the door.

Naturally, Fabien had a convertible. She almost laughed at the predictability.

'You look very pretty today.' He smiled and leaned over to open the door for her. She slid in beside him, digging out her sunglasses. Eat your heart out, Grace Kelly, she thought as the car sped out of the square.

'Where are we going?' she asked as they followed the road over the bridge and out of town.

'First I thought some lunch in Perpignan then we'll go to the gallery.' The wind blew his hair wildly and flapped the collar of his pale-blue cotton shirt. She couldn't see his eyes behind his shades, but she could see clearly the slight dimple in his cheeks when he turned to smile at her. 'It's an exhibition of photographs by a news photographer, Claude Le Gall, who was huge in France between the Wars. Very clever. Very elegant pictures. I am sure you will like them. Are you hungry?'

Sarah nodded and, conversation being too difficult with the noise of the car and the wind, she turned to look at the scenery.

Two hours later, after a delicious salad of artichokes hearts, haricots and tiny quails eggs, plus the obligatory crispy *pain* and a bottle of Côte de Roussillon, she sat back in her chair, replete. She was aware that throughout lunch she'd interrogated him – he'd laughed at one point in mock horror, 'What is this? Do you work for *Le Monde*?' – but he'd been guilty of doing the same. By the time they were nearing the bottom of the bottle, he'd told about how he'd studied twentieth-century art in America and worked in galleries in Paris and Marseilles before coming to Sauzils. 'My family did not approve,' he laughed. 'My father is a tyrant of a man, and wanted me to be a doctor or a lawyer – usual thing. I come from quite an old French family – you'd call it your aristocracy, I suppose – and artists are a lower form of life.'

'What medium do you work in?' she asked, intrigued.

'Oh, a bit of everything. I love to sketch. Oils, too, are an inspiration to me, but I have so little time these days, what with the shop and everything. But what about you, lovely Sarah?' He ran his finger around the top of his glass. 'Tell me about what dragged you from England's green and pleasant pastures to *Les Pyrenees*?'

She was evasive to begin with: she'd wanted to come to see Nathalie, she had wanted to stop teaching for a while and play the violin, but under his gentle questioning, she'd talked about her marriage and the children, and the need to find herself. 'Oh, it probably sounds very silly,' she muttered, though he hadn't taken his eyes off her face as she'd talked, 'but I just had an overwhelming sense that my life had to change. My mother died last year and left me a bit of money, so I thought, now's the time.'

'I can understand that,' he said quietly, a serious expression on his face. He played distractedly with the fork, making rivulets with the prongs on the tablecloth. 'I think us men, we forget just how much women sacrifice while our lives change very little.'

'Do you have children, Fabien?' He sounded as if he was talking from experience.

'A boy, yes. He's ten now but I hardly see him. His mother took him with her when she went to live in Toucy.'

'Oh,' Sarah said with sympathy, not having a clue where Toucy was.

'Yes.' He frowned. 'It was very painful. I speak to him occasionally but she makes it so difficult for me to visit him. Her husband is very tricky, I think, and perhaps they don't want me around.'

Sarah tried to imagine what it must be like. 'But that's outrageous. Don't the French courts have laws about access and things?' She could feel her dander rise. 'In England you'd have rights as the father. You shouldn't be missing out on your little boy's childhood—'

'Sarah, Sarah.' He smiled at her ire and put his warm hand on hers to calm her down. 'It's okay. I see him when I can and maybe it will get better as he grows up. *Alors.*' He shrugged and pushed back his chair. 'Enough talk of difficult relationships and past sadness. Let's go and spend a lovely afternoon with each other, shall we? I can't imagine anything nicer.'

Nor could Sarah. And nor could she remember the last time someone had wanted to spend time with her like this. The afternoon turned out to be better than she could have imagined. Fabien explained how photojournalism was celebrated in Perpignan with a festival called *La Visa pour L'Image* each September and how Claude Le Gall's work would feature then too but, in the quiet intimacy of the gallery, owned by a man who greeted Fabien warmly, she could get up close and really concentrate on the powerful images. Afterwards, they walked slowly through the narrow cobbled streets, and he told her about Perpignan's history, so intertwined with Spain's that it had once belonged to the counts of Barcelona and was the capital of the Kingdom of Majorca, which stretched from the Balearic Islands to Marseilles. He showed her the Castillet Tower and the Palais des Rois de Majorque, then, over coffee, they laughed about how little she'd travelled and how much he had. This, thought Sarah, as she stretched contentedly and watched people wandering past the café, is what new experiences are all about. It was exactly what she had craved. New people, history she knew nothing about, places she'd never seen.

Whether that included the feelings she was experiencing while spending time with this devastatingly attractive man, she wasn't quite sure.

Chapter 23

Unrestricted access to the bathroom. That was another advantage of being on your own and one he'd got used to almost without noticing. David popped his head out of his room again but the bathroom door remained resolutely shut. And he knew of old that Claire hated to be hurried. He tugged at his bow tie. Tight enough to stay up meant it was strangling him; loose enough to breathe meant it would come untied every twenty minutes. That was most definitely a disadvantage. Sarah had had a way with bow ties so David had never bothered.

He gave it another hopeful wiggle and went to see how Tom was faring. Taller than ever, his son's gangling presence made the room feel smaller and David smiled to himself, a little painfully, as he remembered the nights without number of reading stories and tucking in and cuddling when Tom was small and his room large enough to conceal monsters in its distant corners. 'Let's have a look at you, then?'

Tom turned at his father's voice and held his arms out awkwardly at his sides. 'Will I do?'

David looked him up and down slowly. He was taller than David, but the trousers hung low on his narrow hips, so they didn't look too short. His shoulders were broadening out and his bony wrists extended a little way beyond the sleeves of the dinner jacket. With his fair unruly hair and the slight colour he'd acquired out rock climbing, he looked older. His face, still changing shape, seemed longer and leaner. David felt a mixture of pride and pain. His son had become a man. 'You look good.

Very good. If there were going to be any women under seventy there tonight, I'd be worried.'

Tom's face creased up as he laughed, and the boy returned. 'Come off it, Dad. I'm spoken for, anyway. You're the one we should be worrying about. Off the leash and dressed like James Bond. Granny'll be trying to fix you up if you don't watch it.'

'What's all that?' Claire had emerged and, as always, wanted to know exactly what was being said. 'What's Granny up to now? Oh, Dad! You look great. Here – just let me have a look at that tie. There! That's better. You know, I like your hair a bit longer, like that. It suits you.'

Tom pouted. 'Oi! What about me? Don't I look pretty too?'

'Your ego's big enough as it is. I'll say this for you, though: you look better than you did at the school Prom.'

They all laughed, Tom wincing a little, as they remembered the last time he'd worn a dinner suit, but David stepped back to admire Claire in her turn. 'Look at you. You look fantastic! Where's your dance card? Pencil me in right now! I hope they've got an ambulance on standby, because Grandpa's golfing buddies are going to need resuscitation when they see you.'

Claire smiled, smoothing down the sea-green satin of her dress, bought earlier this afternoon after David has dragged her into town and sat like a warder outside the changing room as she half-heartedly tried on various options. It had been worth it. She'd caught her hair up in a matching ribbon thing and the touches of make-up he could detect, not that he was an expert, made her look a bit healthier than she had last night, when he'd picked them both up from the station and taken them home for a take-away curry. She was wearing a dark velvet jacket of Sarah's that had usually been reserved for concerts and funerals, and she'd pushed up the sleeves and adjusted the collar, flicking it up at the back and giving it a much more rock-and-roll look than it had ever had before. David shook his head indulgently.

There was an awkward moment as Sarah's absence suddenly loomed. 'Oh, that's a pretty bracelet. Where did you get that?'

Claire frowned slightly and went to cover it up with her other hand. 'Oh, I wasn't sure whether to wear it. Mum gave it to me before she went. It was Granny Mary's apparently. Do you mind? ' She looked embarrassed for a moment.

David shook his head. 'No, darling, why would I mind? Let's have a look – I don't think I've ever seen it before, but then I'm not great at noticing these things as you know.'

He was aware of a look passing between his children and Claire spoke quickly. 'Oh, you wouldn't have, probably. Mum said she'd found it in Granny's stuff and Rachel didn't want it. She didn't know where it came from either, cos it wouldn't have been Granny's style, really, would it?'

'Well, it looks lovely. ' He was on automatic pilot now. What had that look meant? David frowned and stood back to let the twins go downstairs ahead of him before slipping into the bathroom to check his reflection in the long mirror there.

He tried to smooth down his hair on the back of his neck where it flicked up over his collar. He had put on weight, there was no question, and he eased his cummerbund, tucking his shirt in a bit more firmly so it didn't bulge out any more. Maybe he should go walking regularly with Malcolm and Richard – but he couldn't bear the prospect of any more sensitive New Manism. He turned sideways and scowled. He'd have to do something or none of his work clothes would fit. Maybe jogging again? He turned back at looked at himself straight in the eye. Then suddenly it hit him.

The twins had been afraid to talk about Sarah in front of him, as if he'd break down and be unable to cope. He rocked back on his heels. Was that the impression he was giving them? Is that what everyone thought when they looked at him now? Poor abandoned David. Too dreary to be married to. Someone to be handled with care. What a strange turnaround when your own children start trying to spare your feelings. He took one more glance at the cautious, slightly worried and overweight, dull-looking man in the mirror and he saw, with blinding clarity, what they saw and what Sarah had seen when she'd looked at him and at their marriage. He turned away.

Even Maurice noticed the smile on Sarah's face, though she hoped she hadn't been that obvious. 'I think Sauzils must be doing you some good,' he observed with a raised eyebrow. Sarah was seated on the floor of his study and, for once, he was so often out, he was bent over his desk marking up a score.

'Oh?' she asked innocently, pushing the hair off her face.

'I think so. Not only have you lost that terrible pasty English colour you had when you arrived, your confidence with your part in the second movement has improved no end. I noticed it last night.'

Sarah felt a wave of pleasure. 'Oh, I'm so glad you think so. I've been practising it hard.'

'Mmm.' He put his hand theatrically under his chin. 'I think there is something else going on there too. Yes, you definitely have the look of a woman who is being seduced.'

'Maurice!' The directness of these people always floored her. She called it the French frank.

'Anyone nice?' he asked, going back to his work and pretending not to be interested.

'Mmm, very nice, as a matter of fact.'

'Is he taking you to lots of interesting places?'

Sarah put an elastic band around the papers she had sorted and picked up the wastepaper basket, full now with documents that dated back about ten years. 'Lots. It's been lovely. We've done the *Musée*, been to Spain for the day, paddled in the Med, something I haven't ever done, and he's taking me out again in' – she looked at her watch – 'about five minutes.'

Maurice looked at his watch too. '*Merde*, is that the time

already? Right, I'd better get home. Off you go and put on your lipstick and Sarah' – she turned to him – 'enjoy it. You deserve the attention. See you at rehearsal tomorrow.'

Spontaneously Sarah went over to his desk and gave him a peck on the cheek, before grabbing her bag and heading for the door.

Tonight they were staying in town for dinner and Fabien was already sitting at the bar when she swept in, a bit breathless, a few minutes later. He stopped talking to the barman and turned to smile at her, pushing his sunglasses up onto his forehead, then he put his arm around her waist and pulled her towards him. 'You look beautiful,' he breathed into her hair, 'and you have a smut of dust on your nose.'

Sarah rubbed her nose with the back of her hand. 'Better?'

'Here.' He gently rubbed at the end of her nose then slowly ran his finger down over her lips, moving his fingertip from side to side. She held her breath, the sounds of the bar receding, until his head blocked her view and his lips touched hers. It was only a brief kiss but she could smell his breath and his clean skin.

'Much better.' He smiled, pushing a strand of hair from her face. 'I've wanted to do that for a long time.' Then he leaned down and kissed her again, for longer this time, his tongue gently pushing between her lips. She pulled away slowly, warm with pleasure and embarrassment.

'Fabien! People are watching.'

He looked around innocently. 'Where? This is France. No one cares. Come on, Mrs Uptight English Woman, let's go and eat.' And he leaned forward to whisper in her ear, 'I need the distraction.'

Chapter 24

In a smart, rather urban hotel in Chipping Campden, some eighty smartly dressed people, mostly retirees, were standing around chatting while well-trained staff wove between them with drinks on large silver trays. The noise level was surprisingly high for such well-bred people, but perhaps a combination of Champagne cocktails and upper-range hearing loss meant they'd all cranked up the volume. Claire wondered what Sarah would have made of it – a symphony of light laughter and delighted greetings, over a sustained bass line of commentary about golf, the stock market and the latest planning developments – a hot topic in a town where any change was regarded as 'a bad thing', particularly by those who had moved in most recently.

Claire peeped in through the doorway. At the centre of the hubbub, Anthony held court, charming and affable as ever, with Heather, floating in lilac, darting around and greeting newcomers, steering them from place to place. Leaving Tom and David to hand their coats over in the panelled hallway, Claire plunged in. The room, a modern take on a traditional country house, had an open fire, and it was warm and welcoming after the drizzle outside. She smiled and nodded as she moved through. Many of the people there she'd known since she was tiny, first met when she and Tom had spent the odd day with Heather and Anthony while Sarah was working, particularly if one or the other of them was off school.

She remembered very clearly the week Mum and Dad had been away on a rare holiday to Scotland, when they had just turned seven. They'd been at Sarah's parents' house for a few days then on to David's parents, and what a fascinating contrast that had been. From the shambling comfort of Wilf and Mary's, where they'd watched a peculiar black-and-white film on afternoon television about a man running a nightclub (and which she now knew to be *Casablanca*) while Granny had dabbed at her eyes unashamedly, to the regimented Calamine-lotion dabbing of Heather's stricter regime. There they'd been fed on cod steaks and broccoli and had stories read to them from an annual that had belonged to their dad. Heather hadn't even trusted Anthony to go and pick them up, and had driven his big Rover herself, waiting on the doorstep while Wilf had handed over their bags. Claire couldn't recall where Granny Mary had been.

Claire looked around, more in hope than in expectation that Wilf would be at the party. It seemed a bit mean not to invite him, now he was on his own, even though the two sets of grandparents had never been close. Heather pounced.

'Ah, there you are! You look beautiful, darling, and such a pretty bracelet. Not your usual Top Shop find! Come and say happy birthday to Grandpa before we sit down to eat. You three are on our table, or course, but I know he'd appreciate it, especially with all his friends around.'

'Hello, Granny.' Claire allowed herself to be led over towards Anthony. 'This all looks lovely. You must have worked terribly hard.'

'Oh, this. Well, I wanted to do it at home, of course. But it would be so cramped, and you know your grandfather – he said he thought it would be too much for me, and so he insisted. I've hardly had to lift a finger, although I do like to keep tabs on what they're doing.'

Claire squeezed her grandmother's arm and smiled to herself. Sarah had always laughed about what a control freak Granny was, although Claire saw it more as a desire to please. Her grandmother's kitchen was her sanctuary and she treated offers of help as hostile invasions. Claire and Sarah had only ever just been tolerated there, and Heather was old-fashioned enough not to expect Anthony, David or Tom to help at all. Over the years, they'd all got used to Heather waiting on the menfolk hand and foot, while simultaneously complaining about how little they did. The result was, however, that both her husband and her son had fallen into lazy ways, which infuriated Sarah almost beyond speech.

Mum. Claire fiddled with her bracelet, running the pearls between her fingers, and wondered where she was at the moment. It was so hard, when she called, to have any kind of conversation that didn't veer onto painful ground and Claire knew she hadn't managed their last few calls well at all. There was so much she wanted to say, but the price of calls to France inhibited her terribly. Maybe she'd Hotmail her about this party, when she got back to college.

Anthony held her at arm's length and studied her with a proud smile, then folded her into a bear hug. 'You're lovely, lovely, lovely! And I'm so touched you've come all this way for an old man, when I bet there are queues of handsome young ones to fend off!'

'Happy birthday, Grandpa!' As charming as ever, Anthony had the knack of making everyone feel special.

'Ah – and here are the lads. David – Tom. Look at you both! Where's that photographer? Heather? Come on. Let's have a picture with the lot of us.' He gathered them in, then sighed and there was a short silence as they all thought about the glaring absence in the line-up.

Well, maybe not all. 'Tom, you'd better go behind now! Come on, Claire. Let's have a nice smile. Goodness knows, those braces cost enough. Do stand up, David! Anthony, pull your stomach in! Good Lord – I'm going to have to put you on a diet.'

Heather was on form.

Outside on the terrace, the light was fading already. David closed the long glass door behind him and side-stepped behind a pillar so he couldn't be seen from inside. The riot of voices, laughter and music faded away and he breathed out deeply. God, it was hard work fending off all the questions – particularly the ones that weren't even voiced. Heather had obviously told some of their friends and not others, so there had been a variety of reactions from the people he'd spoken to, from sympathetic and supportive arm squeezing or downright vilification of Sarah, to puzzled queries at her absence usually cut off mid-stream by a meaningful nudge from someone in the know.

Thank God for Claire and Tom. He'd left them working the room like pros, charming the wrinklies, as they called them, and dancing with the most unexpected partners. They'd made a giggly pact, in the car on the way there, to start with the oldest guests and work their way down, with a special prize for the one who got someone to say, 'If I were twenty years younger …' Neither of them seemed especially bothered by Sarah's absence. Or if they were, they weren't showing it. It was a strange situation – he was trying to be strong for them, but he was beginning to think they were doing the same for him. The net result, though, was that he wasn't sure what either of them was really thinking. And maybe the same was true for them. Perhaps keeping a stiff upper lip wasn't helping, after all. Maybe that was what had got him into the whole situation with Sarah in the first place. David shook his head, hoping the cold air would clear his thoughts.

The scent of tobacco caught his attention and he peered off into the darkness where the Cotswold stone paving faded into lawns and herbaceous borders. Yes, he could see the glow of a cigarette tip flare as someone took a long drag on it. A sudden longing to fill his lungs with smoke drove him into the gloom. As he got closer, he made out a short figure swathed in loosely draped velvet. 'Abigail? Is that you?'

The woman turned quickly and, he thought, rather guiltily. 'Oh, it's you, David. Thank goodness. I was afraid it might be

Clive. The doctor's commanded me to give up so I have to sneak out if I want one. Filthy habit, I know, but sometimes ...'

She trailed off wistfully and turned away very deliberately to exhale.

David smiled. He'd known both Abigail and Clive since his schooldays, when he'd shared lifts to school with their son. They must have made the trip up from Epsom, or wherever they'd retired to, especially for the occasion. He remembered Abigail had always had a cigarette between those immaculately painted fingernails in those days, and persisted with the habit even after the most hardened people started giving up. Her raspy, smoker's voice was a testimony to years of obstinate refusal to listen to anyone's advice. She'd always been an original, her quiet, unassuming yet apparently brilliant husband trailing in her wake. But she was thin now, unhealthily so, and perhaps her years of defiance had caught up with her. And here she was, out in the cold on her own, still determined to have her own way.

'Could I have one?'

She turned sharply. 'But you haven't smoked for years, darling. Are you sure? I wouldn't want to be guilty of leading you astray.' A spark of mischief flashed in her eyes and she looked at him challengingly.

'I'm a big boy. And, quite frankly, I would murder for one right at this moment.'

'Well, I shouldn't like to meet my end like that. If ciggies are going to kill me, as I'm told they will eventually, I think I'd prefer to be in my own bed. Here you are.'

She offered the packet. A smile of complicity passed between them and he slid one out, then leaned forward to her proffered lighter. He inhaled deeply. And felt his diaphragm convulse as the urge to cough nearly overwhelmed him. He suppressed it with an effort and felt his eyes sting with tears.

'Cor, Abigail! They're strong.'

'Hmm – aren't they, though?' She sighed contentedly, drawing deeply on her own. 'So, David, what's all this about your little Sarah? Has she gone for good? Or for bad?'

He took a more cautious puff and exhaled slowly. 'Oh, so you know all about it?'

'Not really. I don't expect anyone does – perhaps not even you and Sarah. I know what Heather has told me. Anthony, of course, has been very quiet on the subject.'

He glanced at her. Was this a casual question or did she really want to know?

'I don't know.'

'What don't you know? Why? Where? When? Or how you feel about it all?' Abigail turned to face him full on.

David tried a smile. 'Well, all of the above really. She wasn't very specific. It seems she needed to find herself.' He air-quoted with what he hoped was heavy irony.

But Abigail wasn't so easily deflected. She pursed her lips, the cigarette burning down between her fingers as she scrutinised his face. 'I'll tell you something, David. I've known you for a long time. You were a lovely little boy – always full of fun and ready for adventure. But you're lost. I look at you, and I can't see that little boy any more. You've lost him along the way, or tucked him so far out of sight, he can't be found.'

'Er – not sure I know what you mean.'

Abigail took him by the arm and looked up at him, her face serious and intent. 'Yes, you do. You know you do, if you stop and think about it for even a moment. Sarah's not the only one who needs to look inside herself. You had the twins very young, didn't you? I remember Heather sounding off about it. About Sarah. At the time I thought she just had an axe to grind, you know ...'

'Er, not sure I'm following ...'

She ground the cigarette out with a practised twist of the wrist, in a little portable ashtray she produced from her jewelled bag. 'You and Sarah, you didn't have time to be young together.

164

Don't you see? It's a classic case of having to grow up before you're ready for it. If she'd got it out of her system earlier, she wouldn't have to do it now, and neither would you.'

David shook his head disbelievingly. 'Now, Abigail, surely you can't make a sweeping statement like that ...'

She wagged her finger. 'Do you see? Do you see what you're doing? You're old before your time, David. Or you're pretending to be so, because it's safer. But life is for living. And at full speed too. Look at me. My days are numbered. I know they are. But I'm going to live every single one I have left to the full. Because, believe me, time is too precious to waste on being unhappy.'

David felt his shoulders sag as her words sank in. The image of himself in the bathroom mirror flashed into his mind. His voice, when it came, was a whisper. 'But I don't know how ... I've never had to be without her. I don't think I can ... I don't even know who I am without her.'

Abigail grabbed both his hands in her own and squeezed them hard. 'You are yourself, David. You can and you must work out who that is now. Because if you can't find the man you are, the wonderful, fun-loving, interesting, exciting man you used to be and can be again, the man she fell in love with, how do you expect *her* to find him again?'

The glass door opened and a burst of noise spread across the garden. Framed in the doorway, they could see a man peering into the gloom. 'Are you there, Abi?'

She turned towards David and spoke more quietly. 'He's come to get me. I knew he would. He always does, and he always will.' Then she turned back towards the lights and called, 'Here I am, darling. Just having a little breather, you know.'

Clive snorted gently. 'Oh yes, I know all right. Come on, you wretch. Come and get warmed up – he's going to cut his birthday cake – they've got the fire brigade on hand, just in case.'

Abigail took David's hand and led him in. 'Come on, David. Join the party.'

Chapter 25

Claire slipped off the dress and laid it carefully over the chair. It was so long since she'd worn something so feminine – had it been the school Prom when her mum had talked her into a charcoal silk sheath dress and she'd been too adolescent to admit how great it had made her feel? She wished Sarah had been there to see her tonight. Would she have minded that she'd borrowed a jacket from her wardrobe? She had always looked so sophisticated in it, and Grandpa had told her how like her mum she looked, with her hair neatly brushed and tied back.

It had been a relief to kick off the shoes, also borrowed from Sarah's wardrobe. How the hell did anyone stand up for more than five minutes in heels like that, let alone dance in them? Suddenly she felt exhausted with the strain of putting on a carefree, adult face all evening; acting the grown-up, Dad's companion, and telling people 'Thank you, yes, the course is going well' when all she wanted was to scream that she'd made a terrible mistake, and that she'd give anything to be at art college instead.

Heather, a little tipsy by the end, had embraced her warmly and said something Claire didn't understand about taking after her father, but she had been cut off by a drunk old buffer who lunged at Claire, squeezing her bum and telling her she was as beautiful as her mother and had he been twenty years younger ... another wrinklie point to Claire!

She could hear Tom going into the bathroom, so she'd have to wait to clean her teeth. She yawned expansively. It was only one o'clock according to her watch but she couldn't wait to slip into bed. Unlooping her earrings from her ears, she dropped them onto her dressing table, then carefully unfastened the bracelet Sarah had given to her before she left, the catch fiddly and delicate in her fingers. She ran the chain, with its tiny pearls, across her palm then, picking up the box it had come in, coiled it onto the velvet pad. No, it wasn't really Granny's style – she'd like chunky modern jewellery. Maybe that was why she'd never worn it. Perhaps it was something from years ago when styles were different, although the box looked quite new. She was just about to close the lid, when she noticed the little silk tab and tugged it experimentally.

It lifted under her fingers, and she peeped underneath. There, tucked inside, was a folded slip of paper. A receipt, perhaps. Claire pulled it out and unfolded it carefully. It was a note, and the writing was loopy and thin. And terribly familiar.

Darling Mary,
I know it's the end for us, but I wanted you to have this.
Pearls for our tears.
Yours forever, Anthony.

Claire frowned, confused for a moment, and sat down heavily on the bed. That wasn't right, surely? She must be wrong. Why would Grandpa have given Granny Mary a present? Yet it was unmistakably his signature.

She read the note again, slowly. 'The end for us.' What had he meant? Then she understood, with gut-wrenching clarity. Who else knew about this? Who could she ask? The very idea of Mary and Anthony together was laughable. Did this mean they'd had sex? Grandpa with his half-moon specs and Granny Mary, all crêpe-skin and wrinkles. She felt vaguely disgusted.

Tom would think she was mad, and Dad? Well, it was too unbelievable. As if he didn't have enough to worry about at the moment. Claire dropped the note into her lap. What should she do? She couldn't ask anyone in case she was the only one that knew. The revelation would be explosive for everyone, or did the grown-ups know already? Had they been keeping it a secret, like Father Christmas or what happens to unclaimed dogs at the rescue centre?

What the hell should she do now?

Thinking about it afterwards, Sarah had to admit the evening had been charged from the start. They'd gone through the motions of ordering, but Sarah had moved the baked fish and salad around her plate and stuck with the wine. They'd talked about everything and nothing, but he'd put his hand on hers whenever possible and while they waited for coffee, he had gently run his finger up her arm.

'So, what are you doing over the weekend?' she asked nervously, trying to focus her mind on the here and now, firmly banishing any other part of her life from her mind.

'Well, I hoped I might spend it with you.'

Sarah felt a flood of pleasure. 'What shall we do?' she gabbled on. 'I would love to go back and explore Perpignan a bit more, or what about going up the valley towards Canigou?'

'I would love to go to bed with you.'

The statement was so direct that it made Sarah stop short. 'Oh.' She felt her face grow pink and as she put out her hand to pick up her glass – a sip would stall things – she managed to knock it over and the red wine spread out over the tablecloth, soaking in to the fabric. 'Oh God, I'm so sorry.'

'Leave it. They will clear it up.' Fabien laughed and moved the salt and pepper out of the way. 'Let's go, shall we?' He patted his pocket for his wallet, then with a slight frown patted the inside pocket of his jacket. '*Merde*, I've left the damn thing at home. I'll have to ask Jacques if I can pay him tomorrow.'

'No, no.' Flustered now, Sarah pulled out her purse. 'I'll get it.' And she put her card on the little tray with the bill.

Payment complete, they wandered back through the streets

hand in hand. There were lights from balconies above their heads, and the noise of people eating and laughing. Lanterns hung in trees in the square and light from the bars and restaurants poured out over the pavement. Spring was moving into summer but Sarah didn't notice. She felt as though she was in a trance, being pulled along against her will. No, not against her will, just against her better judgement. But she wanted this. She wanted to be heading towards bed with this delicious man, and she wanted to do something about this heightened sensitivity that was making her ache and her skin tingle. In fact, she wanted it so badly, she put everything else out of her mind. How easy it was.

Fabien stopped outside a door in a square she hadn't discovered before. He let go of her hand as he fumbled for his key. Neither of them said a word as he pushed it into the lock. The apartment on the first floor was dark and smelled of vanilla and lilies. In the light from the window, Sarah could make out huge sofas and oversized lamps with exotic bases, and large canvases on the walls. Instead of turning on the light, though, he drew her across the lounge to the bedroom. Sarah, her eyes more accustomed now to the darkness, could make out a large bed with a white cover, and over a chair hung a jacket. There was no sound as he added the jacket he had been wearing to it and turned to her, her back now facing the bed. Placing his hands gently on her hips, he pulled her towards him. He kissed her hair, her ears, her cheeks and finally her lips. Sarah slipped off her shoes and the wooden floor felt warm under her feet as he slipped the straps of her dress off her shoulders. Moving her hands up she began to undo the buttons of his shirt as her dress slid to the floor.

Suddenly she felt vulnerable and crossed her arms protectively over her breasts. She tried frantically to remember the last time she had shaved her legs or done her bikini line and prayed to God he wouldn't turn on the light. He stepped back to look at her, and she looked away embarrassed.

'Oh Sarah,' he said quietly, 'you look so beautiful.' Gently he pulled her hands away, brushing her nipples almost imperceptibly with his thumbs. Then, taking her in his arms, he fell with her onto the bed, and she was kissing his chest and running her fingers over his back. His skin felt warm and taut under her lips. He was smooth and strong, narrowing at the waist, but she gasped, distracted by the way he kissed her ears and down her neck and shoulder. As his mouth travelled down her body and she began to tingle all over, she thanked the Lord again she was on her back so her stomach at least looked flat. But even that didn't matter as he took her nipple in his mouth and she arched her back.

'Oh God.' The thought barged its way into her mind. 'I shouldn't be doing this.' And as his fingers slipped inside the waistband of her knickers, followed by his warm mouth, she put out her hand to push him away.

'Fabien, don't,' she said, but even she could hear it sounded like a moan, as his fingers slipped inside her.

'Don't fight it,' he whispered. 'You know you want it.'

'Oh God, yes,' she breathed heavily and opened herself up to him.

Chapter 26

David was breathing heavily. No, to be honest, he was panting. A weekly amble round the footie pitch was no preparation for full-on running. Or jogging. Or even trotting, which was all he could manage within minutes of leaving the house.

The diet of take-aways and beer had taken its toll, and after last night's over-indulgence at the party, his head felt like a brick, but Abigail's words spurred him on as far as the postbox at the end of the road, then he gave way and lapsed into a walk. Once he got his breath back he'd start again. His T-shirt was stuck to his back with sweat, he had a stitch and his calves felt as though they were on fire. He hobbled to the corner, then set off again. Only another five minutes and he could stop, turn back and cook a full English for himself and the twins.

It was early when Sarah made her way back through town towards Nathalie's apartment and the market was setting up. The traders glanced at her as she passed. Did she have the look of an adulteress? A woman who'd abandoned herself totally all night so now she was so tired she could barely walk straight? She hoped not and, slightly lightheaded, smiled cautiously at them, swinging her bag and listening to the early chorus of the birds up in the trees.

Knowing she had an important rehearsal later, she had slipped away, leaving Fabien sleeping. His face had been relaxed, his skin stubbly and his hair in a mop over his face. She'd paused for a moment, confused by her mixed feelings, elation and deep, deep guilt.

Carefully, she let herself into the flat, tiptoeing into the kitchen to make a cup of tea. Nathalie's cat jumped lazily off the sofa and came and wrapped itself around her legs and, as the kettle boiled, Sarah opened the shutters a little to let in the morning sun. A man was walking a dog across the square below her, a loaf of bread under his arm. What a gorgeous, gorgeous morning. She smiled to herself, gently rubbing her hands up and down her forearms where Fabien had kissed her.

Carrying her cup of tea, she padded across the hall to her room. Should she shower first? No, she decided, she'd wait until she got dressed later. Keep the scent of his body on her a bit longer. She yawned, and turned to find something on the bedside table to put the cup on. There, still in its small paper bag, was the postcard she'd bought from Fabien's shop for David. Unwritten and unsent. Resting her cup on a paperback, Sarah sat on the bed and slipped the postcard out then, lying back on the bed she held it, her eyes wide open, staring at the ceiling, and stayed like that until ten o'clock when she had to get ready to go out.

Chapter 27

'So, you like Arch Villains, do you?'

Claire started and looked up in surprise to meet the cool, appraising stare of a boy she'd seen round the campus. Tall, vulpine and thin to the point of emaciation, he was perpetually dressed in black with long straight hair in a centre parting and black eyeliner emphasising the pallor of his watchful, clever face. He was an original all right, the unspoken leader of a bunch of wannabees who hung around the darker recesses of the Union bar, talking, smoking, rarely smiling, except at each other.

She was surprised to see him here, alone, in HMV, where she had been listening to a track from the new album with the bulky headphones half on and half off, lost in the plaintive yet angry lyrics that were starting to get this band known. It was divine to escape from the thoughts that had whirled round her head since she'd opened that note in the early hours of last Sunday morning. It had been on the tip of her tongue all through the following day to blurt something out to her dad, but he'd made such an effort for the party and seemed happy to just have them there with him, that she couldn't bring herself to ask him if he knew.

'Er, yes. Yes, I do. It gets under your skin, doesn't it?'

He shrugged and raised an expressive eyebrow. 'Interesting choice of words. I saw them before they released their first album. It was raw. Kind of, er, Dionysian.'

She met his challenging look and thought quickly. 'Hmmm. Pretty dystopian, though. I mean, look at the sleeve art. It's got echoes of Kokoschka, hasn't it?'

There. She'd got him. He nodded slowly, bluffing. 'Maybe. Interesting.' But she saw his eyes flick quickly to the swirling lithographic image. 'So, you're not buying it, are you? Cos I've ripped it. I could, er, burn it for you if you like. Or you could download it off my laptop. Sometime. Y'know.'

She nodded, trying to look thoughtful. Trying not to smile. 'Yeah. Cool. Whatever.'

Somehow, they were walking out of the store together. She had to hurry to keep up with his long strides and she glanced sideways at him. He was staring at the ground, his long hair flapping over his face. 'So. What is it you do then? Art History or something?'

'Nah. Mediaaar. It's boring, though. You?'

He snorted. 'It's all boring. That's the point, isn't it? I'm doing English. Well, like you really. Just hanging out. I write poetry. Play in a band. You know. Just stuff.'

Claire nodded in sympathy. He was right. It was all just boring. 'I draw – mostly.'

'Yeah? Wanna show me some of your stuff?'

Claire thought quickly. She'd been sketching the pigeons on her window sill instead of preparing for a seminar that she almost certainly wouldn't go to. The charcoal drawings looked quite bold and harsh, reflecting the turmoil in her head; the lies and secrets, the ground shifting under her. She could show him those, rather than the series of detailed little life drawings she'd been working on, which depicted her lunch in various stages of being eaten. 'Yeah, sure. D'ja fancy a coffee? I've just got to buy some milk.'

He shook his head pityingly. 'Buy? That's a bit of an alien concept, isn't it? Wait here.'

He darted into a small supermarket, leaving her waiting and wondering on the pavement, then reappeared only moments later with his long coat wrapped tightly round his angular frame.

He strode off quickly and she stared after him, puzzled, until he turned and gestured her to follow with a sharp jerk of his head. She looked around fearfully, then ran after him.

Chapter 28

When the alarm went at six thirty, David was already stirring. He stretched luxuriously, then rolled out of bed and shrugged off his pyjama bottoms. He'd stopped wearing tops altogether – for some reason Sarah hadn't liked him to sleep bare-chested but he much preferred the feeling of being open to the elements. He stretched again and patted his stomach – or rather the place where his stomach used to be three weeks ago. He certainly didn't have a six-pack, nor was he aiming to get one, but the running was paying off. He was starting to look and feel better than he had in, well, years – sleeping well, no more indigestion, energy to spare. He'd really made headway with rebuilding the Alvis in the evenings instead of pigging out on fish and chips. He'd even had to dig out a belt to hold up his trousers. Progress.

He sorted quickly through the pile of clean washing he'd dumped on the floor by the door – what was the point of putting it away when he was going to use it anyway? – and pulled on pants, trackie bottoms and a T-shirt, then rummaged through the pile of sports socks for something approximating a pair. Downstairs, he shoved his feet into his trainers, ate a banana and had a glass of water, then set off. The new iPod he'd treated himself to fitted well into the arm-strap and the sports earphones were as comfortable as the bloke in the hi-fi shop had promised they'd be. David clicked the dial and selected his running tracks, illegally downloaded from an obscure website Tom had recommended last time he'd been home, and set off.

Focusing on the pavement ahead of him, he ran smoothly and economically, his body settling into the now familiar rhythm, with his footsteps, his heartbeat, his pumping arms fusing with the music in his ears. His breath came easily in the early-morning air and almost before he realised, he'd completed his circuit and, for the first time, felt he could have gone on. But work lay ahead and the promise of another initiative from Barry. He walked the final stretch of his route, to cool down, and let himself into the quiet house.

An hour later, showered, shaved and dressed in an unironed shirt, he arrived at work. Doreen wasn't at her normal station, which was pretty much a first as far as David could recall. He glanced around then looked over the reception desk. Her perpetual cup of tea was on a coaster next to her keyboard so she was in, at least. He shrugged and took the stairs two at a time.

Most of David's colleagues were in place already and a quiet hum of activity blended with the staccato sound of fingers on keys and the white noise of fans and air con. He look around. What a dismal spectacle. His sense of well-being started, very slowly, to evaporate and he sat down at his desk, face to face with the photograph of Sarah and the twins when they'd just left primary school. And where were they now? All three of them off in the big wide world and here was he, stuck in the same cubicle in the same office, still playing the safety game. He rubbed his face with his hands and turned the picture over onto its face.

The stack of papers in his in-tray looked even larger this morning than it had yesterday evening, when he'd left that little bit early to get to the Alvis parts place in Kenilworth. Surely those memos weren't replicating overnight? Dispiritedly, he tugged the file at the bottom of the pile and opened it with a sigh. He was downloading his emails, and flicking through the pages in the file, when a door burst open along the corridor that led to the meeting rooms.

'I don't think there's any need for that attitude, do you? All I'm saying is that I'd like you to check with me first before you book your holiday. It's a simple matter of courtesy. I don't think

I'm being unreasonable. I like to run a tight ship here and we all need to pull together. Do I make myself clear?'

David leaned across in his chair to try to see the victim of Barry's latest cliché assault. Doreen was walking hurriedly along the corridor towards him, her head down and her hands clenched into fists at her sides. He jumped to his feet and followed her through the double doors and down the stairs to reception, where she darted behind her desk and, bending down, started to search for something.

He approached cautiously. 'Doreen? Are you ... are you all right?'

A noisy nose-blowing sound emerged, followed by Doreen, suspiciously red-eyed.

'It's nothing. Well, not really. Just Barry being Barry.' She sighed. 'I'd booked for us to go away – me and Dougie – the same time we do every year. You know, David, it has to be regular for us because of ...'

David nodded.

'Well, it seems Barry wanted to schedule in some training days. He's got this American company coming in, and it all clashes. Silly really. I should have mentioned it probably, only I thought ...'

'The insufferable little shi ... Sorry, Doreen, but he is. Look,' he went on comfortingly, 'you stay put. Drink your tea. I'm going to have a word. I'm sure we can sort this out. It's probably just a misunderstanding. There's no reason you and Dougie should have to change your plans, Barry must see that.'

He took the stairs at a run again, indignation fuelling him this time. Doreen was the last person to demand special treatment to accommodate her husband's horrendous disabilities, and Barry of all people, who prided himself on his impeccable 'boss' credentials, should have been more sympathetic. He found Barry in the kitchen, filling the coffee machine while talking on his mobile, and he held his hand up to silence David as he started to speak. By the time he'd eventually finished his conversation with a 'ciao', he had a full mug of steaming coffee and gestured David to follow him to his office.

With the door safely shut behind them, David started. 'I ran into Doreen a moment ago, Barry, and you probably don't realise but she's pretty upset about this holiday business.'

Across the green leather-topped desk, Barry sipped his coffee appreciatively. 'Mmm. The finer things in life. That's what it's all about, isn't it? It's what we all want, and we all have to make sacrifices to get it. That's what people don't understand, you see. I have to think ahead for everyone here and make sure that we're all on message.' He held up his hand to ward off any dissent. 'I don't mind doing it, you do understand. I'm not complaining.'

'Right. About Doreen——'

'That's what I'm talking about, David. Sacrifices. Now, I don't expect everyone to put the company first. That would be silly——'

'Good, because, about Doreen——'

'So that's why I have to do the thinking for some of our' – Barry laughed shortly – 'less committed employees. And I don't mind doing that at all. I sometimes like to think of myself as a kind of father figure——'

'But Doreen and Dougie always——'

'Exactly! But change is good. And I think Doreen will come to see that when she calms down a bit. It's for the best. This American company are supposed to be absolutely——'

David took a deep breath. 'For God's sake, Barry, will you listen! Doreen *has* to go on holiday at that time, because they go to a special hotel that can cater for Dougie's special needs and it gives Doreen a bit of a break. And Lord knows, she's got more right to a break than any of us here.'

Barry shook his head dismissively. 'I think that's a rather sweeping statement——'

'No, Barry, shut up! Are you receiving me? Shut your bloody mouth and listen for a change.' David was aware that he was wagging his finger in Barry's face but he didn't seem able to stop. 'You lay off Doreen. Do you hear me? I don't care if you've got the Queen of bloody Sheba coming in to take the training. It doesn't even have to involve Doreen. What are you going to train her to do? Answer the phone faster? Clip on those poxy little visitors' badges more effectively?'

Barry stood up and brushed his hands together slowly. 'I don't think Doreen would appreciate your patronising comments, David. If she gave her job a hundred and ten per cent she could be a far more effective member of our team, and that's something she should be striving for. And she's not the only one who could do with improving their attitude, I might add.'

'Oh, what? Come off it, Barry. The attitude that needs changing round here is yours. Stop talking in sodding management clichés for once and try listening to people. Doreen doesn't want to be a more effective member of the team. No one in their right mind does. This is a job, Barry. That's all it is. Truly. We come to work, we do it, and we go home. End of story.'

The colour slowly drained from Barry's face and his lips compressed with rage. 'If that's what you think, David, then you haven't understood a thing I've tried to teach you since I was promoted. Yes, me, David, not you. You could have been a contender, y'know.'

It was all David could do not to burst out laughing, but Barry hadn't finished yet.

'But you tackle everything in the same half-arsed, don't-care way. And look where it's got you? I wasn't going to mention it, David, but you've forced my hand. Forced it! You're going nowhere. You've got an appraisal coming up, and I'm not happy with your commitment. It's all gone pear-shaped with you, David. I've been a patient man, I've not been unsympathetic, but I've had enough. There! I've said it.'

Anger rumbled up from the pit of David's stomach. 'Stop it now, Barry.'

'I won't. You've got to be cruel to be kind sometimes. I give this job my all, and when I go home, my wife's waiting for me there, appreciating the effort I put in for the family. These last weeks, you've been coming in here at all hours, you leave when you like, and you don't get on with your work even when you're here. And who do *you* go home to at night, eh?'

David knew, with absolute certainty, if he stayed in that room any longer, looking at Barry's ridiculous comb-over and nineteen-seventies moustache, he'd punch his lights out. 'Barry, you've gone too far,' he said quietly. 'You can take your stupid job and your fucking spreadsheets and your sodding training, and you can stick 'em where the sun don't shine. There – is that enough of a cliché for you? I'm handing in my resignation, right now. Got it? Right – I'm off.'

And he turned and walked out through the door, slamming it shut behind him. In the main office, he was greeted by a sea of astonished faces but, as he walked slowly back to his desk, wondering what the hell he'd just done, he saw Doreen clapping, smiling and crying all at once.

Rather sheepishly, some of his colleagues joined in, but it wasn't, David reflected later, a *Spartacus* moment. The applause petered out far more quickly than it had started, and David cleared his desk in almost total silence.

What in God's name had he done?

Iggy took a long swig from the wine bottle and passed it to Claire, who surreptitiously wiped it before taking a sip and passing it on to Animal. Okay, so they'd bonded in the few weeks since the milk shop-lifting incident. She'd even spent a couple of nights with him in his room. They hadn't actually done it, just had a grope and a fumble, Claire trying to convince herself she was attracted by his thin, white body, so different from high school boyfriends'. But she still wasn't sure she knew him that well yet – where she stood with him. He was so hard to read.

They were at the far end of the sports fields, sitting on the grass, although it wasn't really warm enough to do so. Bella cupped her hands tightly together and inhaled through the space left between her thumbs, the joint clamped between her little and ring fingers. Claire watched carefully. This was a method she hadn't seen before and it might render the smoke less chokingly acrid. She couldn't go coughing up her guts again. It was just too uncool.

'When you off to France, then, Claire?'

'Friday. It'll mean missing a seminar.'

Iggy snorted. 'What seminar? Oh – I forgot. Your conscientious brother.'

Claire didn't really like the sneer in his voice but she couldn't be bothered to say anything. And besides, Tom had been pretty boring about her new bunch of friends. He hadn't made any effort even to get to know them. And they certainly weren't too impressed by his hearty, outdoorsy girlfriend, Gemma. Come to think of it, Gemma hadn't exactly been friendly either and Tom hadn't said anything about that, so they were even.

'Yeah, my brother,' she said in as sarcastic a tone as she could muster. 'And my mum's doing this awful "finding herself" thing. God, it's going to be embarrassing.'

Bella laughed throatily. 'She'll probably be shacked up with some old French guy. And you'll have to call him "Papa". Hey, why don't you bring back some wine? It's really cheap over there. You can get it in cartons, like milk.'

Claire didn't answer. It hadn't occurred to her that her mother might have a boyfriend. Surely not? She couldn't. She just couldn't.

Animal, small and squat to Iggy's lean frame, with matted blond dreadlocks that looked filthy to Claire, took the spliff and inhaled deeply. 'You know,' he whispered, trying not to exhale too quickly, 'your mother'll probably be on a major guilt trip.

Mine was when she left my dad. I did pretty well out of it, as I recall. Take everything she offers.'

'What's your dad like, Claire?' Bella grinned. 'Is he fit? Some old guys are. Look at Johnny Depp. I bet he's all lonely and pining. It's a medical fact, y'know, men think about sex every three minutes or something. He must be gagging for it. How long since your mum left?'

'Aww, puh-lease.' Claire pretended to gag, but could feel tears starting in her eyes. 'Anyway, let's change the subject. My parents are so booooring.' *Which can't be said of my grandparents.*

'Well, they're more interesting than mine, I'll tell you.' Bella shrugged, picking at the hole in her tights with fingerless-gloved hands. Her legs looked scarecrow thin in her shorts, made only more so by the grimy white sneakers on her feet. 'What about you, Ig? What are your parents like?'

Iggy leaned back and rested his head on Claire's stomach. She hoped her tummy wouldn't rumble. 'Me? I haven't got parents. I hatched from an egg. Like a snake.' He rolled over abruptly and started to make hissing noises, his lips drawn back from his sharp white teeth. 'Who needs 'em? Except for money, of course.' And they all laughed. Even Claire.

'Out with your lover again tonight, are you?' Nathalie had teased Sarah mercilessly since that first morning when she'd feigned maternal disapprobation at Sarah's absence during the night.

'Yup.' Sarah smiled defiantly, opening the fridge to find some juice. Nathalie, as she often was these days, was preparing something on the stove, having discovered that Christian not only loved jazz but was also very fond of his food. When she wasn't chopping onions or garlic, she was down at the market selecting the ripest tomatoes or avocados. Sarah suspected that the plump strawberries she brought home in her basket were to be used in some kind of *9½ Weeks* sex game, but she really didn't want to know.

'He's gorgeous, isn't he?' Nathalie went on, popping a raw bean into her mouth. 'I bet you can't keep your hands off him.'

'No, you are wrong.' Sarah poured the orange juice into a glass and returned the carton to the fridge. 'He can't keep his hands off me!' And she scooted out to answer a knock at the door.

The last few weeks had been a haze of rehearsals and bed. And both got better and better. Quite often they hadn't even got as far as the bed. What she hadn't realised was that Fabien shared the apartment with a friend – a women Fabien described as 'needy' and 'down on her luck' – though Sarah had never met her. Fabien was vague, said her name was Valérie, and Sarah was left to imagine her from the toiletries in the bathroom and what must be her bedroom behind the closed door at the end of the corridor. But the possibility of her return at any minute gave their frantic trysts on the sofa or in the kitchen, with Sarah sitting on the worktop, an added frisson.

Sarah couldn't really believe herself. As she stood under the shower, letting the warm water run down her face and over her breasts, she realised she had never felt like this before. Well, perhaps in the early days when she and David had been all over each other, but they had been so young and naive and it had all happened in seedy digs or college bedsits. This was grown up. This was the real thing.

'Hello, beautiful.' Fabien kissed her hair as she opened the door for him, before following her into the kitchen. Cheekily he stole a mushroom from the chopping board and Nathalie playfully slapped his hand and said something fast in French, looking over at Sarah, her eyes sparkling. Fabien answered just as quickly and they both roared with laughter. Sarah smiled uncertainly, a bit irritated to have been excluded from their exchange.

'Let's go. I have booked a little place out on the coast so we need to get going.' He mentioned the name and Nathalie raised her eyebrows.

'Expensive. You must be worth it!' she laughed at Sarah.

'Oh, I am,' Sarah replied, pulling her cardigan around her shoulders. Though the days were warm now, the evenings could be cool, and she'd be grateful for it when they came back later in Fabien's car.

'By the way, I shall be staying at Christian's tonight so you love birds can have the place to yourselves, but behave.' She giggled. 'I don't want you embarrassing the cat.'

'That cat,' Fabien replied, taking Sarah's hand and heading for the door, 'has seen more depravity that any self-respecting pet should.' And they both bolted, just shutting the door in time before a potato hit it.

'Hi Dad, convenient to talk?'

'Of course, darling.' He sounded out of breath. 'Why wouldn't it be?'

Claire didn't take him up on it, the fact that it rarely seemed convenient. 'I just wanted to let you know that we're flying out after lunch.'

There was quiet at the end of the phone. 'You okay to get to the airport or do you want me to take you there?'

'Nah, it's miles out of your way.' Claire smiled. She knew he would have driven to Inverness had she asked him to. 'Anyway you'll be at work and the slave drivers don't undo your manacles until five.' She scuffed the tow of her shoe on a mark on the carpet, expecting him to laugh in agreement, but there was more silence.

'Um,' he started slowly. 'There's something I need to tell you. I've resigned.'

'What?' Claire felt a wave of fear. What was this? Another shattering of life's assumptions.

Her father's voice stalled and she could sense he was trying to sound nonchalant. 'I've been thinking about it for a while. You know, getting off the treadmill.' That sounded bogus. The treadmill was his *raison d'être*. 'It was a slight disagreement with Barry that precipitated it really. Just made me make a decision.'

Ah, thought Claire, so that was it.

'You were fired?'

'No, darling,' he assured her hastily. 'It was all my decision. But I did leave a bit smartish.'

She wasn't sure how to react, burying her own disquiet in concern for him. 'Will you be okay? I mean, have you got enough money?'

David laughed. 'You are an old worrier, aren't you, sweetheart? I'm fine. Honestly. Plenty tucked away to keep you two in the manner.'

Claire looked up as Iggy came towards her, strolling confidently knowing people were staring at him. 'Look Dad, I've got to go. I'll let you know when we get there.'

'Have fun, darling. Oh Claire, just one thing. Tell Tom by all means, but no need to mention the job thing to your mother, okay? She'll only worry.'

Chapter 29

Sarah strained to see over the heads of the crowd of passengers coming through the arrivals door. The twins' flight had been delayed and she'd had to sit for an hour on the scruffy square of grass outside the terminal reading a copy of yesterday's *Daily Mail* she'd bought at the airport shop. It was the first English paper she'd seen since she'd arrived, her only contact with British news being an occasional tune-in to the World Service, which she avoided because it made her feel inexplicably low. Now she gobbled up news of celebrity deaths and scandals with MPs and felt as though she'd been away for years.

By the time the board announced that the flight had landed, she was hopping up and down with anticipation. Naturally she saw Tom first, head and shoulders above the rest and, if it hadn't been for his floppy unkempt hair, he would have been the image of his father. It could have been the David of twenty years ago walking towards her.

'Darling!' She threw her arms around him, trying not to cry as that wouldn't do at all, and he dropped his rucksack to return her embrace warmly, swinging her round off her feet.

'Mum, you look fantastic!' He smiled broadly, his dimples as deep as ever.

'And you need a hair cut,' she laughed, kissing his cheek. 'Where's your sister?'

'Oh.' He turned. 'I thought she was behind me.'

Claire was the last through the doors, and Sarah almost overlooked her. Her clothes were even worse than normal: an eccentric mix of black vest, grey T-shirt and faded black jeans cobbled together and finished off with calf-high Converses. Her hair had grown and hung lankly around her pale face, which was made even more so by thick black eyeliner.

'Sweetheart ...' Sarah only just bit back blurting out how awful she looked. 'It's just lovely to see you. I've missed you so much.'

'Hello, Mum.' Claire let herself be pulled into an embrace but was unresponsive.

'You look like you could do with some sunshine.' There, that sounded safer. 'Let's get you back to Sauzils.' She led the way across the concourse and out into the warm day, bundled their bags into the boot of Nathalie's car, and chatted away nervously as she navigated the bashed little vehicle through the complicated route back to the A9. It seemed odd to have these two people with her now, so familiar to her they were like extra limbs, yet so out of context here. Tom, folded uncomfortably into the front seat, chatted back and explained about the hold-up, filling her in on the journey, asking how far it was to the apartment.

'Not far, we'll be there in no time. I'm getting quite good at finding my way about now actually.' She laughed. Her hopeless sense of direction had always been a family joke. 'I've booked us a lovely restaurant on a balcony for supper tonight. I've been there a couple of times and the food is fantastic.' She didn't say who with. 'We might get back in time to catch the end of the market. Oh, I wish you could stay longer.' She knew she was wittering on, but from behind her sunglasses she could observe Claire in the rear-view mirror as she looked sullenly out of the passenger window. Sarah shot Tom a sideways glance, her lips pursed in a way she knew he would understand, and he smiled and shrugged in reply.

By the time she parked in the square, she'd filled them in on Nathalie and the rotund Christian, playing up the stories of her cooking obsession. She'd described the orchestra, and Maurice – how much she wanted them to meet him – and the cellist with the squint. She talked too about Sauzils and what she'd discovered, trying to impress them with stories about the cherry harvest and how the first cherries of the season were always delivered to the Elysée Palace, hoping that would fascinate them as it had her. Tom had laughed in the right places, but the other half of her audience stayed resolutely silent, only grunting when Sarah enquired how the revision was going for the end-of-year exams.

'I'll probably scrape by.' Tom winced and she knew he wasn't joking. Unlike Claire who grafted to come top, Tom had always scraped by in life, but only because that was all he needed to do: the bare minimum, which left him time and energy to do the things he adored – the band, the sport, the partying. After they'd dumped their stuff and had a wash, they headed out to have a drink and browse the market, which was still in full swing. Sarah felt a warm sense of belonging as people greeted her and she introduced Claire and Tom. The garlic seller, his stall groaning under the weight of huge heads of juicy garlic on strings, waved and smiled toothily, calling something Sarah did not understand, his accent was so strong. Pascal came straight over to their table as they sat down, ignoring people who had clearly got there before them, which thrilled her enormously, and he even managed to make Claire smile with some joke about her wanting her English tea like 'peeess'.

As they waited for their order, Claire even commented on the beauty of the mottled bark on the plane trees and, as she glanced across the square, Sarah felt a sense of relief that Fabien's shop was firmly shut today. He'd told her last night that he was off to Toulouse to meet an artist; though he hadn't taken it too well when she'd suggested that it might be tactful if he stayed out of the picture over the weekend.

'You have left their father, haven't you?' he'd protested. 'They can't expect you to behave like a nun, can they?'

'No,' she'd sighed. 'But nor am I going to rub their noses in it' – an idiom that made him cringe when she explained what it meant.

As the busy Friday atmosphere of the town and the large cups of coffee began to work their magic, the children relaxed. Tom closed his eyes and tipped his face up towards the sun; Claire pulled her legs up and rested her chin on her knees. Putting her hand out, Sarah tentatively touched her daughter's arm, desperate to connect with her.

'It's lovely to see you, you know,' she said again.

Claire turned her huge eyes towards her. 'You too, Mum.'

'How's your dad?'

Claire took in her mother's freckled face and her tanned arms, soft and sleek under the straps of her sundress. Her hair, nearer its natural colour after the orange fiasco, was sun-bleached and appeared to be expensively cut, and she looked fresh and happy. In fact, she looked beautiful.

'I don't know how you dare ask.' Claire could hear the savage tone in her voice and watched her mother flinch in response.

'Claire.' Tom's voice held a stiff warning but Claire was fed up with the pleasantries now, no matter how lovely the town.

'No, Tom, we can't pretend it's all la la and happy. Dad's fallen apart and you know it!'

Tom leaned forward in his seat, aware they'd aroused the interest of the English couple at the table behind, and pushed his sunglasses up on to the top of his head. 'You seem very hung up on this, sis. Actually, I think Dad's okay. We had a great time at Grandpa's party and Dad seemed quite relaxed. He even danced with a woman who looked as though she was about to peg out.'

Claire shrugged. 'Oh, Tom, you just don't see it, do you? That's what it was meant to look like, but Dad's always been great at burying his head about things.'

'Amen to that,' muttered her mother, and looked down at her hands.

'Runs in the family, then, doesn't it?' Claire asked bitterly, angry with Sarah for criticising David, for being Mary's daughter even if she knew nothing of the affair with Anthony, and, most of all, livid with her for looking happy. Sarah turned a questioning look at Claire's tone, but before she could ask her what she meant, Tom was talking again, recounting the story of David's walking trip, embellishing it even beyond their dad's exaggeration.

'Oh God, Richard's always been the most pompous man unhung,' Sarah laughed. 'Dreadful humourless little berk. I can't think what your dad ever had in common with him. Yeats! Hah! David would have loved that!'

Claire felt immediately defensive. 'Well, it wasn't that bad – you're just trying to make Mum feel better. The house is a right mess, and he seems to spend all his time in the garage. And on your wedding anniversary he wasn't even home – probably out drowning his sorrows—' Tom shot her a warning glance and she stopped abruptly. Though he'd been as shocked as she was at the news, Tom had been happy to agree to the conspiracy of silence, at Dad's request, about leaving his job, though she couldn't see why it all had to be hush-hush. 'Mum will worry,' he'd said too, but why shouldn't she? Claire felt a bit peeved if she was honest. Surely Dad would want to have talked to her about it, but, whenever she called recently, he sounded distracted and she could hear the sound of spanners being dropped in the background. There was so much she wanted to say to him, but he always sounded as though he was straining to reach something – undo some ruddy nut probably – and there had even been moments when he'd put the phone down for a moment before coming back with a 'What was that, love?'

'Ah, he's finally doing something with that wretched car, is he?' Her mum's voice sounded amused and that annoyed Claire even more.

'Yes, he is. And why not? He's got nothing else to do.'

'I think he's going to that hill-climb thing,' Tom said vaguely. 'You know, that car event in Shropshire or is it Worcestershire – the one you used to drag us to when we were little?'

'Oh, I quite enjoyed that. Having a picnic in the sunshine and all the lovely old cars.' Her mother put her hand out again and took hold of Claire's arm a bit more firmly this time, not letting her pull away when she tried. 'Claire, if Dad is busy then that is great. I don't want him to miss me. We both needed to get away, even if Dad didn't realise it. It's not something you could possibly understand at your age—'

'Don't patronise me!' Claire folded her arms. Why did everyone seem so happy about this lousy situation? As the argument slipped away from her, she could feel the tears pricking behind her lids. Thankfully her phoned beeped in her pocket and, glad of the distraction, she pulled it out. It was a message from Jess asking how she was.

'Who's that from? A college friend?' Her mum too seemed glad of the change of subject.

'Nah. Just Jess.' Jess and she had been at school together since they had arrived on their first day aged four. She was so much part of the landscape that Claire knew she took her for granted. Good old dependable Jess, now working at a local insurance company. She'd always been the one who was there to go out with. The one who'd she'd shared first make-up and first periods with, whose house Claire had used as a second home, who always knew what she wanted and was happy with that – she'd never have found herself in a hole of a university doing something she hated. Not Jess.

'How lovely. Send her my love when you reply. It's ever so expensive to text from here, though. Hotmail is brilliant, isn't it? Means I can keep in touch. I ought to go online somewhere and check I don't have any messages on the home account, though I don't suppose I will. I'm not even sure I can remember the password. I think I wrote it down somewhere.'

Tom rolled his eyes theatrically. 'Come on then – are you going to show us round or what? We haven't come all this way to sit and drink coffee, you know!'

Sarah dropped some coins onto the tray with, Claire noticed, practised ease, and laughed at him. 'You are uptight Eeengleesh! You need to learn the way of the Med, young man.'

As one day stretched into another, Claire had to admit reluctantly that she was actually enjoying herself. The balconied restaurant had been enchanting, the vines that surrounded them intertwined with lanterns. The town seemed to come alive at night, and it wasn't just the copious amounts of wine that had helped her relax. Sarah, her own face flushed, had admonished her a little bit, but what the hell? She was a grown-up now. On Saturday they did a tour by car but, hot and uncomfortable, they decided to head back and, in Nathalie's flat, they'd had crusty bread and pâtés then headed for the *Musée*.

'You'll like this,' Sarah had said, tucking her arm into Claire's. Well, that was the understatement of the year. Why hadn't Mum mentioned *this* in her letters and messages? From the moment they stepped into the light airy foyer, tucked behind the traditional exterior of the building, Claire felt transported, her skin tingling with anticipation. She let Tom and Sarah go on ahead, they were chatting too much anyway, and drank in the atmosphere: stark white walls enlivened by bold canvases. Here were artists whose pictures she had pored over in books: Matisse and Miró, Chagall and mad Dali, and then, of course, Picasso, wonderful, genius Picasso. She almost didn't want to look in case she saw it all too quickly and it was over too fast. She watched her mother's retreating back – of course, she wouldn't have any idea how special this was to her; she'd never been interested in art. Claire's curiosity had been vaguely piqued by her stories about the orchestra – to Claire, Sarah's music had involved simply playing along to the dreadful squeakings of small children who came to the house for private lessons, delivered by pushy mothers – but that wasn't the same as art in this form, was it?

Claire stood for ages in each room, reading the catalogue and the information about each piece of work, until Tom came back. 'How long are you going to be, sis?' he asked impatiently.

'Ages yet. I've still got four rooms to go.' Let them wait. This was too good to miss.

'Well, our legs are aching, so we're going to the café. Meet us there?'

Glad to have shrugged them off, Claire lost herself once again, marvelling at the collections by artists she'd never heard of, then, before heading to join the others, she spent a fortune in the shop buying posters and postcards. That should brighten up the shithole she called a room at uni.

'The *Musée* was a hit with Claire,' her mother said indulgently over dinner later. They were tucked away at the back of a tiny little restaurant run by a friend of Nathalie's, who'd joined them tonight, all Chanel No.5 and rattling bracelets. Claire liked Nathalie. She liked her brashness and her vulgarity. She liked her chaotic bedroom where Claire was sleeping (Nathalie making room for them by staying at her bloke's), filled with necklaces and scarves, glittery shoes and the strong smell of perfume; she especially like the way she dressed and didn't seem to give a monkey's what anyone thought. She'd already said things about Christian's proclivities in the bedroom, which had made Tom blush beautifully and had earned a reproachful look from Sarah.

'It's quite something, isn't it?' Nathalie enthused. 'It's like living in Paris, though, and never seeing the Tour Eiffel even when it is on your doorstep. I went to the *Musée* once when I moved here but I haven't been since. Your mum appreciates art, though, don't you, Sarah?' Her tone was curiously pointed and her eyes twinkled as she looked at her mother.

'Er, yeah.' And Claire was certain her mother kicked Nathalie under the table.

The rest of the evening was hilarious, Nathalie trying to forge a major flirtation, on Tom's behalf, with the young waitress, despite his assurances that he was very happy with the dismal Gemma. Sarah had been full of questions about Gemma after that and Claire's attention wandered.

'Well, in that case we shall have to find someone for Claire, won't we?' Nathalie dragged her back into the conversation. 'Or do you have some boring boyfriend back there at home?'

'Nah.' She blushed, though she wasn't sure why. 'I've got a group I sort of muck about with.'

'Oh good,' her mother gushed, her face lighting up with the thought that Claire had finally found friends.

'They are known as the Gotham City Crew,' Tom put in, and Claire shot him a sideways glance. Thanks, mate.

'Meaning?' Sarah didn't look so sure now.

'Meaning they are Goths. You know, all drainpipe trousers and black eyeliner. Bloody odd looking.'

'Oh bugger off, Tom; they are my friends.' She stirred her coffee a little harder than was necessary.

'Yeah, but from what I've heard about them, you need to take care. That's all.'

There was a fluttering at the front of the restaurant as someone came in. '*Bonsoir!*' The owner rushed forward, arms outstretched, and greeted the new arrival. He was tall, with dark floppy hair and tanned skin and the sort of good looks that made people stare. Amazingly, he seemed to be heading for their table. Nathalie stood up and offered her cheek.

'Fabien!' she spoke very quickly in French and the man laughed deeply, then pulled up a chair beside them, as Nathalie introduced him to them as a friend of hers and their mother's.

'*Enchanté*. You look just like Sarah,' he said to Claire, scrutinising her under long dark lashes, but there seemed to be a sudden urgency in Sarah to get them home and they barely had time to finish their coffee before she was hustling them out of the door with excuses that they needed to get to bed, brushing off Fabien's offer to walk them home.

Later, when the flat was quiet, Claire gazed up at the ceiling where the streetlight from the square made patterns through the shutters. What, she wondered, had the expression on her mother's face meant when that man had walked in? It was all so confusing. This wasn't how she wanted to think about her parents, or her grandparents, for that matter. Claire thought about the little jewellery box. Of course, Sarah couldn't know about her grandparents' affair and nor could David. There was no way Sarah would have knowingly handed that bombshell to her daughter wrapped in a little note. Claire realised she was terrifyingly on her own with this one.

Sarah felt lousy all morning at the thought of them going, and by the time they headed off for the airport, she could barely speak in case she cried. Tom, sensing her mood, kept quiet too, except for light conversation about nothing in particular, and Claire spoke barely at all. Sarah gave them both the bag of goodies she'd put together – local honey and mustard for Tom, a necklace Claire had admired at the market and which she'd managed to buy quickly when she wasn't looking.

She found a space far too easily at the airport and was annoyed to see the flight was due to leave on time. Why couldn't she have had a delayed hour with them? She was fussing, she knew, when she kept asking if they had everything or wanted anything for the journey, and Tom was patient with his 'No, we'll be fine' until the flight was called.

She embraced them both tightly enough to stop them breathing and watched Tom wave and wander towards the plane. Claire, moving to walk away, turned back suddenly and, dropping her bag, threw her arms around her mother's neck again.

'When are you coming back?' she asked into her neck.

Sarah couldn't speak for a moment. She wanted to reassure her daughter more than anything, to take that expression of anxiety and hurt from her face. But it wasn't as simple as that.

'I don't know, darling,' she said eventually. 'I don't know.' Claire released her and backed away, then she picked up her bag and walked away without looking round. On their way home. It seemed so odd that they were heading back to what was her life really, but one that she now felt so disconnected from. It had certainly made the day of their anniversary easier to bear. So far from home, and with no one around her to remind her, she'd been able to bury it, forget about ways they'd celebrated in the past. Only Wilf, who'd called, had alluded to it but only in passing. Sensitive as ever. But now, being with the children, had sucked her back in and feelings were emerging she wasn't sure she wanted to explore. She turned away and walked back to Nathalie's car, jangling the keys in her hand.

Chapter 30

It was years since David had been to the Shelsley Hill Climb, but for the owners of classic racing cars it was one of the highlights of the season. For a start, it had been going on for over a hundred years, and it meant you could go out and have your car admired by a uniquely appreciative audience. There was always a chance a record might get broken – although it was very much an outside one. For those who weren't racing, it was just a lovely day out, loafing around on a hillside in the middle of the glorious Worcestershire countryside, while a succession of fantastically maintained cars took turns to zoom (hopefully) up a steeply curved swathe of tarmacked drive. For many, the cars were just an excuse to pack a picnic, meet up with old friends, and buy some obscure gifty thing for the car enthusiast. There was plenty to choose from at any one of the many stalls set up alongside the fields where the cars were parked in neatly controlled blocks.

David wasn't sure about going on his own, but it wasn't as if he had many calls on his time these days. Since walking out of the office, he'd spent two days in a state of abject shock and disbelief, followed by another two of complete terror, then he'd thrown himself into working on the Alvis like a man possessed. He was quite keen to show it off, although the upholstery still needed some attention. He had even started to put out feelers to see if he could get some work in one of the specialist garages he'd visited while doing it up.

He wouldn't make a fraction of his previous salary, but his needs were fairly simple these days, and he had salary in lieu of holiday he hadn't taken. But he'd felt so much better since that blow-out with Barry, that he hadn't regretted his snap decision for a moment. The reactions of his friends had been interesting. The men were all for it, especially Phil, who had known how frustrated David have been for some time. The women, however, were much more guarded, and they'd looked anxiously at their own husbands as if to reassure themselves that they wouldn't do anything so rash or financially imprudent.

David arrived at Shelsley good and early, after his usual run. He'd continued to increase his mileage and even he could see that he'd shaped up an awful lot. In fact, that morning he'd had to rummage around in the depths of his side of the wardrobe to find the jeans of days gone by, because the others actually fell down now. He'd laughed when he'd looked in the mirror and had seen his jeans hanging down round his hips and his boxers on show – just like Tom. All he needed was a leather jacket and some shades and he'd look like a middle-aged man in the rapacious clutches of a full-flown mid-life crisis. He shook his head in amusement.

The Alvis had coped well with its first outing for years, purring along the road and handling like a dream, but his hair hadn't. He'd tried to smooth it down but the effort was futile. It was too long anyway and, aware he hadn't shaved either this morning, he thought he must look a sight, but who cared? Once he'd parked and bought himself a bacon roll and a cup of tea, David settled down to the serious business of admiring the cars in contention for the hill climb: Morgans, Jags, MGs, even Tyrells, Ferraris, Minis, all in superb condition and raring to go. He strolled around, chatting with owners and enthusiasts, and recognising some familiar faces from years ago. The sun rose higher in the late May sky and he slipped off his jacket, rolling up the sleeves of his creased pale-blue shirt.

'David? David – is that you?'

The voice stopped him in his tracks, and he turned round to

see a tall, perspiring man, grinning broadly. 'Olly! I don't believe it.'

'Good lord! What is it? Six or seven years? More, I fear. Bloody hell, you're looking fit. You look younger than last time we met. Got a portrait in the attic or something?'

David laughed, but he couldn't help noticing the buttons straining on Olly's stripy shirt. 'Do you come every year? I haven't been since that last time – do you remember the D-Type Audi that Neil Corner demo'd?'

'Fancy you remembering that. I thought you only had eyes for the red triangle?' Olly turned round and scanned the area. 'Penny's with me somewhere. She brought her cousin along for a bit of female company. Is your better half with you?'

David hesitated, then remembered that Olly had barely known Sarah. How strange to meet someone who didn't see him as having half missing. 'Actually, we've split up.' God! It was the first time he'd put it quite so finally and even saying the words made him feel a bit unreal.

'Oh, bad luck. Are you here on your own, then? Join us. Please. Penny's packed enough to feed an army, as usual and, unlike you, I have to watch my waistline. You'd actually be doing me a favour. Where is the dratted woman? Penny? Over here.'

A woman in her mid-forties, neat and dark-haired, came over, a long-suffering expression on her face and a huge picnic basket balanced on her hip. She thumped it onto the grass and straightened up gratefully before looking at David with interest but no recognition.

'You remember David, love? An old regular from years back.'

Penny shrugged, smiled and offered a hand. 'You can't expect me to remember anything about these hill climb days. I switch off entirely, I'm afraid. Are you here on your own, David?'

Olly jumped in. 'David and his wife have divorced.' David winced but couldn't bare to correct him. 'He's here on his own so I said he might like to eat with us. That's all right, isn't it?'

'Oh yes, absolutely. I wonder where Kate's got to. Shall I text her?' Penny turned away and started jabbing at her mobile then turned back to David with a brilliant smile. 'David, my cousin Kate is here with us, do you think you could carry the picnic basket for her, because she wants to find exactly the right spot for us to eat, so we can see the hill but not get too much noise or interruption. Would you mind?'

David shrugged. 'Of course not. It's the least I can do, since you've been kind enough to offer your hospitality.'

David attention was distracted by a woman making her way through the crowd. Tall and dressed in tight jeans with a sort of gypsyish white blouse pushed low on her shoulders, she was weaving her way through the cars and knots of admirers giving flirtatious little glances as she went, and turning plenty of heads – no mean feat in such a gathering where four wheels usually held more appeal than two legs. David followed her with his eyes only gradually realising, as she wove ever closer, that she was coming right over to them. He swallowed.

'Ah, Kate, there you are. This is David, an old friend of Olly's. He's kindly volunteered to be your sherpa while you scout out the optimal spot for the picnic.'

'Oh hi, Dave! Thanks.' Her Australian accent and broad, open smile seemed as exotic, in this context, as a bird of paradise. She tossed two long, dark plaits back over her shoulders and extended her hand, brown and firm, shaking his and meeting his helplessly admiring gaze with an amused one. 'C'mon, let's go exploring. I'm not too familiar with the wildlife over here yet. Could you protect me from poisonous snakes if it came to it?'

David lifted the picnic basket and paused. He glanced at Penny and Olly who were now involved in intense discussion and turned to face her. 'I think I can handle that, yes. No need to be afraid. You'll be perfectly safe.'

She glanced sideways. 'That's just what I'm afraid of.'

And they burst out laughing.

Chapter 31

Sarah's annoyance with Fabien for turning up uninvited at dinner hadn't lasted long. He'd looked as sheepish as a little boy on Sunday night, claiming he couldn't resist meeting her children, and had expressed amazement that she was old enough to have children that age.

'Oh bugger off, you charmer.' She'd tickled him under the duvet. 'Don't give me that hackneyed old line.' He had looked bemused and she couldn't be bothered to explain, much more interested in investigating what else was under the duvet.

To make up for it, he'd promised a round of dinners out, days on a friend's boat on the Med and they even talked about a weekend in Barcelona. Sarah was excited. This is what she had come to France to do.

At work at Maurice's later in the week, Sarah thought back over the weekend. The children's visit had definitely been a good thing and her contact with Tom had increased since. Now she felt she really had something she could say to him, instead of having to explain what she was talking about in her emails. She could update him on the man with the three-legged dog they'd made up stories about while eating breakfast at a café on the first morning of their stay, or Nathalie's new foray into baking pastries, which had resulted in something that the French army might consider deploying in a mortar attack.

There was less contact from Claire, but Sarah persisted, sending off supportive messages to help her through the impending exams. Claire's lack of contact and the complete absence of any information about university life was starting to disturb Sarah.

When they'd pored over course details round the kitchen table all those months ago, Claire had accepted that art school was a bad idea and seemed perfectly content with the media course. 'It will be convenient for everyone,' she'd said. 'You know, for you and Dad to have us both at the same place. It makes sense and I can keep an eye on Tom.'

Sarah rested her chin in her hand and looked out of the window beside Maurice's computer, which he'd kindly allowed her to use to Hotmail the children. Should convenience have even entered into the equation?

'Would you have travelled anywhere to do what you wanted to do?' She asked Maurice later when he came back. His study was now pretty ship shape, the dead wood thrown out and the filing cabinets crisp and alphabetical and in order. Her time with him was nearly done, and she'd have to start thinking about other work. If she was going to stay.

'Yes, of course I would,' he replied without a second's thought. 'Things don't come to you, or at least only for the very lucky. I washed plates in Vienna for six months just so I could study under one particular conductor.' Sarah tried to imagine what he'd been like when he was young – charming and intense and romantic, she suspected. She'd met his wife briefly when they'd gathered in a bar for a drink after a particularly onerous rehearsal. A short, stout German woman, she was gaspingly plain, especially among these slight and wiry musicians. Like a doughnut on a bed of lettuce. 'Why do you ask?'

'Oh, I was just thinking about my daughter and whether she is happy.'

'Ah.' He nodded, putting down the papers he was carrying on top of a pile on the floor. 'The question at the centre of every parent's mind.'

'Oi!' Sarah stepped forward and he jumped back. 'Don't you dare pile them up there!' I've just cleared that area!'

'Good 'eavans, I had no idea you were such a harridan, Sarah,' he said with mock horror. 'I am so sorry. I shall have to take great care from now on.' Slowly, with theatrical precision, he made his way over to a table and placed the pile down carefully. 'Will that do, *madam*?' he asked with heavy sarcasm and a cod English accent, and Sarah smiled and shook her head with despair. She was wrong, Maurice was an on-going project.

Despite Fabien's attentions, the rehearsals had to come first now, and went on later in the evenings as the date of the Festival loomed. Maurice went up a gear in the pressure he put on the orchestra, and had a young flautist running out of the room sobbing after he had slammed down his baton, screeching something at her which Sarah couldn't understand, but which had something to do with her repeated failure to come in on time in bar twenty. Maurice's instructions in French were hard enough for Sarah to follow, but as he became more and more tense so he became more and more unintelligible. She felt as though she was permanently raising her bow in the air for clarification and he was patient enough most of the time, except for once when she asked him what he'd meant and he'd barked, 'That was for the low brass. Mind your own business!' Sarah had cowered and kept quiet, glancing at the others and following their lead much of the time, but she also knew she had never played better. The sound of the piece, now they had practised together so often, was becoming close to magnificent, and each time they rehearsed the slow movement she could feel the hairs stand up on the back of her neck. She'd never played with such skilled musicians and she knew she had raised her game to join them.

Tonight's rehearsal had gone particularly well and, as she packed away her fiddle, loosening the bow and slipping it into its case, she spotted Fabien slouching on a chair at the back of the hall, his hands in his pockets. She smiled at him, but he was gazing around, yawning expansively.

Geneviève at the desk next to Sarah leaned over. 'Looks like you have an admirer waiting for you.' She nodded in Fabien's direction. Maurice, who had come to collect the scores and was standing close by at that moment, looked over too and frowned.

'Mmm, Fabien Renard.'

'Do you know him?' Sarah asked brightly, delighted that there was a connection. She hadn't even thought to ask.

'Oh yes.' Maurice slipped the scores together and shuffled them into a neat pile. 'Everyone knows Fabien Renard.'

'He's gorgeous, *n'est-ce pas*?' Geneviève continued, staring unashamedly.

'You can tell you are an out-of-town girl, then,' Maurice continued, waving at the bassoonist who was calling goodnight.

'What do you mean?' Sarah felt unease in her stomach.

'He is …' Maurice thought for a moment. 'He is like the fox of his name:. Clever and cunning. No one is a greater admirer of Fabien Renard than the man himself.' And he moved away to talk to the horn player. There was silence between Geneviève and Sarah.

'What does he know?' Geneviève asked eventually. 'He looks delicious to me.'

Sarah laughed uncertainly. 'See you tomorrow.' And she headed towards the back of the hall.

'God, how much longer was he going to keep you?' Fabien pulled himself up from his seat, handed her the handbag she'd left at the back with everyone else's, and directed her towards the door. 'I have a table booked at Le Singe Noir.'

'Oh Fabien,' she sighed, 'have you really?' He had gone on about this restaurant for weeks but tonight she would really have preferred to stay in. All she'd had since the beginning of the rehearsal was the bottle of water she'd shot in to buy at a shop while Fabien waited in the car outside, and she was desperate for a cup of tea. Her shoulders ached from tension and she wanted to lie in a bath and then pick at something from the fridge. 'I really need to get home and freshen up. I feel all sticky. Will we have time?'

He sighed. 'If you are quick.'

The evening was not a great success. The restaurant was as lovely as he had described, with a terrace overlooking the sea and an atmosphere of exclusivity. The prices, too, reflected what a treat this was, but Fabien seemed quiet and pensive, Sarah would almost say sullen, and she wasn't really in the mood either. But she chatted on, trying to please him and make him laugh, and eventually he put his hand over hers and told her how lovely she was.

'You look like a different woman to the one I met all those weeks ago.' Then he leaned over and whispered something in her ear that made her blush.

'Well, that probably accounts for the permanent smile on my face,' she whispered, though under the table she had her fingers crossed, hoping he would just drop her back at the apartment tonight and go back to his place. Much as she liked sleeping with him, barely a night went by without him intercepting her as she came out of the bathroom after cleaning her teeth or his hand inching up her thigh even as she was dropping off to sleep. He was exhausting too, wanting to do things with her that, when she thought about them the following day, must have looked ridiculous. What was it with men and fantasies? But rather than come across as boring and middle-aged by turning him down, she always went along with it; she'd woven the story, worn the stockings and the lacy knickers.

'What about these?' he'd whispered in her ear only two nights before, slipping something from a bag beside the bed. At first she hadn't been able to work out what they were – did they make thongs that small? It wasn't until she'd slipped them on that she realised they were crotchless panties and had been about to shriek with disbelief that he could forget it, when his face had darkened into an expression that was a disturbing mixture of passion and aggression, and she'd played the game, burying a vague feeling of disquiet.

'Fabien, do you mind if I just go in on my own tonight?' she asked when they pulled up outside Nathalie's apartment, her hand on the door handle. He'd eventually cheered up, had pulled out a wedge of cash to pay for the meal and, spurning her insistence that she drive, assuring her he hadn't had too much wine, had driven back at high speed, his hand on her thigh all the way.

'You sure?' he asked quietly, slipping his hand further up and under her skirt She could feel herself beginning to tingle and respond, but she fought it, wanting only to rest her head on her pillow and sleep.

'I'm sorry.' She kissed him on the lips and, before he could stop her or she could be dissuaded, slipped out of the car and into the apartment. Her heart sank a bit when she could hear the TV on and found Nathalie curled up on the sofa with the cat. She didn't want to talk. All she really wanted was a cup of tea. Made just the way David made it.

'I didn't expect to find you home.' She dropped her bag on the floor and pulled off her shoes, a pair of high and pinching pink suede stilettos Fabien had bought her. 'No Christianity tonight?'

'No, he's playing at the club, and there's only so much faking enthusiasm for jazz improvisation that I can manage.' She sighed dramatically. 'There's some chocolate gateau on the side if you're interested.'

'Oh God, I couldn't. I'd burst.' Sarah undid the button of her skirt and, walking through to her bedroom pulled it off, along with her top, and slipped on her dressing gown.

'Nice time?' Nathalie called.

'Yes, thank you. We went to Le Singe Noir. Very good food.'

'*Merde!*' Nathalie exclaimed. 'Fabien must be making some money on the side, or selling cheap prints is proving very profitable.'

Sarah yawned. 'I'm knackered, though, I have to say. And no! It's not what you think. Maurice is pushing us so hard at the moment and it's exhausting me. You are going to come to the concert, aren't you? I can get cheaper tickets, I think.'

'I wouldn't miss it for the world. You know that.'

Sarah poured some juice into a glass, and kept her back to Nathalie. 'Talking of Maurice. Fabien came to collect me tonight and Maurice saw him. He said he suited the name Renard and was in love with himself. He wasn't very polite at all really.'

'Oh, ignore him.' Nathalie waved away her comment airily. 'He's just a jealous old man with a dog-ugly wife who can't compete with a man as handsome as Fabien.'

'Well ...'

'No, honestly, Sarah. People have lots of reasons to say things that are because of their issues, not based on the reality. Men like Fabien don't come along very often and you're very lucky you have nabbed him. There are a lot of women who'd happily jump into his bed in your place. Make the most of it, girl!'

'But, how can I make the most of it, Grandpa?' Claire whispered as loudly as she could. 'I don't like the course or the people or the place. It's like living in something from *1984* – all concrete and blocks numbered A, B and C, and half the other students don't even speak English!'

She could hear Wilf sigh at the other end of the phone and she slid down the wall until she was sitting on the floor in the corridor. 'I don't know how I can help, darling. I never went to university,' he said gently. 'In my day you had to be a real boffin – no disrespect to you, of course. You're a very clever girl – so I left the grammar and went into an office and didn't come out until I was sixty-five and wrinkled.' Claire giggled. It was such a treat to speak to him. When the boy from the room below had called up to say her grandfather was on the phone, her first reaction was to tell him to say she was out. How could she sound normal on the phone, armed with this explosive knowledge about Granny? But the moment she'd heard his voice she realised how good he was to talk to. Nothing could change that.

'Have you spoken to Mum and Dad about how you feel?' He went on.

Claire snorted. 'Nah! Mum asked but I sort of fluffed around the subject – I mean, she doesn't want to be bothered with this and Dad has his head in an engine all the time—' She broke off. Did he know about Dad's job?

'Of course they want to be bothered, but how will they know unless you tell them? Very few things in life are for ever and can't be changed. Except tattoos, of course.' He added as an afterthought. Claire's heart beat faster – how the hell did he know? – silly, of course he couldn't, and she tentatively touched the butterfly at the top of her arm, the skin still tender around it, just to remind herself it was still there. She wasn't entirely happy she'd had it done, but Bella had been so insistent that they all had one.

'Your dad mentioned about the car thing when he came over last Tuesday. Sounds like he's all fired up about it. I thought he was looking good too – with all that weight off him.'

So Dad hadn't mentioned anything. Why not? Why did everyone pussyfoot around? 'He didn't tell you he's jacked in his job, then?' she asked, getting some perverse pleasure from lobbing in that particular grenade and waiting for the fall-out.

There was a pause down the phone. 'Has he indeed?' Wilf asked after a while, nonplussed. 'That's brave.'

'That's mad, Grandpa!' Claire protested. 'What's he going to live off?'

'No, it's not mad. And it's not before time. Sometimes you can get so entrenched in a situation that you can't bring yourself to make the change. It's part fear and part blindness. It takes courage to make a change, darling, but maybe it's something you should think about for you. But enough of that. I'm just an old buffer, what do I know? Tell me, what are your friends like?'

Not what you'd expect, thought Claire. 'Oh, okay. Quite nice. Jess is coming up for the night later, though. She finishes work in Stratford at five so she'll be here by seven.'

'That'll be nice. She's a lovely girl. Now I need to run along, dear. I'm meeting a friend for a walk by the river and I only wanted to say hello.'

'What friend?' Claire felt a little peeved to be brushed off.

'A lady friend, actually. I met her at an event at the Civic Hall. She'd called Sally.'

'A girlfriend, Grandpa? You old goat!'

'No, Claire.' He laughed gently. 'A lady friend. Someone to play backgammon with or bore on to about my sciatica. It can get lonely on your own sometimes.'

No shit, Sherlock, thought Claire, after saying goodbye warmly and going back into her room. Even Jess's imminent arrival wasn't much to look forward to. She'd been asking for ages if she could come up and Claire had finally caved in – but what the hell was she going to do with her? There was some boring film on at the Arts Centre, and she certainly couldn't introduce her to Iggy, even though he'd said to bring her along later for a drink. Jess wasn't their type at all. Strongly suspecting she herself wasn't either, if they only knew, Claire took in the unopened books on her desk, and, sighing deeply, slouched down into the chair and opened the first one. '... equip you with the theoretical and practical tools to examine the relationships we have with contemporary institutions, media forms and practices, and communications and cultural institutions,' she read. It was as if all her hens had come home to roost. That vague feeling of unease she'd had from the moment the university UCAS forms came through and she'd had the letter of acceptance was now a jangling, deafening warning bell. This was not art school. This was not what she wanted to do, but she could see no way out.

She'd wasted everyone's time and her parents' money. They'd be livid – that is, if they had time to notice.

Slamming shut the book, she looked up at the poster from the *Musée* Blu-Tacked on her wall. It was a black-and-white photograph of Salvador Dali wearing what must have been a brightly patterned shirt, sitting by the sea, his head thrown back in an arrogant pose that said 'Look at me, I'm at the top of my game.' Well, I'm right at the bottom of mine, thought Claire, suddenly standing up and grabbing her jacket. Stuff this for a game of soldiers, I'm off for a spliff. Dutch courage. And she went out of the door, slamming it behind her.

Jess pulled up in her little Peugeot outside the accommodation block right on seven, just as Claire knew she would. Claire could see her through the net curtains at the window, and stood in front of the mirror for a moment, feeling a bit dizzy and light-headed, which wasn't very surprising. Iggy had finally answered her text asking where he was, after she'd tried all the obvious places, and she'd unearthed him on the other side of Campus in a block she'd never been into before. She'd knocked tentatively and the door had been opened to reveal a small room, much like her own. And there was Iggy, lost somewhere behind five or six bodies and a fog of sweet dope smoke. She hadn't stayed long, intimidated by the people she didn't know and who barely glanced at her, and getting no support from Iggy, who was slumped in the corner, out of his head, his skinny arm draped around a girl she didn't recognise who he snogged virtually incessantly. She was surprised by how little she cared, but she did manage to nick a couple of drags from his joint, though, which he had silently proffered, saying only ''Bout time you bought some, innit?' as she slipped out again.

'Jess, how lovely to see you!' She flung her arms around her friend a little too enthusiastically, and made a mental note to calm down or Jess would think she had gone mad.

'Claire!' Jess, a little plump in her jeans and V-necked T-shirt with a little lace camisole, embraced her back and Claire flinched as she pressed down on the raw tattoo. She smelled fresh and clean. 'Look at you, girl, you've gone even trendier! You make me feel like a right country mouse.' That's cos you are, thought Claire, a little astonished by her own cattiness.

'Phew! They don't go in for decoration, do they? Is it any better on the inside? I suppose you can get posters up and stuff – make it really cosy. Actually, I've got you something for your room – little pressie. Hope you like it!'

Claire could imagine what the little pressie would be like – pink, sparkly, girlie. Typically Jess, in other words. How would it look with the band posters, the grafittied sheet she'd fixed to the wall and the postcards of vorticist art she'd Blu-Tacked in a line all round the room. She felt a surge of guilt. 'That's so nice of you. You shouldn't have – really. It's just as grim inside. And the rooms are tiny. You can have my bed – have you got a sleeping-bag in that bag? It looks like you've got the kitchen sink! Come on, let's dump your stuff and we'll go and find a drink.'

Jess didn't say much about Claire's room, and for the first time, Claire could see it through someone else's eyes. It smelled bad, for a start: of stale washing, sour milk and cigarettes. Claire threw open the window and avoided Jess' eyes. The view wasn't helped by the headless doll that Iggy had stood on the window sill. He'd thought it was so funny, and had wrapped it up and presented it to her as if it was a gift, and he'd laughed and laughed and so had all the others when she'd torn off the paper. And she'd laughed too, although she'd felt like crying. There were clothes all over the floor, the decoration she'd put up, she had to admit, made the gloomy little room more oppressive still. She felt a wave of despair.

Chapter 32

David had just got in from the shops when the phone rang. Dumping the carrier bags on the floor, he grabbed for the receiver. 'Hello?'

There was a pause. 'Er, hello. I'm trying to get in touch with David Lewis. Have I got the right number?'

Her accent was unmistakeable, but she sounded surprisingly hesitant. David felt a rush of pleasure and anticipation. 'Yes, this is David. Kate? Is that you?'

'Yes! Oh great. That's a relief. I hope you don't mind. I got your number from Olly.'

'No, it's lovely to hear from you. Er, how are you?'

She laughed – the full, throaty laugh he'd heard at Shelsley, and had thought about since. 'I'm good, thanks. Really good. You? Whatcher been up to?'

'Oh, you know, this and that. I stopped working recently and I've been catching up on all the things I've been meaning to do for ages. Working on the car, getting out to see old friends.' David squeezed his eyes shut. That sounded rather more constructive than it actually was, but Kate didn't need to know that he'd been doing all the jobs round the house that Sarah had been on at him about for years, doing more work on the car, watching cricket in the afternoons on Sky, and steadily increasing his mileage with the eventual aim – unthinkable only months ago – of doing a charity half-marathon at the end of the summer. As for the old friends – well, none of them were around during the day, since they still had proper jobs, and he could tell that his mates' wives were starting to regard him as a potentially subversive influence on their house-trained partners. 'How about you?'

'Oh – loads of stuff. I'm trying to pack in as much as I can before I go on my way. I've been doing a bit of waitressing, just to stoke up the finances, but I want to see everything, so I've been up to London a couple of times. Done all the sights. I've been to some great gigs too. The music scene is amazing here. I've been going to yoga classes, and I'm crewing for some old guy I met the other day – he's sailing his yacht over to Portugal, and he needs help, so I thought, hey, why not? He's going to pay my airfare back too.'

'Wow – that's amazing. Do you ever sleep?'

There was a short pause, then her voice came, warm and amused. 'Why, yes, I do sleep – occasionally. But I can usually think of something better to do. So – anyway ...'

David felt he was teetering on the edge of a cliff. Should he take the step? Could he? Why shouldn't he? Why the hell shouldn't he? 'So, er, Kate, would you ...? I was thinking, it might be ... Maybe we could—'

'Oh, thank goodness! I was afraid you were going to give me the brush-off. You English guys are so hard to read. Yes, whatever you were going to ask, I'd love to. Are you free next Tuesday?'

David pushed his hair back and smiled broadly. He felt suddenly exhilarated. 'Yeah, Tuesday would be great. Shall I come and pick you up? We could go for lunch somewhere. There's a lovely pub by the river just outside Oxford. Have you been to Oxford yet?'

'No, but it's on my list. That'd be great, Dave. Let me give you my address ...'

As David wrote it down, he was still telling himself that he was just being friendly to a relative of an old friend who happened to be staying in the same town. Just showing the sights to a foreign visitor, passing through. But at the same time, he was thinking that, in Oxford, there was very little chance he'd run into anyone who knew him. Or Sarah.

Feeling very loving and matey towards her friend, Claire tucked her arm into Jess's and they headed off towards the Union building.

'How's things in the whacky world of insurance then?' Claire asked, dipping her finger into the froth of her lager and licking it off. Jess was sitting very upright and looking around her, fascinated.

'Oh, all a bit dull compared to this, I expect.' Jess sipped her coffee. 'But I've applied for a promotion – into the underwriting department. Bit more money, cos I want to start saving for a house. Can't live with Mum and Dad for ever.'

'Oooh, how grown up.' Claire took a swig, the taste unpleasant on her tongue. 'Why don't you move in with what's-her-name – you know, the speccy one who threw up on that school trip to Birmingham?'

'Stacey?'

'Yeah. Didn't she rent a flat or something?'

'No, her mum died and she moved back in with her dad. Don't you remember?' Jess's expression was puzzled.

'Nah, don't remember that. And how's Debbie? Still with that jerk who sold cars?'

'Stuart? They're getting married. Come on, Claire, you must know that! Didn't you get an invite? We're all going. The reception's at some lovely hotel near Broadway. I went with her to choose the dress. Oh, it's beautiful.'

Claire felt a mixture of disappointment that she hadn't been asked – but then she hadn't been in touch with Debbie since A-levels – and relief that she wasn't going to have to endure some sickly wedding with bridesmaids and pink flowers and confetti. 'Wouldn't wanna go anyway, to be honest,' she laughed, and then, thinking of something, began to giggle. 'Hope the bridesmaids don't wear orange! What with Debbie being a ginga and all!'

Jess didn't smile. 'We are actually. And it's apricot.'

Claire couldn't stop herself and burst into painful giggles. After that, the conversation was a bit stilted, and Claire could feel herself getting sleepy. She waved at a girl she recognised from her seminar set but she glanced away. Perhaps she didn't know who she was.

Claire looked back at Jess and the laughter fell from her face. This was never going to work. Jess, with her neat hair and her lip gloss, stuck out a mile. She'd tried so hard, but it was all wrong. For the first time, in all the years they'd known each other, Claire felt ashamed of her best friend.

It was harder to know what Jess was thinking. When she'd set eyes on Claire earlier, there had been an expression of – what? – disapproval? Concern? Their lives were so different now.

'I'm not keeping you from revising, am I?' Jess asked anxiously after a while.

'God no! Anyway, I haven't done a thing. Don't really care about it.' She picked at the black nail varnish now almost completely peeled off her short bitten nails.

'That's not very good, is it?' Jess asked. 'I mean, I don't really know about these things, but aren't the first-year exams important?'

''Not really. And anyway they'll be a breeze. The whole course is just bullshit about magazines and newspapers. I'll buy a copy of *Heat* before I go in.'

Jess frowned again and was distracted by the bizarre vision that was Animal coming towards them, his T-shirt ripped and his black jeans tight over his stocky legs. He ruffled Claire's hair.

'Hi, Cas. This your mate? There's a party over in Kendal tonight. Block 6. You comin' or what?'

'Certainly am.' Claire smiled. This would show she had mates. 'You up for that, Jess?' Jess's face had an expression of uncertainty but she shrugged acceptance.

'Sure, should we bring some wine?'

Animal threw back his head and laughed, without replying, and Claire laughed with him.

'Can you show me round a bit?' Jess asked, as they made their way from the café. 'Like where you go to your lectures.'

Oh, Christ. Claire was having trouble remembering herself, and racked her brains as they went round the campus.

'And this is the media resources block.' She tried to sound blasé as they wove between the buildings, avoiding students on bikes.

Jess was gazing round her, open mouthed, at the glass and steel structures towering above them, each named after some rich benefactor or other. Claire could see how impressed she was. Well, she herself had been impressed when she'd come here for her interview, but now she wasn't sure she cared.

'Miss Lewis. Can that really be you?'

Claire spun round. Shit! That had been the risk of coming here – running into one of her lecturers.

She smiled uneasily. 'Hello, Dr Routledge.'

The short, thin man with his normally smiling, rather wrinkled face, who had interviewed her all that time ago, feigned surprise. 'So you remember my name! I thought you must have been struck down with amnesia. Tell me, have you received the notes and emails I've been leaving you?'

'Er ... Not sure.' Claire thought about the succession of letters she'd peeped at without taking them out of the envelope, and the emails she'd deleted.

'Well, there have been plenty of them. We need a little chat, you and I. I think you owe me ...' He stopped and went through a pantomime of counting up on his fingers. 'Well, do you know how many essays you've failed to turn in so far? I don't think I've had one since January. You've got a good deal of catching up to do. Those essays will form part of your module assessment for the year, on top of the exams. You have heard you have exams coming up, haven't you? Next week, as it happens.'

He stopped, and looked at her with a mixture of exasperation and indulgence. 'Come on, Miss Lewis. You made a very promising start to the year. Don't throw it away.'

Claire was looking at the ground, aware that Jess had witnessed it all. She could feel the threat of tears and bit her lip hard. 'I understand,' she mumbled.

'Listen, come and talk to me. I don't bite. If there's something bothering you, just come and tell me. Pretending it's not happening won't make it go away. You're going to have to deal with whatever it is sooner or later. And believe me, later is always worse. Make an appointment with my secretary on Monday.'

Claire nodded silently, and he strode into the building at a vigorous pace. Jess said nothing as they walked back to the hall of residence.

'Why haven't you been going?' Jess asked eventually as they sat with a cup of tea made with some milk that was definitely on the turn.

Claire sighed. 'Because I hate it.'

Jess frowned. 'What, the course or the place?'

Claire looked around the room and out of the window and the nothing view. 'Both really, but especially the course. It's not what I want at all.'

'Well, couldn't you ... I don't know ...?' Jess stumbled a bit. Bless her for trying to help, thought Claire, but what did she know?

'It's not like changing your job, you know. There's all the complications and Dad and Mum, and Tom, of course.' Not to mention the detail of Granny and Grandpa's little tryst, too appallingly shameful to discuss here.

'Tom wouldn't mind! Seems to me that he's the one getting the best out of the place and you're the one suffering because you thought it would be easier if you were both at the same uni, you said so yourself last summer. That was your whole reason for coming here.'

Claire rubbed her eyes and yawned. 'I know, I know. But what does it matter now? It's only a degree. I'm sure I can stick it out.' The thought made her head ache, though.

Jess shrugged. 'That's up to you, but stop trying to please everybody all the time, Claire.' She put her hand on Claire's arm. 'Three years is a big chunk out of life to waste doing the wrong thing.'

A couple of hours later they set off for Kendal block. Claire had fallen asleep on her bed so she wasn't sure what Jess had done in the meantime, but when she woke, Jess had changed into a skirt and white top. She had mentioned earlier that she was hungry and asked if they were going to eat, but Claire couldn't think of anything – supper these days was usually a Pot Noodle or a bag of crisps, but at least it meant she could fit into tight, tight drainpipes like Bella's. Jess must have gone to the shop because she had a bottle of white wine tucked under her arm.

'How was the trip to the South of France, by the way?' she asked as they headed across the campus lawns in the twilight, the thump thump of music coming from various open windows.

'Crap. I think Mum has some fella. Or at least some froggy creep turned up and she got all embarrassed.'

'Oh. I saw your dad in town the other day. He looked great – much thinner and sort of younger.'

Claire shrugged. 'Whatever. Come on, it's in here.' The party was spread over several rooms and a corridor. Claire recognised hardly anyone, but, taking Jess's arm, made her way through the crowd towards a table where there were some cans, a couple of empty bottles of vodka and several empty bottles of Smirnoff Ice. Paper cups, many half chewed and crumpled, lay on their sides in the rivers of spilled beer. Taking the bottle from Jess, Claire unscrewed the lid and, selecting the least crumpled cups, filled them full with the warm wine.

'Keep the bottle with you,' she said, pushing it into Jess's handbag, 'or someone will nick it. Now, let's find Iggy.' Pulling

Jess's hand again, she made her way across the room and, after several minutes, found him in a corner with Animal and Bella and the girl he'd been snogging earlier.

'Yo, Cas,' he said. 'This your mate?'

'Yeah. Jess, this is the crowd.' Claire had to shout a bit to be heard over everybody and the volume of Sisters of Mercy emanating from the speakers in the corner. Jess looked around the room at the motley selection of people. She's so out of place, Claire thought, sipping her wine. I shouldn't have brought her.

'Is Tom here?' Jess mouthed.

Claire snorted her drink. 'Hardly! He's all loved up, so he'll be down the pub having a half of bitter cos he has to get up early to do something hearty like climbing.' Claire couldn't hear Jess's reply, but it was something like, 'Sounds a better option to me.'

The volume of the music went up a few decibels and, as the wine hit the spot, her plastic beaker replenished from Jess's handbag, though Jess hadn't made much headway at all with her own drink, Claire began to dance about with Animal. She tried not to splosh her drink everywhere, but it seemed so incredibly difficult and so incredibly funny trying not to. Time seemed to pass in a blur, but she knew it included slipping off into someone's room for a spliff. Jess wouldn't mind if she was gone for a moment and, besides, she wouldn't approve of the bloke who was snorting a line in there. When she emerged again, her head dazed and spinning, she couldn't see Jess anywhere and, when Iggy pulled her into his skinny arms, planting an unexpected kiss on her mouth, she sort of forgot about her and quite some time must have passed, much of it spent dancing frantically to Marilyn Manson and laughing wildly – so wildly, in fact, that she was aware quite a few people were looking at her.

Iggy had his arms round her again and she was hazily aware that he was kissing her, his breath a mixture of fags and beer, when she felt a persistent pulling at her arm.

'Gerroof,' she shouted without taking her lips from Iggy's, but whoever was pulling wouldn't stop.

'What the f—' She turned around irritated to see who it was, to be met by a red-faced Jess, her eyes a pool of tears, being jostled by people dancing around her.

'I'm off,' she shouted above the music.

'What?' Claire could feel Iggy pulling her back towards him but she needed to hear what Jess was saying, she knew that.

'I said,' Jess shouted very slowly and very loudly, 'that I am going back home. See you.' And she turned and headed out of the door. Worried now, Claire pulled herself from Iggy's grip and stumbled after Jess. People kept banging into her – or was she banging into them?

'Jess,' she called, just catching her before she headed through the fire door at the end of the corridor. Her eyes were puffy now and the mascara she'd put on so carefully was a smudge.

'You can't go.' Claire tried to take Jess's hand. 'Come back and have another drink!'

'What?' Jess's face looked harsh and mocking. 'And stand in the corner with it for an hour or more waiting for you while you are draped around some ludicrous-looking boy who seems pretty confident he's going to get into your knickers tonight? No thanks. I think I'll spend the night in my own bed if you don't mind.' She pulled at the handle of the door again.

'Please don't go.' Claire felt a bit panicky and very sick. 'I'm sorry. I didn't realise. I thought you were talking to someone or dancing.' Surely she had been, hadn't she?

'No, Claire, I wasn't and half the time I didn't know where you were. But I do know that you've really changed and you're not my mate any more. In fact, you aren't being a very nice person at all. See ya. Call me when you find Claire again.' And she disappeared through the door.

Chapter 33

David woke with the light and stretched. He hadn't done that for years – woken up exactly when he felt like it – and it was amazing. Kate had this theory about sleep – something about your body self-regulating after a while if you listened to it. He'd laughed at first. She had so many theories. But she'd looked a bit offended so he'd given it a try, and she'd been absolutely right. All these years he'd been bound by someone else's timetable and he'd never explored what he wanted to do. It was liberating, and when he'd told her so, her hazel eyes had sparkled and she'd kissed him full on the lips – the first time. There had been plenty of those since.

He picked up his watch from the bedside table. Nine thirty. That was a habit he couldn't give up, despite her urging. He really didn't feel comfortable unless he knew what the time was. And, he'd argued, she wouldn't like him to be late picking her up. They were going into London again today because she wanted to go on a river trip along the Thames to Greenwich. That was pretty conventional for Kate and, although David hadn't been for years, at least he felt he could take the initiative and organise it for her. Some of the things they'd done together had been completely new territory for him, things in the past he would have dismissed as not his sort of thing – the peace festival in Leamington Spa, the salsa class (though his performance made sure it was only the one), the late-night screenings at The Picture House in town, eating Dim Sum in a multi-floor restaurant off Leicester Square where all the other customers were Chinese and she'd eaten chicken's feet. It had been like a mystery tour, the last few weeks, yet David had never felt so alive. Somehow he had found himself in a relationship. Had it really been that easy? Thrilled by it all, he conveniently buried any reminders of Sarah. Of their wonderful early days together. It made it so much simpler.

And he wasn't the only one to notice the change in him. Claire and Tom had both commented, although with completely different reactions – Tom had seemed genuinely pleased that David was getting out, although David had carefully avoided any mention of Kate. Claire, however, either had guessed or was just not prepared to accept the reality of her father changing. She'd been quite off with him on the few occasions they'd managed to speak on the phone. The usual enquiries into how her revision was going had been brushed aside quite curtly. David shrugged and slipped on a T-shirt. She'd be all right. Claire had always worked so hard at school and was so amazingly organised, she'd ace any exams that came her way, something her brother had not always managed, and David had told him to take a leaf out of Claire's book. Tom had predictably greeted the suggestion with silence.

He checked his reflection briefly in the mirror and ran downstairs. The feeling of anticipation at seeing Kate was as if he'd had a jolt of strong caffeine – wired, as the twins would have said.

Claire was still feeling a bit wired when she arrived at the examination room just after half past nine. She'd got a couple of hours' sleep curled up on a large cushion in Iggy's room, but had set her alarm early so she'd have time to flick through her notes and a couple of books she'd taken out of the library last week. She had a pack of new gel pens and a bottle of water. And a sense of complete unreality.

She looked round at the other students, waiting outside. She recognised a few people from those first weeks of lectures – Lydia smiled briefly and turned away to her group of friends – but there was no one, really, she could talk to. Not that she wanted to. There was an air of fevered anxiety about them, a bit like there had been before A-levels, all that time ago. Most were chatting in groups – laughing too loud and trying to look relaxed. A few, like her, were standing on their own, some obviously running through their revision in their heads, others looking sick with nerves. In the pit of her stomach, Claire began to feel something a little like nausea, a lot like fear. She'd been in this place for a year and yet she was still waiting for her life here to begin. When she was with Iggy, when they spent sweaty nights squeezed into a single bed, exchanging kisses, his breath reeking of tobacco, it felt like she belonged somewhere, but now it was as if she was here by accident and no one was interested in her at all. Even Jess – good old reliable – hadn't called or returned her texts all week.

She took a loud shuddering breath, like someone who'd been under water for too long, and a group of over-made-up girls looked round at her, then exchanged glances. The doors opened and the students streamed in, slipping into the single desks and laying out their pens. Silence gradually fell and, as the invigilators gave out the papers, Claire took a sip of her water and squared her shoulders. How hard could it be? She'd swanned through every exam she'd ever taken. It was just a question of technique. And anyway, she didn't even care.

'You may turn over your question paper … now.'

The rustling of paper died away, but the rushing noise in her ears grew louder as she scanned the questions.

'The idea of the fourth estate remains ambiguous and subject to context. It is also resilient and the key to defining the media's democratic role, if it is to have one.' Discuss.

She bent over the paper, trying to find something that looked familiar, a word or phrase she could latch onto.

Media spaces provide an awareness of the remote space. State what you understand by the term 'awareness support' and briefly describe how awareness of a remote space is provided by two examples of media space systems.

She looked up, her breath starting to come fast. Around her, the other students were making notes or underlining key words. She looked at the paper again. What the hell was a 'media space system'?

She could feel sweat prickling her armpits and she was sure she was going to hurl. She picked up her pen, then put it down again. Maybe. She checked the front of the exam paper, just in case she'd strayed into the wrong room. Shit. She was supposed to know this stuff. What was the fourth estate? Something to do with journalists, she seemed to remember. But what were the other three estates? She rubbed her face and picked up her pen again. Two hours.

The hall was dark, the blinds shut against the evening sun, and a gantry of lights directed at the stage made it warmer than was comfortable. Or perhaps it was just nerves. Sarah couldn't remember the last time she had performed to this number of people. There must be eight or nine hundred at least – she'd never been very good at approximating such things – but because of the glaring lights she could only see halfway back up the hall anyway. The mood backstage had been jittery, with musicians gabbling and laughing nervously, commenting on each other's formal attire and complaining how hot they were in long skirts and white blouses, or suits and bow ties. Sarah had borrowed a blouse from a friend of Nathalie's who was clearly smaller round the bust, and she'd spent the last two nights stitching an approximation of a skirt from some cheap fabric she'd found at the market. Versace it wasn't, with its elasticated waist and a shape that made her feel like a Victorian governess.

'Mmm, very chic,' Fabien had commented drily when she'd posed in it for him. 'Don't bother going in to fashion design, will you?' Then he'd produced a little box which he'd handed to her with a kiss. 'Wear these. They might stop you looking completely like a crow.' Nestled inside the silk lining of the box was a pair of tiny stud earrings – an aquamarine stone with white gold around it.

'Oh Fabien, they're beautiful,' she'd gasped and, climbing onto the bed, she'd lifted them carefully out of the box and put them in her ears. 'How do they look?'

'Understated and elegant. Just like you.'

Sarah had felt a wave of affection – could it even be love? – towards him. 'Thank you so much.'

Fabien had shrugged in his Gallic way. 'Now take off that hideous skirt and come here,' he'd growled, and she'd shown her appreciation as best she could.

Now, the audience hushed in anticipation of the arrival of the orchestra leader, and Sarah touched the earrings for good luck. She hoped Fabien could see her do it and it would please him. He'd said he would sit near the back, but she'd already spotted Nathalie four rows from the front, waving manically.

Alexandre, the first violin, swept on to the stage and bowed ostentatiously.

'Such a show off,' whispered Geneviève out of the corner of her mouth. Then, through the doors, came Maurice, resplendent in white tuxedo, a crimson handkerchief in his top pocket, and for once his hair oiled back and under control. The volume of applause surprised Sarah. She'd known he was held in high regard, but perhaps Geneviève had been right when she mentioned backstage that there would be representatives from national French orchestras there, even one from Vienna, who were trying to lure Maurice away from his precious Sauzils. His face was serious now and he frowned deeply as he bowed to the audience. Then he turned towards the orchestra and the applause fell silent. He scanned the musicians, checking everyone was prepared and giving time for the mood to change from excitement to concentration on the mammoth task ahead. Then, he lifted his arms, his baton poised and, almost noiselessly, the musicians lifted their instruments in preparation. Sarah could feel her hands shaking and she breathed deeply. You can do this. You are a professional, you are confident; this is the greatest thing you have ever done. Do it for Tom and for Claire. Do it for Fabien who's watching you now.

Then Maurice brought his arms down and the opening bar erupted into the silence of the hall.

Chapter 34

'What do you mean he wasn't there?' Nathalie was making a cup of tea for Sarah, who was stripping off the ghastly skirt and blouse at last and putting on a dressing gown.

'Well, afterwards,' she called from the bedroom, 'we were clearing up and by the time I'd finished the hall was empty, except for a few stragglers.' She came back in to join Nathalie, tying her hair up to let the air cool her neck. The night heat was intense and her shoulders ached.

'Perhaps he had to get away. I'm sure he will call in a minute and explain. *Tiens*. You deserve this, my girl. What a superb performance. I don't think I have ever seen such a great performance at the festival. Maurice looked like he was on fire!'

'I think he was. I don't know how he coped in that jacket. The sweat was pouring off him by the end.' Sarah sipped at the hot liquid gratefully. It was too weak, of course, but despite her best efforts, she hadn't managed to persuade Nathalie that she liked her teabag in a little longer than five seconds. How did the French drink their coffee so strong but fail to get it with tea? She paused and sat back on the armchair, letting the tension run out of her. She'd have liked her dad to have been there. He'd have been so proud. And her mum. Her mum would have been transported. Suppressing the urge to cry, she took another sip of her tea. She missed them, she realised with a surge of emptiness. She missed having people around her who knew her well and who could make a decent cuppa.

David had made good tea. That first cup, left by the bed when he went to shower, was the rock on which she built her day. Was he making tea for himself now he was on his own?

By the time she went to bed, her whole body craving sleep, there was still no word from Fabien. Perhaps Nathalie was right and he'd had to get away. He was working tomorrow and it was late now after all. That would be it. But, as she slipped under the cool sheets and lay back against the pillows, the waves of fatigue washing over her, she could feel a germ of disquiet.

When Sarah woke, she was already able to feel the heat through the shutters of her room. She'd thrown off the sheet in the night and her skin felt clammy. She knew she had slept deeply, when she had slept, but in between she'd been woken by someone shouting underneath her window, and then again an hour later by confused dreams about Fabien arriving at home in Stratford and Pauline from next door inviting him in, even though Sarah asked her not to. David had been welcoming, and Phil had been there with a strimmer, but then David had been crying and Sarah had woken with a start.

Her clock said nine thirty and she turned on her back and yawned. Her head felt heavy, as though she'd had a night on the razz, and she didn't have the energy to move. She was due at Maurice's at ten, as usual, but, despite his boundless energy, he was sure to be lenient today, wasn't he?

She checked her mobile for a message, and saw with relief there were two. Of course Fabien would be in touch. Why wouldn't he? But the first was from Tom asking how the concert had gone, and the second was just an upgrade reminder from the mobile phone company. She replied to Tom as enthusiastically as she could, wishing him luck with the last few exams, and sent Claire a similar message. Shame Claire hadn't texted this morning, but perhaps she was out of credit. She'd have to check that the monthly direct debit had gone through to top up her daughter's phone.

Standing under the shower, letting the cool water run off her hair and down her back, she felt a strong sense of anticlimax.

She hadn't noticed what effect the build-up to the concert had had on her; on the entire orchestra, in fact, but by the end they had been wired. Perhaps that was why the performance had been so dynamic, driven by sheer nervous energy. Hot again almost as soon as she came out of the shower, she padded around the empty flat in her bra and knickers. Nathalie had left a message before she went off to work asking if there was any word from 'lover boy' and to have a good day, but despite the cat, who ignored her and slept in the heat, the flat was quiet. Suppressing a sudden sense of what felt terribly like loneliness and homesickness, she slipped on her cotton shift dress and flip-flops, tied her hair up in a clip on top of her head, and let herself out of the flat into the searing heat of the morning.

Making her way towards Maurice's, she found herself diverting so she would pass Fabien's shop. Perhaps she'd just drop in and say hello. She'd never done that before – well, not without letting him know first – but it would only just have opened and wouldn't be busy. He probably hadn't wanted to wake her before, and it would give him a chance to explain why he hadn't waited after the concert.

The streets were quiet, it still being early for this nocturnal town; the gift shops owners were just beginning to put out their postcard racks to attract the tourists driven from their beds by a northern European body-clock and the intense heat. Stratford would be busy by now, Sarah thought, then reminded herself that she needed to get some milk to take to Maurice's. Perhaps she'd treat herself to a croissant, too. She'd been too high then too knackered to eat last night and her stomach was now rumbling in complaint. Opening her purse she saw she was almost out of cash, so stopped outside the bank to withdraw some Euros. She slipped in her debit card, punched in her PIN and waved at the man from the *tabac* who called in greeting as he passed. She turned back to the cashpoint screen: *Unable to process your request. Please refer to bank.* That was odd. She'd deposited

Maurice's pay only three days ago. It should be showing by now. Damn. Reluctantly, she pulled out her credit card. Only for use in an emergency, she'd always told herself, but she wouldn't take out much, enough to tide her over, and she could always transfer it back when she'd sorted out the bank mix-up. She slipped it in, and tapped in her usual pin number. David had said she ought to use another one, but what was the point?

Unable to process your request. Odd. And very annoying. Bloody computers must be down. Forgoing the croissant, she picked up some milk, and headed into the square.

She could see the shop was closed as soon as she turned the corner. There were no racks of artistic postcards of lavender fields or moody shots of shells, and the white shutters were up. Stuck to the door from the inside was a note which Sarah translated falteringly. 'Closed today for personal reasons. Many apologies.' Crikey, she hadn't even thought that something may have happened that had called him away. Now she felt terrible, and quickly sent him a text asking if everything was okay.

Maurice was buoyant, elated by success. The phone rang for most of the morning and thankfully, he'd bought *pains au chocolat* for them to share in celebration. People dropped by in between calls and embraced the little Frenchman, declaring the previous evening a triumph. Sarah, too, received her fair share of praise.

'She finally came good, didn't she, after all my hard work?' Maurice asked cheekily, winking at her. She lobbed a screwed-up ball of paper at him from across the room.

'I was just a little rusty, that was all!'

'And,' asked a rotund gentleman who had arrived bearing Champagne, 'will you stay with us until the next performance in Toulouse at the end of August? The plan is Stravinsky, *n'est-ce pas,* Maurice?' Both men looked at her expectantly.

'I, er … I don't know,' replied Sarah. 'It's a tempting idea, though.' And it was. She'd relished the whole experience, felt she had grown, achieved something. The thought of doing it all again appealed enormously.

'That's if Maurice hasn't been seduced to Vienna, *n'est-ce pas, mon cher Maurice*? What would Frau Greta say about that?' Maurice simply shrugged and mumbled a reply.

Finally there was some peace, and Sarah busied herself, even though there really wasn't much to do now. She packed up the scores from last night to return to the music library, and made a pile of Maurice's correspondence, hoping he wouldn't notice she kept checking her phone for a reply to her text to Fabien.

'Problem?' he eventually growled.

'What? No, no,' she laughed lightly. 'Just hoping to hear how the children have got on with their exams, that's all.'

'Mmm.' His tone was circumspect. 'Not mooching about that Renard, are you? The man is a thin-weight. Is that what you call it?'

'Lightweight. And I think you are wrong, Maurice. We've had a lovely time together.'

'Did he come to watch you play last night?'

'Yes, I think so.' Sarah hated herself for her uncertainty. 'Yes, I'm sure he did. He just had to leave early.'

Maurice waved his hand. 'Maybe, but the only thing he's a master of is the art of making a woman feel good. For that he could get an award.'

Sarah frowned, torn between defending Fabien and desperate to know what Maurice was referring to. 'How do you know?'

Maurice laughed drily. 'This town is small, and even though the shutters are closed and people hide behind them, they know what's going on. It's human nature, isn't it' – he tapped the end of his nose – 'to stick this where there's something interesting to investigate?'

'Well, I think you are wrong,' she said again more stridently this time. 'He is a very generous man.' Maurice looked at her for a moment.

'Yes, Sarah, I am sure you are right. Now I must go home. Greta and I are going to spend the afternoon at the vineyard of a friend. If I don't get there on time to pick her up, I will be made to suffer!' And he made his way to the door.

After tidying up, and with no word from Fabien, Sarah decided to go back to the apartment. She'd raid the fridge and make herself an early supper, followed by an early bedtime. Perhaps she'd even curl up with the English novel about a holiday in Cornwall she'd found in a second-hand shop. It was old and battered, perhaps left by a holidaymaker, but she rather craved the comfort of an easy read. In English. It was exhausting listening to a foreign language all the time. The afternoon was still awesomely hot and she dodged from shade to shade as she headed across town. She knew she was taking the wrong route back, but somehow her feet were directing her towards Fabien's place. It was pointless because he probably wouldn't be there, but she'd give it a try.

The square was quiet, except for a couple of boys playing football between the parked cars. She couldn't see his car, but sometimes it was hard to find a space and he could well have left it streets away. The blank first-floor windows gave nothing away so she rang the bell and waited. She was about to turn away defeated when the front door opened and a tall woman with shoulder-length dark hair opened it. She was handsome, even beautiful, in an unmade-up way, and her curvaceous figure was emphasised by a tight skirt and sleeveless white shirt. Her legs and feet were bare and brown. This must be Valérie, the elusive flatmate he was helping out. What man wouldn't? thought Sarah wryly.

'*Oui?*' the woman asked, her voice soft and lilting.

'*Je suis* Sarah,' she said hopefully, expecting a smile of recognition. Fabien was bound to have mentioned her.

'*Qui?*'

'Sarah. *Le* …' – she tried to remember the word – '*amie de* Fabien?' Still nothing. '*La girlfriend? Et vous êtes Valérie?*'

'Sarah?' The woman frowned. '*Non, desolée, je ne vous connais pas.*'

Sarah sighed. This was going to be tricky. She wasn't going to be able to ask where he was – or understand the answer – so she thought quickly. She'd leave him a note, so, in her best Franglais, accompanied by a good amount of arm movements, she fabricated a story about having left her cardigan and could she collect it? Her gesticulations must have worked, because Valérie, if that was who she was, opened the door wider and turned round to go back upstairs to the apartment. Once they were inside she shrugged and went back into the kitchen to carry on with whatever she had been doing before.

Sarah glanced around the room. Fabien's shoes, a beautiful pair of fine leather ones he'd bought recently, were strewn on the floor and copies of old newspapers and magazines lay on the sofa. There was a glass on the coffee table, with the dregs of red wine in the bottom. Cautiously, feeling like an interloper, Sarah made her way towards his bedroom. The room was dark, the shutters not yet opened, and it smelled stale. The bedding was ruffled up, and his boxer shorts lay on the floor where they had fallen. Sighing indulgently, she picked them up, laying them on the chair. Of course there was no cardigan of hers in here, so she straightened the bedding and plumped up his pillow and moved round to do the same on the other side, where she usually slept – strangely the other side than she had been used to with David. She picked up the pillow and, as she did so, she could feel something smooth hook onto her fingers then fall onto the white sheet, a pool of red silk. She dropped the pillow and picked it up – a camisole as light as a feather, with black lace around the edge. For a moment she thought it might be hers, but it couldn't be. It was nothing Fabien had ever bought her. Without thinking, she brought the fabric to her nose and smelled it then dropped it quickly onto the bed.

Confused, and with a growing sense of unease, Sarah left the room. She could hear Valérie humming in the kitchen and the sound of cupboard doors shutting. She was about to make her way out when she glanced down the corridor. For once, the door to Valérie's bedroom was open but, to her surprise, instead of a bed she could see the corner of a desk. Glancing back to the doorway of the kitchen, she quietly made her way towards it and carefully peered round the door. The desk was quite big and covered in papers and a computer keyboard and monitor. So big, in fact, that it almost filled the room, which was so small there was barely space for the chair. On the wall was a pair of shoddy, makeshift shelves covered in books with titles she didn't understand but none of them on art or artists from what she could tell. The papers on the desk were bank statements, or blank sheets with scribbles and numbers. A flatmate and no bedroom. Did Valérie sleep on the sofa?

Sarah was about to turn away, trying to figure out what the set-up was here, when her eye was caught by the corner of a photograph peeking out from under the bank statements. Glancing back in the direction of the kitchen but consumed with curiosity, she put her hand out and lifted the paper to reveal the picture. There was more than one but it was what they showed that made her heart pound and the bile rise into her mouth.

The pictures were of her and each taken from a slightly different angle. She was asleep on Fabien's bed, her body sprawled out, one arm behind her head. Her mouth was slightly open, her lips swollen and her hair was splayed out wildly on the pillow. Her legs were apart and she was naked, except for the pair of pink crotchless pants.

Claire's heart was pounding. She knew what the tablet was – well, she'd read the leaflet that she'd been given at Freshers' Week and some girls at school said they had taken them – but she'd never actually held one.

'Oi.' Iggy folded her hand over the tablet. 'We don't want everyone wanting one, do we?' he shouted into her ear.

The thump of the music from the speakers seemed to match her anxiety. Around her, people were dancing wildly, bottles of water in their hands. She had no idea where she was, having lost her bearings as he'd led her through the streets of the city. The heat was intense and already she could feel the sweat running down her back, even though she was wearing only a light vest. This was supposed to be the post-exam celebration, but that was a joke. She couldn't think what there was to celebrate. Animal and Iggy had howled with laughter about how badly they had done in theirs, but they weren't even on the same course as her, so that was no comfort.

'Not 'ad one before?' Iggy shouted again. 'E-virgin, are you?'

'Oh yes, of course I have,' Claire mouthed back. 'Just not seen one ... this colour before?'

Iggy looked bemused and shrugged. Then he leaned towards her ear again. 'As a special gift, my little virgin, I'll treat you to this one, but next time, you're forking out.' Claire nodded. She'd meant to give him some money, for the weed, but her card had been refused at the cashpoint earlier in the day and she couldn't phone Dad cos she was out of credit. In fact, she'd been thinking about going to find Tom when she'd bumped into him outside the campus supermarket, a letter in his hand. His bike was propped against his leg and he looked fit and brown in his shorts.

'Hang on,' she'd said to Animal and ran over to him.

'Yo, sis.' He'd looked up, his eyes shining. 'Christ, you look like shit.'

She'd looked down at her jeans and T-shirt. Well, it had been the only thing clean. 'Thanks. Listen, can you lend me a tenner? I've got no credit on my phone and I need to call Dad cos the cashpoint wouldn't give me any cash. And our allowance was due on Tuesday, wasn't it?'

'And you used to be Mrs Frugal.' Tom, with painful slowness, had drawn a note out of his pocket and waved it tantalisingly. 'The reason you have no money is cos you're spending it too fast with that weird bunch.' He'd jerked his head towards Animal, who was looking at the ground and scuffing his foot. 'Luckily I, like a good boy, have still got some credit left over from last month.'

'That makes a change,' Claire had huffed. 'Please, Tom, I'll pay you back.'

He had stalled theatrically. 'So what's in it for me?'

But Claire had snatched the note before he could withdraw it. 'Thanks,' she shouted back as she ran off, and she thought she heard him shout back, 'Take care.'

Was she taking care now? 'C'mon,' Iggy urged. 'It's a bit of a laugh. Much more of a kick than a spliff. Time you moved on, my girl.' He looked around, a bored expression on his face and, fearful that he'd just move away and leave her standing here with this crowd she didn't know, she breathed deeply and threw the tablet into her mouth, swilling it down with some water from the bottle he handed her.

She wasn't sure what she'd been expecting, but what there was was a great, fat nothing. She danced with him for a while, hoping that it would appear as though it had taken effect, and tried to mimic the people around her who looked like they'd had a big hit. How pathetic would that be, to be immune to Ecstasy!

Then someone seemed to turned up the music. There was a whoosh in her head like a rush of air, and her heart started banging against her chest, matching in her head the intensity of her dancing. What a fantastic beat! Iggy kept pulling her towards him and she threw her arms around his neck. She was really hot now, but it didn't seem to matter. What a lovely bloke he was to bring her here and look after her! Wasn't she lucky to have friends like that?

'What? Sorry – can't hear what you're saying.' David gestured incomprehension and pointed at his ears. 'Is there somewhere quieter we could go?'

'What?' Kate shouted back. 'Oh, never mind – look they're coming on.'

Kate grabbed his hand and pulled him after her, weaving her way through scattered groups in the audience, then barging past them as they got closer to the front. David turned to apologise to a women whose toe he must have crushed, but the crowd had closed up behind them already. The support band had been loud enough, even when they'd been at the back, surely it couldn't get any louder? In fact, he'd felt the thud of the bass even when they'd been walking down the stairs to the standing area. Kate had turned to look at him and, just for a moment, he'd expected a look of complicit horror at the volume, but instead of reflecting his own mood, her face had been alight with excitement. He smiled ruefully. This would be Sarah's idea of hell.

At the back, when they'd eventually filed into the arena through the huge doors, there had been plenty of space and, although it was warm, at least there had been a nice breeze reaching them from the outside. Ahead, closest to the stage, he'd seen a wall of bodies and shuddered inwardly at the very idea of being in that crush. But that's where he was now, towed in Kate's wake.

The lights dipped and a terrific roar went up from the crowd. Lights started to pulse up from the back of the stage, playing against a huge silk screen that had been dropped in the temporary darkness. It looked a little bit like Pathé News clips of the Blitz. He looked around. Was there anyone here, apart from him, who would have any idea what Pathé News was?

A throbbing bass beat started to ripple across the auditorium. Evidently it was recognisable to the fans, although, to him, it just sounded like a steam train with hiccups. All around him people started to jump up and down – even Kate, who turned to grin at him. It was unbearably hot now. He could actually feel the heat radiating from the bodies packed in around him and he cringed as an anonymous sweaty arm pressed up against his. Against the white silk, the silhouettes of the band were projected huge and arrogant.

If only he'd brought ear plugs. The singer was screeching and the crowd around him were joining in. He'd been wrong about the noise level. It was even louder now and he felt himself physically tensing up as though to repel it. His shoulders were stiff and he could feel the start of a headache. Great! Would he end up with tinnitus, like Beethoven?

Kate was clearly having a great time, so there was no prospect of slinking off early. For some reason, she seemed elated at the idea of having her ears battered into buzzing numbness. He looked enviously at the lucky buggers at the back who'd been sensible enough to book seats. They looked so comfortable. But not quite as comfortable as if they'd been sitting in a nice, quiet pub or, even better, at home.

David sighed heavily. He'd never let Kate talk him into some damn fool thing like this again. He turned his attention back to the stage. The silk drapes had been released from the top and cascaded to the ground. He almost laughed. The musicians – well, if you could call them that – looked tiny compared to the huge projected images he'd just been looking at. Didn't they realise how daft that whole effect had made them look? As they went into another song, Kate cheered, her arms in the air. Yet to him, it sounded exactly the same as the last one. And the one before that. God – he was bored already.

From behind, there was a surge from the crowd, pushing him and everyone else forward. He turned round angrily. That was very irresponsible! It forced him hard against Kate's back and she looked at him over her shoulder, her face flushed and bright with enjoyment. Then she very deliberately reached her arms behind her, got hold of the belt loops of his jeans and pulled him against her gyrating bottom. He gasped with a mixture of surprise at her brazenness and of raw, unexpected erotic pleasure. He could feel himself getting hard. And evidently so could she, because she reached back and took hold of him, rubbing her hand against his fly, still dancing and leaning back against him.

David felt himself get hot, then cold, then hot again. He looked around but no one was paying any attention, even if they could have seen in the crush. Oh, what the hell? Tentatively at first, he put his hands on her hips and pulled her closer. The noise, the sweat, the heat, the other people – none of it mattered. He could smell her hair and feel her back through her thin top as she writhed against him. God, she was gorgeous. His heart pounded.

Chapter 35

Sarah was up at six the following morning. Her sleep had been fitful, and at three she'd made herself a cup of tea and taken it back to bed. Once again – it must have been for the tenth time – she'd steeled herself to look at the pictures she'd taken from Fabien's and hidden in her bedside drawer, but that didn't make any difference to how sick they made her feel. She looked like a tart. Willing, salacious, gagging for it. With her arm thrown back behind her head, it appeared as if she was tied up, something Fabien had done a couple of times and she'd gone along with. She thought she'd taken off the knickers but she must have fallen asleep with them on. So why had he taken pictures? For kicks? Perhaps he was going to show them to her later as part of a game?

Out of the shower now, she picked up the photos and took them into the kitchen. She opened the shutters, lit the gas ring, and watched as the flames licked across the images, the photo paper curling up and distorting her body as it burned. Then she briskly scooped up the ashes and dropped them into the bin.

'For fuck's sake, what's that smell?' Nathalie shuffled out of her bedroom a short while later, squinting in the sunlight. 'Is the building on fire?'

'No, it's nothing. I just dropped some kitchen roll on to the gas.'

'Why are you up so early?' She yawned, stretching her arms. 'It's like dawn.'

'Things.'

'Well, I'm back to bloody bed,' she grumbled and shuffled back into her room.

Sarah watched her go, then, picking up the phone, went back in to her bedroom to call the bank. She didn't want to speak to David about the cashpoint not paying out – that would be a very odd reason to call him after all these weeks – and besides, he'd only get at her for not keeping an eye on the account. But why would she? The account had been comfortably in the black when she'd left – David made sure it always was – she was spending within her pay from Maurice and she knew what she'd put in the bank from Mum's bequest. Hard to believe, but perhaps David had overspent, but then he'd have been paid last week, wouldn't he? She dialled the number and, as she waited for it to click through, she thanked the Lord for phone and internet banking.

'Hello, can I take your postcode please?' The soft, Scottish voice sounded warm and reassuring. No wonder the Scottish dominated call centres.

Sarah said it automatically, then gave the rest of her details. 'Can I have a balance of the account please?'

'Certainly, madam, just one moment while I take a look.' There was a pause and Sarah watched the dust particles dance in the shaft of sunlight dance. 'You are up to your overdraft limit, and we have …' – there was another pause – 'we have payments that we have had to refuse, I'm afraid.'

Sarah's face felt hot and her stomach lurched. How could that be? What the hell had David done? 'Are you sure?'

'Yes, madam, I am sure. You have had several large payments going out of your account in the last week or so. Let's see now.' She sounded like a teacher. 'Eight hundred pounds to Sand Dreams Holidays. That was on the ninth. Six hundred pounds to El Barca Hotel Barcelona. It's a joint account, isn't it? Is your husband away at the moment?'

Sarah didn't understand what she meant. 'I don't think so, why?'

'Well, several of the payments appear to be cash withdrawals from a bank in France. A place called Sauzils?'

'Well, yes, that's where I am. We're ... we're separated.'

'I see, madam.' There was another pause. 'That explains why you haven't received any letters from us. I have a note here of two being sent to you in the last week. It seems we haven't been able to process a regular monthly direct debit to the Halifax. Would that be your mortgage repayment, Mrs Lewis?'

'Yes. Yes it is.' Sarah swallowed hard. She'd have to use her credit card. 'And could you just check the balance on my Visa card please?'

'I'll just call up that screen. One moment.' Pause. 'Up to your credit limit, I'm afraid, Mrs Lewis.'

'What!' This was beyond a joke. 'But how? I haven't used it!'

'There seem to be cash withdrawals, and some online transactions. Yes, there is one large one here for two thousand pounds.'

'How?' Sarah gasped weakly.

'It's hard to say, madam. It appears to be a company in Antwerp.'

'Right.' Sarah was distracted, her mind racing. 'Thank you. I'll call you back.'

'But, Mrs Lewis,' the Scottish lilt persisted, 'in view of the seriousness of this, I will need to put you on to one of our account managers. Mrs Lewis, would it be all right to hold?'

'Er, no. I mean, I'm abroad and this is on my mobile. I will call my husband. He will call you back later this morning.' And before she could say anything else, Sarah snapped her phone shut.

Her hands shook and she did a mental calculation. Perhaps Maurice's cheques had bounced, but no, she'd have known. Could David have moved the money somewhere else to spite her, or cut her off? But why would he do that? Was his anger so deep?

How could it have happened? Whatever the reason, the ramifications of her situation began to seep in. She must have sat for ages, her eyes fixed straight ahead. The immediate problem was that she had 20 Eurocents in her purse, and no means of getting any more. She picked up her bag and emptied the contents out onto her bed, searching in vain for the odd note that might have gone astray, but there was nothing except old receipts and tissues. Among the detritus were cards from restaurants she'd been to with Fabien, including that little fish place in Perpignan and Le Singe Noir with its exquisite menu where he'd told her she was beautiful. Perhaps she had got through more money than she had imagined – David always said she was hopeless with it – whipped into irresponsible extravagance by the power of her passion. But except for one occasion, Fabien had always paid. He'd funded all their romantic nights out.

Sarah looked at her watch. It was still too early so she killed time by making another cup of tea, her mind distracted, exploring every possibility. Finally, steeling herself when she thought it wasn't too early, she dialled home. It took a moment to click through then she could hear the ringing tone. She could picture the phone in the hall ringing, a sound once so familiar to her, but now she couldn't remember what it sounded like. And it rang. Sarah frowned and looked at her watch again. He couldn't have gone to work this early, surely? Had she got the hour wrong?

'I'm off now,' Nathalie called from the corridor, then she popped her head around the door. 'Will you be with Fab—' She stopped suddenly as she took in the handbag contents scattered on the bed, and Sarah sitting perched on the edge of it, her head in her hands. 'Hey, what's up? I told you you'd got up too early.'

'I'm in deep shit.'

'What?' Nathalie crouched down in front of her and rubbed her hand gently up Sarah's arm. 'What's up? It is Fabien?'

'I've got no money.'

'Oh that!' Nathalie laughed dismissively. 'Don't panic. We can find you another job, no problem. I'll have a word with my boss. And besides, your French is pretty good now – perhaps Sylvie will be able to give you something to do. Things get really busy in town now that the tourists are descending, and she has such lovely things. Or, I know, have a word with Fabien. His shop is always—'

'No,' Sarah sighed. 'What I mean is our bank account is empty. Worse than empty. Up to the wire. I can't get any money out and the worst part is I don't know why.'

There was silence. 'Has David …?'

'I don't know. I can't get hold of him.' She looked up at Nathalie. 'I've got the most horrible, horrible feeling in my stomach.' Neither of them said anything but simply looked at each other.

'Might Fabien lend you some money? He seems to have loads and he adores you?'

'Fabien?' Sarah thought of the photographs, so intimate and so damning. 'I don't think I can ask him that. But anyway, I have to find him. I went to his place last night. He wasn't there but' – she paused – 'I met his flatmate.'

Nathalie frowned. 'Flatmate?'

'Valérie?'

'Valérie?' Her frown deepened. 'Tall, dark, good-looking?'

'Yes.'

'Oh.'

'Oh?'

'Only I thought … Oh, it doesn't matter.'

Sarah stood up and Nathalie followed, but she wouldn't meet Sarah's eye. 'It does matter. Who's Valérie?'

'I just thought she was off the scene, that's all. Well, we all did …'

Sarah could feel a strange pain. 'Is she his girlfriend?'

'Sarah, she's his wife.'

The pain was suddenly in her stomach. 'Oh shit. But I thought that was years ago.'

Nathalie reached out and touched her arm. 'I really thought they'd separated. It's been on and off for years and I'd heard she'd gone back to Marseilles. Honest or I would never have invited him over that night.'

Sarah was trying desperately to process this information. 'So why was he having a relationship with me when she was around? I mean, we would go to his flat and stuff.'

Nathalie didn't appear to have an answer to that and took hold of Sarah's hands. 'Perhaps she's only just back.' She warmed now to her theory. 'Perhaps she turned up out of the blue and that's why you've not seen him in the last couple of days. Maybe he's trying to sort things out. She's a very tricky woman, I gather.'

Sarah's head hurt as she tried to assimilate all this. Fabien with a wife? He'd said that was over years ago, and yet they'd come and gone to the flat and there was no hint of a wife. And what wife would open the door as calm as you like, as Valérie had done yesterday, and let in a woman who described herself as her husband's girlfriend?

'I don't believe you.' Sarah felt suddenly resolute. 'There must be some mistake. Have you met her?'

Nathalie had dropped her bag now and was fidgeting with her hands, distressed by what she'd revealed. 'Yes, years ago. It was always an odd relationship. She had lovers and he ...'

'Had lovers?' Sarah asked quietly.

'Yes, a few, maybe.' She hurried on: 'But not like this. I've never seen him so happy.' Sarah looked at her friend sceptically. 'I just thought he'd be good for you.' Nathalie's voice was almost beseeching now. 'A fling after David. Someone to make you feel good, reassure yourself that you are still attractive. I mean, you had fun, didn't you?'

'I had fun, yes, but I think it might just have been the most expensive fun I ever had.' She turned back to her bed, panic seeping through her whole body, and began to stuff her things back into her handbag. 'I have to find him,' she said again.

'He could be anywhere.'

'Then I'll look everywhere. He has to open the shop sometime.'

Nathalie picked up some coins that had fallen onto the floor and handed them to Sarah. 'What will you do for money?'

Sarah could feel the sweat beginning to prickle at the back of her neck and she lifted her hair, clipping it onto the top of her head without thinking. 'Fuck knows. Maurice still owes me for the concert, I suppose, but that'll be a pittance.'

'Here.' Nathalie fumbled in her bag. 'Let me give you some. God knows, it's the least I can do.'

'No, no really, I'll be fine.'

Nathalie thrust some Euro notes into her hand. 'Don't be ridiculous. You can't get by with nothing. Now I've got to go to work, but I'll call in a bit and, for God's sake, let me know what happens, won't you?' Sarah nodded then a thought came into her head.

'But he said he had a son?'

Nathalie stopped at the door and turned. 'Son?'

'Yeah a little boy that his wife took away when she moved ... north.'

Nathalie shook her head slowly. 'No. I don't know of any son.'

Chapter 36

David stood in the shower, eyes closed, letting the water cascade over his head and body, trying not to think about how he was feeling. Back home at last, he could give way to the exhaustion, combined with that slight sense of tingling unreality that follows a night with virtually no sleep – although that wasn't something he'd experienced for years, probably not since the twins had insisted on camping in the garden that time. He frowned at the memory and attempted to push it out of his mind. Thoughts like that didn't fit well with last night.

He'd spent the whole of the gig in a state of tension – and not just due to the noise, the crowd, the heat. From pretty early on it had been blatantly obvious that he and Kate were going to have sex. She was clearly up for it and, once he'd managed to overcome the Jiminy Cricket voice of his conscience, he'd been impatient to leave and just do it. He felt as though he was going to explode with the feelings and frustration and anger and longing in him. Surely sex with a willing woman would sort him out. It wasn't even just the sex itself he wanted, although he certainly wanted that. It was the release he longed for and the retreat into something simple and wordless, to wash him clean of all the complicated and painful stuff he couldn't even bear to think about any more. He wanted to lose himself in her.

And for a while, it had been like that. They'd gone to her place. Neither of them had drunk much and neither of them said much on the way back. That had suited him. Her hand inching up his thigh as he drove them home was enough to bounce him out of any final reservations he had. This was a huge step, after all, to

have sex with another woman after all these years. But Sarah ...
He had turned to Kate and looked into her dark eyes. Sarah was
probably doing exactly what she wanted. And now so was he.

There hadn't been any time wasted on tenderness or discovery.
As soon as she'd closed the door behind them, she'd pulled him
close then they'd stumbled together into her bedroom and fallen
onto the unmade bed. The rest of the night came back to him
in flashes. The spicy scent of her skin, the feel of her ribs under
his hands, her musky unfamiliar taste and the way she cried out
above him, throwing her hair back and digging her fingers painfully into his chest.

She'd made everything so simple and straightforward. And the
way she felt was ... he smiled as he remembered the pleasure of
losing himself in that fantastic, supple, silky body. Any anxieties
he might have felt beforehand – although he'd barely even admitted them to himself – had been blown away after the first
time. After that – well, he couldn't help feeling pretty pleased
with himself. Yet something ... something ...

He soaped himself down now. He should be feeling satiated,
and on one level he was. But he hadn't found that uncompli-
cated place he was looking for, apart from those few seconds
when he'd forgotten everything. And when she'd nestled up
afterwards, fitting her long body against his, it just didn't feel
right. Lovely though she was, he'd wanted nothing more than
to turn away. Put some space between their bodies. But even he
knew that wasn't on. He'd done what was expected: caressed her
hair, returned kisses.

But when they woke he'd lied about an appointment, and left
before she could make him breakfast, trying not to look at her
disappointed face.

And now here he was, home again. And although the shower
could wash away some of yesterday, he was left with an uncomfortable sense that, in some way, it had marked him and that
things were more complicated than ever.

The truth was, he'd had sex with Kate to forget. But he couldn't help remembering.

From her position at the window, Sarah watched without seeing the people passing through the square. The entire morning had been spent pacing the flat, going over in her head every moment she could of the months she'd been in Sauzils. The trips out, the cafés she'd been to, the exhibitions at the *Musée* and shopping in Perpignan. It had all been a blur of late nights and irresponsibility. She'd been so swept up by it all, perhaps she really had lost her mind. Over and over in her head she went through what the bank had said. Why oh why wasn't David answering his mobile? She had to speak to him. To see the bank statements.

Risking her credit again, she dialled the bank once more. Another pacifying Edinburgh burr came on the line. 'Can I have your postcode please?' Sarah rushed through the security check. 'Can you tell me about cash withdrawals please? Recent ones.'

There was a pause. 'I have withdrawals showing here for four hundred euros on the eighth, ninth, tenth and eleventh of this month.'

Sarah trawled her brain. She hadn't. She couldn't have. Fumbling, her hands shaking, she pulled out her purse. Her card was there, innocently poking out of its snug credit card pocket.

'When?' she desperately asked the woman at the other end of the phone. 'What time of day, I mean, was the money taken out?'

'Let's see now. A variety of times. There is one at five fourteen. Another quite late in the evening and ... oh, here's one, a transaction at two a.m.'

Sarah thought she was going to be sick. 'Thank you.'

'Anything else I can help you with?'

'God, no thank you.'

She put down the phone quickly and rushed to the bathroom where she threw up the little that was in her stomach, then retched and retched. 'I've got to find him.' She repeated like a mantra, splashing water on her face. Back in her room, she picked up the phone again and, scrolling through her numbers, found the one she wanted. Again it took a while to connect, then she could hear the ringing tone at the end of the line, then a click.

'Proton Systems. Can I help you?' Sarah couldn't imagine how many times she had heard that voice.

'Doreen? It's Sarah. Sarah Lewis.' There was silence for a moment.

'I know which Sarah.' Her voice was matter-of-fact, not harsh as Sarah had expected.

'How are you?' she asked falteringly, not sure what to expect.

'I'm okay.' The response was cool, so strange from a woman who'd shared almost all the family's tragedies and joys over the years. She'd even come to Mary's funeral last September. 'And you?'

'Yeah. Can I speak to David please?'

'David? Sarah, David hasn't been here for weeks.'

The hair on Sarah's head tingled. 'What on earth do you mean?'

'Hang on a minute.' Sarah could hear Doreen talking to someone who'd come into reception, signing them in, then she came back on the line, her voice low, almost whispering. 'Sarah, when did you last speak to him?'

'When I left. We sort of agreed we wouldn't be in touch unless it was an emergency. And this is an emergency.'

'He left, walked out. Had a huge bust-up with Barry.' She said the name so quietly Sarah could barely hear her. 'It was sort of about me really. Barry had been vile about my holiday and David came to my defence.' Sarah felt mild surprise. Yes he thought the world of Doreen but confrontation just wasn't his thing. 'I've had the odd text from him and he seems okay but I don't know anything else. Have you tried ringing home?'

'Yes, I tried earlier. He's not there.' There was silence from both of them. A heavy, pregnant pause.

'Look, I've got to go. There's couriers and all sorts here. Let me know if I can help.' Doreen put the phone down. I don't deserve that kindness, Sarah thought, unclipping her hair and, twisting it painfully, clipped it up again. Hardly daring to risk running out of credit on the phone again, she dialled home, but still no reply, then, steeling herself, she dialled Fabien's mobile number. It rang and rang, not even going to his voicemail. Pulling her flip-flops from under the bed and grabbing her bag, she let herself out of the flat.

Chapter 37

Against his better judgement, David had been doing some thinking. A good hard run had made everything seem easier. Kate, good fun and undemanding; just enough work to keep him ticking over; his running. He didn't really need anything else. Why was he trying to complicate matters when that was the very thing he didn't want? Without him having to do very much at all, he was building a new life. And it was a pretty good one, all things considered.

It was getting hot as he'd started into the home stretch. The sensation of pushing his body just that bit further was fantastic. He felt alive and tingling. Kate was going to come round later and they were going out to the cinema and maybe a meal. He'd pop into town and maybe get her some flowers.

He could hear the phone ringing as he fitted the key in the lock and quickly opened the door, scooping the mail up before stacking it on the hall table with the rest of the stuff. The call, from the Alvis garage in Worcester, offering him some temporary work, put a spring in his step, despite the eight miles he'd just run. After all these years of desk work, to think he was making money from doing what he loved! Life was good. He'd get over Sarah. Life was going to be good.

He was feeling well-disposed towards everyone as he strolled up Bridge Street an hour later. Handing back the company car had been a sort of freedom, although hadn't it seemed so important once? And there was always the Alvis when he needed to go any distance, and what a stylish way to travel! Even the *Big Issue* vendor felt the benefit of his largesse, although he would have to be a bit more cautious with money now he didn't have a regular salary with benefits. David smiled to himself. All that stuff had once seemed so critical but, now, he realised, there was so much more to life than he'd known before. He laughed drily. Perhaps Sarah had been right with her 'I need more' speech.

He slid his cashpoint card into the machine. Sarah had normally had the job of withdrawing cash for them both for the whole week, when he'd been stuck in the office on the outskirts of town. He keyed in his pin and waited.

Unable to complete transaction. Refer to bank.

Damn – he must have got the number wrong. He inserted the card once more, keyed in the pin – her birthday, he was sure it was right – and chose Balance Enquiry, to make sure. The screen flashed and he felt a kick to the pit of his stomach.

£6556 OD
Nil available credit.
Refer to bank.

It couldn't be. They'd had at least twenty-five thousand in there, what with his last pay check, Sarah's mother's money and salary in lieu of holiday. He'd been meaning to open a deposit account and transfer it. He stepped back, aware that a queue had formed behind him. He rubbed his head. What the hell had happened? Had he lost his cheque book? Had Sarah …? Shit! What the hell had Sarah been doing?

He felt completely numb as he waited at the enquiries desk. His mouth was so dry, he could hardly get his words out.

The teller frowned at the screen. 'Yes, Mr Lewis, there has been some activity on your account from France. Have you been abroad lately? Obviously, if you haven't, then we have to suspect that someone has your details. It's a big problem these days.'

'My wife,' he murmured. 'She's living abroad.'

How *could* she? How bloody could she? Not only had she

dumped him, but she was ripping him off too. He could feel a pulse beating in his temple and he clenched his fists. 'Can I put a stop on the account? Can I prevent any more money from going out?'

The teller turned the screen to show him. 'Well, unfortunately, you've exceeded your overdraft limit already so there's no possibility of any more cash being withdrawn, either by yourself or by your wife. Of course, if you have credit cards, they can still be used, provided the credit limit hasn't been exceeded.'

David stared at the neat rows of dates, words and figures. In the space of a few weeks, she'd bled their account dry. Withdrawals in the middle of the night, up to the limit each time, until there was nothing left. She'd taken out all her money and his into the bargain. Had that been her plan all along?

'Mr Lewis, would you like to speak to your account manager? The thing is, I notice that you've got some direct debits due – is this one a life assurance? The mortgage perhaps? You'll need to make some arrangements. I could make an appointment for you ...'

She'd left him with nothing. Nothing at all. Wordlessly, David shook his head and stumbled outside.

It was pointless going to the shop, which would be closed today. Typical, Sarah muttered to herself, irritation mixed with panic, how the French pay no heed to market forces. Just go their own sweet way, opening and shutting their shops when they feel like it. In the corner of the square a man was having a row with a boy on a moped. She could hear a dog yapping through an upstairs window. Poor sod, it must be hot as hell in there. With more determination than she meant to, she pushed the doorbell, then stepped down from the doorstep, putting her shoulders back ready to face who ever might open the door.

Nothing. She waited for five minutes, pressing the bell again, once, twice, three times almost manically. He had to be there.

'*Ça suffit, Madame!*' An upstairs window was flung open and an elderly woman leaned out, her hair wild and her expression wilder. '*Arrêtez! Il n'y a personne! Ça ne sert à rien!*'

Sarah turned away. *Try the shop. Try the shop.* Dodging pedestrians, she hurried through the streets. As she turned into the Place de L'Eglise, she collided with a woman carrying a bag of groceries. Courgettes and lettuce went flying. '*Excusez moi, Madame.*' Sarah dropped to her knees, frantically picking up vegetables, then scampered after tomatoes rolling down the pavement. As she ran she trod on two or three, their red juices squirting out under her flip-flop.

'*Imbécile!*' the woman screeched and, dumping what she had collected back into her arms, Sarah ran as fast as she could out of the square, stared at by people who'd stopped to see what was going on. Tears blinded her as she ran and she turned her ankle in one of the *caniveau* drains down the side of the street, trying to avoid someone walking out of their doorway.

As she turned into the square she could see the shop was closed. Of course it was. Hobbling towards it, wiping the tears from her cheeks, she dared not look over towards the café in case Pascal saw her. The street was busy with people: tourists with bum bags, shorts and brown legs; shoppers with their groceries in carrier bags. Sarah passed them all and peered in through the darkened windows. The shop looked tidy and untouched in the murky light. Fabien's desk was empty, the till drawer open.

'*C'est fermé.*' The little man from the shoe shop next door came out, tidying the rack of sandals outside his door. 'It is closed.'

'Yes, I can see that.' Sarah sighed. 'It'll be open tomorrow, I suppose?' She looked at the stickers on the door for some sort of explanation about the mess she was in.

The little man shrugged. 'Who knows? It hasn't been open for days. Several people have been knocking.'

'So' – Sarah faltered – 'the owner hasn't been here?'

'The owner? Ha! Haven't seen him for years. He is too busy sitting on his yacht all day counting his munnay.' The man waved his hand despairingly. 'Bah!'

'But Fabien ...'

'Oh, Monsieur Le Renard? He just works here. Well' – he looked over at the empty shop – 'when it suits him.'

'So it's not his?'

'Nah! That man could not run a – what do you call them? – ice-cream shop if he wanted to.'

He turned away. 'Perhaps,' Sarah asked, desperate to know more, 'perhaps he's gone to another gallery elsewhere?'

The man shrugged, and straightened a card displaying the price. 'What would he know about art? About as much as I do!' And he cackled and disappeared back into his shop.

Maurice found her two hours later curled up on the chair in his study. She thought he'd gone to Toulouse – he'd said he was going to – and there was nothing here for her to do except dust and tidy the already tidy piles, but somehow she'd gravitated to his quiet haven. She must have fallen asleep because she started when she heard him come into the room.

'Sarah, you almost gave me a heart attack. What are you doing?' He dropped his things on the table and came over, perching on the chair opposite. 'You look terrible.' Briefly she explained about the money, not mentioning her growing suspicions, avoiding the subject of Fabien all together.

'Oh, *merde*.' Maurice ran his hands through his already awry hair. 'And I cannot help you. The concert money has to come through the right channels. It's not for me to pay and they always take ages. I didn't realise things were so difficult for you.'

'They aren't. Usually.' She fiddled with the tie on her dress. 'Maurice, you said something about Fabien, about him being cunning. What do you know about him?'

'Ah.' Realisation dawned on Maurice's face. 'Have you been lending him money?'

'No. I fear he may have been helping himself.'

Maurice rubbed his face with his hands. '*Mon Dieu*. I knew he had targeted women before. Usually foreign and usually naïve. No disrespect, Sarah, but he is charm itself, isn't he?' Sarah blushed. 'I had heard he got them to, well, give him a comfortable life. Pay for things. I never thought it was more than that.'

'Oh God, I've been such a fool. I really thought he cared about me.'

Maurice leaned forward, his brows knit in concern. 'The thing about foxes, Sarah, is that they are one of the few animals that kill for the hell of it, not just for a meal. Let one into the hen house and they will keep going until there is nothing left.'

Sarah bolted from her seat and grabbed her bag, heading for the door. 'Take care!' he called after her.

Almost out of her head with panic, Sarah walked urgently through the town. It was beginning to get dark now and people were trickling into the restaurants and bars. Sarah, ignoring the curious glances, made her way into each one, trying to find the familiar dark-haired man. Some of the restaurateurs greeted her, but shook their heads when she asked if they had seen him. Eventually she found herself in the square of his apartment. There were no lights at his windows, and the street lamps made strange shadows through the trees. She tried his doorbell again and, when there was no answer, sat down on the step, hunching her knees up under her. Her stomach rumbled as she realised she hadn't eaten all day, and anything that had been in her stomach she had puked up. Her skin felt clammy in the evening heat and the air felt close, as though one of the spectacular storms that broke out at night over the Pyrenees was about to shatter the evening air.

Chapter 38

'Who cares, anyway? It's all crap, really, isn't it? I mean, loads of people don't even do degrees, anyway.'

'Yeah – whatever. Where's Iggy? Have you seen him?'

Claire wasn't sure Bella could hear her reply above the jukebox and the general hilarity of the Union bar. Bella was gnawing on her nails and just shrugged. 'Dunno. I mean, it's not like it's even important to me. I—'

'Well, if it's not important,' Claire snapped, 'why the fuck do you keep going on about it? You're not the only one, y'know?'

Tears started to well up in Bella's smudgy, over-made-up eyes. 'But that's why I thought you'd understand. Cos it's you and me. It's different with the others. I mean, Animal's scraped through – just – and Iggy, well, he's just a genius so he didn't need to work. But ... what am I going to tell my mum and dad?'

Claire looked at Bella's pale face for a moment. She almost felt sorry for her, although Bella could be a right moody cow at times. But the person she felt sorriest for was herself. How had she gone from being the golden girl to a loser, about to be chucked out of uni just because she hadn't been able to answer any of the stupid questions on the poxy exam paper? Oh yeah, and because she hadn't gone to a single lecture or seminar, or handed in a single essay since the start of last term. Still, at least she didn't have to worry about what her parents would say because, unlike Bella's, they clearly didn't give a toss.

She patted Bella abstractedly on the back, looking round for a means of escape. 'Oh, there he is! I'll just go and, er ...'

Iggy had stalked into the room and was looking round. She

could tell from the look in his eyes that he'd scored something. She left Bella behind and pushed through the crush in the bar towards him. She was aware of people watching her, nudging their companions and pointing her out. Her shameful performance in the exams was already passing into departmental legend. She held her head high, sucked her cheeks in a bit, and swaggered over to Iggy.

'Well? Did you get it?'

Iggy looked down at her, his usual scornful smile in place. 'Hello, Iggy. It's nice to see you, Iggy. Thanks for risking life and limb to score, Iggy.'

He was right, of course, but she felt a wave of irritation. It was all right for him. He'd be here next year. He didn't have anything to worry about for the rest of the summer. He didn't have that sick heavy weight in the pit of her stomach she'd had since she'd gone to look at the department noticeboard. He didn't understand at all. But she forced a smile otherwise, capricious as ever, he might decide not to let her have any. And, God, she needed it.

'Sorry.' She pouted, putting her head on one side. 'I'm just so wound up, y'know, and I could really do with relaxing and having a laugh. Thanks for doing the business. You're a star, Ig, you know you are.'

'That's more like it. C'mon.' He patted his pocket in satisfaction. 'Let's get out of here. Is Bella coming?'

Claire glanced back towards the bar where Bella was slouching in despondency. 'Don't think so. She seems fine to me. Besides' – she took Iggy's arm as they started to walk out – 'all the more for us!'

Iggy snorted and shoved her playfully. 'You're a piece of work, you are. A total nutter. That's what I like about you. You don't care about anything, do you?'

Whoosh! The now familiar sensation started to engulf her. The music felt like it was coming from inside her, part of her body, yet it was all around her too. She could feel her face break into a wide smile she couldn't control, but everything was fantastic. She moved her head slowly – lovely and slow, like moving in water – to look at Iggy. God, he was so beautiful. She loved his face and his smile was like looking into a mirror. He was the best person she'd ever met. She made her way over to him. He'd got a drink and he was holding the plastic glass up to the light. It looked amazing. She had to go and look at it too.

Giggling, she wove past the chairs. It felt a bit like how surfing looked on telly and she stretched her arms out, feeling the air rushing between her fingers as she swayed towards him. She couldn't help stroking people's faces on her way over. They felt so soft and detailed on her fingers. One girl, she didn't know her name, slapped her hand away but Claire just smiled. 'You've got no idea what your head's into,' she said and moved on.

Iggy stretched out his arms and they stood holding each other for ages. She wanted to hug everyone. She wanted to kiss everyone. If only Bella was here too, it would all be perfect. Everyone should be here.

How much later was it? She wasn't quite sure. But Iggy was saying something about another party. She nodded in time with the music and also with her heartbeat, and his too, which she could feel all over her body. This was all so important. She had to make sure her whole life was like this, because it would be so much better if it was. He took her hand and suddenly they were outside and the air was cool, but it felt perfect. She was looking up at the sky and it was so amazing, she wanted Iggy to stop and look at it too, but now they were in another place – someone's room, but she wasn't sure how they'd got there, and that was really funny. And she was laughing, and someone handed her a drink and it tasted fantastic, and even if she closed her eyes she knew what colour it was, because she could taste it.

*

After an hour or more, Sarah's bottom was numb and cold. She'd watched cars come and go, people letting themselves in and out of their front doors, and nothing. He could be out of the country even. She laughed cynically. He can probably afford to be, she told a cat that came to rub itself against her. This was pointless. She was just about to stand up and go when she heard a car come into the square. Its roar was unmistakable.. It pulled into a space, and she waited, crouched on the step, hidden by a Renault in front of her, until she heard the door slam and footsteps coming towards her. Thankfully he was alone. As he came into view she stood up and noticed with cynical pleasure that he started.

He put his hand to his chest. 'Hell. You made me jump, creeping up like that.' He put his arms out as if to embrace her but she stepped back.

'Good. No wife with you tonight, then?' she asked, feeling intimidated by his height in the darkness.

He paused, searching her face the, theatrically, he looked behind him. 'No wife that I can see.'

'Fabien, how did you do it?'

'Do what?' He looked down at his keys to select the right one for the door.

'My money. How did you get hold of my money?'

He stared straight at her, his face half shadowed in the darkness, the whites of his eyes and his linen jacket the only brightness. 'I don't know what you are talking about.'

'Yes you do. You've emptied my account.'

He stepped closer to her and bent down slightly so his nose was level with her chin. 'How could that be, little English woman?' he said quietly. 'Perhaps you've just been a little careless. Some people can be very unscrupulous, you know.' His voice sounded hard.

She swallowed. 'How unscrupulous do you suppose?'

'Oh well, that would depend how careless you were. Leaving

things where other people can find them. It's a bad world out there. These days it's so easy for people to find out all about you, you know.' He straightened up and crossed his arms.

'I didn't tell you anything.'

'Oh but you did, little Sarah. You told me so much without realising you had.' He took her chin in his hand and rubbed his thumb over her skin. 'That's what is so adorable about you, your innocence. Like a little girl.' Sarah, disgusted at herself for tingling under his touch, pulled away sharply.

'I don't get it. It *was* you. It had to be. So how did you do it, Fabien?' She hoped to goodness she was right because standing here in the darkness, the square empty of people, she felt exposed and vulnerable.

He shrugged. 'I think you are deluded. I don't know what you are talking about, and there you go blaming me for your own carelessness. Did you leave your card lying about? What about your pin number? I bet you have that on a teensy bit of paper' – he put his fingers together – 'in your bag in case you forget it. Just where wicked people can find it.'

Sarah put her shoulders back, uncertain now that she'd got this right. 'No. Never. I wouldn't be that stupid.'

'Well.' He shrugged again. 'Who knows? I'm not your Sherlock Holmes.' He gazed up at the sky through the trees, making a show of studying the stars. 'Someone could have slipped your card out when you weren't looking and whipped it away and taken down all those essential little numbers!' He laughed a deep belly laugh, making a fool of her.

'But how would they know my details? My pin number, for example?'

Fabien looked right at her. 'Birthdays, it's always birthdays, little Sarah. Your own, Your children's . . .' Had she told him the twins' birthday? She couldn't remember. Could it have been one of those nights over a couple of bottles of good wine when she'd nattered on about her life under his gentle questioning?

She began to shake, unsure of everything now, whether he was lying or whether he had just told her how he'd done it. He moved towards the building, his key ready to put into the lock. 'But how could you order things online?' she asked, following him, needing to ask before he went inside, and knowing that when he did that was her last chance.

He turned back and sighed as if addressing a little child. 'You aren't going to let this drop, are you?' She could see his frown in the half light. 'What does it matter now?' he asked quietly. 'Any fool can steal your identity. You gave so willingly, didn't you, Sarah? So generous with yourself – how could anyone resist? And then you'd fall asleep, wouldn't you? That lovely deep sleep of yours when I could watch you and find out all about my little English woman from her provincial little town with her neat little handbag all ordered. Addresses, email addresses … so fascinating to read.'

Sarah gasped, horrified by his exploitation and her own stupidity. 'You bastard,' she breathed.

'And the delicious thing is, Sarah, my willing little *putain*, I've made sure you can't prove a thing.'

Sarah spluttered, speechless. He put his key into the lock. 'But why?' she whispered finally, hoping he had heard. 'Why did you do it? I thought we had something. I thought it was real.'

In the darkness, she could see a smile spread over his face, the smile she had once thought charming and sexy. Shame overwhelmed her. 'Real?' he sneered. 'What on earth does real mean? You wanted an adventure, a bit of excitement after your oh-so-dreary marriage. You women are all the same. I gave you what you wanted and I got my reward.'

'Why all the lies, though?'

'Lies?' He paused.

'The son you clearly don't have. Being an artist. Valérie, for fuck's sake. Is there anything about you that is credible?' Now she felt deep, intense anger.

'Yes of course. I know who I am. But telling stories amuses me. It was entertaining to watch you believe it all.'

'And the photographs. Did they amuse you too, Fabien?'

'Oh yes, the photographs! Did you like them? Valérie said you'd found them.'

Sarah found the collusion unbearable and, in her deep loathing, she wanted to hit him, to strike out and hurt him too, but in the dark now she felt afraid and intimidated. 'You've taken away not only my money – and my husband's' – she felt braver saying the word – 'but you've taken my dignity too.'

'No, Sarah, you gave that away yourself. I'm done with you now, and I need a glass of wine. *Adieu*, Mrs Lewis.'

And, letting himself into the building, he shut the door firmly behind him.

Chapter 39

This was the best fun she had ever had. Wasn't everyone gorgeous! Claire wasn't quite sure where Bella had got to, but Animal and Iggy were either side of her as they made their way across campus to Iggy's friend's place. She had a vague idea it was a third year, so that seemed grown up. How did Iggy know a third year? But she was too busy telling them in minute detail about the exam questions.

'So unfair really. I mean, wouldn't it be better if we didn't have all this exam shit?' She stopped, realisation dawning as cars whooshed past her through puddles from an early-evening shower. She held her arms out, welcoming in the notion. 'Just each person finding their own way in life. Everyone just happy and, oooh Iggy, aren't you just the most delicious thing ever?' Wasn't his face so unusual and handsome in this light? She kissed his eyebrows, then linking arms with them both, she pulled Animal and Iggy into a dance. '"Follow the Yellow brick Road, Follow the Yellow Brick road, la la la la la la la, because because because because because of the wonderful things he does!" My mum used to sing that to me, and we used to dance around the kitchen to it! Ha, and now Mum's off shagging some frog!'

The people inside the party all seemed lovely too. And her favourite band playing on the CD! The room thudded and Claire's head thudded too, but she didn't care. This was going to be magic! She felt dreadfully thirsty and, pulling Iggy's arm, made her way over to the kitchen. Unable to find a mug, she turned on the tap and held her head under it, holding back her hair. 'Oh, that was good. I need some more.' She cast about then, spotting a bloke on the other side of the room with a beer can, she went over to him. He looked beefy and handsome. 'You look just the kind of bloke my parents would like!' Gosh didn't her laugh sound loud? 'Can I have a swig?' She couldn't be sure he'd said yes, before she pulled it out of his hand and swigged it back. It tasted warm and a bit disgusting.

'Oi, steady.'

'Thank you, sweetheart.' She handed it back. 'Do you think I am beautiful?'

He looked at his mate and winked. 'Gorgeous. Fancy a dance?'

'Yippee!' What a great idea. She pulled him by the hand and they made their way towards the music, which was throbbing out of the speakers in the next-door room. This bloke looked so warm and friendly, she threw her arms around him and thrust her hips to the beat. No wonder other people did this, it felt so good.

They must have danced for quite a long time, stopping every now and then for some water. There must have been twenty or so people there and she was loving another girl in the group, who was dancing as wildly as she was. 'You are lovely!' she shouted in her ear. 'Will you be my best friend?' It really made sense that she should be when she loved to dance like this. The lights were so bright and vibrant, and now they were playing Iron Maiden. Fantastic! She'd never realised before.

'Here,' someone bellowed down her ear. 'You must be thirsty, love!' How sweet of them. Claire turned to a bloke who was holding out a plastic beaker of beer. She shouted back her thanks, and holding on to her new friend for balance, swigged it back then tossed the beaker into the crowd.

Sarah pulled the suitcase out from under her bed, then wrenched open the drawers, throwing their contents into the case.

'Nathalie, it's all too complicated to explain,' she answered distractedly to her friend who was hovering by the door. 'He didn't admit it outright, and he says I can't prove anything anyway and he's right. But I know he did it. I've got to get home. I can't call David about it – there's too much to tell him – I just need to get home.'

'On what?'

Exactly. On what. Sarah stalled, a couple of dresses on hangers in her hand. 'I don't know. Perhaps I can ring Dad. He'll help. I'm sure he will.'

'Maybe, but do you want to explain it all?' Nathalie had spoken what she felt.

'No.' Sarah dropped the dresses in the case. 'No I don't. Oh fuck, what a mess.'

'Look. You're a very old friend and I love you. And I'm sorry for being partway responsible for this.' Nathalie found a bit of bed to perch on that wasn't covered in clothes, papers and cosmetics. 'Let me give you the plane fare. I'll call up now and see if we can get you a seat.' Sarah couldn't argue. Nathalie wasn't to blame for this, but the truth was Sarah had nothing with which to buy a ticket.

'Would you?' she asked slowly, sick at having to beg like this.

'Yup, I'll look for a flight now.' And, touching her friend on her arm, she left the room.

Sarah's heart pounded. Pulling things from the bedside table, she made a small pile of paperbacks she had read to leave for Nathalie, a pathetic payback for bailing her out, then turned back to sort out the odds and ends scattered there. A small beaded bracelet from Perpignan, a silly badge that had made her laugh when they'd travelled to a town further up the valley, the tag from a skirt they'd bought in Sylvie's shop. All bits Fabien had bought her. Or had he? She put her hands up and, with more aggression than she meant, she pulled the aquamarine and white gold studs from her ears and dropped them back into the empty box. Then, she threw it all into the waste paper basket.

Nathalie put her head around the door. 'I've got you on the dawn flight. We'll need to leave at something silly o'clock so you'd better get your head down for a couple of hours.' She held up her hand before Sarah could object. 'Don't argue. I'm taking you there and that's final.'

Claire was finding it hard to focus but why was no one helping when she tried to grab hold of them? She could feel herself shouting, but the music was so loud they couldn't have been able to hear her. It seemed to thud, or was that her heart?

Someone pushed past her and she grabbed at them. 'Can you help me?' They couldn't hear either, and shook her off. She could make out the door, and made her way slowly over to it, elbowing people out of the way. 'Please' – she grabbed the arm of the beefy bloke she'd danced with earlier. 'Can you take me home?'

His friend roared with laughter. 'Think you've just pulled, mate!'

'Now a bloke can't pass up an invitation like that, can he?' He handed his beer to his friend and, taking Claire's arm, led her back along the corridor to the stairs.

'Oh God, I don't feel good.' Her heart was thumping too hard. Would it just burst out of her chest?

'You've been doing too many Es, my lovely. They're bad for a girl.' He was slipping his hand under her T-shirt at the small of her back. She pushed him away. She had to concentrate on her heart thumping. Oh God, what was happening? Where was Iggy?

'Over here.' She hurried, pulling him along. 'It's over here.' She had to make sure he knew where she lived. She'd be okay if she could just get into bed. Suddenly the poxy little room seemed the only place on earth she wanted to be. Except for home. She really wanted to be at home.

'I've buggered up my exams,' she muttered to him as he

trotted beside her. 'Completely buggered them up. They'll throw me out. Oh shit, oh shit. Have you ever done that?'

'God, you're a laugh.' He didn't sound so nice now, and she was glad she could see her block coming into view. 'Got anything to drink at your place?'

'Here. Now, where's my key. It's here, I'm sure it's here. Oh help me.' She fumbled with the lock, why wouldn't the damned key go in? 'I'm here now.' The bloke seemed to be trying to follow her in. 'No, no thanks. Thanks for seeing me back.' And before he could come any further, and with all her strength, she shouldered the door shut. He banged hard, but Claire put her hands over her ears. The blood was pounding and pounding in her head, whooshing like a river around her brain.

Oh God. Muuuum.

Chapter 40

'How much to Stratford?' The fat man in the cab looked her up and down appreciatively and gave an outrageous price. Sarah rolled her eyes and moved to the cab behind. The handle of her suitcase was hurting her hands and, in her sleeveless dress, she felt chilled in the early-morning air. The second cabbie's price was slightly better and, after haggling for a moment, she stashed her bag and violin case in the boot, jumped in with relief, and rested her head against the back of the seat. She hadn't slept at all, even before they'd left for the airport, and she was beginning to feel dizzy and lightheaded.

The BRMB morning show was playing on the radio – not a programme she'd ever listened to – but the Birmingham traffic reports were strangely comforting. The intense familiarity of the airport, the signs, even the driving on the other side of the road, gave Sarah a sense of terror at what she was about to face. Yet combined with this was immense relief that she was home. It was still very early, England being an hour behind, but already there were courier trucks hurtling past as they edged onto the motorway.

The cabbie turned down the radio. 'You look tanned. Where you been on holiday?'

'France.' Then she closed her eyes so he wouldn't ask her any more questions, and he soon turned up the radio again.

What would she find when she got home? She hadn't been able to call ahead to warn David, her phone now firmly out of credit, so perhaps she'd wake him. She could imagine his familiar, sleep-crumpled face and something inside her ached. If he didn't hate her already, he would now. The radio was playing a track that was loud and tense and she could feel her shoulders tighten in response.

As they came off the motorway towards Stratford, she leaned forward slightly in her seat. The trees were bursting with fresh greenness and gone was the starkness of the winter when she had left. So, life had gone on without her. But, as they came over the bridge, she glanced towards the spire of Holy Trinity behind the trees and the swans serenely swimming on the river by the boathouse. She must have seen them a million times, and here they were still, waiting for her.

'Stop here, please,' she said just before the house, and handed over the last of Nathalie's cash, which she had changed from Euros at the airport. The cab driver helped her out with her cases and she winced as he slammed the door loudly before driving off up the road. Then everything was still. She looked about her. Nothing had changed, but why would it? Pauline's bedroom curtains were closed, her newspaper recycling box ready for the bin men to collect. Of course. It was Wednesday after all. Sarah noticed there was no box outside their house, a chore that had always been David's to perform. She also noticed there was no car outside either. Could he have gone away on holiday? Perhaps that's why he hadn't chased her about the bank account. He might even be somewhere, stranded, with no access to any money. Either way, she had no key, an important detail she'd completely overlooked. Damn. She put her finger on the bell, realising that she'd never rung her own doorbell before, but then ringing doorbells was becoming a regular occurrence. Her stomach ached as she thought about the last time she'd stood waiting and waiting at someone's front door.

No response. No familiar sound of footsteps coming down the stairs into the hall. Perhaps he'd gone to see Tom and Claire, though that would be an odd thing to do in the middle of the week and they must be about to break up for the holidays. She ought to know details like that. She headed round towards the back door, her shoes crunching on the gravel in the silence of the morning. Then, dumping her bag and violin case on the step, she made her way round behind the garage and cautiously lifted the large stone under the fern. There, as always, among the wood lice, was the spare key.

The kitchen was still when she let herself in, the only noise being the familiar hum from the fridge. Everything was as she had left it, except for the air of neglect. The plates she had collected over the years on the dresser, and the quirky tin hen on the window sill she'd bought from a craft market in Devon. There were two upturned coffee cups on the drainer. From two different times, she wondered, or had he been entertaining someone? She felt strangely uneasy at the thought. On the table was a *Times* showing yesterday's date, so perhaps he hadn't gone away, and on the worktop, on top of the bright blue bread bin, was a pile of unopened bank statements.

Walking through to the hallway, she felt she was home, yet it wasn't her home. A jacket of David's was dumped as usual on the chair, a lazy habit of his, but it hardly mattered now, and she picked it up and hung it on the peg under the stairs. The sitting room had an atmosphere of total neglect. The cushions on the sofa were squashed, and there was a glass and a mug on the coffee table. TV listing magazines were strewn on the floor and the curtain fabric and furniture, once so familiar to her, now looked old fashioned and worn, after the freshness of the South of France. The room smelled stale and she opened the windows onto the garden to let in some fresh air. The lawn needed mowing and the roses had taken a battering from the overnight rain. All the bushes needed dead-heading.

In the corner of the room her computer sat ignored, its cover dusty from weeks of neglect. Yet it jumped into life when she pressed the button and she sat down in front of it, too frozen in terror for a moment to log on and see what she might find. To order anything online surely Fabien would have had to supply her email address for acknowledgement of the order, but, she realised now, there was one obvious way he could have found that out – from Nathalie's computer, always turned on in the flat and open on her email page. Any fool could have looked in her email address book when no one wasn't looking.

Not to mention the fact that Sarah had it written on a piece of paper in the handbag he seemed to have made himself so familiar with.

It took an agonisingly long time to load up, but eventually she clicked the send and receive button and emails cascaded down the page, all dating back to the day she had left. There were messages about store cards and supermarket promotions; messages from friends who'd included all their contacts in a round robin about global warming, plus messages from people she'd rarely communicated with who hadn't even known about the split and were just 'touching base'. Then online order confirmations started to download, dating from about a month ago. '*Confirmation de votre command. Merci pour …*' Sarah read them in mounting horror, the details, laid out incontrovertibly in front of her eyes, worse than she had feared. A drip drip drip of online shopping orders, starting with small amounts then mounting as he had obviously became bolder. At first it was books and CDs, three or four shirts, a couple of pairs of Armani jeans. A pair of leather shoes costing nearly two hundred pounds – were they the ones that he'd shown off with such pride? – a gold ladies' watch and a Louis Vuitton bag, paid for in dollars; stereo equipment, a laptop, two digital cameras and a mobile phone. And on each order, as she clicked on the details, a different despatch address was given, and one she didn't recognise. In London. How clever he'd been. Mustn't raise suspicions by having things ordered abroad, but then it became obvious he'd been able to fly in to collect the goods, because next appeared the aeroplane bookings with e-ticket orders, to destinations all over Europe. Faceless, identity-free travel.

Then came the holidays, two-day packages in hotels she'd never heard of, and all dated within two or three days of when they were booked. Sarah could feel the sweat under her arms, her reaction a mixture of indignation, and amazement that he had been so audacious. The dot.con king indeed.

She looked at her watch. She'd have to call the bank as soon as possible, but wasn't the damage already done? The shoes worn, the holidays taken? Had Valérie gone on them with him? There had to be a way to prove Sarah had ordered none of this, hadn't there? There was protection from this kind of fraud, wasn't there?

Fraud. She dragged her suitcase up the stairs. He'd been a fraud all right.

Their bedroom was unchanged too. Reliably similar with the rose-patterned curtains and the white duvet. The bed was roughly pulled up, her pretty decorative cushions left on the chair. He'd always thought they were pointless. Perhaps they were.

Without opening her case, she pulled off her dress and under-wear and, turning on the shower, she closed her eyes and stood under the hot cascade of water, trying desperately to wash it all away: her stupidity, her relationship with Fabien, the betrayal, the whole bloody mess.

She was standing at the top of the stairs in her dressing gown. David had known the moment he walked in that something was different. Even the air smelled different, but when he saw the violin case propped up against the wall, it confirmed what he knew already.

Her hair was wrapped in a turban made from a towel, the way she always did it, and her tanned face looked wide-eyed like a child's.

'Hello, David,' she said quietly.

He felt a confusion of emotions. 'Where the fuck have you been?' he growled. 'I've been trying to call you on your mobile.'

'I turned it off. I've run out of credit.'

'Yes, that happens when you run out of money.' He could hear the snarl in his voice, but who was he really angry with? Her or himself for the stupid hope he felt when he saw her there.

'I've got something to tell you,' she went on.

'Too right you've got something to tell me!' He slammed down his keys on the hall table. 'What have you done? What the hell have you done with our money? You've left me with nothing. Less than nothing. All your mother's money. All my salary. It's all gone. They showed me at the bank. Do you have any idea how much you've spent? I don't know why you've even bothered to come back. I've got nothing left to give you. The cupboard's bare, Sarah.'

Standing there with his hands on his hips, David glared at her. The night he'd just spent with Kate receded in his mind as he struggled to see something familiar in the woman standing before him. Then her face crumpled and she raised both hands to her head in a gesture so familiar it made the breath catch in his throat.

'Look, I'm sorry. I don't know what to say. It's ... it's complicated, what's happened. It wasn't me. Surely you didn't think it was me who spent all that money?'

'What do you mean? Of course it's you.' David could feel his anger rising. 'The money's been siphoned off from our account from the South of France. How can it not be you? Cos it sure as hell hasn't been me.' A thought flashed through his mind. 'Unless ...'

He could see Sarah's eyes pleading with him, such a change from the cold indifference she'd shown in the days before she left, all that time ago, when he'd pleaded with her. 'Unless you're trying to tell me this was an accident? Did you lose your bank cards? All of them? In one go? Come off it, Sarah. I wasn't born yesterday.'

She wilted visibly, despair radiating from her. 'Sort of.

Someone got hold of them and used them without my knowing. I'm sorry. I'm so sorry. I didn't know what to do.'

David sighed. Maybe there was a chink of hope after all. He felt himself getting businesslike and shrugged off his jacket, dropping it on the chair. Sarah began to descend the stairs cautiously. It reminded him of Claire as a child after she'd been told off and sent to her room. 'If someone stole your cards, then we should be able to get something back, at least. Did you report it to the police? Did you notify the bank?'

She wouldn't meet his eyes. 'No, I didn't. I don't think it's going to be as straightforward as that.'

'For God's sake, Sarah. You're talking in riddles. Were your cards stolen or weren't they?'

She raised her head and looked him squarely in the eye. 'They were taken from my bag by someone I trusted,' she said quietly. 'And who found out my pin number and all my details. That's why I didn't tell the police or anyone. Because my card wasn't even missing. I promise you, David, I had no idea until I couldn't get any money out myself.'

David felt his arms go cold. 'Then we're screwed. We're utterly screwed. If you gave someone else your pin number, there's no come-back at all. You've basically given all our money away and there's not a single thing I can do about it. How could you be so fucking stupid? Who the hell was it? Nathalie? Did that stupid bitch do this to you?'

She shook her head wordlessly.

'So what have you come back for? What do you want from me, Sarah? Do you expect me to sort it all out for you? You know I haven't got any money for you. Your "trusted friend" took care of that. Always assuming there was a friend, that is.'

'Of course there was! Do you think I'm lying to you?'

He shrugged and pushed past her to the kitchen, a huge hurtful anger in the pit of his stomach. 'I've no idea, quite frankly. And actually, I don't really care. You've got yourself into some kind of mess and, after everything you've dumped on me in the last few months, you seem to expect me to sort it out.' He felt a wave of utter desolation that pricked at his eyes and he turned away from her to the kettle. 'You know what? I think you'd better go. I really don't want to talk to you any more.'

He could feel her there, looking at him, but he didn't look round until he heard a ring at the doorbell. They both turned and, through the glass, he could make out Kate's long hair and cherry-red cardigan. This was the last thing he needed.

'That's someone for me,' he said quickly and went to open the door.

Kate was smiling broadly, as usual. 'Hey! Long time, no see! You left your sunglasses. I thought you might need them.' And she slid her arms round his back and kissed him. David was aware of a movement behind him and he untangled himself, stepping outside to join her.

'Listen, this isn't a very good time,' he whispered urgently. 'Thanks for the glasses and everything. Can we meet later? I've got someone here and it's ... I'll explain when I see you. I've had some bad news.'

Kate's brown eyes opened wide in sympathy. 'Sure – is there anything I can do? What's up?'

Behind them, the front door swung open and Sarah, pale beneath her tan, stood in the doorway. She'd taken the towel from her hair and it hung in wet tendrils around her face. She looked small and vulnerable compared to the athletic woman beside him.

Kate stepped back and looked quickly between them. 'Right. What's this, David? Is there something I should know?' She sounded annoyed.

'No – not really. I mean. Kate, this is my wife who's just arrived back unexpectedly from the South of France. She was just leaving.'

'Hang on?' Kate's voice was sharp. 'Wife or ex-wife? I thought you were divorced, Dave.'

'Divorced?' Sarah asked confused. 'Have you started proceedings?'

David didn't answer and turned back to Kate. 'That's right. I'm not divorced. My wife here walked out on me. Your cousin assumed I was divorced the day we met and I didn't correct her – or you. I'm sorry, but I didn't think it would matter to you.'

She frowned, and for once her unrelenting 'no-worries' attitude seemed to slip for a moment, before she pouted, then tilted her head to one side. 'Actually, I don't think it does. But I don't fancy sticking round while you two are slugging it out.' She theatrically looked at her watch, in what David could tell was a false insouciance. 'Anyway, I'm already late for work. Gimme a call once you're free.' She glanced at Sarah. 'Okay, lover?'

And she walked back to her Mini, parked at a rakish angle at the end of the drive, swinging her hips more than was strictly necessary.

David turned back to Sarah and folded his arms defiantly. She didn't look anywhere near as angry as he would have expected. Interesting. He looked at her narrowly. Of course! It was a man. That was why she was being so cagey about the pin number. Still pale, she was breathing fast.

'I see,' she said slowly. 'So we're divorced now, or as good as. And was there anything else you were going to tell me? Like leaving your job. Doreen told me.'

'Why should I tell you anything? I don't owe you any explanations.' He looked at her coldly. 'Who are you to question me when you've handed out our bank details to a man you've been shagging.' The fact that she didn't deny it was all the answer he needed.

He watched her start to cry but, unexpectedly, felt no sense of triumph, only an empty, empty feeling of regret. She turned back into the house and he followed, closing the door behind them. No point in sharing the disintegration of their marriage with Pauline and the rest of the neighbours. In the hall now, he prepared to interrogate her, but sighed as the phone rang and he snatched it up impatiently.

'Tom? What's up?' He'd never heard Tom sound like this, or at least not since he'd fallen out of a tree as a child and hadn't been able to feel his legs for a few moments. It was shrill with panic.

'Dad, it's Claire. She's in hospital. I'm here with her. She's bad. The doctors are trying to . . . I don't know what's wrong, but she's taken something. Dad, you've got to get here.'

'What hospital? We're on our way.'

He felt Sarah's hand grasp his arm and he could smell her perfume. Tom's voice was trembling with the effort of holding back tears. 'And Dad, they say you should contact Mum.'

'Oh God. It's all right, Tom. She's here with me now. I'll explain later. Just tell me what you know and we'll be with you as fast as we can.'

As Tom falteringly explained, David felt himself turn icy cold, his whole body tense with terror. He replaced the phone and turned to Sarah. Everything else was irrelevant. 'It's Claire,' he said, struggling to keep his voice calm, seeing her eyes widen with fear. 'She's in hospital. It's serious, apparently. We'll need to take your car.'

Without speaking she bolted upstairs and came out moments later, as he opened the garage door, dressed in jeans and a T-shirt, her hair almost dry now, blonder and sun-bleached. In her hand were the keys, and her bag was over her shoulder.

'I'll move the Alvis out – okay?'

She nodded tensely and slipped past him into the garage, looking curiously at the gleaming drop-head parked behind the dustsheet-covered shape of her own car. He reversed out automatically, his mind fixed on Tom's shaking voice and the awful words he couldn't bring himself to share with Sarah just yet.

He opened the driver's door. 'I'll drive,' he said as calmly as he could, and Sarah got out without a word. He felt her search his eyes and recognise the fear in them. And cursed the fact that she knew him better than anyone else in the world.

Chapter 41

Thankfully her car started after a couple of goes. They barely spoke as they pulled away, leaving the Alvis on the drive. How ironic. After years of nagging that he shouldn't let it die from neglect, it had taken Sarah leaving to galvanise him into action. It looked resplendent, but to travel in it now on such a journey seemed wrong. It was a car for fun. They both knew that.

Everything she wanted to talk about, everything she wanted to ask him – about that woman at the house, his job, the money – meant nothing now. All she could focus on at this second was getting to the hospital. Every traffic light seemed to take for ever to change, and every driver in the rush-hour queues, which had built up since she'd come over the bridge earlier, was a prat who shouldn't be allowed on the road. The summer rain started again, making people hurry as they dodged puddles in their in-appropriate shoes. The wipers made a fwump fwump, smearing the windscreen as she peered through it. They were well clear of Stratford before the sickness in her stomach had receded enough for her to ask.

'What else did Tom tell you?'

'That she is in intensive care.'

Sarah gasped. 'Has she had an accident?' She leaned forward in her seat.

'The details Tom gave me were sketchy, but they think she's taken a drug overdose.'

Sarah looked at the side of David's face to see if he was covering up anything. She'd always been able to read his face, because he could never hide anything. It was thinner than before, the skin lightly tanned. His hair was longer, and he'd lost weight. How unbearably odd that in this nightmare she couldn't help noticing he looked good. He was staring intently at the road, an expression of suppressed pain she knew only too well. 'What else did he say? I know that's not all he told you.'

He sighed. 'Tom said she was very poorly. They think she's reacted badly to something she took and the next few hours are critical.'

'Stop the car!' Sarah shrieked and, as he pulled in to a lay-by, she opened the door and threw up into the verge.

The tears slowly fell down her cheeks for the rest of the journey. They didn't speak, except every now and then she could hear herself saying 'Oh God'. How could their beautiful, clever daughter have wanted to take her own life? How had they missed the signs?

David stayed resolutely silent, an arm uncharacteristically rigid, clasping the steering wheel. The only signs of his turmoil manifested in how close he drove to the car in front and the way he swerved out into the fast lane. He pushed her little car to the limit, driving it as he had his high-spec company saloon.

'Poor Tom,' he said suddenly. 'He's probably all on his own at the hospital. He's too young to cope with that.' And he accelerated even harder.

Finding a parking space in the hospital car park took an age. Overweight and pregnant women, looking stupid and bovine, seemed to have taken them all, then were waddling like happy ducks over to the ante-natal outpatients. It was all Sarah could do not to scream at them to get out of the way. Her hands were shaking now and, as the door of A&E slid open, she hurried through them and past the reception desk, desperate to find Claire. Were they too late?

David grabbed her arm. 'Hang on. We have to say we are here.' Then, very calmly, he told the nurse behind the desk who they were.

'Come with me.' A dark-haired woman with a kind face came round to them. 'I'll take you to your son.' Her gentle tone was reassuring, but the fact that she seemed to know all about the situation was not. She led them through several corridors, all with identical doors. Her white clogs squeaked on the linoleum floor. Then finally they pushed through double doors into the intensive care unit. The reception area was brightly lit, people in hospital scrubs hurrying through doors either side, revealing brief glimpses of rooms with wires and equipment.

Sarah stood frozen as David and the nurse talked to the woman behind the desk, who pointed along the corridor. They followed her directions and, as they turned the corner, she saw Tom, slumped on a rigid chair, alone in the clinical silence. He raised his head as he heard them and jumped up, relief all over his face. Down each cheek were weals and scratches, raw and red with congealed blood.

'Dad? Mum, how come you are here?'

'Oh, my darling boy. What the hell has happened to your face?' Sarah took him into her arms and, as she did so, his body gave way and, as he hadn't since he was a little boy, he sobbed into her T-shirt. Sarah gently rocked him in her arms, whispering reassurances that they were there now. He smelled of sweat and fear, but she buried her face in his hair, kissing him and summoning the courage to say the words.

'We're too late, aren't we? She's dead, isn't she?'

But in her arms she felt him shake his head urgently. He looked up, his face red and ravaged. 'No, Mum, she's hanging in there.'

'Oh God, Tom, tell us what's happened.' Gently she pulled him down onto a chair and sat beside him. David crouched in front of them both. Wiping his nose on his sleeve, Tom began to speak, the words tumbling out of him without prompting, as he found comfort in at last being able to share the agony of the last few hours.

'It's been horrendous.' He sniffed and wordlessly David handed over a crumpled handkerchief, always in his back pocket. 'Someone woke me this morning saying Claire was in her room screaming and acting crazy, as though she was on some mad trip.'

'But I thought …' Sarah faltered. 'I thought she'd taken paracetamol or something – a suicide attempt.' She couldn't believe she'd voiced the word. 'That she'd …'

'No, no, Mum.' Tom's eyes were red now, raw from crying. 'No, I think she took an E with that fucking crowd she's been hanging out with. Maybe at a party or something.'

Sarah's momentary relief was immediate replaced with horror. 'Drugs?'

Tom nodded wordlessly. 'Thank God someone knew where my room was. Anyway …' His mouth made an odd grimace as he fought back the tears again. 'Anyway.' He swallowed. 'They said I had to get over there quickly because she'd gone all weird. When I got there she'd barred the door and there were people outside, sort of banging and shouting at her to open up.' He looked up at Sarah and David. 'God, she was like a Claire I didn't know. She's never behaved like that. Well, me and this other bloke sort of threw ourselves against the door and eventually I squeezed in and she was … she was …' He stopped and jiggled his leg. 'She was cowering in the corner. Sort of like a wounded animal.' There was a noise from David like a stifled sob.

'I tried to talk to her, Dad, but she was looking at me as if she didn't know me. And when I tried to touch her, she just went for me, screaming and tearing at everything. The posters on the walls, her books. She picked up a chair and threw it at the window, shouting, "Leave me alone." She just wouldn't see it was me … hence the face. She got hold of all her pens and went for me.' He tried to smile weakly. 'Eventually an ambulance arrived. It seemed to take for ever. At least they let me ride with her, but even the paramedics couldn't control her. She was so strong. She was like a prisoner or something.' He struggled for a comparison. 'Or like a cornered rat. I think she wrecked the back of the ambulance and, then when we got here, they sort of brought us in the back way somewhere and she was running and screaming and throwing her arms about knocking trolleys flying. I think she even punched a doctor.'

There was a pause and he jiggled his leg again, scrunching up David's handkerchief. 'What happened then, son?' David asked quietly, rubbing Tom's knee.

'They took her into a room and I couldn't go in, but a nice nurse told me they had managed to restrain her and sedate her. It seemed to take ages for her to stop shouting. About an hour I think.' He looked at David searchingly. 'I tried to call home but you weren't there and your mobile wasn't on.'

David looked down at the floor. 'No. I'm sorry.'

'Oh, Tom.' Sarah could hardly breathe. 'Where is she now?'

Tom jerked his head to a door a bit further along the corridor. 'In there. There's about a hundred people in there with her but they won't let me in. The nurse said her blood pressure and temperature were sky high and they're trying to get it down.' He paused and none of them spoke. 'It's going to be really critical,' Tom said eventually. 'The doctor said he'd wait to talk to you when you got here, but that her organs might pack up. He wouldn't really answer my questions because you two are down as her next of kin or something.' Again his face crumpled. This big strong son looking so much like a little boy. 'God, the not knowing. It's been awful.'

David watched silently as Tom – tall, strapping, confident Tom – buried his face in Sarah's neck and broke down in tears. She smoothed back his hair, just as she had ever since he'd been tiny, and gently kissed his bruised and scratched face, murmuring words of comfort that David couldn't hear. From the compression of her lips, David could tell she was close to tears again herself, but holding them back, the way she had when Tom had broken his leg that time. So much history. He moved closer to them and, hesitantly, put out his hand to rub Tom's back, Sarah's arm, then changed his mind.

'How the hell has she got involved with drugs?' he tried to keep the anger out of his voice. 'Did you know anything about it?'

Recovering slightly, Tom shrugged and sniffed. 'Dad, drugs are all over the place. You know that. But ...' He hesitated. 'We haven't really seen much of each other this term. I feel terrible about it but it can be hard. I mean, we're in different departments and we have different friends so ... And the people she's been knocking around with ... well, they're not my type. I don't even think they're Claire's type. And after the exam thing—'

'What?' David and Sarah asked simultaneously.

Tom looked up sheepishly, clearly not sure he should be letting on. 'She ploughed them, basically. People are saying she didn't write a single word, just drew pictures on the page, but that just might be gossip. We only got the results the other day and I hadn't even had a chance to talk to her, but it's spread like wildfire.'

Sarah looked confused. 'But she's always worked so hard in the past – her A-levels and things. I thought she was enjoying the course? She never said anything.'

There was a long, uncomfortable pause. 'Well, neither of you were really listening, were you?'

'Tom! I came as soon as I heard. What's happening? Is she all right?'

A tall girl with fair hair and a clear, high-cheekboned face was hurrying towards them. Her look of concern told David exactly who this was.

Tom disentangled himself from his mother and straightened up. 'Gemma! You got my message.'

They stopped slightly awkwardly, obviously about to embrace

but feeling it might be inappropriate. Tom took her hand. 'Mum, Dad – this is Gemma, my girlfriend.'

David felt a surge of something – pride mixed with envy, perhaps, and a sense of time passing too fast. In his mind, Tom was still a gangling, moody adolescent. The Tom standing in front of him now, protective of the girl beside him, was a young man, clear-eyed and confident, who'd just coped with a horrendous ordeal. Had he looked like that himself, all those years ago, when he and Sarah had first been together? Had they really been this young when they'd fallen in love? Sarah was shaking Gemma's hand and they were talking quietly. Then David, too, shook her hand. Would her face, one day, become as familiar to him as his was to Wilf, he wondered, or Sarah's to Anthony? Families went on, didn't they? That was what they were supposed to do. David squeezed his eyes tight. His family: falling apart at this very moment. And behind the doors, his little girl was fighting for her life. A sense of utter powerlessness swept over him.

Sarah's hand on his arm made him open his eyes. She motioned with her head over to the seats and they left Tom and Gemma talking quietly together..

'She seems nice,' Sarah said at last.

'Mmm. Tom looks happy.'

'Poor Tom. What he's been through! And poor, poor little Claire! Our baby.'

Sarah's shoulders began to shake and David, instinctively this time, pulled her close. 'Where's the consultant? I wish someone would tell us something. It feels as if we've been here hours.' But a glance at his watch showed it had been less than thirty minutes. He looked up and down the quiet corridor, with its constant whine of artificial lighting and the smell of cleaning fluid, his eyes drawn to the door of Claire's ward. He clenched his fists, willing himself to feel how she was. Surely he should be able to sense it. But all these months, according to Tom, she'd been floundering and he hadn't even realised there was anything wrong. How could he have been so blind?

The swing doors bounced open and a small, curly-haired woman in scrubs appeared, followed by a nurse. She looked up and down the corridor, then directly at them. Her blue eyes looked tired but assessing, and she came over. 'Mr and Mrs Lewis? You're Claire's parents?'

They both nodded, wordlessly, too afraid for social niceties.

'I'm Dr McKenzie and I've just taken over the care of your daughter.' She pulled up another chair and sat down facing Sarah and David who had taken Tom's seat. The nurse stood by watchfully. Dr McKenzie paused for a moment, her face serious, and made eye contact with them both as though weighing up how much to tell them. 'We are concerned about Claire. She's taken or been given a number of drugs and she's reacted badly to the combination. Her condition isn't stable yet and the next four hours will be decisive. When she was brought in, she was very distressed indeed. Your son may have told you. We've given her a sedative that works very well in these situations and doesn't react with what she's taken already, so she's unconscious now and that's how we want it to stay for a while. We're monitoring her very closely, but our main concern is to bring down her body temperature and her blood pressure.'

David could feel Sarah start to shake and put his arms round her shoulders to pull her close. 'Will she be all right?' His voice sounded so much more controlled than he felt.

The doctor dropped her eyes for the first time and looked down at her hands. David followed her gaze and found himself, stupidly, thinking how clean her short-nailed hands were. Of course they would be. He forced himself to concentrate on what she was saying, as if he could pick more meaning from the careful words by sheer force of will. 'We don't know yet. We're doing everything we can but these situations are, by definition, unpredictable.'

'What's the worst that could happen?' he heard himself blurt.

'Her body is under enormous strain. It's obviously a concern that there might be permanent damage to her organs and her brain, but we can't tell at the moment.' A sob left Sarah's lips and the doctor reached for her hand. 'Do you know of any underlying conditions that Claire might have?' she asked gently. 'Does she have a heart condition, for example? Anything you can tell us will be a help. We need to know if there are any possible complications to look out for.'

David suddenly couldn't think. 'Well, her grandmother died of an aneurysm, but she was in her seventies. Nothing else, I don't think. Nothing we know of.'

The doctor nodded. He had to ask, although he feared the answer. 'These ... these drugs ... Can you tell if ...? I mean, she's not a regular user, is she, because I'm sure she wouldn't. She's not that type.'

'It's impossible to say, Mr Lewis. This may very well be the first time your daughter has ever experimented. Your son told us she had been at a student party, so possibly she took a synthesised drug there, but they can have very unpredictable effects and, the trouble is, these young people think they're perfectly safe. Almost as if they're not real drugs at all. We see cases like this all too often. Or, and I'm afraid this is another possibility, someone may even have slipped something into her drink.'

'That'll be it,' Sarah said urgently.

'Well it's a possibility, but the most dangerous combination is amphetamines mixed with alcohol on top of anything else she may have taken last night. And that's my concern at the moment.'

'Can we see her?' Sarah's voice was barely audible.

The doctor turned her calm, level gaze on Sarah once again. 'Normally, I'd say no. But I'll just go and take a look at her. I'll be right back.'

She disappeared back through the doors as quietly as she had come. David stared at a mark on the floor. This wasn't making any sense. The woman had used words he couldn't believe were being associated with his daughter. The minutes stretched out wordlessly between Sarah and David. It felt as though breaking the silence would rupture their absolute concentration on their daughter, near yet so distant and in a place they couldn't reach. David was acutely aware of the sound of Sarah's breathing.

The doctor reappeared, holding the doors open, and smiled for the first time. 'You can come in, but only for a short time. Please be careful of the drip.'

They stood up in unison and David felt Sarah reach for his hand, taking it in her short, strong fingers. She'd stopped crying now and led him forward with quiet purpose.

Under harsh lights and surrounded by drips, monitors and breathing apparatus, Claire looked like a broken doll. They moved forward cautiously and just stared. Pale, and thinner than he had seen her in years, her hair stuck to her forehead with sweat, she was frighteningly still. Her nails, still bitten even after years of effort with foul-tasting lotions, were painted black, the varnish chipped off here and there. She was in a blue hospital gown, there were scratches on her cheeks and it looked as though her earring had been ripped out, leaving a livid tear on her earlobe.

Beside him, Sarah dropped his hand and raised both her own to her mouth.

'What have I done?'

He was uncertain which of them had said it, confused for a moment. Then he realised that Sarah had voiced the thought that had just entered his head.

Chapter 42

Sarah pulled the bedroom door closed quietly behind her. Claire was sleeping gently, her pale drawn face relaxed at last, after the turmoil of the last thirty-six hours. They'd gone back to the campus with Tom in the early hours once they'd dared to leave Claire, but had returned to the hospital as soon as they woke the next morning. Little had been said between times. Sarah did her best to straighten the mess Claire's fit had made of the dismal little room and her sleep in Claire's narrow empty bed had been fitful and wracked with dreams; David's night on Tom's floor had not been much better.

After a breakfast of thin coffee in a plastic cup from the hospital vending machine, they'd sat again in the corridor, barely speaking and watching the clock, looking up every time the door opened, hoping it might mean good news. Any news. Dr McKenzie had come past to tell them there was no change and that she was going off her shift, and Sarah had wanted to clutch on to her and not let her leave. Then Sarah must have dropped off, because she had woken with a panicky jolt as the doors of the intensive car unit had opened and a different doctor had come out. With light auburn hair and freckles, he'd looked even younger than Tom, and Sarah had almost ignored him, sure that the plump little middle-aged nurse with him must be more reliable.

When he'd told them that Claire was conscious and was tired but alert, Sarah had let the sobs come, and the young doctor had stood awkwardly, fiddling with his fingers, as the tears poured down her face. As he had when Mary had died, David simply held her and let the storm pass.

They had finally let them bring Claire home, but only after they were happy her body was functioning normally. There had also been the obligatory meeting with the psych, 'normal procedure in these cases' they were told, and the interview had taken place resolutely in private with David and Sarah left excluded and wondering outside. Claire had sat, silently, in the back of the car with Sarah as the four of them made their way home. At one point Sarah had put her hand on her daughter's leg and Claire had let her body slump and she had rested her head on her shoulder.

'I feel like shit,' she'd mumbled.

'Yeah, never a good idea to mix your drinks,' Tom had said over his shoulder and they had all smiled wryly. As usual, Tom had managed to lighten the mood, to bring them all back to something approximating normality.

After a shower and something to eat, Tom had gone off to see some friends in town – old school friends of both his and Claire's – who'd want to know how she was. He deserved a break after the drama he'd been through. The man who kissed her on the cheek, and said 'Glad you're back, Mum,' before heading out of the front door, seemed years older than the boy she'd seen off at the airport in Perpignan. He and Claire had had a moment upstairs so heartbreakingly touching that Sarah hadn't been able to watch. He had gone through hell for Claire and it would change their relationship for ever.

Sarah wandered into the kitchen. She felt as though she had crash landed but she could feel her familiar routine return instinctively. Every urge was to start tidying, to begin a shopping list of fruit and veg for the totally depleted stocks, to launch into the ironing pile of crumpled clothes so stiff and dry now they must have sat there for weeks. Perhaps David's girlfriend wasn't the domesticated type. Had she been in here doing the jobs that were Sarah's? And were they Sarah's now anyway? Her heart did a little leap of anxiety and she pulled a pencil out of the pot and began to scribble down things she'd need to get.

Then she remembered there was no money to buy them with. What a God-awful mess.

'The bank manager wants to see us first thing in the morning.' David came into the kitchen, and they stood and looked at each other. 'I finally got through to the branch and I explained about stuff.' He paused. 'He was okay. Quite sympathetic in a way, but he said there would be no clawing back the money that was drawn out as cash because the ... the person who took it had knowledge of your pin number and had your card.' He paused. 'Christ, Sarah, how could you have done that?'

'I didn't.' She looked down at her list and began to doodle on the edge of the page. 'He was clever and—'

'What? Seductive?'

Sarah flinched. 'What about the credit card?' She asked quietly.

'Well, apparently, and he's not sure yet, anything ordered online we should be able to get a refund on because the responsibility was with the merchant. You will have to assure them tomorrow that you didn't order any of it. Or did you? Was it presents and stuff?' His face looked curiously pained.

'No. No. I only found out when I got home yesterday morning and looked at my emails. He must have got all the information from Nathalie's computer.' She stopped. Here she was explaining details about a place, a situation he hadn't been a part of but which had nearly ruined everything for him.

'In the meantime, they have agreed to extend the overdraft until we can get something sorted.'

'We don't have to tell the children, do we?' Sarah couldn't bear them to know, not when Claire had been through so much already.

David looked hard at her for long minutes. 'No. No, we won't tell the children nor our parents, but whatever happens we have to pay back the bank. He said we can talk about it tomorrow but the bottom line is we can't live on a massive overdraft with no funds available.'

'Of course not.' She didn't want to ask about his job and why he had left, but the obvious solution hung in the air. 'We could remortgage to raise the money.'

'I'd need to get a job to be able to do that. And why should I get any old job to get us out of a mess you created?'

There was a knock at the front door and through the glass they could make out the distinctive silhouette of Wilf.

'Oh God, I completely forgot to call him.'

David opened the door and the elderly man hurried through, his face ravaged with concern. Sarah didn't think she'd ever seen him look so distraught and panic-stricken.

'I've just met Tom in town. He's told me what happened. How is she?'

Sarah put her arms around her father's neck and gave him a warm hug. 'She's okay. They say it will take her a few days to recover completely, but she's okay. She's been through a terrible ordeal and she needs to rest.' Wilf held her very tight. 'How are you, Dad?' she asked gently

'I'm okay darling. I'm okay.' He released her slowly. 'But I've missed you terribly. Thank God you were here. How come you came back without letting us know?'

Sarah caught David's eye over her father's shoulder and he shook his head mouthing 'no'.

'I just needed to come back,' she replied, realising, as she said it, that it was the truth.

'Well, it's good to have you home. David, old son, how are you?' He put his arm round David's shoulders and they embraced rather awkwardly.

'Better now, thanks, Wilf. Can I make you some tea? I think there's milk.'

Suddenly it felt difficult, as though she too were a guest. 'Er, no there isn't. I'll nip down to the corner shop. I could do with some air.' And, picking up the keys, she let herself out.

The lady in the shop was wreathed in smiles when she walked in. 'Good to have you back. Were you on some sort of sabbatical?' she whittered on. ' I've heard people do that. Sounds like a lovely idea but my George won't hear of it. A weekend on the South Coast is the best I get. That husband of yours looks like a dish of fish. I see him out running everyday. Stops in to get his paper on the way home and the weight has fair dropped off him.'

'Yes. Yes, hasn't it?' Sarah acknowledged, another piece in the jigsaw of David's new life slotting into place. She put a few carrots into her basket, milk and bread, mentally totting up how much she had left in her purse from Nathalie's loan. That was someone else to be paid back. They could defrost something for supper from the meal-for-one stocks that she had made before she left. As she made her way back down the road, she winced at the thought of how patronising that must have seemed to David. Here you go, some lonely meals to keep you going. I'm just off to find myself. No wonder he was so angry. She turned the corner into the driveway and her heart raced. There, parked next to her little car, was Anthony's imposing silver Mercedes.

She could sense the atmosphere even as she opened the front door. She dropped the keys on the hall table and headed for the quiet voices in the kitchen. Wilf and David were leaning against the worktop on one side of the room with Heather and Anthony in a similar pose on the other. It was almost a stand-off and everyone looked rigid and ill-at-ease. Despite the mercy visit they were making, the antagonism between them was tangible. Were they still angry at Sarah? Then, Sarah realised, she hadn't seen her father and her in-laws in the same room together for years. How had that been allowed to happen?

'Hello?' she said, breaking the silence and trying to smile. 'It's lovely to see you.'

Anthony, ever the gentleman, stepped forward. 'Sarah. How lovely to see you too, even in such terrible circumstances. David called earlier and we came straight over.' Sarah looked at David.

He shrugged, his expression as bemused as hers. 'Sorry, I was going to tell you.'

'Well, thank you for coming. I'm sure David's told you she's sleeping and needs to be left in peace, but can I make you some tea?' She headed towards the kettle and began to busy herself with cups. 'I had to nip out for some milk, I'm afraid, but it'll be ready in a moment.' She could sense Heather ticking away like a bomb behind her.

'Would you like Darjeeling as usual, Heather?' she asked over her shoulder. 'I'm sure there's some here still.'

David opened the tin, kept especially for his mother's occasional visits, and sniffed. 'Still smells as vile as ever,' he joked. Why were they both trying so hard to lift the atmosphere?

'No, I haven't been over since you left,' her tinkling voice broke in pointedly. 'But we've been feeding David in Campden, haven't we, dear?'

'Well, yes, I've been over on the odd occasion.'

There was a pause and the air of expectation, the silence before the bomb explodes, made Sarah clench her fists in anticipation. As the kettle reached boiling point and the switch flicked off, Heather opened her mouth on cue and the diatribe began.

'I don't know how you can come back here, calm as you please, and start making tea, after all you've done.'

'I—'

'You walk off into the sunset, no regard for anyone, leaving behind a God-awful mess and then, just like that, turn up again just as everyone is beginning to get used to the fact that you have gone. Do you have any idea what you have done?' There were little red marks of excitement on her cheeks. Anthony crossed his arms and looked down at the floor, and Sarah noticed that Wilf was gripping the side of the worktop.

'Mum,' David growled and stepped forward, but Heather held up her hand.

'No, David. It's about time that your *wife* – she almost spat out the words – 'took some responsibility for what she has done to this family.'

'Heather.' This time Anthony interjected, his voice firm, but Heather, hand on hips, was not going to let up. There was fire in her eyes and they were unwavering on Sarah.

'I don't think you have anything to say on the subject, do you, Anthony?' she said without looking at him. Sarah looked at her father-in-law in confusion, but his gaze was fixed somewhere in the distance. 'You, the expert on pleasing yourself at everyone else's expense.'

What the hell was this all about? Suddenly Sarah was too exhausted to be bothered with her mother-in-law, not when her daughter was upstairs recovering from an experience that was both her and David's fault, and theirs alone to sort out. 'For Christ's sake, Heather,' she sighed, 'this isn't the time. Yes, David and I have things we have to talk about, but that's our business, and for the moment there are much more important issues to deal with. We all need support through this, not more trouble.'

'I'll tell you who it is that needs support.' Heather narrowed her eyes. 'Claire for a start. No wonder that poor little child in bed up there had to go to such desperate measures to get attention, while her mother was off being a tart.'

Sarah gasped and the whole room seemed to atrophy.

'Then there's David, poor dear man. How could you do that to my son? I can only assume it must be genetic. Because the other two people who have had to suffer most here are Wilf and myself.'

David and Sarah looked at Wilf in confusion. His face was ravaged with grief. 'Heather, don't,' he said quietly, his voice cracking. 'Just leave it alone. It's in the past.'

'What?' David's voice sounded uncertain and hesitant.

'It may be in your past, Wilf. She's dead, after all. But I have to live with it every day. The gnawing reminder of it all. The whole bloody nightmare.'

'What the hell is this all about?' Sarah felt fearful of the situation that was unravelling. 'Is this about Mum?' She looked at Heather, then at Wilf. ' What you said before about her and ... her and other men?'

Wilf shook his head, then seemed to droop. 'Yes, but there was only one other man, darling. Only one that mattered,' he said quietly. 'And that was Anthony.'

Chapter 43

David heard himself laugh harshly. Everything seemed to be moving slowly, while his mind raced to comprehend what he was hearing. He heard Sarah gasp, as if from a long way away, and looked from one to the other of the players involved in this awful, unbelievable farce.

'It can't be,' he heard himself saying, loudly, as if speaking loud enough would will it away. 'I don't believe it. You're joking, aren't you?' But the expressions on their faces told him everything he didn't want to accept. Wilf looked as though he'd had the wind punched out of him, weakened and resigned and terribly, terribly sad. Anthony had adopted his usual pose, arms crossed and looking hard to the floor, a technique he had of simply pretending to be somewhere else. But the tension in his shoulders proved he was far from detached now. Heather looked as though she couldn't believe she'd spoken, but her eyes were fixed on Anthony, as if daring him to contradict her, with a glittering fury David had never seen before.

Slowly, slowly, David started to join the dots. A hundred questions he didn't want to know the answers to jostled for position. But other facts were starting to make sense, for the first time: Heather's constant drip drip of criticism, her taunting Anthony about being vain, constantly reminding him of their age difference. Perhaps that explained why both sets of parents had managed to avoid each other for years. Everything he had believed ... everything he'd thought about his family. It was all based on lies. Had it permeated their lives too? Was that how they'd reached this point? Him and Sarah? And Claire too? Deception on deception?

Sarah spoke at last, her voice low, as though trying to calm a child. 'Dad, is it really true?'

Wilf nodded wordlessly, and Sarah crossed the room to stand at his side, squeezing his arm gently. David looked across at her but she wouldn't meet his eye, seemingly unreachable. Layers of emotion and loss stretched between them and he felt his ears humming, as though he were on a train that had just sped into a tunnel. He looked around the room, not sure where he fitted in any more. One part of him was livid with Heather for dredging this up, now of all times, yet he could feel her pain. And his father? Suddenly he was angry.

'Dad? What the fuck is this about? This is huge ...' He couldn't get the words out. 'In fact, it's bloody monumental ... When ...? I mean, for how long did it go on?' He tugged his hands through his hair, shaking his head in disbelief.

Anthony shrugged. 'Your mother spoke out of turn. Heather, this was certainly not the right place, nor time.'

Heather turned to face him. 'But when is it right, Anthony? When?' She was trembling now, her voice tight and bitter. 'For years I've carried this knowledge with me. Your infidelities were bad enough but you said they never meant anything. And I believed you. I never made a fuss. And I kept on washing your shirts, even when I could smell another woman's perfume on them. But this. I knew it was different, even before I realised it was *her*.'

A groan that was almost a whimper escaped from Wilf's lips, and David saw Sarah hold him more firmly, as though afraid he would sink to the floor.

'Anthony,' Sarah said coldly, 'David asked you a question.'

Anthony shifted his weight onto his other foot, but kept his arms tightly across his chest. He looked at them all from under his brows and took a deep breath. 'You shouldn't have done this, Heather,' he said, glaring at his wife again. 'They have enough on their plates without our problems. It's too bad of you.'

David moved across to his mother and gently rubbed her arm, looking over at his father, seeing him, coldly, not as the long-suffering and teasing and tolerant figure he had, but as a serial philanderer: pathetic, cruel and selfish.

'Dad, I don't think you have any right to tell Mum what she should and shouldn't do, do you?'

'Anthony.' This time Sarah almost shouted. 'David asked you a question. When did it begin?'

'I suppose it was an attraction from the beginning,' he muttered. Heather closed her eyes in pain. 'I don't see any sense in raking this over. It was all done with years ago. We knew it was wrong and we ended it. That's all you need to know.'

'Oh, for Christ's sake!' David snapped. 'Mary was my mother-in-law. Sarah's mother. From the moment you crossed that line you made it our business too. And all these years – was it going on when the twins were small? All those Christmases we spent together?'

'Is that why you stopped coming when we invited you?' Sarah said slowly.

'Yes, yes, it was too difficult.'

Heather almost spat. 'Too difficult for whom, Anthony?'

'Is that why you've given Sarah such a hard time, Mum?' David turned his head to her. 'Because of Mary?' He shook his head. 'You've let them ruin your life, you do realise that, don't you? What a mess!'

'They *have* ruined my life and that's why I couldn't bear to see it happen all over again with her.' She jerked her head towards Sarah. 'So you want the facts?' She had an almost manic expression of triumph in her eyes, as though she'd waited years to unburden this. 'It was before he retired, when the twins were very small. That place in Ebrington; the chocolate-box cottage that was supposed to be my dream.'

Wilf's head sunk lower.

'That's where they met up. It had been going on for some time before I found out.' Her voice sounded tight and high. 'I stayed on once alone after the weekend. Anthony went back to London. I was clearing up and I found a scarf in our bedroom. I wasn't sure to begin with, but that scent she always wore – Guerlain, wasn't it?' She directed this at Wilf who didn't move. 'I couldn't believe it at first. She'd been in the house before many times, obviously. I'd invited her, for God's sake. You'd all come over to visit. She'd come with you, Wilf, as our guest. I'd cooked for her and shown her the garden. Taking my hospitality while all the time—'

She broke down at last into noisy sobs and David put his arms around her. They all watched her grief uncomfortably, except for Anthony, who had turned to look out of the window, then Sarah asked quietly, 'And you, Dad? When did you find out?'

Wilf, hands deep in his pockets, cleared his throat. 'I knew there was someone. I didn't know who but I never questioned her. She was ... she was so lovely,' he said pleadingly, as if to explain. 'Like a vibrant flame. It was me she came back to. Despite everything, it was me she wanted to be with. And I was with her at the end ...' He tailed off in his turn and David caught Sarah looking at him but couldn't read her expression.

There was a cough and, looking briefly at Heather, Anthony began to speak into the silence, falteringly. 'It wasn't sordid, the way it must sound to you. It wasn't like that. I admit that there had been other women. But she was different. So intense, so joyful. It was agony for me too, you must see that? And having to be there with her at parties, at tea with our grandchildren and to pretend to be normal! It was almost a relief when we were found out and the pretending was over. She was an extraordinary woman. But Wilf, she did love you. I knew she'd never leave you. She made that perfectly clear from the start.'

Her eyes puffy and sore, Heather spun round and spat, 'And how does that make me feel, do you think? Well, I'll tell you. Unwanted, unloved, undesired. Did you ever stop and consider my feelings? Either of you? I can never forgive you for that. She may be dead, but the thought of you two together, laughing at me, betraying me ... it sickens me still! You can never make up for it. Never.'

Wilf was shaking his head sadly. 'But, Heather, it's in the past. I know how much it must have hurt you. I do know, because it was the same for me. But the only time we have is now, and our time is very short, shorter than any of us realises. Look at little Claire. We could have lost her. You do realise that, don't you?'

'But they betrayed us both!' Heather shrieked. 'How could you have taken her back the way you did?'

Wilf spread his arms beseechingly. 'Because I loved her. I truly did. And I truly do now. I wanted her to be happy. And even if that meant letting her go sometimes, well, that was the price I had to pay. She loved me, in her way. It was enough for me.'

Heather shook her head slowly. 'Well, it wasn't enough for me. And I pity you for accepting so little. She made fools of us both, and now your daughter has done it all over again to my son. And I won't sit here and smile, and welcome her home. I can't and I won't.' She stood up. 'Anthony, it's time we were going. David, let me know how my granddaughter is, will you?'

She waited pointedly for Anthony who, with an apologetic glance, got up to follow her, his usual vague expression in place once more.

David followed them to the front door, though Heather had already opened it and was striding off to the car. He watched as it disappeared down the road. His mother's corrosive anger hung in the air. Back in the kitchen, Sarah was standing silently next to Wilf and they were holding hands. Fear gripped his stomach. What the hell lay ahead for them all now?

Chapter 44

In the last forty-eight hours, Sarah realised, her life had changed utterly. She'd come home before she'd mentally prepared herself to do so; she'd been introduced to a woman David was now having a relationship with – a scenario that hadn't entered her self-absorbed little head; her daughter was upstairs recovering from someone having slipped a Mickey Finn into her drink; there was no money in the bank thanks to a man she thought liked her – loved her? – and now she'd discovered her mother and her father-in-law had been conducting a love affair under everyone's noses. It was laughable. Almost.

David and she had barely spoken yesterday evening once Anthony and Heather had left, Heather rosy-cheeked and high with the excitement of her revelation, Wilf had been taken home by David, rejecting her suggestion he stay for supper, but not before he had apologised over and over again, as if this mess were his fault, and Sarah had had to reassure him again and again that she was okay; that she would recover from the shock. 'Don't think badly of your mother, will you?' he kept repeating and Sarah, unable to admit to him that she had more in common with her mother than he would ever know, could only shake her head and say, 'Of course not, Dad'.

The news that the 'man' Wilf had mentioned was Anthony had rocked her to the core. It was devastating, disgusting, almost incestuous? She was having to revise everything. Did she condemn Mary for this, for hurting Wilf so much? She knew she should but she didn't, though if she'd found out before she'd left for France, she might have been less forgiving. Oh, how easy infidelity could be.

But it was while she was hanging out washing later in the afternoon that the laughable obviousness of it struck her. Of course Mary and Anthony would like each other, be attracted even, wouldn't they? Sarah and David had been, hadn't they? And each had traits in common with their mother and father. It was an attraction repeating itself, one step removed.

That night she'd prepared to head off to Claire's bedroom floor with a sleeping-bag but, exhausted by the extraordinary events that had unfolded, she'd caved in to David's awkward, off-hand suggestion that she sleep in their bed. Even though she'd fallen asleep before he'd come upstairs, she'd woken stiff and sore, having unconsciously held her position on the edge of the bed all night so as not to move near to him. That, on top of everything, would be too weird.

The morning was clearer and fresher than Sarah's mind and, while everyone still slept, she tried to busy herself with normality. Where did life go from here? Owing Nathalie an update on events since she'd got home, she fired up her computer and sent off an email with more news than Nathalie would have been expecting, but held back on the issue of her mother and Anthony. Somehow that seemed too raw and personal for sharing.

'Hi Mum.' Claire put her head around the door, her hair dishevelled and her vest and pyjama bottoms hanging loosely over her too-skinny frame. 'I brought you some tea.' She placed Sarah's favourite china cup on the desk and, without asking, sat gently in her mother's lap, cupping her own steaming mug in her hands. Sarah, deeply moved, simply put her arms around her daughter's tiny waist and they sat like that without speaking, head to head.

'Feeling okay?' Sarah asked gently after a moment and felt Claire nod. 'Wanna tell me about it all?' but Claire just shook her head slowly.

'Later. Not just now. Later.'

The bank manager looked half their age and Sarah felt like a criminal seated in his characterless cubicle office later that morning. He referred to the computer screen neither David nor she could see, and almost transaction by transaction, went through the history of the last few weeks.

'So you say these withdrawals were not made by yourself, Mrs Lewis?'

'No, as I explained, someone had got hold of my card and correctly guessed my pin number. Then' – she shivered at the terrifying audacity of it all – 'simply put the card back in my bag.'

'And how were they able to do this without your knowledge?' he asked, looking at Sarah.

'He was a friend.'

'A friend?'

'Yes, a friend, or at least I thought he was,' she added quietly, and David moved awkwardly in his seat.

'You have the option to pursue this with the police, you know, Mrs Lewis.'

Sarah glanced at David. 'No. I can't prove a thing.'

'As I explained,' he went on, 'the bank cannot be responsible for card transactions at a teller machine when your card and pin number have been used while still in your possession, especially if your personal information was available.'

'But it wasn't!' she protested. 'It was just a lucky guess.'

He looked sceptical. 'Either way, Mrs Lewis, the pin number was correct. In future, perhaps you should choose one that's not so obvious. However, as I explained to your husband yesterday, we may be able to refund the credit card transactions. Your ... friend chose his purchases carefully and they have been used already, you say – the flights and such like – but we do have some redress with the merchants.'

By the time he shook their hands weakly and they stepped

back out into the summer sunshine, Sarah felt as though she'd had a mauling from the headmaster. He'd made her feel even more foolish than she felt already, before offering the olive branch of an extended overdraft, at some cost, in view of their 'good banking history', on condition that they could give him 'a date when the issue could be resolved in some way'. They stood on the steps of the bank, people jostling past dodging tourists wandering slowly with maps and confused expressions and then, without consensus, found themselves wandering towards the river.

David didn't speak until they had crossed the foot bridge and were on the towpath. On the other side of the river the theatre dominated, its reflection playing in the water. The willow trees hung down in an Olivier-style theatrical bow, and the geese and swans slowly and imperiously ignored the narrow boats with their bright tubs of summer plants decorating their roofs.

'We'll have to use most of our savings,' he said eventually. It wasn't a question.

'Yes. Sorry.'

'I don't want my father to know about this. I don't want anyone to know about this. One scandal in a family is enough and I don't want any more pressure on Claire.'

'No, of course not.' They walked on in silence, beginning to cross the grass.

'What was he like?' he asked suddenly.

Sarah looked over at him, but his eyes were on his feet. 'He was charming and I fell for it.'

Again silence, then he bit. 'Did you need to be charmed?'

'It was nice, yes.' Was that enough explanation? Probably not. Despite the mistakes she had made, David still needed to understand why she had fallen for Fabien. 'He made me feel good and special. He made a fuss, planned things, outings, you know. We went out to dinner.'

'On our money.'

Sarah winced. 'Well yes, but I didn't know that at the time.'

Then the one that had been hanging in the air since she'd come home: 'Did you sleep with him?'

The chatter, the people around them, the boats and the hum of traffic, normal life, seemed hugely at odds with his quietly worded question.

'Of course I did.'

'Was it good?'

She sighed. 'It was okay.'

'Okay?' He laughed scornfully.

'It was different, that's all. I've never been with anyone else but you.' She faltered, confused by discussing something that had been just a part of their marriage, something that she had now shared with someone else.

'So it's true what they say about the French, then?' he asked tightly. 'Seems like he had it all, hey? Fucked us both, come to think of it.'

Sarah gasped in horror at his venom. She'd never heard David speak like this, so bitterly and angrily. She stopped in the middle of the grass and turned to him. 'Well, how was it for you, then? Don't tell me you didn't sleep with that woman. So don't give me all the grief. You can't take the moral high-ground here. What do you want me to say, David? Yes, it was fantastic? The earth moved?' She could feel her emotions rising, precipitated by exhaustion and fear and the tension of the last few days. In her head everything was driven away – Fabien, the photographs, her wanton abandon – by images of David and the tall, pretty woman who'd arrived at the door the morning she'd got home.

Suddenly she felt very possessive. Kate had stolen a part of David from her, just as Mary had stolen a part from Heather, and Anthony had stolen a part from Wilf. No wonder Heather felt so bitter.

Sarah realised with a sickness to her stomach how much pain she had caused David. And how much she deserved the pain he had caused her.

Chapter 45

They walked home in resentful silence, taking great care not to brush against each other or to bump hands. David's shoulders were tense with anger – as much with himself as with Sarah. He'd promised himself he wouldn't start on at her but he'd done it anyway. The spectacle he'd witnessed in the kitchen between Heather and Anthony had persuaded him of how terribly corrosive it was and he was determined that he wouldn't make the mistake Heather had, devoting every waking moment to recrimination and emotional blackmail.

So much for what he wasn't going to do. But he still hadn't worked out what he *was*. Sarah's words had confirmed what he already knew. Whether he and Sarah had a future now or not, could he just forgive and forget? Swallow the rage and resentment and go the Wilf route? It was too big to think about so he simply didn't, concentrating instead on the ramifications of what the bank manager – unimpressive little twat – had told them.

They rounded the final corner and crossed the road to the house. The sun was getting higher and the day would be a hot one. He'd put off his run until later. As they went through the gate, he saw Appalling Pauline appear from around the side of her house and scuttle towards them.

'Sarah, lovely to see you back,' she said, leadingly, but they both kept quiet. 'Anyway,' she bustled on, 'just a small thing, can I ask you to do something about the loud music coming over the fence. I can even hear it in my conservatory.'

Indeed there was loud music and David turned to look at Sarah. She was looking up into his face, her expression completely unguarded as she listened intently. She looked like a stranger – a beautiful, confident, untouchable stranger – and he simply stared, taking advantage of the fact that her thoughts were elsewhere.

'Do you think …?'

'Let's go and see.'

They brushed past Pauline, leaving her spluttering like a guppy, and hurried into the house. If Claire was outside in the sunshine, David told himself, that would be a good sign. It would mean everything was going to be all right for her. He'd been making these pathetic wagers with himself ever since Tom's phone call that awful morning. Had it only been a few days ago? It seemed to David a symbol of how powerless he felt, that he was hunting for signs and omens that could prove the universe was on his side. He followed her to the kitchen, he shook himself. Here he was, Mr Rational himself, acting like a superstitious caveman.

Peering through the window into the sunny garden, he felt a wash of relief. Claire had got the sun-lounger out of the garage, found the cushions and was out there with a mug of tea and her sketchbook. Thank you, universe.

'Oh, thank goodness,' Sarah sighed. 'Shall I make us a cup too, and maybe we can go out and sit with her, all casual-like? See if she'll talk.'

'Good idea.'

David put down the post he'd picked up in the hall – including an official-looking letter for Claire – and set two mugs on a tray. It didn't feel right for Sarah to just take over, like before. Everything had changed, after all, even if it didn't look like it from the outside. Tea made, David took the tray and followed Sarah out. Claire looked up briefly, then returned to her doodling.

'We thought we'd join you in the sunshine. Hope that's all right.'

Sarah's forced jollity made David wince, but he could understand it. The last few days Claire had spent almost all her time upstairs in her bedroom and had been monosyllabic and, although

312

she was starting to return some of their affectionate gestures, she still seemed distant and preoccupied. He looked up into the crab apple tree in the corner. If those two sparrows flew off together, she'd talk to them properly today. He watched them hop along the branch, hunting for insects, then they flew away – almost simultaneously. He turned to her.

'How are you feeling? Sun doing you some good?'

She smiled weakly. 'Mmm. Thanks.'

He glanced at Sarah and saw her looking sidelong at him. This was ridiculous.

Sarah reached forward and took Claire's thin little arm, but she shrugged away and her T-shirt sleeve moved to reveal a small tattoo. David opened his mouth to exclaim in horror, and spotted Sarah about to do the same. Glancing at each other swiftly, they exchanged a look of complicity. Not now.

Sarah found her feet again. 'Darling, won't you tell us what happened? What went wrong? Was it ... was it us separating? Me going away?'

David looked quickly at Sarah. The expression of guilt on her face was agonising. She had assumed it was her fault, he suddenly realised. Whereas he had been feeling it was down to him – that it had all started to go wrong for Claire when he'd been left 'in charge'. He sat back in the cast-iron chair, looking from Claire to Sarah, wondering what would happen next.

Claire took a sip from the mug she was staring into. 'I hated it,' she said in a low voice. 'I hated the course. I hated the place. I hated my room. I hated ... feeling out of things. I hated it almost before I got there.'

There was a stunned silence. 'But you didn't say?' stammered Sarah. 'I had no idea. Did you, David?'

'Of course you had no idea. I barely did.' Claire picked at the remaining varnish on her nails. 'But by the time I'd worked out why I felt so awful, you two were too busy with your own thing to pay any attention. I couldn't talk to you, either of you.'

David was aware of Sarah turning to him again, but couldn't bear to meet her eye. Claire went on.

'I don't even know if uni is where I want to be. Well, obviously not that one. I couldn't go back after ... well, after everything. And I don't even want to. I never fitted in there. And it was ... it was a shock. No one was really interested in me.'

David winced. Had she really been so miserable, and he hadn't even seen it? 'But you had Tom. Did he know how you were feeling?'

Claire snorted. 'Look, part of why I did that course in the first place was so I could keep an eye on Tom. Sensible Claire and Daft Tom. That's what it's always been, hasn't it? I've always been the one. Taking dinner money. Knowing when homework was due in. He's hopeless. Well, he was, anyway. I thought ... I don't know, I suppose I felt responsible for him and I thought it would be easier if we were together. We always have been, haven't we?'

Sarah looked aghast. 'So you thought we wanted you to look after Tom? Is that it?'

Claire shrugged. 'Partly. Partly it was me. I'm just ... I worry, y'know. I worry about things when I can't even control them. And not knowing how he was, if he was somewhere else. I don't know if I could have handled it.' She laughed bitterly. 'As it turned out, *I* was the one who couldn't cope. Tom was fine. I could see that from the start. Loads of friends, Mr Popular, all sporty and adventurous. I was the one that messed up this time.'

David shifted uncomfortably. All those years, when they'd fretted about Tom. Their concern must have rubbed off on her. He squeezed his eyes closed. Well, he'd wished for her to open up and now he'd have to deal with it.

'Claire – sweetheart – you haven't messed up. I know it must feel like it, but really, it's not. Sometimes things go right, and sometimes they don't. Mostly everything's been all right for you.

314

But life isn't one thing or the other. It's a mixture and sometimes you make mistakes and have to sort them out. But if things do get difficult – well, that's what we're here for.' He sighed. 'Only I think we're the ones who messed up this time ...'

Sarah picked up as he trailed off. 'We never wanted you ... never expected you to look after Tom. He's always got himself into scrapes, I know, but he gets himself out, doesn't he?'

'That's more than I did,' Claire muttered. 'I keep thinking about what I must have been like the other night. Scratching Tom's face and everything. *I* did that to him. And I didn't even know what I was doing. How can I ever trust myself again?'

'It wasn't you, darling.' Sarah was leaning towards Claire intently. 'It wasn't. The doctor told us that the drugs you were given could make anyone react that way. It was like a ... I don't know ... an allergic reaction or a really severe side-effect. I know – we both know – you would never have acted like that. We both know you wouldn't take drugs yourself. It was some stupid, irresponsible prank.'

Claire turned to face them both, her expression set and determined. 'Oh, but I did. I did take them. Not everything. Someone did spike my drink. At least, I assume they did. But I did take drugs in those last few weeks. And it nearly killed me. You see? You don't really know me at all, do you?'

David reeled. Beside him, he heard Sarah's sobbing breath. Suddenly, he knew that what he said next would be terribly, terribly important.

'But Claire,' he said slowly, 'you're here now. You're alive, thank God. And now you know, you know the drugs didn't help you at all, although it might have felt like it at the time. You've learned something because of what you've been through. Loads of people will never understand that the way you do now. And you can build on that. Because it's never too late to change your life. That's the mistake so many people make. We can sort this out. But we have to know ... you have to tell us everything because we can't guess. I'm sorry. I'm so sorry that I wasn't listening properly before. I should have seen the signs, maybe. But tell me … tell us now.'

Sarah took over. 'Daddy's right. The important thing is that you're here with us. And you know we love you and we're so proud of you and how brave you must have been. The important thing is to get strong again – then you can think about what to do next. There was a letter – let me get it for you.' She got up and went into the kitchen.

Claire flicked a glance at her mother's retreating back. 'Dad, can I tell you something?' Her voice was urgent.

David leaned forward, looking at his shadow on Claire's face. 'Of course, darling. Anything.'

Claire put her empty cup down slowly. 'It's about Granny Mary.'

'Oh?' Oh God, Sarah and he hadn't even got round to discussing what, if anything, they should tell Tom and Claire. Did she know already? Had she heard the discussion the other day?

'And Grandad Anthony'

He faltered. So she knew.

Claire sighed as Sarah reappeared with the brown envelope and some sunblock. 'Here, put some of this on. You don't want to burn.' She looked at the two of them in their tense silence 'What? What is it?'

'She knows about … Mary and Dad.'

Sarah's arms dropped. 'Oh, David, you didn't tell her? She doesn't need any more worries at the moment.'

Claire shook her head emphatically. 'No – you don't understand. I've known for ages. So you do know? Why the hell didn't you tell me?' She sat forward on the chair. 'Why did you give me that bloody bracelet if you knew?'

Sarah sank down beside her onto the sun-lounger. 'What do you mean? What bracelet?'

'That bracelet you gave me before you left, the one with the love letter in it.' Her face was twisted now with pain. 'Didn't you have the courage to tell me? Was this some kind of joke, Mum?'

Sarah shook her head in disbelief. 'There was a note in the bracelet? I had no idea – I didn't even get it out of the box when I gave it to you. I just assumed it was one of Grandpa Wilf's presents that Granny hadn't wanted.' She looked for support to David. 'Your dad and I have only just found out about all this. Grandma told us yesterday afternoon. We're as horrified as you are.'

'Oh Claire, sweetheart.' David's chest hurt. 'What an awful burden for you. Does Tom know?'

'No. No, I haven't told him. I didn't know what to do. But the more I thought about it, the more it sort of made sense. The way Grandma sometimes talks and gets at Grandpa. And we never used to see them all together, did we?'

'No, we didn't?' Sarah sighed. 'How could we all have missed it?'

'The thing is, it's only a shock for us,' David put in. 'They've all known for years and Wilf, certainly, has moved on. Maybe in a way it's good that we all know now and perhaps we owe it to them not to dig it up again. Although I don't think Grandma will ever get over it. You're right, she does like to torment your grandfather.'

'Maybe he deserves it,' Sarah said softly. 'We need to tell Tom but I don't think this ought to go outside the family. For Wilf's sake more than anyone's.'

'But what about Aunty Rachel?'

'Especially not Aunty Rachel,' David said and realised he'd spoken in unison with Sarah. They both smiled cautiously. It didn't need explanation. David watched as Claire took her mother's hand and felt a pain. How ironic. If only Claire knew how phoney the family was now.

Sarah seemed to brace herself. 'Oh, here's your letter. It looks official.'

Claire took the envelope and, frowning slightly at the university crest, tossed it to the ground and lay back. 'It'll just be them confirming that I'm out on my ear. I can't even bear to read it.'

David could feel Sarah beside him, itching to know what it actually said. Would she be able to resist nagging at Claire about it? He heard her intake of breath. No, of course she wouldn't.

'Well,' she started lightly, 'maybe it's time we thought what you might fancy doing next anyway. Have you had any ideas?'

'No, Mum. As a matter of fact, I haven't,' Claire replied witheringly, but Sarah wasn't dissuaded. 'I mean, with your A-levels there's quite a bit open to you, isn't there? History of Art, or Philosophy or something. Do you remember how you loved that book, *Sophie's World*. Gosh, we couldn't stop you reading it even after we'd put the light out.'

David saw Claire's expression close over. 'Look, love, we don't want to rush you,' he placated. 'But you're a clever girl. You could find something – I don't know – something you really enjoy. There are loads of courses available. Far more than when we were starting out—'

Claire got abruptly to her feet. 'I can't talk about this now, so please stop bugging me. I always wanted to go to art college. You knew that, so did the school, but somewhere along the way it was sidelined. "Oh, you're too clever to do that," you all said and I sort of buckled cos I didn't know better. "Why don't you get a sensible degree and you can always teach?" And then, like an idiot, I got that thing about having to look after Tom.' She threw her hands up in a feeble gesture of resignation. She looked so cross with herself. 'I don't know what I want to do yet. I don't want to think about it and I certainly don't want to talk to you about it. But I know what I don't want. And that's to go back to university. Don't you see?'

She turned and walked back into the house.

'That went well, I thought,' said David heavily.

Sarah, too, got up and went inside, leaving David on his own in the sunshine. Over in the crab apple tree, a solitary sparrow was looking at him with its head on one side.

'Oh, piss off!' David muttered.

Chapter 46

'I'll be back once I've cleared everything up,' Tom had said reassuringly before he left, filling the doorway of her room with his lanky frame, his scratched face healing now. 'Carl's having a party tomorrow which I don't want to miss and most of my stuff is still in my room, so I've got to get back.'

Claire knew that, but over the last few days the house had seemed terribly quiet without him. He was the only person of the four who wasn't carrying a trauma around with them – he'd even taken the news of his grandparents' affair with an incredulous snort. Even Claire felt she was coming out the other side better than her parents were. The atmosphere was as heavy as lead. Suppers were the most unbearable, Sarah pussy-footing around apologetically, behaving as though the house wasn't hers and checking with David 'was it okay if she …'. Their conversations were curt and polite, information given on a strictly need-to-know basis, so Claire, in despair, had taken to putting her plate on a tray and going through to watch TV in the other room, a move that had elicited concerned looks and enquiries about her well-being.

To be honest, everyone was being stiflingly kind to her. Rather than give her the out-on-your ear letter she'd been expecting for her appalling showing in the end-of-year exams, the university was being remarkably accommodating. While realising that she could not continue the course she was enrolled on, they would be 'willing to discuss moving to a more suitable course, particularly in view of your excellent educational record to date'.

'That's good of them,' Sarah said, picking up the discarded letter from the kitchen table.

'Yes, but, like I said, I just don't want to be there.'

'I know, darling. I know.'

When they weren't checking on her every move and state of mind, they were asking about who had supplied the drugs or slipped the stuff in her drink. At first it had been quite overt. 'Tell us who it might have been,' her dad had asked, his very touching concern coming out in an heroic desire for vengeance; but she had, with all honesty, been unable to tell them. So much of that evening had simply disappeared, thank God, and the only memories she had were like running a film very fast through her head. Then, once they had given up on that tack, her parents had started to ask innocent-sounding questions. Who lives in the block the party was in? Your mates, who do they mix with, then? For a couple who had separated, they sure as hell sang off the same hymn sheet when it came to child interrogation. In fact, watching them together made Claire smile. Despite the absurd atmosphere between them, they worked imperceptibly like a team, moving around each other as they did chores in a dance that had developed over years of living together. Having Dad around all day, except for the odd afternoons he spent at the Alvis garage, seemed odd, but Claire didn't dare raise this topic on top of everything else and ignored the whispered conversations between them that stopped the moment she walked into a room.

The question of her 'mates' was a moot one indeed. There had been the occasional text from the few normal people in her department, such as Lydia, asking how she was and, touched, Claire had replied gratefully. From Iggy, Animal and Bella there had been nothing so far and, rather than be hurt, Claire found herself cynically amused. Their lack of concern seemed to sum up their superficiality. Perhaps they thought she was going to shop them.

It was some days later that a message finally popped through from Iggy: *How r ya doll?* Claire left it for twenty-four hours before replying: *What do you care? I could have died. Thanks for nothing.* Unsurprisingly, there was no response.

Her mood was twitchy, though, and there was something that was bothering Claire more than Iggy's selfishness or even her parents' issues. For a while she ignored it but, by late Thursday morning, she knew what she had to do and, grabbing her bag, she headed into town. David was out somewhere and she dodged Sarah's questions by shouting 'I'll be back by teatime' and slamming the front door. Her familiar old bike was hidden behind the gleaming Alvis in the garage but, after a bit of a wipe down and some attention to the tyre pressures, it was good to go and she swung her leg over it and headed down the road. The warm air blew in her face and she realised how, over the last few months, she'd stopped doing normal things like walking or sport. Even meeting mates for coffee or going shopping. Iggy and the crew, the drugs, her hatred for the campus had pulled her into a hole she hadn't even realised she was in. Now she wanted sun on her face and her energy back.

She pulled up outside the imposing office building and, abandoning her bike against the railings, headed through the revolving doors to reception.

'Can I help you?' A dark-suited lady looked over her glasses at Claire, taking in her crumpled cotton dress, flip-flops and canvas bag.

'I'd like to see Jess Young please.'

'Department?'

'Motor claims, I think.'

'And you are?'

'Claire Lewis. A ... friend.' Claire clenched her hands around the strap of her bag. Would Jess even be there and if she was would she want to see her?

'Hello. I've someone in reception for you.' A pause. 'Um, Claire Lewis. She says she's a friend.'

Claire perched on the hard, bright-red sofa and looked around the modern reception area, her wait agonising. She jumped each time the lift opened, but Jess seemed to appear from nowhere because suddenly she was standing in front of Claire, smart in a neat skirt and pink blouse. She looked at Claire without speaking for a moment, her eyes searching.

'*Are* you a friend?' she asked eventually.

'No. You're the friend.' And with that, Claire threw her arms around Jess's neck and Jess put her arms around her in reply.

'I'm so sorry,' Claire sobbed.

'Stop it,' Jess sniffed back, laughing through her tears. 'You'll get me fired!'

Jess couldn't take a very long lunchbreak, so they simply sat under a tree in the sunshine by the river and Claire did all the talking. Jess nodded occasionally and, as they parted, she replied 'you too' to Claire's 'love you lots'. Jumping back on her bike, Claire whizzed back down the road, slipping in and out of traffic as it waited to filter onto the roundabout, singing at the top of her voice. Whatever else, she was back on track with Jess and that was all that mattered.

The house was quiet when she let herself in and she was about to creep upstairs when her mother called from the lounge.

Claire sighed. 'Yeesss?' She pushed open the door to find Sarah at the computer, surrounded by print-outs.

'You got a moment?' She turned to her daughter, a pencil twisted in her hair and her eyes sparkling with excitement.

'Yes.' Claire looked at the mess cautiously. Had she been drinking?

'I've been doing some research.'

'Oh yeah?' Claire dropped her bag on the chair, cautious but intrigued.

'Here are some details on art courses.' She thrust out some documents enthusiastically, watching Claire's face for her reaction.

Claire wasn't sure what her reaction ought to be. 'But I don't understand.' She took the sheets from her mother. Each one featured courses offered by various art colleges: St Martin's, The Slade, Camberwell, Bristol, Liverpool. 'I thought you didn't want me to do an art course. You always said it was too unpredictable.'

'I know I did and I was wrong.' Sarah's face looked flushed. 'I was putting some clean laundry in your room earlier and I saw your notebook on your bed. I'd forgotten how talented you are.'

Claire perched on the arm of the sofa and faced her mother. 'Yeah, but you're just biased. All your geese are swans.'

'Maybe. That's a mother's prerogative. Who else would think you were great if your mother didn't?' Claire put out her hand and rubbed Sarah's arm in sympathy. Granny Mary had had enough love to think everyone was wonderful. Maybe too much love for everyone in the end. 'No,' Sarah continued, 'even I can see that you have immense talent, Claire, and I know Dad thinks so too.' She sighed. 'I did lots of stupid things while I was away, the first might have been going in the first place, but while I was there I met a man—'

'I know you did, Mum.'

'No ... not that kind of thing.' Claire could tell Sarah was avoiding her eyes. 'No, this was a man called Maurice – you didn't meet him when you and Tom came over and I wish you had. He runs the orchestra of the region and is the most superb conductor. When he let me join and play, I sort of blossomed and I loved every moment of it. I realised that I had almost missed the opportunity to play the violin as I should play it, and instead I'd become bogged down, like Dad had in his job, with what I thought I ought to be doing.'

'But you both did it for us. To bring up Tom and me.'

Sarah nodded slowly. 'Yes, to an extent we did and maybe now's our chance to spread our wings, but you have the chance to do that too.' She leaned over and picked up some other sheets.

'You are too late to start in September, but maybe that's a good thing. It will give you time to put a portfolio together and to find the course you want. It will also give you a gap year.'

'But ...' This volte-face was doing Claire's head in. It was too much to assimilate but she could feel her excitement rising. 'But what about Tom?'

Sarah smiled. 'Tom is having a ball, falling in love and doing all the things he adores. Perhaps it's time that you went your own ways. You'll always have each other just not be in each other's pockets. He needs you and always will, but you don't need to be in the same place all the time. You'll cramp each other's style. Besides, and this is important, a year away would give you time, darling. Time to be your own person not who you think you ought to be. I never did that because things were different for me then – though, believe it or not, I was more bloody-minded than you and insisted I went to music college. You need space, though. Go away and see things before you have ties that bind you.'

Overcome with delicious anticipation, Claire threw her arms around her mother's neck. 'And,' Sarah whispered into her neck, 'you realise there are some ties you never want to unravel from.'

A noise came from the kitchen and they both looked up.

'Oh, Dad must be home.'

'Ties that bind you.' David had heard enough. Quietly he let himself out of the back door and started walking, without purpose, along the road. *Ties that bind you*, she'd said. *Ties that bind you*. Sarah's words to Claire wounded him more than anything else she'd said or done so far. Worse even than ... he couldn't think any more about that. More than any of her weary explanations before she'd left, that summed up her view of their relationship and consigned it neatly to the pile of things to be discarded. Like those bags of clothes for the charity shop she used to assemble from time to time, sad and unwanted – old shirts, clothes the children had grown out of, sale mistakes, dog-eared books. And the ties that bind.

The phrase drummed itself into his mind with every step he took, the words turning over and over. Ties – things that choked you, stopped you, kept you in place. But ties could be good, couldn't they? The ties of marriage? He'd always assumed they would last for ever. Sarah obviously didn't.

He found himself crossing the bridge before he'd given any thought to where he was going. How many times had he and Sarah walked these pavements, pushing the double buggy, holding the hands of jumping toddlers, carrying bags of shopping, going to see friends. She was everywhere he looked. He stopped and stared at the river flowing by, swans and ducks looking at him hopefully. *Ties that bind*. By then, the words had lost all meaning. He stopped. Where should he go? He knew what he *ought* to do. There was something he had to sort out.

He turned back to the house, quickly and purposefully this time. He had the keys to the Alvis in his pocket. No need to go back in and disturb anybody. *The ties that bind*. The house looked exactly the same, but in David's head everything was altered. All the time she'd been away and even more, he realised, since the moment he'd seen her on the stairs again, he'd been nursing the hope, belief even, that she'd be back. Even during his relationship – was that what it was? – with Kate that was what he'd been counting on. But with those four words, his hope had simply evaporated. He felt empty.

He drove to Kate's faster than he should have. He had to apologise, put things right and explain how he'd chickened out of telling her the truth about his marriage. God, he'd been a bastard.

He phoned her on the way and was alarmed to hear pleasure in her voice. Had she assumed he'd cut and run? David realised uncomfortably that he had no idea what she assumed. He didn't really know her at all. Finding a parking space in front of her little shared house in Old Town, and hoping she was alone, he avoided his own eyes in the rear-view mirror before he turned off the engine.

On the doorstep, he felt dizzy and put out a hand to support himself against the wall, his head down. She opened the door and, smiling, slid her arms round him and pulled him close. 'I knew you'd be back,' she breathed in his ear. 'I just knew it.'

What? Did she? How, when he'd had no idea himself until half an hour ago? This wasn't right at all. He pulled away uncomfortably and followed her in.

'Look,' she said, as they went into the tiny kitchen where coffee was dripping from a filter machine, and filling the room with a sharp, appetising scent, 'I'm not going to ask. I just don't want to know. I don't need to.'

David tried to smile, but his face didn't feel quite right. 'But I owe you an apology, at least. I should have said something, but I ...'

He trailed off and sat down opposite her, squinting in the light streaming through the window. She reached across and took a heavy pottery mug from the drainer, poured in some milk and topped it up with coffee, then passed it to him. He felt like a total shit. Kate was sweet and undemanding. She deserved better than him.

'I'm sorry, Kate, that I didn't explain things properly. It started at Shelsley. Olly just assumed we were ... I was divorced, but it wasn't like that and I didn't know how to explain. It was a peculiar situation, you see ...'

She shook her head and placed a finger against his lips. Involuntarily, he pulled back. 'Dave, like I said, it doesn't matter to me.' Her voice sounded too upbeat, with that irritating Australian lift at the end that made everything sound like a question, as if anything was possible. 'I was a bit surprised is all – but from the look on your face, so were you. It's your business

– it doesn't have anything to do with us. All that matters is that you're here. Okay?'

She sat back and stretched luxuriously, looking at him challengingly. David felt uneasy. This wasn't going right at all.

'But I came here to explain. Sarah left for France – some finding-herself mission – I never wanted her to go. She just landed it on me.'

'And?' Kate sounded puzzled.

'And now she's back.'

Kate searched his face and, gradually, her expression changed as she read his meaning. He saw her body tense and a look of anxiety crossed her face 'But—'

'And then there's my daughter,' he rushed on, hoping he wouldn't have to spell it out. 'She's been in hospital – we think someone spiked her drink. We had to rush over, it was awful. She's okay but we needed to take care of her.'

Kate nodded and pressed her lips together. 'We? I see,' she said slowly.

He could see tears glittering in her eyes. 'Kate, it's been wonderful. You are great fun to be with. A great girl.'

'I think you'd better go.' Her hands were clasped so tightly her knuckles were white.

'But the thing is, I'm not going back to her. It's not like that. I know now that Sarah – my wife – doesn't want to be with me any more, but I just don't think you and I are right together. I had no idea—'

'Dave, stop. I was the one who had no idea. No idea I was just a stop gap. Someone to mark time with until your real life started again.' She looked straight at him, her eyes brimming now. 'You haven't been honest with me. You're a cheat, messing about with people's feelings. Don't expect me to forgive you just to make *you* feel better. You not going back doesn't somehow make it bearable.' She stood up now and looked down at him, his coffee going cold on the table. 'I don't get any of this crap, but I do know that you're more tied to her than you realise. I can't compete with whatever you had ... sorry, have with her.'

There was silence, then she turned her back on him, and started to fuss in the sink. 'Please go.'

He got up silently and let himself out.

Back in the car, he turned on the engine but this time looked at his reflection for a long time before he pulled away. Where to now?

Chapter 47

Where was he? David had come and gone much as he pleased over the last few days, but even by the standards of this new regime it was late for him to be back. Claire had gone into town with Jess, wreathed in smiles when she left, and though Sarah should have been relishing the respite from the constant pressure, instead she just felt lonely. She had been unable to settle all evening, not eating but just picking from the fridge, and channel-hopping on the TV between a drama that she'd missed the first part of and an inane reality show that made her despair for the future of the human race. She knew her mood was half out of anxiety in case he came back and they had to face their first real time alone, but what surprised her was her concern about where he was. Her ears were on full alert for the sound of his feet on the gravel, and every time she heard a noise she jumped.

To pass the time, she went through her credit card statements. Where was Fabien now? Was he conning some other poor cow who'd succumbed, romancing her at Le Singe Noir and taking pleasure in paying with her cash? Then she wrote a long overdue message to Maurice, hoping he was okay. 'You were right about Fabien,' she added, 'but I was fooled by his charm. It should have left a sour taste in my mouth about Sauzils, but it hasn't because my memory of working with you and my experience with *La Mer* and the orchestra also made it one of the best times of my life. Thank you for having faith in me. I did run away to France and then I ran back. Maybe now I will stop running.'

She leaned back in her seat. Yes, it had been the best and the worst of times, and now she wanted David to walk back in the door, to connect with him again. She'd been selfish and she'd been stupid, and now she had a shed load of work to do to win back what she'd so nearly lost.

She could sense he was about to put the key in the lock before she actually heard it, and then there he was, standing in the doorway of the lounge. His hair looked wild and untidy, which made him seem younger, but his face was tired and drawn.

'Hiya.' She tried to sound light. 'Want a cup of tea? I was just going to make one.'

'No thanks. I'm not staying.'

Sarah stopped. 'Oh?'

'I've been thinking.' He fiddled with his key. 'You were right. I understand now that you had to get away and I realise I can't behave like my mum has done with Dad, making him suffer for the rest of his life because of what he did wrong. I don't want to and, more to the point, I have no right to.'

'Well, I—' she began, but he held his hand up.

'No, Sarah. You are a superb mum and you have been a wonderful wife, but I've made up my mind. I'm giving you your freedom. Letting you go, before we end up hating each other.' With that, he turned and left the house, closing the front door quietly behind him.

Chapter 48

Sarah ticked off every half hour through the night. She heard Claire come home at one, but didn't go to meet her, fearing she'd ask where David was. For the rest of the time she watched the light on the ceiling, asking herself if David had done this in the empty bedroom when she'd left for France. Had he looked over to her side of the bed and seen the plumped-up pillow and the emptiness?

Eventually she heard the dawn chorus and the first cars on the road, people who started early shifts or drove miles to work to jobs in offices, all so like David's had been, where they wrote reports on computers and had meetings and then left again to come home to their families. Dutiful and disciplined.

Her heart feeling hollow and unable to stand it any more, she swung her legs out of bed and, after splashing water on her face, slipped on a pair of cotton trousers and a light fleece over her T-shirt, tied her Converses and, leaving a brief note for Claire on the hall table, headed out of the back door to the garage, clicking the door quietly behind her. Grateful that Claire had given her bike some attention, Sarah manoeuvred it out of the garage door and after a bit of a wobble of unfamiliarity, headed off down the road. Her mind felt numb with disbelief and she simply let the breeze hit her face. The traffic was minimal this early and it took her only a few minutes to get to Maidenhead Road. She was less fit than she'd thought and had to push the bike for a while, her head feeling dizzy from the effort of pedalling up the hill. Hot now, she propped the bike up against the fence and slipped off her fleece, tying it around her waist, then headed into the field and followed the footpath up the Welcombe Hills to the obelisk on the hilltop. What she needed was a dog to make the most of the bushes and the long grass. Perhaps she'd get one. They'd never had a dog, despite the twins' nagging, but had stuck to guinea pigs and a cat called Boris who was fat and cantankerous. David had been the only one he'd shown any affection to. Now she was on her own she could choose what she wanted.

On her own. It was unbelievable really; everything had turned on its head. How could she have assumed he'd be there for her? Following the path worn by previous walkers through the grass, she headed up the hill past the familiar fallen tree where it grew steeper. By the time she reached the bench she was out of breath and sat down gratefully. The sun was warm now, drying the morning dew but her Converses were damp. The landscape looked misty, with the promise of a glorious day, but who cared? Everything had changed since she'd last been here and met that woman who had known her mother. What was it she had said about never moving away, because this place was part of her landscape? Sarah could see now she was right. It was, as much as her children were. As much as David was, or at least had been.

Leaning her elbows on her knees, she squinted into the distance, running through her head what he had said, the events of the past few days, her time in France which now seemed so unreal.

The peace engulfed her, and for over an hour she welcomed the space to explore her despair, which made it all the more irritating when she spotted the top of someone's head coming up the hill. Damn. She didn't want to be disturbed, to have to make polite conversation about the weather. She averted her gaze, trying to will them to move off to another path but, when she turned back, there he was. His lovely familiar face, the body, as lean now as when they had first met, standing only ten feet away.

Neither of them said a word, but her stomach fluttered with fear. She couldn't mess up this scene. 'How did you know I was here?' She ventured after a while.

'I found the note you left Claire.'

'But it didn't say where I was going.'

'It didn't need to. I knew you'd be here. It's where you always come to think.' The old predictability felt comforting now, a point of reference.

She didn't want to ask. 'Where have you been?' She braced herself for his reply. Please God, not with that woman.

David rested his weight on one leg in that familiar stance, resting his hand on his knee. 'At Wilf's.'

'Oh.' She could have wept with the relief. 'What did he say?'

David sat down beside her on the bench and looked out at the morning view and the sunshine glinting off roofs and barns. 'Oh, lots of things,' he said eventually. 'He's a wise man, your dad.'

'Yes, isn't he? A lot wiser than his daughter.'

David leaned forward and put his elbows on his knees. 'He could teach us both something. I don't think I've been too sensible either.'

'What do you mean?'

'Oh, you know, too blinkered on the career-to-pay-the-mortgage path.'

Sarah looked sideways at him, his hair curling slightly on his collar. She hadn't seen it that long since they were students, when they'd first met and he'd let her cut it for him; those days when they never gave a thought to the future, when every second was exciting and every touch made her tingle. It had. She knew it now but she'd forgotten. Now here she was, not sure where she stood and too afraid even to touch him. 'But you've enjoyed it, haven't you? You've got on.'

'Yeah, I met the bills, but I'd lost the bigger picture. Barry being a prat and me walking out was actually a wonderful relief. The decision was made for me because I'd lost sight of what was really important.' He glanced towards her, but she was looking ahead again.

'You've certainly made up for all those years of being sensible in the last few months,' she said and her voice sounded tighter than she meant it to.

'You're not the only one who can do what they want,' he retorted, and Sarah turned her face away quickly as if to deflect the barb. 'You can't bugger off to "find yourself" or whatever it was and expect me to just tick over. And what are you going to do now you're back?'

'I don't know,' she said quietly

'Do you even know what you want yet? Would you have come back at all if that bastard frog hadn't helped himself to my salary?' He was almost shouting now.

Sarah put her head in her hands, unable to bear his onslaught, all the more so because she deserved it. David leaned back and put his elbow on the back of the bench, sighing loudly in exasperation. 'Well, one thing's for sure, we'll have to sell the house.'

So he was confirming it. He wasn't coming back. 'Yes, I suppose so, but you know I'll pay the money back, don't you?'

'Whatever.' He sighed deeply. So she was confirming it. She wasn't coming back. 'You'll need to buy somewhere of you own, won't you? Unless you're going back to France.'

This was all moving too fast for Sarah. 'And what will you do?' she ventured. 'Will you buy somewhere with that woman?'

David turned to her sharply. Did he detect something in her voice? 'Would that bother you?'

Sarah took a deep breath and held his gaze. 'Yes. It would. Terribly.'

'I couldn't. For one thing her accent would drive me mad,' he replied, holding her gaze.

'Are you saying it's over? With her, I mean.'

He shrugged. 'It never really started.'

Sarah took a deep breath. 'I know I don't have rights to anything here after what I did, but I don't want this to happen. I don't want it to be over.' She searched his face for some reaction.

'Why?' He tried to stay impassive. Ties that bind, she'd said. Ties that bind.

'Because I want to be with you.'

Every part of him wanted to believe her but none of it added up. 'I don't get it. You walk out on our marriage leaving me guessing. Have a fling with a con man and then come home with your tail between your legs. Then I walk in last night and hear you say to Claire that you felt tied down. What were your actual words? "Go away before there are ties that bind you," I think you said.'

Sarah gasped, but the expression on his face was one of defeat and despair. 'I didn't realise you'd heard.' Sarah shook her heard is disbelief, trying to remember what she had said, but knowing she had to tell him her actual words last night. Restore his faith.

'You always used to tell the children not to pick up fag ends of conversation. You didn't hear the important bit.' She could feel a smile growing on her face. 'What you missed, my darling, is what I said to Claire after that. That if you leave it too late to be carefree, there will be ties you don't want to unravel from. Ever. Listen, David.' She turned her whole body towards him, willing him to understand. 'We got married terribly young – you know that – we were only just older than the twins are now but we did it because we adored each other – we didn't want to be without each other.' She laughed wryly. 'Perhaps we just met too soon. But the thing is, neither of us had the chance to explore the world as Claire or Tom can now. The twins have been our life, but we missed out on so much. When I went to France, I *had* to go. We had gone stale, you and I – you must see that now.'

David nodded. He knew he understood it and that she was right. He gritted his teeth, hardly daring to ask. 'And do you still adore me now?'

Sarah couldn't stop herself and put her hand on his tanned cheek, warm in the morning sun. 'More so than ever, because of everything between us and everything we have been through. But

I had to go away to realise that. And even though I was forced to come back, I would have come back anyway. The urge to be away had run its course. Can you forgive me? For all of it?'

He put his hand under hers and gently pushed it away from her face. Her stomach clenched. But instead of rejecting her, he laced his fingers between hers and held it tight. 'Funny. That's what Wilf said last night. He said the strength of marriage is about compromise. Growing together. That when you love someone, you have to forgive.'

'Perhaps we both should have talked to him before.'

'We didn't know then that he had anything to say.' David shook his head. 'I'm still trying to come to terms with all that. Dad and stuff. But it's funny, you know, Wilf told me before you left that I had to let you spread your wings and it's only now I realise what he meant and why he said it. He told me he always kept his arms open for Mary and that was why she came back, but I had to be sure you really wanted to, Sarah. That you came back for *us*, whatever the circumstances.'

She could feel her body sag as she dared to release the tension. 'I've been a complete fool.'

'No, you haven't. I did stifle you. I didn't think about our marriage. I got complacent and let it bob along. You are so much a part of me, I forgot you were your own person. I didn't see what you needed. I didn't even think about it. And I needed change forced on me.' He paused, suddenly afraid. 'Us having been with other people. Can we handle that?'

All Sarah could think about was the hideous image of David touching someone else. 'I can't bear the thought of you with her.'

'It makes me crazy too to think of you with him. It makes me feel sick with jealousy, if you want the truth. I'm not going to pretend it's okay because it's not.'

'No. I know.' There was a long silence.

'We've got a long way to go to get back to where we were, haven't we?' Sarah asked cautiously.

'I don't want to be back to where we were. It wasn't right for you and it wasn't doing either of us any good.' Silence again. 'We've got a lot of forgiving to do, haven't we?'

'Yes. Do you think we're strong enough?'

'We've got to be.' He looked at the beautiful face he knew so well. 'I love you so much that I can't let you go.'

Very slowly and cautiously, they moved towards each other and rested their foreheads gently together, not speaking, just relishing the familiarity.

'I still think we should sell the house, though,' he said after a moment, and Sarah pulled back suddenly.

'What?'

'Why don't we go and live somewhere we've always wanted to. Make a break. The kids don't need us to be here any more and I'm not sure I can face another twenty years living next to Appalling Pauline.' They both laughed. 'What about somewhere beside the sea? You've always dreamed about that. Let's make our lives the way we want them to be.'

Sarah caught the excitement in his voice and saw his eyes sparkle. This wasn't the face of the man who'd walked in from work religiously at five past six every night of his working life. Could she lose the view from this hilltop that she now realised was the part of her landscape? Yes, anywhere could be her landscape so long as he was there. 'My my, David Lewis, how you've changed!'

He looked sheepish. 'You're not the only one with dreams, I just didn't realise as quickly as you did that I had them. We can be a bit slow, us men.'

'Okay,' she said challengingly. 'Let's do a shopping list of dreams, then. You go first.'

'I want to do more with cars.' He clasped her hands between his in his enthusiasm. 'I've loved working on the Alvis and you were right – again – I should have done it years ago.'

She nodded. 'Fair enough. I want to travel more. Not just

safe package tours from the *Sunday Times*. They do have running water in Peru, you know.' She shot him a glance.

He smiled, knowing full well what she meant. 'Okay, okay. Point taken.'

She nudged him gently. 'But I would like to go to Rome, if the offer's still there. I've got the guidebook after all!'

'We haven't actually celebrated our anniversary, have we?'

'No, but we will. Oh, and I want to play in an orchestra. Regularly. Not teaching. Not quartets for weddings. I want to do it seriously. I did do something worthwhile in France. I played Debussy's *La Mer* with the Ensemble de Roussillon, you know.'

'I wish I'd been there.'

Sarah paused guiltily. 'I wish you had too. It's given me more confidence. I can do it. I'm not just there to teach grade one, or be at home making cakes and do the ironing.'

'Well, no need.' He pointed theatrically to himself. 'Here I am with my apron. I can run a house now, if you can bear to drop your standards a bit?'

Sarah laughed. 'You didn't do much bloody ironing, though, did you? That pile was weeks old.'

'Well, there'd be no ironing. If we don't have proper jobs, we can be like students again.'

'Yeuch! Eating off yesterday's plates? No chance!' Sarah looked thoughtful. 'But you're right, there are a few things I don't want in my life any more. I don't want to have my hair all middle-aged and sensible.'

David ruffled it gently. 'Don't go too radical, will you? I love your hair. Me, I don't want to work in an office again with idiots and targets and appraisals.'

'No. I can see that. I don't blame you.'

'Your turn.'

Sarah glanced at him to gauge his mood. 'Er ... I don't want to pick up your pants every day?'

He smiled broadly. 'Does that mean I also have to put the loo seat down every time too?' Sarah shoved him with her shoulder.

'Yup. And you can put your sodding nail clippings in the bin while you are at it.'

'Only if you stop using my razor to shave your legs and for once don't overfill the sodding bin bags. Makes them a nightmare to tie.'

Sarah laughed. 'I can see we have our work cut out.'

David stood up and held out both hands to her. 'Well, what are we waiting for? Let's go home and get started.' And, pulling her to her feet, he held her hand tightly and they headed back down the hill.

The Gap Year for Grown Ups

Five Ways to Spot You Need a Break from Your Life:

- The washing machine begs for mercy when you fill it … again.

- They paint a personalised parking space for you at the supermarket as a reward for your loyalty.

- You can not only finish your husband's sentences for him, you can start them as well.

- The kettle breaks at the office. And you are all still talking about the calamity a week later.

- Your hairdresser starts cutting your hair without even bothering to ask how you'd like it.

Ten Great Escapes:

Okay so you can't really escape from life, but here are some places and experiences that are wonderful to run away to and you'll come home restored and ready for the next bout:

- Cherry Pick: Head to Céret – the novel was loosely based here, a delightful little town at the foothills of the Pyrenees in south-east France. The region around Céret is major fruit producer, in particular famed for its cherries. The first of the season's pick is, by local tradition, sent to France's president. Céret hosts a cherry festival each year with such oddities as cherry beer and a cherry stone-spitting competition. The cherry season is during the end of April and May. At this time, the town is at its most picturesque.

- Enlightenment through shopping: the perfect dirty weekend escape – or you could just go with your flexible friend. Log on to the delicious boutique site www.mrandmrssmith.com and think global. New York? Why not ... Hire a bike in Central Park from the Loeb Boathouse. Go ice-skating at the Rockefeller Center from October to January, or until March in Central Park. And squeeze in a few crustaceans from the NY Oyster Bar in the cellars of Grand Central Station. Then there's the shopping – Barney's on Madison Avenue, and the altar to consumerism that is Fifth Avenue.

- Sleepless in St. Petersburg's: The White Nights. From late May to early July, the nights are bright in St Petersburg, with the brightest period, the White Nights, normally lasting from June 11th to July 2nd. The White Nights (Beliye Nochi) are a curious phenomenon caused by St. Petersburg's very northerly geographical location: (roughly on the same latitude as Oslo, the southern tip of Greenland and Seward, Alaska). St. Petersburg is the world's most northern city with a population over one million, and it stands at such a high latitude that the sun doesn't descend below the horizon enough for the sky to grow dark. In fact, night becomes curiously indistinguishable from day, so much so that the authorities never need to turn the city's streetlights on!

- Snip at Cnip: The Cnip Village Grazing Trust Campsite has to be the furthest you can get from the madding crowd for the cheapest overnight stay. And the location is idyllic. This remote campsite, on the western coast of the Isle of Lewis in the Outer Hebrides, is owned by the villagers of the Cnip crofting community and seems like the last place on earth. Stand on the dunes of Traigh na Beirigh and gaze out over the aqua-blue water watching the sunset. The entertainment? Birdsong and waves lapping. The fact that there is no website says it all. 01851 672265.

- Calmer Chameleon: run away from the stress of the daily grind at Rivendell Buddhist Retreat Centre – you don't even have to be one to escape to this centre of meditation and calm in the Sussex countryside. Surrounding the house is a lovely garden, beyond this lie fields and woodland. This provides an ideal peaceful environment to learn to meditate, practice yoga or to find out about Buddhism. Tel: 0208 688 8624 www.rivendellretreatcentre.com

- Music to Your Ears: Orkney's St. Magnus Festival was founded 31 years ago by Orkney's most celebrated resident, composer Sir Peter Maxwell Davies. Held every year in late June, when the days are long and the sunsets spectacular, the festival brings out the community spirit in everyone. A circus tent springs up in the car park, symphony concerts are held in the sports centre, and churches on far-flung islands host chamber concerts with both audience and performers arriving on the same ferry.

- Run away to sea and crew a tall ship. These magnificent boats are crewed by amateurs (working alongside the pros of course!) and voyages take you to the Spanish Maine, the Western Isles, the Caribbean and the Azores. Splice the main brace, cap'n! www.tallships.org 02392 832 055

- Turkish Delight: Tucked away in the centre of the City of London is Ironmonger Row Baths – rated in the top five Turkish Baths in the UK by the *Financial Times*, which describes it as 'cheap, cheerful and unashamed'. The baths are a haven of relaxation and include a steam room, a series of three hot rooms of varying temperature, marble slabs for great value body scrubbing and an icy plunge pool. There are also two relaxation areas: one is a resting room with proper beds and the other is a television room. Tel: 0207 253 4011 www.aquaterra.org

- Fly off to Mauritius with a clear conscience - Responsible Travel (www.responsibletravel.com 01273 600 030) is about sensitively supporting the host country's environment, social and economic policies, whilst minimising visitors' own negative impact in these three areas. The tour is a balance of eco-tourism and volunteer experience where visitors have the opportunity to get involved with the community. You're also given the opportunity to offset your carbon footprint by sponsoring a plant in a designated conservation area. Accommodation is at small, family-run guesthouses or hotels, locally owned and run by local people. All food is purchased locally from small independent retailers or markets to ensure money is put directly back into the economy and to reduce unnecessary packaging and waste. Feel better now?

- Not just for Yoof: the Youth Hostel Association have some wonderfully located properties but none better for a true escape than Skiddaw House – a fantastic get-away-from-it-all in the peace and tranquillity of the Northern Fells of the Lake District. Once a pair of shepherd's cottages in a spectacular remote location, the bunkhouse is surrounded by wild, rolling fells with miles of walking and cycling opportunities. It has basic, comfortable accommodation with a special and unique atmosphere. Best of all, you'll have to walk or cycle to get here – access is via tracks/paths, torch advisable after dark. Battery lighting and no phone facilities, plus negligible mobile phone signal. Perfect! Tel: 07747 174293 www.skiddawhouse.co.uk

Annie Sanders, 2009

Acknowledgements

The fun part in writing this book has been dipping in to the pick 'n' mix of life. Some bits have come from our own experience but we've needed the help of other people where we were ignorant. Thanks must go to Simon Hogg and Cal Dagul for their invaluable musical input; Priscilla Chase and Tudor Summers – the man with his head under the bonnet of an Alvis; Lynn and Dick Shone and L'Office de Tourisme de Ceret for their help with local colour; Charlie Okell and Graham Martin for the university information, plus Marie-Laure Legroux for correcting our French. There are certain extreme situations described in the book which (thankfully) we don't have any experience of, so we turned to the experts. Thank you to the National Drugs Helpline, Dr Jeremy Shearman, Simon Bennett – APACS, and Freddie Baveystock for telling it like it is.

And, of course, greatest thanks to Mary Pachnos, Sara O'Keeffe and all at Orion, for their unswerving support.